The Path Through the Woods

Emma Sinclair

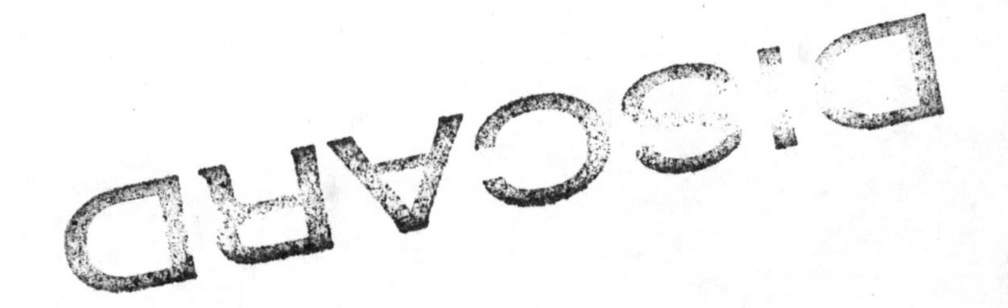

Copyright © 1999 by Emma Sinclair

First published in Great Britain in 1999 by
Judy Piatkus (Publishers) Ltd of
5 Windmill Street, London W1P 1HF

The moral right of the author has been asserted

A catalogue record for this book is available from the British Library

ISBN 0 7499 0499 2

Set in Times by
Phoenix Photosetting, Chatham, Kent
Printed and bound in Great Britain by
Butler & Tanner Ltd, Frome, Somerset

To Geoff, for his patience and help.

Chapter One

They had no idea of the impending disaster; it was just another aircraft heading home across the Suffolk countryside on a tranquil August evening.

Suddenly the engine cut, surged with a roar, cut then surged again.

Working late on the harvest, field hands from the Women's Land Army looked up in alarm. Smoke was trailing from the bomber; it was losing height rapidly; airmen were baling out and those watching could feel only a sickening horror as parachutes failed to open. In the village of Thornley people came from their cottages to stand, paralysed and helpless, as the Lancaster decended towards the cluster of houses.

A terrified woman rushed into her farmhouse and up the stairs to the children's bedroom. Grabbing the youngest and nearest from her bed, she looked through the window and froze. The bomber was now on fire and heading straight for her.

Suddenly it banked and plunged out of sight behind trees. The deafening crash was followed by a thick black column of smoke. The child in her arms whimpered while the six year old in the other bed was screaming with fear. Turning quickly as her husband rushed into the room, Diane Fenton groaned: 'Those men! Oh, those poor men.'

John Fenton caught his breath, gasping, 'I thought you and the girls . . . oh, God! Telephone for help. I'll go and see what can be done.'

Still holding one child and heedless of the screams of the other, Diane followed him from the room. 'Was it a Fortress?'

'No. A Lancaster.'

'John.' Diane's bright blue eyes were anxious. 'It crashed in the woods . . .'

He turned and shook his head. 'No, the field. I saw it clearly.' She stared at him stupidly for a moment, then her face relaxed and she breathed a deep sigh of relief.

1958

Thérèse, called Terry for as long as she could remember, stood on the edge of Five Acre Field.

Under a large, hazy sky the flat landscape of ochre-coloured stubble stretched away before her, ending in a blue-green horizon of trees. Four days ago the ripened corn had rippled in a golden sea; now the harvest was cut, and straw bales were being lifted on to a tractor-drawn cart. Her father and two farm hands were working tirelessly on this exceptionally warm September day, but warm as it was, summer was almost over and Terry felt sadness tinged with anxiety.

Brushing a windswept tangle of fair hair from her face, she turned back along the nettle-bordered track where tractor wheels had carved deep ruts. A small trim figure in a loose blue cotton shirt worn over navy trews and canvas shoes, Terry could hardly be called pretty, but many would admit she was attractive when made up. Today she wore no make up over her suntanned complexion and frowned as she contemplated the new life awaiting her.

It was one thing to be a carefree student on a teacher's training course but another to take on the responsibility of teaching as a career. Could she do it? Was it what she really wanted to do, or had she simply drifted into the whole thing because her parents had expected it of her?

Glancing at her watch, she started walking more quickly, past the outhouses and the black wooden barn, past the woods to her right and on until she came to a nineteenth-century red brick house covered now with Virginia Creeper. Lynwood Farm had been bequeathed to Terry's father after the accidental death of his widowed and childless cousin almost twenty years earlier and with it had come ninety-eight acres of arable farmland, six of woodland and four of rough pasture which flooded most winters when a nearby meandering stream overflowed its banks.

Making her way to the front drive, Terry smiled at her brother who was leaning against the Morris Traveller. Tall for his thirteen years, with colt-like limbs shooting out from an Aertex shirt and cotton shorts, Eliot's expression was thunderous and his voice bitter with disappointment.

'It isn't fair! First she was leaving at nine, and now it's almost ten. At this rate, by the time we reach Woodbridge, sort out the dinghy and launch, the tide will have turned. It's typical of Marisa. She has everyone hanging about and doesn't care whose plans she upsets.' He turned fierce blue eyes on his sister's soft grey ones. 'Why don't we just go and leave her here? Who cares if she misses her stupid train?'

Slowly coming to the boil herself, Terry managed to raise a calming hand and told him to be patient. 'Don't worry. I'll fetch her right now.'

She entered the small flagstoned vestibule with its row of Wellington boots and went on into the wide hallway dominated by a grandfather clock. A Victorian hallstand stood like some strange tree with branches sprouting macintoshes and shabby jackets; the oak table beside it was cluttered with paperwork and magazines, and somewhere among all this was a telephone.

Leaning on the banister, Terry called up to her elder sister: 'If you don't come at once you'll miss that second train as well. Either way, I'm leaving now with Eliot. It's his last day and you know I promised I'd sail with him. Marisa? Did you hear me?'

'I'm almost ready.' The voice from the bedroom sounded unperturbed. 'Won't be a jiffy.'

'A jiffy will be too late. Ready or not, we're leaving.'

'Oh, for goodness' sake, don't fuss so!' A trim young woman appeared on the landing, carrying a small suitcase. Her reddish-brown hair, now swept back in a neat chignon, complemented green eyes. The elegant beige suit, worn with high-heeled patent leather shoes and matching handbag, set her worlds apart from the farm where she had been raised. Ice cool and almost attaining beauty, Marisa had been snapped up by BOAC and trained as an air stewardess almost a year ago.

After unhurriedly descending the stairs she set down her suit-case and glanced around. 'Well, where's Mother? I presume she intends to say goodbye?'

Terry winced inwardly. Before she could answer Diane

appeared from the kitchen, severe and smiling as though unaware of Marisa's pointed remark.

'Sorry, darlings, it took longer collecting the eggs than usual. The hens have come up trumps today.' She placed her hands on Marisa's shoulders and sighed. 'So, you're off. Don't make it so long visiting us again. Now take care and have a safe trip, my dear.'

'Well, that does rather depend upon the pilot,' Marisa replied 'Anyway, must go. Goodbye.' Barely touching Diane's proffered cheek, she followed her sister out to the Traveller where Eliot was already settled in the back, arms folded firmly to show the world he was still sulking.

Diane told Marisa. 'Ring as soon as you return to England. Promise, now?' You know how much we worry about you.'

The oft-repeated phrase received the oft-repeated answer. 'I will, I promise. 'Bye.'

Diane watched as the car moved away. In her late forties, she was still a good looking woman with only a few grey hairs among the blonde and eyes as blue as ever. At last she turned and walked back into the house.

As Terry eased the car along the drive and out into the narrow lane, Marisa fumbled in her handbag for a cigarette and lit it before leaning back. 'Worry be damned! She can't wait to get rid of me. But I daresay she'll weep buckets over Eliot when he starts at boarding school.'

'Shhh!' Terry's lips tightened. 'He'll hear you,' she whispered. 'And it's time to change the record. This fixation that you're not loved is boring and utterly wrong.'

'You think so?' Marisa gave a wry smile. 'When you used to cry, you were hugged. When I cried, I was told to pull myself together.'

'Nonsense. We were treated exactly the same with no favouritism shown to either of us.' What's the use? thought Terry. Her sister was in one of her moods and nothing would lift her out of it.

They drove in silence along a lane which was bordered by their own wood; on past the square-towered church then down the slight hill into the High Street with its two pubs, four shops and oak-beamed sixteenth-century cottages. Having eased their way through the watersplash, scattering wildfowl in all directions, they proceeded along the street then out through a maze of narrow lanes until they reached the main road.

Marisa drew on the cigarette as her mind dwelt on a distant summer's evening when the loud roar of an aircraft had set her screaming with fear. She would never forget it, never forget how their mother had rushed straight into the bedroom but instead of comforting her, had picked up Terry instead. On that evening, at the age of six, Marisa knew that, had a choice been necessary, then she would have been the one left to die. That hurt had festered over the years into a terrible emotional wound which she had borne without a word to anyone. It went far too deep for that. From then on, whichever direction her mother wished her to take, she had wilfully chosen the other path, culminating in a glorious family row a year ago when she had gleefully announced that BOAC had accepted her for cabin crew training and that she was glad to be leaving home at last.

'Mother's jealous, of course,' she said now, stubbing out her cigarette in the ash tray. 'Jealous because I have a better life than she ever did. I'm independent, live in London, have masses of friends, travel and meet interesting people. She, on the other hand, has spent most of her life on a farm and running a house. When did they ever have a social life to speak of? Sad, really. Her looks have been wasted. Let's face it, Dad's not much to write home about.'

She lit another cigarette and smiled. 'Wonder what Mother looked like as a bride? Frumpy, I suppose, with her old aunt influencing her dress sense. Pity they didn't bring any photos with them when we left Guernsey.' She paused and, turning to her sister, saw Terry's disapproving expression. 'You know, we don't have to love our parents just because they are our parents, and we don't have to let them control our lives.'

Terry sighed. 'If you say these things simply for effect then I'm singularly unimpressed. The truth is that if anything happened to either one of them you'd be heartbroken. You love them more than you know. As for, controlling us . . .'

'They did a pretty good job on you.' Marisa smiled wryly. 'The Dame Edith Harting School for Girls . . . dear God! You'll spend your days with spotty pubescents and dowdy females and wind up an old maid. You should be in London, not wasting your youth in a backwater like this hoping some man will rescue you.'

After this Marisa fell to silent brooding. Love? That was something she had neither felt nor known. Perhaps she was incapable of it. Was that possible? After all, she had never wanted for men, her looks guaranteed that, but she simply could not fall in love. Perhaps it was because they became serious too soon and she was immediately put off.

'I'll tell you one thing,' she said. 'If ever I give up my independence for marriage, it'll be money behind it and no other reason.' She glanced at her watch. 'We're late. Can't you step on it?'

'Have a heart,' said Terry, 'I only passed my driving test two weeks ago.' She smiled and added, 'I collect my car tomorrow evening.' Her father had given her a loan to buy a second-hand Austin and she was over the moon. It had been a necessary purchase since reaching the Dame Edith School would have meant two bus journeys and long waits in between.

'How old is it?' asked Eliot, suddenly taking an interest in the conversation.

'Nineteen.'

'What?' Marisa laughed. 'You're wasting good money on a pile of old junk?'

Terry shook her head. 'Not so. One careful owner. He bought the car brand new in 1939, was killed at Dunkirk. His widow never learned to drive nor could she find the heart to sell it, so it's been up on blocks and covered with tarpaulin all these years. Sad. I felt I was being vetted by her. She was such a dear, said she hoped I would be as happy in it as she and her husband had been.'

'And she's going to call it Sally,' scoffed Eliot.

'You're joking, of course?'

'No.' Terry glanced at her sister. 'This woman and her husband were great fans of Gracie Fields so they called the car Sally. She hoped I would too. I said I would at the time because I thought it would make her feel better. But now I'm keeping my promise.'

'People who personalise cars are positively weird,' said Marisa disparagingly. 'Sad people who probably can't have children.'

Twenty minutes later they arrived at the ancient river port of Woodbridge, drove down Market Hill, dominated by the Elizabethan Shire Hall, then on past the old quayside buildings of the town's maritime past, and finally drew up at the station.

The train was just about to leave and in a breathless rush all three ran from the car to the platform, Eliot ahead with the suitcase, Marisa teetering as fast as she could behind him while Terry just watched helplessly, convinced they wouldn't make it. The guard raised his green flag, held the whistle to his lips and paused as Eliot opened a carriage door. When Marisa and the case were safely inside, the whistle blew and the train moved forward.

After watching until it was out of sight, brother and sister turned and walked back to the car, Eliot fuming that Marisa hadn't even the grace to wave goodbye, and Terry accepting that such a thought would not even have occurred to her sister.

It was almost eleven-thirty by the time they reached the small and unfashionable sailing club where John Fenton kept a small clinker-built dinghy. The tide was on the turn and it took a precious fifteen minutes to prepare *Firefly* and launch her from the trolley stern-first into the Deben. Terry hoisted the rust red mainsail while Eliot looked after the jib.

Pointing into a light wind they tacked their way seaward past old wharves and the famous Tide Mill until Woodbridge slowly gave way to fields and woods.

Adjusting the jib, Eliot leaned out slightly to balance the dinghy but his eyes stared towards Sutton Hoo on the far bank, his mind on its necropolis and the famous Anglo-Saxon ship burial which had yielded treasures of the age. Among them had been a helmet of iron, bronze and silver, its nasal guard and eye slits sending a chill of fear through him the first time he had seen it at the museum.

Since that day he had suffered strange dreams in which the dead chieftain had risen from his grave. Always dressed for battle and wearing the terrifying helmet, he would stride like a giant across the Deben and over the low-lying fields to Thornley, to a bedroom in a farmhouse . . . Eliot's bedroom.

Fearing the dream was a portent of disaster to come, he had never spoken of it to anyone. Today, however, he spoke of the archeological find to Terry because they had always been close and she had always listened to him.

'They say he was King Raedwald of the East Angles. When he died they brought him by river from his palace at Rendlesham, then laid him in the ship with all his treasures about him. Now they plan to excavate the other barrows.' He looked worried. 'I don't think they should, I don't think it's right. They should have left Raedwald in peace.'

Terry looked surprised. 'Eliot? That's not like you. I thought you wanted to be an archeologist. Oh, hang on. Changing tack ... ready about.' As *Firefly* turned towards Woodbridge, she adjusted the sail, sat back and smiled at him. 'You would watch *Curse of the Mummy's Tomb* the other night!'

'It was daft.' Eliot glanced up at the jib sail thoughtfully. 'Anyway I've changed my mind about archeology. I wouldn't mind being an actor, or even a barrister because that's much the same as acting only you get paid more.'

They sailed on in silence until the tide became low and the mellow afternoon sun turned the Deben to shimmering liquid gold.

Having checked on her mare, Diane entered the large pinewood kitchen which had changed little since she'd arrived here twenty years earlier. The black cooking range had a good fire burning in it; the well-scrubbed pine table in the centre had a bowl of Michaelmas daisies on it; herbs hung in bunches from the ceiling to dry and on the dresser were Kilner jars ready for bottling fruit and tomatoes in the morning.

At the threshold she took off her boots and slipped into house shoes. Having no downstairs cloakroom, it was necessary to wash her hands in the utility room where she cleaned the eggs every day before packing them in cartons and selling them to the local shop. As she dried her hands and rubbed on handcream she tried not to think about life without her beloved son. For all his years, he was still her baby and always would be. Kingsmead! It was miles away and Eliot would be miserable, she just knew it. He loved his home and his friends, most of whom would go on to the Grammar. But John believed that a good boarding school, albeit a minor public school, would turn his son into a well-educated and rounded man. Diane privately wondered if it would turn him into a nervous wreck.

But as she started preparing the evening meal a rare feeling of contentment settled over her. Marisa had gone. She spent little enough time with them these days but when she was here the tension became almost unbearable.

Now Diane's nervousness would end, and the stress vanish.

Only the guilt would remain to haunt her, along with the memory of one terrible evening. Marisa had been two and a half at the time. Could a two year old retain memories? Hardly. Yet those green accusing eyes, those terrible tantrums, and later the speech impediment which, thank God, had slowly vanished, seemed to imply she did.

For all that she worried about her, Diane felt much happier with Marisa out of the house.

The hall telephone rang. She wiped her work-worn hands on a kitchen towel, walked briskly to answer it and stiffened on hearing Brigadier Rashleigh's authoritative tones.

'Just ringing to remind John about the Parish Council meeting tonight. Desperately important that he's there. There's a strong feeling in the village that we must settle the issue of the Lancaster memorial once and for all. Will you tell him for me?'

'Yes, of course.' Too worried to say more, she replaced the receiver and stared at the flowered wallpaper for a full minute. Oh, Lord, not again. Why, oh why, had that bomber crashed on their land? Why did past burdens only weigh more heavily as the years went by? Why could she not feel free of them? If only she had a close confidante, someone she could trust to listen and somehow, by the act of listening, share that burden. But she had no such friend, and there were some things no confidante should hear.

She wandered into the sitting room, casting her eyes across faded armchairs, a tall oak book case and upright piano, then sank on to the sofa. Why couldn't John have been here to answer that call? Now she would have to tell him the bad news and he would hit the roof.

It was well after five-thirty when Terry drove uphill through the narrow streets of Woodbridge where Georgian fronts masked sixteenth-century houses, past the church and Shire Hall once more, and finally made her way out of town. Her face felt tight and sore from too much sun; she longed for a hot bath and hoped that her father would try to spend a little time tonight with Eliot before he left for boarding school the day after tomorrow.

Glancing at him, she could only guess at her brother's feelings for both she and her sister had been educated at the local Grammar School where they had been happy and went on to pass exams at advanced level. But for the son of the house, their father had decided otherwise. Terry felt for the boy; his long silence spoke more loudly of his fear and misery than any words he might have uttered.

New schools, she and Eliot both! Marisa's warning hammered into her brain. 'You're just not cut out for it. Children need a firm hand and you're like marshmallow. They'll sense it straight away and lead you a merry dance. Frankly, sister dear, you simply don't have it.'

Marisa was right. Like it or hate it, she was right. All the confidence along with the good looks had been bestowed on one sister and not the other. Why had the genes not been distributed more fairly? As it was, no one ever imagined they were sisters.

They were four miles from Thornley now and heading through a small hamlet towards the crossroads. Suddenly a large dog sprang from a garden and chased across the road in front of them. Terry hit the brake, swung the wheel to the right then saw a car turning into her path. Too late to avoid a collision, she braced, felt the shock course through her body and was thrown forward against the steering column.

Chapter Two

After the crash came the stillness. Shocked, Terry slowly looked up, immediately thought of Eliot and turned to him anxiously. He was pale, staring in disbelief, but unhurt. She sighed with relief, then saw a young man getting out of the other car, a Rover. He stood shaking his head for one moment before walking towards the Morris.

Tensing, Terry waited for an angry tirade against 'idiot women drivers', but when he opened her car door she saw only concern on his face as he asked, 'Are you all right?'

For a moment it seemed her voice was imprisoned in her throat but at last she managed a faint, 'Yes . . . I'm all right.' Her wrist hurt, though, and she felt an ache in her neck. 'Are you?'

He ran a hand through light brown hair. 'Better than the car, I think.'

Finally managing to move, Terry climbed out of the Traveller, stared with dismay at the dented rear door, then turned her attention to the Rover. The headlight was smashed and glass lay on the ground. 'I'm sorry, so terribly sorry. A dog came out of nowhere and . . .'

'Didn't it just! The only one of us to come out of things unscathed, it seems.'

Unconsciously rubbing her painful left wrist, Terry wondered how she would explain the state of their car to her parents, and began on the business of exchanging names and addresses for insurance purposes. Casually dressed in open-necked shirt and brown jacket, the man wrote the details in a small black notebook. As she studied the clear grey eyes in his tanned face she thought him handsome, probably in his mid-twenties.

He glanced at her address. 'Thornley! Funnily enough I've just come from there. I was on my way back to London after staying with relatives. You probably know the Rashleighs?'

Terry's face brightened. 'Of course I know them. Fiona's an old friend.' Feeling this called for polite introductions, she held out her right hand. 'I'm Terry Fenton and this is my brother Eliot.'

'Alastair Hammond.' He frowned as he took her hand. 'You look pretty shaken up and I notice you keep rubbing your wrist. Is it very painful?'

She shrugged and lied, 'Not really. I must have twisted it somehow. It'll be fine. Fine.'

'I don't think so. Come on, get into my car and I'll take you back to Thornley. We'll fetch your car later.'

'But you're on your way to London. I couldn't possibly . . .'

'I can't go to London now until the headlight's fixed. So get in.'

After helping her into the Rover, he and Eliot pushed the Morris away from the corner and left it safely at the kerbside before they all set off for Thornley. Glancing at Terry's expression, Alastair laughed off her further apologies.

'The dog it was that died! Or in this case lived to cause havoc another day. Don't worry, I've been in far worse scrapes and anyway it isn't my car. I borrowed it to escort Fiona to a ball, then stayed an extra day. Now I'll have to stay a little longer. Work can wait, that's all.'

She wondered what he did for a living that he could be quite so casual about it but could hardly ask. Eliot however was all questions, much to her embarrassment.

'What'll you say to Dad?'

'The truth,' replied Terry shortly.

'He'll be hopping mad.' Leaning on the back on her seat, he stared at Alastair. 'If you want the car fixed quickly then the garage at Boxham does a pretty good job. Dad swears by them. What do you do in London, Mr Hammond?'

At this Terry tried to hush her brother only to hear Alastair murmur something about car manufacturing. Really? Odd! Wrong type and wrong class for an assembly line, she thought. Strictly public school. Wrong place for car factories too. Pen pusher then, and not a well-paid one either since he had no car of his own.

'Are you married, Mr Hammond?'

This question brought dark looks from Terry even though turning her neck proved a painful exercise.

'No.' Alastair smiled.

'Do you live alone then?'

'Oh, Eliot, do be quiet! It's rude to ask so many questions.' Terry's head was hurting now. She could hardly wait to get home and dose herself with Aspirin.

As Eliot sank into reluctant silence Alastair answered his question. 'Yes. In London. It's pretty rare for me to come here.'

Terry could imagine that it was. Good-looking young bachelors were in short supply in this part of the world. At college most of the student teachers had been women and the few males on the course were already attached or about to be. Even Fiona Rashleigh had fared little better. In spite of finishing school, coming out balls and the London Season, poor, overweight, warm-hearted Fiona, who smelled of saddle soap rather than Chanel No. 5, had ended up high and dry in the marriage stakes. At least she could turn to Alastair. Poor relation or not, he was acceptable enough to be trotted out whenever the youngest daughter of Brigadier Rashleigh needed an escort.

Dragging her mind back to the car, Terry said, 'Eliot's right about Boxham. My father always goes to Gordon Price. He'll pull out all the stops and get you on your way.'

'I just need the headlight fixed for now. I'll take it to a Rover specialist when I return to London. Have you always lived in Thornley?

'Since I was a baby. We came here from Guernsey just before the war. Do you like Thornley?'

Alastair shook his head. 'Pretty place but not for me. All the talk at the Hall is of horse shows and hunting. Frankly I couldn't wait to get away.'

'Oh, dear,' sighed Terry. 'And I've dragged you back at your moment of escape. Sorry.'

He laughed. 'Don't worry. If this Gordon Price is all you say he is, I'll be out of here first thing tomorrow morning.'

She smiled wistfully, a little hurt that he should still be so eager to flee. 'Gordon will make your wish come true, you have my guarantee.'

John Fenton was in a dark mood as he took a much-needed bath. This was the busiest time of year for him and he could have done without Rashleigh's latest broadside. He towelled off, put on grey flannels, white shirt and sober tie, and carried his jacket down the stairs, placing it over the back of a kitchen chair. Taking a beer bottle from a cupboard, he poured brown ale into a glass and watched grimly as the milky effervescent head began to settle.

'The man's got a damned cheek, mooting this one again! What's changed since last time?' We can't have a path through the wood and that's that.'

Diane stubbed her cigarette out in a half-filled ashtray and prayed that John would not let anger get the better of him. It was wont to cause raised eyebrows at a Parish Council meeting.

'Be careful,' she murmured. 'Don't antagonise Rashleigh or anyone else. Simply say you don't want people wandering on your land. It's perfectly reasonable. They must accept it.'

'For Christ's sake, don't you think I've been all through that?'

A tall, taciturn man with dark hair now turning salt and pepper grey, John Fenton's voice and general demeanour were strangely at odds with his present life as a hardworking farmer toiling on the land. It was a life he found increasingly prosaic, unlike the exciting war years when Thornley and Lowdham Market had hummed with American and British airmen.

Those were the days, he thought. The days when they used to invite pilots to the house and Diane would help run the local Red Cross canteen. But the Americans were long gone, and the airfield from which Flying Fortresses had bombed Germany was now closed, its runway covered with weed-filled cracks, its empty buildings an eyesore waiting to be removed. Later, when RAF Boxham had been put on a Care and Maintenance footing, Thornley and Lowdham had drifted back into the usual tenor of life in the countryside made famous by Constable, while John Fenton had been condemned to live out his years feeling bitter about certain choices he had made when young.

Knowing his secret thoughts and true, hidden nature, Diane too had come to regret the past. She checked the oven; an appetising smell of casserole and braising vegetables filled the kitchen. After setting plates to warm, she put table mats and cutlery on the table. The evening was chilly and with a constant fire in the range they never dined anywhere else these days. Only at Christmas was the dining room used for meals, leaving it free for sewing, studying or checking accounts and other matters related to the running of the farm.

Dusk was turning to darkness. As she closed the curtains, Diane glanced at the wall clock anxiously. 'Where on earth are they?'

Pouring herself a dry sherry she sat on the Windsor chair opposite John and, filled with apprehension about the coming meeting and a growing anxiety that something had happened to Terry and Eliot, picked up the rumpled *East Anglian* and made a pretence of reading it.

Ten minutes later they heard wheels on the gravelled drive. Diane almost ran to the front door, opened it then stood on the porch step watching in puzzlement as Eliot climbed out of a damaged-looking Rover and walked towards her, shouting, 'We've been in a car crash!'

'What?' Hand at her throat, Diane stood in the hall light and saw a strange man climb from the driving seat. Only when he helped Terry out did her tense shoulders fall with relief. 'What happened?'

As John appeared at the door, a pale and contrite Terry explained how the accident had come about then introduced Alastair to her parents. Relieved that the situation was not as bad as it might have been, John contacted Gordon Price while Diane set an extra place, insisting that Alastair stay for dinner.

'It's the very least we can do,' she said. 'Anyway it's too dark for you to drive on to Thornley Hall without headlights. My husband will take you there.'

'That's kind of you,' murmured Alastair, glad of the beer John had pressed into his hand. 'But truly, I can walk. You've enough on your plate, having to collect your own car.'

'We'll collect it later,' said John, at his most charming. 'The Hall's almost a mile from the village. It's no trouble dropping you off.'

Crêpe bandage now binding her left wrist, Terry was aware of Alastair's eyes on her throughout dinner. Although his stare made her feel self-conscious, she was glad he had stayed. It meant a temporary reprieve from accusations of careless driving which she knew would come from her mother, if not her father. She of all the children had been the closest to him and he was everything to her. 'Daddy's girl,' her mother used to say in a slightly sarcastic tone. Nevertheless, crashing the Traveller just two weeks after passing her test might be too much even for him.

Making pleasant conversation with Alastair, John nevertheless thought it ironic that he should perforce be grateful to a relative of the very man who was currently making his life a misery. But one look at Terry's face dispelled his darker feelings. It could have been so much worse, this accident. Look how pale she was, his little girl, the one who had always adored him as he adored her. He loved Eliot, too, but his son was his son and the love John felt for him could not be expressed in the same way.

Marisa was a different matter, he thought as he helped himself to potatoes. He cared for her, of course he did, but she was independent and wilful, lacking Terry's warmth and vulnerability, traits which meant he had not been happy for his 'little girl' to go to London where she might be led astray. Even the teacher's training course had only been a bus ride away since he wanted her home safely each night. To this end he had now forked out for the second-hand Austin, pretending it was a loan. No sense in making waves for Marisa to splash through.

Smiling and chatting, he felt a churning in his stomach as his thoughts turned to tonight's meeting.

The small room which had been added on to the Victorian church hall in 1922 was cold and smelled musty. Time something was done about it, thought the Chairman of the Parish Council, but the coffers were bare and so they patched and replastered and made the best of things as they had during the war years.

Gerald Rashleigh had been given the rank of Brigadier during the First World War and this along with his squirearchy background gave him a natural air of authority which he wielded over the villages of Thornley and neighbouring Boxham. A large-built, grey-haired, ruddy-faced man in his early seventies, he tapped a fountain pen on the table top with growing anger, well aware of the tension in the other Councillors seated about him. His pale eyes stayed fixed on John Fenton.

'I don't understand your attitude. Damn it, man, is it so much to ask?'

John looked down at his Minutes and said in a quiet, tense voice, 'You did ask me and I gave you my reasons. In case you've all forgotten I gave up one acre of land for the memorial site, and did so gladly.'

Rashleigh threw down his pen. 'But what's the use of it without access through the wood? The field's completely landlocked.'

'Gentlemen,' said John testily, 'I've said it time and time again and I'll say it once more. I will not have people walking through my wood. In my place, Brigadier, neither would you.'

Rashleigh leaned forward in his chair and growled, 'A narrow path is all it would need. If it's money you're worrying about, then damn it, Fenton, I'll pay for the path and the fencing of it myself!'

'I don't need your money,' snapped John. He could feel his heart pounding and sweat was breaking out on his brow. 'You all seem to forget that I shoot in the wood. What would happen if I hit someone by accident? I'm sorry, but you must understand my position.'

The Vicar shuffled in his chair, cleared his throat and said, 'Everyone in the village feels strongly about building a memorial to those young men. We must find a way.'

'The only way,' snapped Rashleigh, 'is a path through Fenton's wood from the gate in Harvest Lane.'

John wiped his forehead with a white handkerchief then placed it back in his trouser pocket. 'There is another way. I'm prepared to offer you a different site for the memorial, and one which would be more convenient for people to reach.' With that he delved into a battered briefcase, produced a roughly sketched layout of the village and pointed to the land which lay east of the church on the Boxham Road. 'Better all round, surely?'

'Short Furlong?' Rashleigh shook his head. 'But what's the point in that? The bomber crashed . . .'

'I know where the bomber crashed,' John cut in, anger slowly getting the better of him. 'But access to that site through my wood is out of the question. It's up to you. Take my offer or leave it. I refuse to discuss this matter again.'

The publican of the Bell Inn looked unimpressed. 'We already have a war memorial on the green. To place another close by would be ludicrous, and would only create the impression that the crew were buried in the churchyard, which is wrong. Their bodies were sent back to their own homes.'

Another local farmer disagreed. 'I can understand Mr Fenton's objections and I think we should put his offer to the vote.'

'Very well,' said Rashleigh. 'All those in favour of the Lancaster memorial being place on the field known as Short Furlong?'

The farmer and John Fenton raised their hands.

Rashleigh smiled with satisfaction. 'And those against?' When the other hands went up, he declared the motion defeated and it was duly noted in the Minutes.

John shuffled to his feet and snapped, 'Well, that's that. I hope you'll forgive me, gentlemen, if I absent myself from the rest of the meeting but my daughter was in a car accident this evening.' As he had anticipated, this news was received with shock and concern by everyone except Rashleigh who knew it already. Assuring them all that Terry was shaken but not badly hurt, John left the room, made his way out of the church hall and stood for one moment breathing in the fresh night air. His heart was still pounding.

Rashleigh slammed down his pen on the table and folded his arms, angry that for once he was not going to have things all his own way. 'Isn't that just like the man? Accident my foot! It was a mere bump and no one was hurt. No, we've ruffled his feathers, that's all.'

The Vicar frowned. 'Ruffled or not, we can't force him to anything. It's understandable. No farmer wants the general public wandering all over his land.'

The silence which greeted this remark left another hovering in the air to stab at the Brigadier's conscience. *And in his place, Brigadier, neither would you.*

After a restless night, Terry finally drifted off to sleep at cock crow and was awoken at seven-twenty-five by a tractor engine and shouts from the farm hands. She lay still for a moment listening to the bustle of a new day. The sound of the tractor began to fade away as it headed once more into Five Acre Field, dragging the hay cart behind it.

Slowly easing herself out of bed, she headed for the window noticing that the day was much cooler. In a landscape dominated by huge skies, an east wind sent grey clouds chasing across the sun but the clouds were high and it seemed they would be spared rain. How different from yesterday's sunny warmth.

Yesterday! She smiled at the memory and recalled the way Alastair had looked at her during dinner. How tense her parents had been, though. Were they very angry with her? Would her father go back on his word and refuse to loan her the money for the little Austin after all? Dear God, how would she cope then, hanging around for country buses to reach the school? Useless. Especially in winter. She would have to take a bed-sitter in Lowdham, if she could find one. Her thoughts returned swiftly to the accident and Alastair. Soon his car would be fixed and he would speed off to London.

'And that,' she murmured sadly, 'is that.'

She glanced at her left wrist and unwrapped the crêpe bandage. The swelling had gone down but it still hurt. Later, having bathed, and breakfasted on tea and toast, she walked into Eliot's room to be faced by his trunk and a pile of new clothes. And there it was, the dreaded white bundle of name tapes each reading ELIOT FENTON, just waiting for her. She had promised to sew them on his new uniform for her mother. Well, she had a good right hand and would manage well enough.

At half-past ten Diane entered the room and frowned. 'Time you had a rest if you want that wrist to get better. You have visitors so I'll take over for a while, then we can check off the inventory together before I take the car to the garage. The insurance company are sending a Claims Form. Your father will have to take Eliot to Kingsmead in the Land Rover tomorrow. 'Visitors?' Terry looked at her questioningly. 'Who?'

'Fiona and Alastair. And they've brought that wretched dog with them. I told Fiona to tie it up outside, so make sure it stays there. It's Mrs Godwin's morning to clean. She'll want to do the kitchen floor, so don't get in her way. Off you go. Make haste.'

Terry rushed into her bedroom, and stared in dismay at her reflection in the mirror. Her sunburnt face had no make up, her hair was untidy and the blouse she was wearing was only fit for a jumble sale. Painfully she changed into her favourite blue over-shirt which had sleeves ending at the elbows, slapped a little cream and powder on her face, added a touch of lipstick then brushed her hair vigorously. When she had finished she wondered why she had bothered. In any case, hadn't Alastair already seen her looking her worst after sailing? As far as he was concerned she was right there with Fiona.

A smell of coffee permeated the air as she walked down the stairs and entered the kitchen. Fiona, Alastair and Eliot had made themselves perfectly at home around the pine table while Mrs Godwin was chatting on as she poured coffee from a percolator into Diane's best porcelain cups. 'The owner of that dog should be prosecuted! Letting the animal run all over the place, causing accidents.'

'Well, hello again,' said Terry hoping she sounded casual. 'How are things going with the car, Alastair?'

He stood up, saying, 'It won't be fixed until around noon. So I thought it would be a good chance to find out how you were. Is the wrist any better?'

'Oh, yes,' she lied. 'Fine now, thanks. I'm fine. I hope you are.' How ridiculous she sounded! She stood awkwardly, trying to think of something else to say, but no words would fill the empty void her mind had suddenly become.

'It's kind of you to be so concerned.' Now she sounded like the Queen. In an effort to cover her nerves she turned to Mrs Godwin. 'Coffee! Marvellous. I'm gasping.'

Dressed in a baggy purple mohair sweater over trousers which, in turn, were encased in Wellington boots, Fiona was already helping herself to a second chocolate biscuit. 'Speaking of dogs, I'm afraid I forgot that this must be the only farm in England without one. I've committed the faux pas of bringing Max. Thought the walk would be good for him. Your mother seemed rather put out. Odd that. She likes horses yet hates dogs. Why?' Brushing a strand of lank, mouse-coloured hair from her forehead, she pushed it back into the untidy bundle which passed for a chignon.

Sitting down at the table, Terry picked up her cup and said, 'She's allergic to dog hairs apparently. Has been since childhood. They bring her out in a terrible rash if she isn't careful.' She turned to Alastair. 'Luckily cat's are no problem so what we lack in a canine population we more than make up for in feline.' She nodded towards the Windsor chair where, on the shabby cushion, a large tabby lay curled in sleep beside the warm stove. 'That's Thomas, the boss of our three house cats. Out in the barn there are four semi-wild mousers. Well, four at the last count.'

They lapsed into an awkward silence, horribly aware of the disagreement between the two fathers, which was slowly absorbing the village. Last night both men had returned home filled with anger. In the case of Terry's father that anger had slowly turned to relief. 'I made them realise tonight that the issue is over, once and for all.' But Gerald Rashleigh had stormed into

Thornley Hall and bellowed across the drawing room: 'I'll see that memorial raised on the crash site, come hell or high water. Fenton won't best me, by God!'

Aware that Mrs Godwin was waiting to clean the kitchen and hovering without a hint of subtlety, Terry said brightly, 'How about a walk? Poor Max must be miserable tied up out there.'

'I'll take his lead,' said Eliot, rushing out to the large Golden Retriever who, tied to the trunk of a silver birch, now quivered with excitement at his approach. 'Good boy, good Max,' he murmured, bending and stroking the wide head. 'Poor old thing, being tied up.' Slowly he unwound the lead from the trunk and was almost knocked off his feet by the excited dog. The others emerged from the house, putting on jackets and chatting, then they all headed down past the chicken run and outhouses towards the wood.

Ten minutes later, Diane entered the kitchen and looked about her in surprise. 'Where is everyone?'

'Gone to take that dog for a walk.' Mrs Godwin was scrubbing the tiled floor, her round face red with effort. She paused, looked up at Diane then reached into the pocket of her floral overall for a handkerchief. Wiping her nose, she sniffed, thinking that Mrs Fenton seemed anxious. 'Something wrong?'

Diane tensed, irritated by Mrs Godwin's manner. The woman was slapdash too, unable to hold a candle to old Mrs Shotley who had stayed on after Arthur Fenton's death to prove herself a treasure to the household. 'Which way did they go?'

'Towards the wood. Saw 'em through the window.' She stood up, sighed and rubbed her aching back. 'I've finished in 'ere, so I'll go up and do the bathroom. By the way, you need more Vim.' Diane was not listening. Walking to the window, she cursed beneath her breath. *Damn Fiona! How dare she bring that wretched dog with her?*

Armed with cleaning materials, Mrs Godwin made her way up to the bathroom. Her employer seemed very out of sorts today. Nothing unusual in that, mind. Not much of a marriage this one. She should know, having cleaned here two mornings a week since 1955. Very little got past her, she boasted proudly.

Sometimes she wondered about the family who had appeared in their midst after the death of Arthur Fenton. Lucky they had been, leaving the Channel Islands just before the Germans invaded. But that was all she knew about them. All anyone knew it seemed.

Finally she shook scouring powder into the old white enamel bath and got to work on that stubborn stain beneath the taps.

Pulling on his leash, so that Eliot found it hard to control him, the Retriever nosed his way through last year's fallen leaves, his instinct to flush out game now stronger than ever. In the end Alastair took over, calling him to heel with such authority that Max swung around with wide eyes, crept closer to him and walked more slowly.

The sun was out, a stiff wind rustled through beech leaves now on the turn and Terry, seeing the beauty of the woodland, began to relax at last.

'But why can't we let Max run free?' Eliot wanted to know.

'Because,' said Terry, 'if he races off to our left he could end up at the Rashleigh's paddock and frighten the horses, and if he chases too far ahead he could run on to the field where the tractor is working. We'll let him off by the stream. All he can do there is get wet and muddy.'

They walked on, chatting casually until Fiona stopped in the middle of the wood, saying, 'It was about here that Arthur Fenton was found shot dead. Daddy never believed it was an accident, you know. He reckons it was suicide.' Her expression changed. 'Oh, hell, I shouldn't have told you that! Don't repeat it, will you? Please, please, Eliot, Terry, don't repeat it or I'll be in real trouble.'

Alastair's eyes gleamed with amusement. 'You can't drop little tidbits like that without the main course. If it's mystery or scandal, I want the full works. Won't tell a soul. Cross my heart and hope to die . . . or whatever.'

'Everything's a joke to you, isn't it?' sighed Fiona.

'I won't repeat it and neither will Eliot.' Terry glared at her brother. 'On pain of death, Eliot?' When he nodded, she went on, 'Why would my father's cousin want to kill himself?'

Finding herself in the unusual position of being the centre of attention, Fiona warmed to her theme. 'Well, according to my parents, he married a woman who was considerably younger than himself and was over the moon when he learned he was to become a father. Tragically, his wife died in childbirth. The baby died as well. That's when Arthur changed from being a contented farmer to a recluse. Then one day, Mrs Shortly found him about here, shot through the neck. It was assumed he must have tripped, but my father didn't believe it. Arthur, he said, was too careful with guns. Come to that, it wasn't the shooting season – unless he was after rabbit.' She shook her head. 'No, it was suicide. But, of course, no one dare say as much, whatever they thought.'

Poor man, thought Terry as they walked on. She had always known of the accident, of course, and as children she and Marisa had thought that Arthur's ghost haunted the wood. They had been afraid of him then. Now, she felt a deep pity for the relative who was buried in the local churchyard. It was a sad way for her father to come into a legacy. Strange to think that but for this tragedy, she and her family would still be in Guernsey. They would have been there during the German occupation. What a thought!

They came out of the wood and stood watching the tractor ploughing the far end of Five Acre Field ready for the winter wheat to be planted. At the woodland end, however, stubble produced harvest mites which covered Terry's hands, just as they covered the windows of the farmhouse at this time of the year. She brushed them off, hoping no one would mention the site of the bomber crash. With two feuding fathers, a diplomatic silence would be wisest.

'During the war a bomber crashed just over there,' said Eliot.

Alastair's eyes followed the outstretched hand. 'Ah, so that's where it happened.'

Terry felt her heart sink. Clearly Brigadier Rashleigh had wasted no time in telling his nephew how selfish John Fenton was to block a route to the memorial site. What must Alastair think of her family now?

Eliot spoke on in blissful ignorance. 'It was a Lancaster returning from a raid over Germany. My friend told me the bodies were carried to our barn afterwards.' He turned to Terry. 'When I asked Dad he said it was true but didn't want to talk about it.'

Feeling she must now speak, Terry murmured, 'Apparently it was heading for a bomber station in Norfolk. I didn't know about the crew being taken to the barn. I didn't know anything really.'

She lapsed into silence, thinking that this was just a place where a bomber had crashed. That was all. It had happened a very long time ago and she had known nothing of the details. But, with all this talk of the memorial, things had changed. Only the other day

Mrs Shotley told her the crew had been in their twenties. Until that moment it had been another remote incident that had happened during her childhood, as the war had happened. Now, the shock of hearing about the youth of the crew had brought home the true extent of the tragedy and she felt saddened by it.

'My father wants this memorial as much as everyone else,' she said. 'It's access to the field that's causing the problem. But I daresay all will be resolved quite soon.' Walking on, she tried to make her voice light, signalling the end of the subject. 'We'll edge our way around the field towards the stream then Max can be let off his lead.'

The stream which ran through both Fenton and Rashleigh land was shallow, insignificant and almost weedbound. Even so, in winter it spilled on to muddy pasture which in spring gave way to wild flowers. For Terry it had always been a favourite spot and she had swapped the daisy chains of childhood for watercolour paints, spending hours capturing this gentle scene which was given focus by an old white windmill. Rundown and long since defunct, it stood broken-sailed on the far edge of her father's property, a sad reminder of a different age. Now, like the plough horse, it was no longer loved or needed.

Alastair stood staring across at it. 'Can we see inside?'

Terry shook her head. 'I'm afraid not. Dad keeps it locked. It's in a dangerous state.'

'He ought to sell it,' said Alastair. 'People are always doing up old windmills and turning them into homes.' He glanced at the dog. 'Can this poor devil be let off his leash now?'

Released at last, Max bounded about in wild excitement, jumped straight into the stream, nosed into weeds then emerged wet and muddy to shake himself over everyone. Eliot threw a stick. Max raced after it; stopped so fast he almost did a somersault, picked it up in soft jaws and ran back to Eliot, where he sat waiting with it in his mouth until it was taken gently from him and thrown again.

Fiona looked pleased. 'He presents well. Won second prize at the Lowdham Show last year, did I tell you?'

The wind blew more keenly here and Terry pulled her jacket close about her as they walked along. Alastair noticed and laughed. 'What's that saying? "When the wind's in the east, the fish bite least"? Give me London any day.'

Fiona threw the stick for Max and said, 'Your trouble is you don't know how to live in the country. The only horse power you're interested in moves on four wheels.'

'Come to a meeting sometime,' he said. 'You might even like it.'

'God forbid.' She turned to Terry. 'My cousin has no soul. Motor racing is the breath of life to him. Not beauty, not trees or green fields or animals. No soul. Well, come on. We mustn't be late getting to the garage.'

'You see what I have to put up with from my bossy cousin?'

'Second cousin,' Fiona corrected him, as she put Max back on his leash.

'You're lucky, both of you,' said Terry. 'We've no relatives at all.'

'You must have,' said Alastair. 'Everyone has. Love 'em or hate 'em, they've sure as hell got 'em.'

'We haven't,' said Terry. 'Both my parents were only children. My mother was orphaned at thirteen and my father's parents were dead before I was born even. The only relations then were my father's cousin, Arthur Fenton, and Mother's aunt in Guernsey who raised her. But she's dead, too, so now there's no one. You're lucky. Believe me, you're lucky. It must be wonderful to have cousins and aunts and uncles.'

They returned by the shorter route along the top end of Five Acre Field, past the mare's small paddock and the black barn until they finally reached the farmhouse. Eliot, who had become quieter and quieter during the latter part of the walk, said goodbye to Fiona and Alastair, stroked and patted Max in a poignant manner and went indoors.

'He seems upset,' said Alastair as Terry led them along the drive to the gate.

'He's off to boarding school tomorrow.' said Terry. 'He's never been away from home before, you see.'

Alastair did see. He too had been to public school. 'Things have changed at my old alma mater . . . no more fagging, thank God! My younger brother had a better time of it than I did. I'm sure Eliot will find it a happier experience than he expects. Tell him that from me.'

'I will.' After an awkward pause, she said, 'Well, I hope you're car's fixed and that you have a safe journey home.'

He nodded. 'Thanks for the walk. I enjoyed it immensely.' For a moment it seemed he wanted to say more; she prepared herself for what it might be, but then he turned away. 'I'm glad we literally ran into each other. Take care when you drive again. Goodbye, Terry.'

Deflated, she watched as he caught up with Fiona and Max, then turned and walked back to the house, wondering what he had been about to say which he had then thought better of saying.

Chapter Three

The Dame Edith Harting School for Girls stood in well-kept grounds just three miles from the small market town of Lowdham. A gaunt, Victorian Gothic building it had once been a Carmelite convent but in 1928 had been purchased by a local benefactress and turned into an 'academy for young ladies'.

With a stomach full of butterflies, Terry drove her little black Austin through the imposing gateway and along a drive bordered by rhododendrons. To her right lay games fields, to her left a gardener's lodge, and beyond that the grey stone building itself. Passing the main entrance she turned to the rear of the school where several cars were parked between the Art and Crafts Room and the newly built Laboratory. There was one space left; she moved into it and switched off the ignition.

She sat for some time checking her face in the rear mirror. Had she put on too much make up perhaps? Was the grey skirt and blue woollen twin set suitable or was it dowdy, as Marisa had insisted when the outfit had been purchased especially for this very day? Combing her hair, Terry wished she had put it up. Too late.

Finally summoning up enough courage to leave the car, she made her way to the front of the school, walked up a flight of stone stairs and entered the large oak-panelled hallway. By twenty past eight she was seated in the Head's study, meekly listening to the formidable grey-haired woman who wore a black academic gown and sat squarely behind a large oak desk.

'As you already know, Miss Fenton, you'll be Form Tutor to the Lower Second but will take the Upper Second for History and English also. You've prepared your lessons well, I hope? We did discuss the curriculum. Here's a copy of the timetable. You must get your girls to copy it out first thing today.'

Miss Yeats removed her wire-framed spectacles and wiped them on a soft cloth which she kept on her desk. Piercing brown eyes stared out from a sallow make-up-free complexion. 'We didn't discuss the subject of Art, but since you did well in this I'd like you to take the second forms for Art also.'

If Terry had any objection, it was clearly to go unheeded as Miss Yeats went on in her clipped impatient manner.

'Then there is the annual play. You'll be expected to take a prominent role in helping to produce this. We're doing *The Tempest* this year and pride ourselves on our high standards of acting and direction.'

Miss Yeats placed her hands in front of her and looked thoughtful. 'I like to think of this as a happy school, Miss Fenton, but happiness is born of strong discipline. A disciplined class is a class which learns well, so absolute control is essential, which means you must command the girls' respect at once.' Her eyes narrowed. 'You are very young. I've never taken on anyone straight from college before. But we lost Miss Halford quite suddenly and I was left rather high and dry.

'As we discussed at your interview, this will be a trial year for you. Out of a class of twenty-one, six girls have been kept back until their work is up to standard. So, for everyone's sake, I hope my faith in you proves to be well founded.' She glanced at her watch and walked to the door, still speaking. 'We haven't much time, so I'll take you to the Staff Room and introduce you to your colleagues and then on to meet your form.'

Feeling more ill at ease than ever, and wondering what on earth had happened to Miss Halford, Terry bent to pick up her bulging briefcase then followed quickly as Miss Yeats moved from her office, along an oak-panelled corridor which smelt of beeswax, and into a comfortable-looking room which was filled with old leather armchairs and several occasional tables.

Terry glanced about her. A corner niche caught her eye. She assumed it had once contained a statue of the Virgin Mary. Now it was empty. Against the far wall stood a coat rail, already full, with only one hanger remaining. Above this was a shelf containing a strange collection of dowdy-looking hats. Several women stood in a group, chatting; they turned curiously as the Head introduced the new recruit.

Shaking each hand, Terry realised that probably only two women were under the age of forty. Polite words and smiles belied the coolness of eyes which registered disapproval of someone straight out of training college mixing with experienced teachers such as themselves. Suspecting that when she left the room they would turn to each other with grim expressions, Terry followed the Head out and the door closed behind them.

Miss Yeats strode ahead, her voice echoing along corridors which once had been silent. 'When you've checked the register see that everyone files into the chapel for assembly which starts at nine-fifteen sharp.' After showing her where the chapel was, Miss Yeats reached a classroom and stopped. 'And this, Miss Fenton, is the Lower Second.'

As Terry's heart started thumping, Miss Yeats opened the door. The sound of girlish chatter stopped immediately and there was a noisy shuffle of chairs as twelve year olds in grey gym slips stood quickly to their feet.

'Good morning, girls.'

'Good morning, Miss Yeats.'

The Head let her keen eyes travel over the class as she said, 'I hope you all had a good summer and have returned ready for work. There is much to do. This is Miss Fenton, your new Form Tutor.'

'Good morning, girls,' said Terry, hoping she was mixing friendliness with authority in those three little words, but her spirits began to fail as twenty-one curious sets of eyes were turned on her.

'Good morning, Miss Fenton.' The collective chorus sounded unenthusiastic.

When Miss Yeats had gone, Terry smiled at the girls and said, 'You may sit.' As they did so she walked to her desk, reminded herself that she had taught classes during her training and this was no different. Before her lay the register and the familiar two inkwells, one blue and one red. Opening the register, she dipped the nip of the pen into the blue ink. The familiar smell of classroom assailed her nostrils; old wood and that extra unidentifiable ingredient that shouted 'school'. 'Well, now, the best way for me to get to know you all is for each one of you to stand up when I call your name.'

As each girl stood, Terry looked up at her, smiled and then put a mark beside the name. All who should be present were. The class then filed out and made its way in silence to the chapel.

On a raised platform, Terry joined the rest of the staff who were standing behind the Headmistress, hymn books at the ready. The music teacher struck the first chords on the piano and young female voices filled the Chapel with 'Praise My Soul, the King of Heaven', which had been adopted as the school hymn.

After prayers and a 'welcome to the new school year' speech from Miss Yeats, the girls filed out and Terry returned to her classroom. The door was open, the girls waiting inside. It was impossible not to hear their comments as she approached.

'I think she's pretty.'

'Plain as a pikestaff, if you ask me!'

'At least she's a lot younger than Miss Halford.'

'Idiot! She's middle-aged. Into her twenties at least.'

Terry entered the room, and the class fell silent.

The first period was given over to the copying of the term's timetable, which gave everyone some settling in time and a chance for Terry to become acquainted with her pupils and appoint class monitors. When the first lesson began, she asked which books they liked reading at home. Three put up their hands, saying Enid Blyton, the rest slouched in their chairs and just stared at her in silence.

On a note of growing despair, Terry walked among them and spoke of the English authors and poets she would be introducing them to during the term. The bored expressions before her did little to add to her confidence as monitors handed out books to each girl.

She could almost hear the silent groans as she drew their attention to Alfred Lord Tennyson's poem 'The Brook'. 'We shall read it first, and then discuss it. I want every girl sitting up straight and concentrating. Helen Turner will read first.'

Helen stood up, a sniggering smile revealing braced teeth. 'I come from haunts of coot and hern . . .'

Someone at the rear of the room giggled.

Knowing and understanding the silent conspiracy that was going on throughout the reading, Terry chose to ignore it. Slowly the atmosphere changed and with the ending of the poem she drew the girls into a discussion, smiling with them when they found something amusing then explaining it. With more understanding the poem was read through again and this time no one giggled. With a small sigh of relief Terry observed her quiet class, all with eyes fixed on the books before them. At least their little conspiracy was over. A disturbing thought crossed her mind. Just what had happened to Miss Halford that they knew about and she did not?

When the school day was over and girls filed out to waiting cars or made their way to bus stops, Terry returned to the Staff Room to find Miss Martin of Science and Chemistry talking to the red-headed Maths tutor of the Upper School.

'Well,' Miss Martin said as she turned to Terry with a friendly expression, 'how did you find the notorious Lower Second?'

'Notorious?' Catching the look that passed between the older women, Terry asked, 'Did Miss Halford find them notorious?'

'She found them impossible!' said the Maths tutor.

'What happened to her?' At their silence Terry frowned anxiously. 'She isn't dead, is she?'

Miss Martin laughed at this. 'Good heavens, no. Miss Halford crossed swords with the Head over the failure of the Lower Second to learn anything and said it would take a saint to teach such imbeciles. In short, Miss Yeats called an emergency meeting of the Board of Governors and the upshot was poor Miss Halford was dismissed. Unfairly, in my opinion. So be warned.'

The red-headed one turned to Terry. 'You have your work cut out with that class.'

Terry frowned. 'They didn't seem so bad to me. Oh, yes, there are problems – many of them are not up to standard, especially in reading – but calling them imbeciles and destroying their confidence couldn't have helped matters.'

Miss Martin smiled and said she absolutely agreed, while the other tutor wondered why it was that all greenhorns thought they could change the world. It did nothing to endear this young newcomer in their midst to the rest of the staff.

Then staring through the window on to the small car park, she frowned.

'Oh, by the way, Miss Fenton, does that black Austin belong to you?' Terry said that it did. 'Then please be more careful where you park it in future. That space is reserved for our Music tutor. She was most put out this morning and means to complain to the Head if it happens again.'

Shooting a reproving look at her colleague, Miss Martin slipped on a grey coat and green felt hat, piled papers and books into a large battered briefcase and smiled sympathetically at Terry as she left the room.

Suddenly feeling she had lost an ally, Terry walked to another window and looked down on to the playing fields. Mellow sunlight burnished leaves on the chestnut trees and swallows swooped and twisted in the air above in preparation for migration. As she watched, it dawned on her that everyone expected her to fail. That she would be out of here by next July, if not earlier. Well, she would see to it that they were wrong.

Never so glad to arrive back home as she was on that golden evening, Terry stood for a while smelling woodsmoke then entered the kitchen, which felt excessively warm, and placed exercise books on the table ready for marking later. Her mother was seated beside the range, drinking tea from the large beaker usually reserved for her father. She seemed pale, hunched and cold in spite of the cat sleeping on her lap.

'How did it go?' asked Diane, as though her thoughts were elsewhere.

'I'm not sure, to be honest. The girls, who are supposed to be monsters, were fine but the other teachers made me feel like a rather difficult ten year old. All except one.'

Diane's blue eyes looked sympathetic as her long fingers stroked the purring cat. 'Well, you're very young and I daresay they are . . .'

'Old and set in their ways,' snapped Terry.

Diane frowned. 'Oh, dear, have you been trying to teach grandmothers how to suck eggs?'

'Of course not, but when pupils are backward they need encouragement. From what I've gathered my predecessor did just the opposite.'

'And you'll put it all right, of course.' Diane smiled. 'Well, you have youth on your side and that's good, but youth in itself can be galling for older people, especially if mixed with arrogance. When the young think they know better than those with a lifetime's experience then watch out for fireworks, my girl. There's freshly made tea in the pot. Pour yourself a cup.'

Thinking her mother excessively touchy, Terry felt stung. 'I'm not arrogant. And I'm not stupid enough to behave as you seem to think I've done.' She poured tea into the cup already laid out for her, added milk and a little sugar, then stirring the tea gently, settled herself in the Windsor chair opposite Diane. The fire was too warm. Yet still her mother looked cold.

'You need these women on your side,' Diane was saying. 'So be prepared to swallow your pride and lean on them a little. Let them see you welcome their advice.'

'Hmm. I'm sure they can't wait to give it.' Terry drank her tea in silence then frowned at her mother. 'Are you feeling all right?'

When Diane said she was just a little tired, Terry kissed her on the cheek then ran up to her bedroom with the exercise books, keen to mark the first essays of her first day. The room felt chilly after the kitchen's heat. Switching on one bar of her electric fire, she sat herself at a small oak table which had been found in the attic a week ago and settled to work.

Diane meanwhile left the warm kitchen. After settling the hens for the night, she wandered past the old stables which used to house their two plough horses. One stall only remained in use now and belonged to her chestnut mare. She walked on to Dauphine's paddock with a bucket of water and watched as the chestnut mare trotted across to drink.

At fifteen hands, the horse had been her pride and joy for seven years. Hardly in the league of Rashleigh's thoroughbreds, Dauphine was gentle and steady as a rock, so Diane had never had any qualms about Terry or Marisa riding her once they were tall enough. Even Eliot was now able to take her around the paddock. Dauphine loved it all as much as she loved a good fuss. Fussing her now, Diane's mind was dwelling on something else, her visit to the village earlier that day.

The postmaster, usually full of chat, had unsmilingly handed her some stamps then turned away on the pretext of being busy. Next she had walked to the Thornley Stores where three women stood waiting to be served. Their conversation faded to nothing as she entered and, having barely acknowledged her, they kept their eyes averted. After being served politely and efficiently, but more as a stranger than one who belonged, she had practically collided with Lydia Rashleigh who was just leaving the newsagent's with a copy of *Horse & Hound* under her arm. Smiling thinly, Lydia had protested she had no time to stop and climbed into her Land Rover without further ado.

Shunned! As Diane stroked the mare's neck she felt an ache in the pit of her stomach. She had been shunned!

The sun had gone down by the time she left the paddock. Diane took the path by the cornfield and stood gazing across its emptiness, thinking how peaceful a scene it was. Impossible almost to believe in the horror of that summer evening all those years ago. Impossible or not, the row over the route to the memorial site was clearly the talking point of the village and, as a consequence, she and John were now social pariahs.

She tried telling herself that it didn't matter, that it would all blow over. But it did matter, it mattered dreadfully. For twenty years she had striven hard to be accepted into a community which looked on strangers with suspicion. Busy as she had been with the farm, she had found time to help with charity fund raising, the annual church fête, the Harvest Festival which had been held last Sunday, and was on the church flowers rota. She and John had become well-liked and respected. Now this! Where was it all going to end?

Slowly she turned her head to see the wood shadowed by the gathering dusk. An icy chill shuddered through her body.

Oh, God, where was it all going to end?

At ten-past nine Terry heard the telephone ringing in the hall. She lifted her head wearily from the exercise books, expecting one of her parents to answer, but the ringing went on. Sighing, Terry rushed down the stairs and picked up the receiver. 'Lynwood Farm.'

'At last! I was about to give up. That is you, isn't it, Terry?' Taken aback to hear Alastair's voice, she answered, 'It is. Who's this?'

'Alastair Hammond. Remember me?'

'Yes, of course I remember. How are you?'

'Fine. And you? How's teaching?'

'Well, I think I've got the pupils exactly where they want me. There are things they can't teach you in college.' Why was he ringing? What did he want?

'Look, there's a meeting at Snetterton this Sunday. I just wondered if you'd like to come along with me?'

'Meeting?' Light dawned through the mists in her mind. 'Oh, motor racing, do you mean?'

There was a slight pause, almost as though Alastair could hardly believe her words. '*Is* there another kind? You do like motor racing, I take it?' His tone implied she must be abnormal otherwise.

'I don't know the first thing about it,' she blurted, then asked herself why she hadn't lied. Marisa would have done. She would have waxed lyrical about the sport if Alastair had been on her shopping list. 'Still, it sounds fun.' Now Terry was lying.

'Good. You'll come then?'

'Well . . . I . . . Snetterton? Isn't that in Norfolk?'

'Just beyond Thetford. I'm coming to Thornley late on Saturday night, staying with the Rashleighs so that I can zip up there first thing in the morning while the roads are empty. Say you'll come?'

'Very well,' she said cautiously.

'Good. Seven o'clock then. Wear something casual.'

'Like a dressing gown? Seven o'clock? Are you mad?'

'Don't farmers' daughters rise at cock crow?'

Terry smiled wryly. 'Not if they had the sense to throttle the cockerel!'

On Saturday morning, Terry heard the postman, walked into the hall and picked up the mail from the floor. Two were obviously bills, one was in Eliot's handwriting and another had 'States of Guernsey' stamped on it. Curious, she stared at the latter, wondering who on earth could be writing from an island where they no longer knew anyone.

Handing the letter to her mother she stood waiting for her to open it, but Diane paled as she stared at the envelope and, to Terry's disappointment, pushed it into the pocket of her cardigan.

'A letter from Guernsey and you're not itching to open it?' Terry was astounded. 'Well . . . who can it be from?'

'I've no idea. Get your breakfast or you'll be late.' Diane tore open Eliot's letter. 'Had you taken a position with a state school, you wouldn't have had to work on Saturday mornings.'

Terry sighed. 'I need a degree to work in a state school. Dad wouldn't let me stay on for that and well you know it.' She walked into the kitchen, drank coffee, managed half a slice of toast then rushed out, climbed into her car and drove away.

When she returned at lunchtime and sat down to home-made chicken soup, cheese, salad, pickles and newly baked bread, Terry quizzed her mother on the letter once more.

Diane looked guarded and cut a slice of bread. 'Oh . . . that. It was to inform me that the church where my aunt is buried has decided to move the tombstones to one side in order to cut down on maintenance. It seems that grass cutting has priority over respect for the dead these days. Anyway they need permission from any living relatives of more recent burials and that's what this letter is about. I've written back saying that since we cannot tend the grave we have no objections. What else can we do?'

A shade disappointed, Terry glanced at her father, expecting him to say something, but he kept his eyes on the newspaper and his thoughts to himself. 'Well,' she sighed. 'I'm going to ride Dauphine. Weather's too good to be indoors.'

When Terry had left, Diane stared across the table at John's grim face. 'Did I do well? Good God, what next! I thought we had seen the last of those letters years ago.'

'Burn it,' he said. Seeing her indecision, he leaned forward and repeated, 'Burn it as we did the others.'

'But this one's different. This one could be really dangerous.' I think maybe I should reply, saying . . .'

'Believe me, I know what I'm doing. Burn it, and trust in my judgment.'

Diane's bright blue eyes narrowed bitterly. 'Trusting in your judgment has got me where I am today.'

'Then you should thank God for it,' shouted John, fist smashing down on the table, causing Diane to start. He slid his chair back noisily and stormed towards the door.

She cried out, 'I thank God for our luck, not your judgment.'

He paused for one moment, gave her a look which froze the marrow of her bones, then walked out, slamming the door behind him.

That evening, Terry's mind was too much on her meeting with Alastair to concentrate on anything else. His phone call had come as a surprise. Whereas Marisa cast off admirers like old socks, she herself had been out with only three members of the opposite sex. First there was the callow farmer's lad from Boxham her father had deemed Neanderthal, then a publican's son from Lowdham who suffered from halitosis, and the Vicar's son who had disappeared among the Dreaming Spires. Once up at Oxford he had never been in touch with her again and she couldn't have cared less.

Alastair was a different kettle of fish. She liked him more than she should since they hardly knew each other, but he had been in her thoughts and she wanted to remain in his. What exactly did women wear to race meetings? The last thing she wanted was to have him think her an embarrassing idiot.

Hauling clothes from her wardrobe and drawers, it was only a matter of minutes before her bedroom looked as though thieves had broken in. Something casual, he had said. Trews and a sweater? What was his idea of casual? She decided to play safe and tried on a moss green, softly gathered woolen skirt, with a cotten blouse in exactly the same shade. Over this she flung about her shoulders a mustard lamb's wool cardigan, and decided her mother's liberty silk scarf would add the finishing touch.

Walking to her parents' bedroom, she sat down at the 1930s-style light oak dressing table and opened the small right-hand drawer where Diane kept accessories neatly packed away.

As she removed the top three scarves Terry's eyes fell on an envelope. She drew it out and stared at it in puzzlement. The letter from Guernsey. Why was it hidden away in this drawer? Most letters ended up in the old roll top desk until they were no longer needed.

About to put it back she paused and, curiosity getting the better of her, took the letter from the envelope and started reading it.

My dearest Diane,
Since you have never answered any of my letters I can only assume that you sold the farm and moved on, in which case I wonder you never informed me.

If this is not the case, you will be reading these words and, please God, might be moved to answer, if only to put my mind at rest that you, John and the girls are all well and thriving. You see, my dear, when I waved goodbye to you and watched the ferry sail away all those years ago, I had no idea I would never see or hear from you again.

Diane, is it because you, like some other islanders who left before the invasion, believe that those who remained fraternised or even collaborated with the German soldiers? If so, you cannot know how it was here or how deeply wounded I am that you might be thinking such things of me. Yet it seems you must, otherwise I would have heard from you, surely?

I lost my beloved Denis two years ago and widowhood has not been easy, but I've been lucky in having Meg who was only four when you left. You would be proud if you saw her now. She's a nurse and has been a wonderful daughter and companion to me. I shall miss her dreadfully when she goes to London in November to take up a position at Guy's Hospital. Still, the young must be allowed to spread their wings, I suppose. It would be so marvellous for her to meet her only relations. It would also set my mind at rest knowing she has family in England who will take an interest and make her welcome. She'll be in the nurses' home at Guy's for a short while so I'm enclosing her telephone number just in case this letter does reach you.

I sold the greenhouses when Denis died, couldn't cope with all that on my own. I still live in the old house though and do summer Bed and Breakfast. If you came over to see me there's plenty of room for you all. How quickly the years have flown and how much I miss everyone and the times we had in the old days.

Please do write to me. I lie awake at night wondering if you are all safe and well.

Your loving cousin, Grace

When Terry had read the letter she sat quite still. The walls of the room seemed to have receded into the distance and, for one strange unreal moment, she felt caught in a time warp. Then the walls returned to normal and she could hear the ticking of the alarm clock on the bedside table.

In disbelief, she read the letter again then stared at her reflection in the mirror, trying to make sense of everything. A dead aunt, her mother had said, but no mention had been made of any cousins.

Why? Grace sounded a sweet, sad person trying to reach out to her family. Why then was that family ignoring her and denying her very existence?

She glanced at the letter once more, the letter she was not meant to see, and recalled how her mother had lied about its contents. All that nonsense about tombstones. What kind of imagination could conjure up anything so weird, and for what reason?

Someone was coming. Quickly committing Meg's London telephone number to memory, Terry replaced the letter in its envelope, and put it back under the scarves before closing the drawer and switching off the light.

Racing back to her own room, she heard her father's footsteps on the landing and stood quite still, hardly daring to breathe. The light in the master bedroom came on once more. She heard him walk inside and shut the door. Feeling like a criminal on the run, Terry sank on to her bed, trembling a little. Later she roused herself, wrote Meg's telephone number in her address book while she could still remember it, and lay back on her bed.

Lies! All these years her parents had lied to her and now she had uncovered the lie. How would they react if she confronted them with this fact? Unthinkable! Marisa might rise to the challenge but she lacked the courage to face their anger which, given the years of lies, would surely be dreadful.

Better by far to wait, and trust that Meg would prove to be the key which could unlock this mystery.

Chapter Four

Alastair arrived at ten minutes to seven the following morning and grinned as Terry appeared at the door.

'Not too early, am I?'

He was, but she was glad of it; glad to get out of the house, and the sooner the better. How on earth could she spend a normal Sunday at home with this new knowledge hammering away in her brain? It had kept her awake most of the night and she had finally got out of bed at half-past five, drunk three cups of tea, bathed and was dressed by six-thirty.

Misreading the situation, Alastair cast an appreciative eye over her and smiled. 'Well, as I live and breathe, a woman who is not just on time but ahead of it.'

The shock of the letter had overshadowed Terry's initial nervousness and excitement, now all she wanted to do was go. Silly remarks flew straight over her head. It was cold; the morning sun was a red glow to the east still and the day was not fully light.

Looking past Alastair, she saw a sleek roadster in Racing Green and wanted to know what had happened to the Rover.

'Oh, that.' He grinned again. 'Only borrowed it because I drove this one into an embankment.'

'What?' Terry stared at him but all her brain would take in at that hour was his sports jacket, unbuttoned over a check shirt and plain green tie. 'Couldn't have gone down too well when the Rover met a similar fate. Hope I haven't destroyed a friendship.'

'She'll get over it. Anyway, I paid for the repairs, didn't I?' With that, Alastair started towards the car, thinking that, in some strange and subtle way, Terry had changed from the shrinking violet he'd assumed her to be.

Collecting her short woolen jacket, she waved unsmilingly to Diane who was walking towards them from the hen house, then climbed into the vehicle and settled back in the low soft leather seat.

She had never been in a sports car before. Not for the world would she let him know it, though. The roof was down, it would be a cold drive. She tied her scarf about her head; her own, not the Liberty silk she would have liked. The thought of asking her mother for it had completely slipped her mind after reading that letter.

Wondering now about the mysterious 'she' who had lent him her Rover, Terry turned to Alastair as he started the ignition. 'Watch out for pheasants. They're all over the place. Oh, and remember the ducks at the watersplash.'

'Pheasants and ducks. Right, ma'am.' Alastair eased the car along the drive, out through the gates and down the hill. Once clear of the village he put his foot down hard on the accelerator. As he sped along twisting country lanes towards the Al40, Terry wondered how long the car could hold the road.

'You like to drive fast,' she shouted above wind and engine.

'Have to. We've a way to go.'

'Why the hurry? Race meetings don't usually start at the crack of dawn, surely?'

Alastair changed down at a sharp bend and once round it pushed the stick into top gear, accelerating on the straight stretch. 'There's a lot to do. Check out the car for one thing, then practise for the qualifying laps for another. It all takes time.'

She stared at him stupidly until light slowly dawned. 'You mean, *you're* racing?'

'Of course. Why else would I be going?'

'To watch?'

He laughed. 'Christ, no. If I'm not taking part then I don't want to know about it.'

Terry hunched in her seat and tried to take this in. As exciting as it should have been she felt crushingly disappointed that he could take her so much for granted. They would not be spending the day together. She would stand alone in some wind-blown field while he raced around a circuit, having the time of his life. For a moment she was angry, but such was his boyish enthusiasm, the anger soon melted away.

'Are you racing in this?' she asked.

He shook his head. 'The car's being transported by my team.'

His team! Impressed, she decided to ask no more questions that might make her seem an idiot and, turning her head, watched the countryside flashing past instead. Not so long ago he had walked away from her at the gate and she'd never expected to see him again. Now here she was, hurtling into Norfolk with him on on a chilly autumn morning, off to a day of motor racing.

Wondering what the day would bring, she began to relax, a contented smile on her lips.

'What are we to do about you?' Lydia Rashleigh glared across the walnut table at her daughter. 'Is it completely beyond your powers to let a man think you're interested in him and perhaps encourage his interest in you? We've spent time and money in order that you should make a good match, yet you throw it all away and let that Fenton girl seize the advantage.

In Thornley Hall's elegant dining room, Emily poured coffee and listened to the argument raging between her mistress and Miss Fiona. No one minded her presence for she had been with the family for thirty years, watched the three Rashleigh children grow from babyhood and seen a once thriving estate reduced to a third of what it was, with many fields being rented out or sold off and the household staff reduced to herself and a young and fairly useless maid.

Fiona sat in her large sweater, hair tied back, face ruddy and clean of make up, eyes wide with astonishment. 'What on earth brought all this on?'

'God give me strength!' sighed Lydia. 'Do I have to spell it out for you? We're not getting any younger, and your brother will inherit this place one day. So where does that leave you? Think about it, dear. We can't afford to settle enough on you to give you financial security for life.'

Fiona shrugged. 'Oh, that. Don't worry about it. I'll have my riding school. I've found the right place. If Daddy will just start me off with a loan . . .'

'Stop it! Riding school indeed. I'm speaking of marriage?'

'I thought you were speaking of finance.' Fiona's round face split into laughter. 'Oh, Mummy you're a hoot at times. I couldn't marry Alastair if he were the last man on earth, and if you think he wants to marry me then you're living in cloud cuckooland. Anyway, it's out of the question. We're cousins.'

'Second. That's no impediment.'

The laughter drained from Fiona's face. 'We like each other in our own way and get along as cousins do, but that's all. Now may I eat my breakfast in peace?'

Emily smiled to herself and glanced at the Brigadier who was concentrating on his kedgeree. Keeping his head down again, she thought. Once he had ordered men 'over the top', but he knew better than to join battle with mother and daughter.

Lydia sipped her coffee slowly, a grey-haired, intelligent-looking woman some six years younger than her husband, thread veins criss-crossing the cheeks of her florid angular face. Her husband was useless to her on such occasions, but he knew the problem just as she did and worried about it in the same way. If only Alastair would get this racing nonsense out of his system, then Fiona might see him in a different light and make more of an effort. What hope was there of that, though, if Diane Fenton's daughter got her claws into him first?

Diane! Lydia had never liked or trusted that woman. There was something about her which seemed at odds with a tomato-growing background in Guernsey. As for John, what had he been before inheriting the farm? No one really knew, save that he had gone to Guernsey from England, married Diane there and ended up working in a market garden. Ordinary working people, that's all they were in spite of their 'cultured' accents. Awkward, though, never quite knowing where to place them in the scheme of things. Not at her dinner table certainly, even if Diane did like to play the lady.

She smiled at the thought, remembering the war years when many could be forgiven for thinking Diane in charge of the Red Cross rather than Lydia Rashleigh, wife of the Squire. How that woman tried it on, and how people were taken in! And then there were all those young pilots constantly invited to Lynwood Farm for lunch or tea at weekends. Well, that was all over, thank Heaven, and the Fentons' social life with it, but now John was flexing his muscles against her husband just as his daughter was scheming to steal Alastair away from Fiona.

Lydia's fingers tightened on her fork as she pushed it into the kedgeree. The very idea of her nephew mixing with that family was utterly unthinkable. If the Fentons thought they could hitch their horse to the Rashleigh wagon, they would have to think again.

She glanced at her silent husband and then at her daughter who was eating too much and too quickly as usual. Didn't anyone care? Well, even if they didn't, she would make sure that Diane and John did. The Fentons were about to be roused out of their smug complacency.

With six races scheduled, Snetterton was awash with vehicles and drivers as Alastair led Terry along a line of racing cars to where three men were standing beside a sleek green sports model. It was similar to the one she had arrived in.

Having been made aware that this was the new Mk. 7 Terry was then introduced in turn to Alastair's brother Sean, the chief mechanic, and the car's designer. Politely the three men acknowledged her but their show of interest was brief as they returned to discussing the car and racing programme. It was Sean, just twenty-four, who finally took pity on Terry and turned to her, smiling.

'You've had a long trip and an early start. I daresay you could do with a coffee?' Bending to a picnic hamper which stood on the grass, he opened the top and produced a large thermos flask. 'Did you enjoy the ride? Alastair has the earlier model, though, not like this marvellous machine. Dad's over the moon with the seven. Won't come to the meetings, though. Doesn't like the idea of Alastair racing even if it is for Hammond's.' This last sentence was whispered as he poured coffee into a plastic cup and offered it to her.

She took it from him, her mind clearing from the fog which had suddenly enveloped it. Hammond's! Hammond Motors produced one of Britain's most popular sports cars. 'Dad' then had to be Sir Angus Hammond! Idiot! How could she have been such a fool? Of all the people converging on Snetterton, she must be the only one who stood in ignorance as to who was who and what was what; and of all the women the least sophisticated and worldly.

At last Alastair returned to her, saying, 'Time to get started.' Removing his jacket, he pulled on overalls and a helmet before climbing into the Mk. 7 and driving off to the starting grid.

In a strange world of roaring engines and car fumes, Terry

stood watching as vehicles zoomed around the circuit during their practice laps and slowly found herself caught up in the excitement of it all. A Lotus spun out of control and crashed. Heart in her mouth, she watched as the driver freed himself from the wreckage. Relieved as she was, excitement had now turned to fear, not helped by a horrifying crash in the first race when another Lotus was hurled into the bank, sending wreckage flying all over the track. As the driver was thrown out she stifled a scream then relaxed when it was clear that he too had escaped serious injury.

How on earth could she watch Alastair? But she did. He was in the ten-lap race for sports cars and Sean stood beside her with lap chart and stop watch in hand while Alastair raced the Hammond flat out in an effort to take the lead. Pushed back as another car passed him at Coram Curve, he gradually fell back in the field to finish without a place. His bitter disappointment was as nothing to Terry's utter relief that he was still in one piece.

As he watched Alastair climb out of the car and heard him uttering obscene oaths about its cornering powers, Sean's calm words belied his own true feelings. He would rather race himself than watch his own brother risk life and limb. But one son racing was one too many for their father, and Sean had resigned himself to a more pedestrian way of life even though it fought against every impulse in his body.

Having watched Alastair put his life on the line for the sake of speed, yet realising that she had nevertheless thrilled to his skill, Terry felt her emotions had been turned inside out and hung out to dry. Later, when they finally set off for Suffolk, away from the noise, crowds and car fumes, she only knew that she was excited to be with him, even if he was pushing the car to a heart-stopping seventy on some stretches of narrow dark country roads.

Still filled with the energy of racing, Alastair was alert, exhilarated and felt the need to celebrate, even though he had not triumphed. Talking non-stop, he relived every moment of the race until, on arriving at a small remote village, he pulled up at the Old Moat House Inn for dinner.

Seeing at once that it was a fashionable establishment and feeling they were both under-dressed for the candle-lit restaurant, Terry sat beside a roaring log fire in the bar sipping sherry while Alastair drank a large whisky and soda wishing it was winner's champagne. Time was when it would have been; when he had been first past the flag and fame was following.

'Did you enjoy today?' he asked, all too aware that he was no hero in her eyes. When she said she had, he felt she meant it even so and was spurred on. 'There's the Three Hour Race in October. How about coming along for that one?' Before she could say yes or no, he added, 'Anyway, think about it.'

'How long have you been racing?' Terry asked.

He looked thoughtful. 'I started rallying when I was about eighteen, I suppose. Oxford put paid to that, but after graduating I just picked up where I left off and went on from there.'

'Sean says that your father wants you to give it up. Will you?' He stared into his drink and smiled wryly. 'There comes a time when you can't. I began to think I'd already crossed that particular Rubicon, but lately I haven't had the success I started out with and so . . .' He sighed, knowing that to give it up was like giving up on life. 'Dad's no spring chicken and means to hand the company over to me pretty soon. Not that he'll ever retire from it completely, but he's had a spell of ill health of late and has been ordered to rest. Which means I'll spend far more time in Coventry, leaving the London office to Sean. Once I'm that involved then racing's out anyway. But I can't give up the game completely. At the moment I'm trying to persuade my father to produce a racing car using the lines of the seven but with improved cornering and a souped up engine. He's still not convinced.'

Draining his glass, Alastair ordered another Scotch. When Terry declined a second sherry, he returned to the subject.

'Even if he does agree, I know he'll get someone else to drive it. Lucky bastard, whoever he is.'

Terry's eyes softened. 'I can understand your father not wanting you to race, though.' Coventry! It was so far away.

Alastair looked glumly into his glass. Today had been the Archie Scott Brown Memorial Trophy and Archie had been his hero and rôle model. The shock of his death in May still hit hard, and the order from Sir Angus Hammond that his son would race no more had come as no surprise. He understood it. Having built up Hammond Motors into the thriving business it was today, his father needed an heir he could rely on, not some hot shot who thought only of the next race. After some anxious moments and much pleading, however, Alastair had been granted a stay of execution until the end of this year.

The head waiter crossed to them and said, 'Mr Hammond, your usual table is ready.'

Following him to the low-beamed restaurant, they settled at a candle-lit corner table. A shade embarrassed, Terry glanced around at dark suits and smart cocktail dresses and thought she looked like a waif who had wandered in from the fields.

'You've obviously been in here before.' she murmured, glancing at the menu.

Alastair nodded. 'I sometimes look in en route from Snetterton to Thornley.' Suggesting pâté with fillet steak to follow, he turned his eyes to the wine list, suddenly aware that Terry was more attractive than he had first thought. Yet charged as he was with the sexual energy racing always gave him, he knew her to be the wrong woman for him just now. Odd choice, he thought, when he could have asked any one of his other girl friends along; girls who would party until the late hours then go with him to a quiet unfashionable hotel for the night. So why on earth had he chosen Terry? But he had, and here she was in a simple blouse and skirt, managing to look radiant and asking what he had read at Oxford.

'Classics,' he answered. 'Waste of bloody time in my line of work.'

She shook her head vigorously. 'No, never in a million years. Just because you don't need it in your work doesn't mean it isn't important. I would have given anything for a degree, but my father was completely against it. Two years at college was long enough, he said.' She smiled. 'He's pretty short-sighted about these things. Doesn't mind my being a teacher, in his book that's one up from typist or secretary, but he thinks a degree is wasted on women, saying they get married and never think or use their education again. You see? Hopelessly old-fashioned.'

Alastair shrugged. 'He's right after all. Attractive women do marry and invariably give up their careers. Let's face it, Terry, no man likes a blue stocking.' Unaware of her cold stare, he went on, 'And, be honest. You wouldn't give up the chance of marriage for teaching, surely?'

'I haven't given the matter any thought,' she snapped angrily. Seeing his startled look, anger slipped from her and she smiled. 'How on earth did we get on to this subject anyway?'

Alastair smiled. 'It's certainly a prickly one, by all accounts.'

At that moment the pâté arrived. After claret was poured into their glasses, Alastair raised his and said, 'Here's to you and a lovely day. We'll have another bottle after this.'

Alarmed at his words, Terry waited until the wine waiter was well out of earshot then whispered, 'Do you think that's wise? From here on, the roads are nothing but narrow twisting lanes.'

He reached out and took her hand, frowning. 'Enjoy life. Don't be so grave.'

'It's just that I don't want to find myself in one!' His touch had sent a small tremor through her body and her snapped reply was in instinctive defence against it.

He sighed and withdrew his hand. 'Very well then, one bottle it is, and I shall deliver you safely to the bosom of your family, have no fear.'

Her heart sank. Why had she allowed shyness and nerves to make her sound so stuffy? Why could she not learn tact instead of practically accusing him of drinking too much and driving too fast? How many times had Marisa told her to play up to men? 'Forget honesty. They hate the truth.' But Terry could not simper and mew in order to make a man feel important. She was what she was and that was that.

It would be a bitter thing to lose Alastair because of it.

'Oh, for goodness' sake, stop wandering around and sit down.' Diane was trying to read but she and John were both on edge as they listened in vain for the sound of an approaching car.

'It's past bloody midnight!' For the umpteenth time he walked to the sitting-room window and peered out into darkness. 'Not a sign of them. God, if only I'd known, then . . .'

'Then what?' Diane gave up trying to read. She was tired and the fire had gone out long since. 'What would you have have done about it?'

John fell silent, staring along the drive to the lane beyond, tapping his fingers on the white wooden sill and remembering Lydia Rashleigh's words earlier that day. It had happened as they were filing out of church, both horribly aware that everyone was waiting to see if the Rashleighs and the Fentons would cold shoulder each other.

The church stood on a hill overlooking Thornley and a keen

wind had cut about it from the surrounding countryside. The customary chat with the Vicar was over when Lydia walked across and whispered to them that they really must not worry. At first it seemed she was referring to the rift, but then she went on to say, 'I'm quite sure Alastair will get her back safely even if he is a terror on the roads as well as the track. It's why we don't like Fiona going out with him. After Silverstone . . . when he had that accident . . . well, it was the limit. I said to her, never again. So I *do* know what a worry it is for you.'

John had stared at her like an idiot before the truth dawned on him. 'Do you mean Alastair is a racing driver?'

Lydia's eyes had widened as she'd put her fingers to her mouth and murmured, 'Oh, dear. You didn't know? Sorry. I wouldn't have said anything had I realised. No, no, that's wrong too. Far better to put you in the picture. I'm afraid he's a speed king and doesn't always make a distinction between a racing circuit and a country lane.' She touched him gently on the arm. 'But don't worry. I'm sure Terry will be all right.'

As the Rashleighs had walked to their car, he and Diane had made their way down the stone steps which led from the rear of the church to the High Street. Still feeling poleaxed, they climbed into the Morris Traveller and from that moment on had not known a single moment of peace.

At last John saw the headlights of a car; the sound of wheels crunching on the gravelled drive sent relief to combat his anger.

Diane jumped up from her chair and said, 'Well, they're home, thank God. Now let's go to bed. No sense in embarrasing the girl.'

'You go. I want to speak to Terry.'

She gave him a withering look. 'John, you can't do that.'

'I can't spend another day and night like this one either. Go to bed and leave this to me.'

'We can talk about it tomorrow, for goodness' sake. You'll only antagonise her if you play the heavy-handed father now.'

Seeing he meant to stand his ground and knowing him for what he was, however, Diane walked quickly up the staircase and into her bedroom, leaving the door open so that she could hear and intervene if things became too heated.

Alastair saw the light in a downstairs room and felt his heart sink like lead. No nightcap, no heavy petting beside a glowing fire, nor even here in the car for the moment he switched off the ignition another light appeared in the hall and the silhouette of a man appeared in the doorway.

'Is that you, Terry?'

Tense with embarrassment, she called out, 'Yes.' She heard Alastair's long drawn out sigh and simmered with rage. This was the end! How dare her father treat her like a child and embarrass her in such a manner?

'Reception committee,' murmured Alastair as he led Terry to the front door. He smiled at John and saw a possessive father who looked on all men as potential despoilers of his daughter. It was no time to hang around. Bidding Terry and her father a hasty good-night, he walked back to the car and drove away.

Watching in dismay as the tail lights disappeared through the gate, Terry swung round, eyes blazing.

'Why did you do that?'

John glared at her. 'Do you have any idea what you put us through today? As soon as we heard, we were both sick with worry.'

'Heard what?' Frowning, she stared at him but he moved into the sitting room. She followed, threw her jacket over the back of an armchair and repeated the question. 'Heard what, for goodness' sake?'

John told her then added, 'Apart from the danger to you as his passenger, we all know what racing drivers are like and the type of girls who hang around with them.'

For one long moment she just stared at him. 'And what is that supposed to mean?'

'That you're out of your league, Terry, and we love you too much to watch and do nothing.'

She sighed and felt anger slip away. Her father's face revealed his intense worry and it was her fault for not putting him at his ease. 'Look, I can understand your anxiety if Mrs Rashleigh said such things, but they're simply not true. I had a marvellous time among friendly people. As for Alastair, he's a perfect gentleman and doesn't drive like a bat out of hell on our roads.' She turned her face at this last little lie, but angry at the harsh things said about him, found herself rushing to his defence. In that moment she knew she was in love. 'Anyway you needn't worry,' she added in a bitter tone. 'When a man sees a woman being treated like a child, he's hardly likely to ask her out again.'

John walked slowly from the room then paused. 'We love you too much to hope that he does.'

Lowdham Market was mainly one long street of sixteenth- and seventeenth-century houses and shops which sloped gently uphill where it widened on to the large Green. Here, dominating the whole scene, was the ornate wool church of St Saviour, its square tower visible for miles around, its high hammer-beamed nave protected by castellated walls.

Halfway up the High Street, Terry stopped her car outside a newsagent's, felt the chill of the misty October air and, entering the shop, purchased a copy of the weekly *Lowdham and District Chronicle*. Without glancing at the headlines she placed it folded on the passenger seat and continued on her way. Driving on up the hill, she noticed lights in the windows of Georgian houses surrounding the Green and thought how quickly the daylight was fading as autumn approached.

October! Four hellish weeks had passed since that day at Snetterton and still no word from Alastair. It was over, she told herself, over before it had even began. Her father had killed it and she would never forgive him.

Thank goodness she had the school play to occupy her mind and had also won a difficult battle with Miss Yeats for permission to give her backward girls extra tuition after school. The Head had insisted on the parents paying for this, however, and to those who baulked at forking out, sent sharp letters warning that she expected higher standards from their daughters. To Terry it had become a barbed victory, albeit a necessary one.

It was quite dark by the time she reached Thornley. Lights from the ancient cottages were welcoming even if their inhabitants were less so these days. She slowed almost to a halt at the water-splash, peering through the headlights' beam to see whether ducks were swimming in front of her or not; a flurry of wings and loud squawking told her they had scurried away and so she drove on and up the small hill until she turned through the opened gates to the drive. Lynwood looked inviting enough, a beacon of home and hearth to warm a soul on this dark chilly evening, yet she hated the thought of entering.

The coolness between herself and her parents over Alastair went on and on. She wearied of it but her father's implacable attitude made it impossible for her to climb down. Why should she when he was in the wrong and would do the same thing again?

At first she had told herself that Suffolk was a long way from London and since Alastair probably spent much of his time between the capital and Coventry he could hardly keep driving to Thornley. But as the weeks had passed and the telephone had not rung for her, she knew she had been given the brush off, not because they lived so far apart but because Alastair had seen the expression on her father's face.

On top of all this were the lies! Years and years of lies. Why? What on earth was so wrong with Grace and her daughter Meg that they were treated as though they had never existed? And why was it that Terry herself still felt wary about asking?

Enough was enough! Today she had stopped off on her way home from school to buy the local newspaper with the intention of searching for a small flat or bedsitter. Independence! Marisa had it so why shouldn't she? Of course, Lowdham was hardly London, and even if she could find one in a market town, a lonely bedsitter was not the same thing as sharing a decent-sized flat with friends as her sister did.

As she got out of the Austin, it dragged at her heart to realise that only weeks ago she had been perfectly happy to go on living in the home where she was raised. But that was before the letter and Alastair. Now she felt trapped and alone.

Checking household accounts at the kitchen table, Diane heard Terry's car outside and braced herself for the tension this hitherto gentle and dependent daughter would bring into the house with her. It was all she needed. Aware that Terry blamed her and John for Alastair's silence, she longed to speak her mind, to tell the girl that had he been truly interested he would have telephoned come hell or high water. But how could she? How could she hurt and humiliate Terry in an effort to shift the blame from where it truly belonged?

Had it happened to Marisa she would have weathered it all like an old sea captain. But it wasn't Marisa, it was Terry, the vulnerable and gentle one, and that was why the whole thing was so painful.

If only John would soften his stance, she thought. But, in his book, he had prevented his daughter from certain disaster and she could sulk as much as she liked as far as he was concerned. 'Why blame me because some cavalier Jack the lad has no further interest in a girl who's decent when he likes them fast?' was his attitude.

Between the two of them, Diane quietly despaired.

The door opened and Terry entered, weighed down with a large leather briefcase, shoulder bag and a stack of exercise books under her arm.

Diane removed her spectacles and pinched the ridge of her nose, a sign that she was tired and low in spirits. 'Hello, dear. Did you have a good day?'

Although Terry loved teaching, no day at Dame Edith Harting could ever be classed as good. She shrugged. 'So, so.' She dropped her belongings on the clean floor and lifted the cat off its favourite chair for a cuddle and stroke. Thomas purred sleepily into her ear, heavy, soft and lovable. She would miss him when she left home.

'Is that the local paper you have there?' asked Diane

Tensing slightly, Terry tried to sound casual. 'Yes. I stopped off in Lowdham.'

'That was thoughtful of you.' Diane smiled, and stretched out her hand. She rarely shopped in the village now, preferring the anonymity of the local market town. 'They've always sold out by Friday afternoon, which is when I usually go in.'

Unwillingly, Terry handed over the *Lowdham and District Chronicle*, thinking how typical was the assumption that she would never have bought it for herself. She was still their little girl with nothing of her own, not even her privacy, not even her newspaper. Yes, it was time to leave and gain her independence before she lost her nerve completely.

'Well, I'll go up then,' she said as Diane's eyes scanned the front page. 'Hope there's enough hot water for a bath?' Since her mother was now too engrossed in reading to answer, Terry left the kitchen and had just started up the stairs when she heard a strangled cry and ran back again.

Hand clutching her throat, Diane's shocked voice could only just murmur. 'Dear God . . . dear God . . . how dare they? How dare they?'

'What? What is it?'

'Why didn't you warn me?' Slowly Diane stood up and glared at her daughter. 'I see now why you bought it. Well, you shouldn't have wasted your money on such a rag. Why . . . I wouldn't give it dustbin room! That's where it must go, right now, before your father sees it.'

Bewildered, Terry took the paper from her and glanced at it. The offending item wasn't the headline story but a front-page column there for all the world to see.

Thornley At War Over Memorial

A feud between two landowners has shattered the peaceful village of Thornley. For months now, Brigadier Rashleigh, Chairman of the Parish Council, has led the villagers in a bid to place a memorial on the site where a Lancaster bomber crashed in 1943, killing all seven crew members. The scheme, however, has been blocked by one man, Mr John Fenton, who owns the field where the bomber crashed.

Mr Fenton is claiming that he does not wish the public to walk on his land and refuses to give permission for the memorial to go ahead. Mr Tom Steel, who owns the bakery in Thornley, told our reporter: 'We all think it's a disgrace. Those young men gave their lives for our freedom but Mr Fenton can't give up a few square yards of land for a memorial to their memory. Disgusting!'

Neither Mr Fenton nor Brigadier Rashleigh was available for comment.

Jaw dropping with astonishment, Terry shook her head. 'But . . . but it isn't true. It isn't like that at all. They've made it seem as though we don't want the memorial. No word about the problems with access. It's libellous. And what's all this about not being available for comment? Has anyone from the paper approached Dad?'

Diane looked pale and let her fingers trail across one cheek as she always did when worried. 'Well . . . there was a phone call about a week ago. Your father doesn't know about it, I didn't want to worry him. Someone from the paper asked if he could speak to Mr Fenton about the matter and I said certainly not. It was all over and had nothing to do with them. I thought that was the end of it. It never occurred to me they would print such an article without discussing the issue with the one person who was most concerned.'

Terry sank into the Windsor chair. 'Poor Dad. It's wicked, utterly wicked. He's being pilloried for something he can't help.'

'We all are,' snapped Diane. 'Take that paper to the dustbin before he sees it.'

Even as she spoke the kitchen door opened and in walked John, his boots covered in mud from the ploughed fields, his navy boiler suit smeared with oil after getting to grips with a troublesome tractor. He glanced at the two women, saw their serious expressions and took it to mean yet another evening of sulking.

'Damned thing's playing up again. Anyway I've done what I can tonight. Light in the barn isn't good enough. I'll get back to it first thing in the morning. But I daresay I'll have to fork out for a new one.' As he spoke he eased off his boots by the doorstep, left them in a small alcove, put on shoes then moved to the kitchen sink. Wiping oil from his hands with white spirit, he then plunged them into warm soapy water, something that usually troubled Diane who insisted that using the utility sink was more hygienic. Not a word from either of them. He sighed and turned.

'All right, what's up this time? You could cut the atmosphere in here with a knife.'

Terry glanced at her mother and took the bull by the horns. 'Here, read this.'

'No, don't, John. Just throw the damned thing away.'

Frowning, he wiped his hands on a kitchen towel and took the paper from Terry. 'You both sound highly dramatic. What am I to read then and which page is it on?' His eyes went to the headline first before catching the offending column. When he had finished reading, his jaw worked but he was silent.

'Sue them,' said Terry. 'It's libel after all. As for Mr Steel, well . . . you think you know people then you find out how wrong you are.'

John glanced at his daughter without really seeing her. Then he said in a quiet, strained voice, 'Damn them to hell. If they want to make a circus out of this they'll have to do it without my help. We say nothing, do you understand, Terry? Nothing at all. That way it will soon blow over.'

He waited until she'd left the room then turned to Diane. 'Did they approach you?' When she nodded and explained, his eyes blazed with anger. 'Why in God's name didn't you tell me? We can't afford this, not after all these years.'

She was shaking as she always did when he was like this. 'What should we do, though? People are getting angry . . . it's looking so odd.'

He glared at her. 'We stick to our guns. There is no alternative. You know that as well as I do.'

Suddenly feeling the desire for a strong drink, Diane walked into the sitting room, picked up the whisky decanter and poured a double measure into a crystal tumbler. Trembling, she stood before the oak mantel and drank. The alchohol warmed her; slowly the trembling stopped. If only the terrible foreboding would stop also.

'What the hell do you think you're doing?' The whisper came from the threshold where John stood glaring at her. 'This is no time to drink. Keep your wits about you. Start by cooking the dinner, why don't you?'

Diane took another sip, then put down the glass and reluctantly returned to the kitchen where she started peeling potatoes. John followed her, read the article again then hurled the paper across the floor, shouting, 'They make me out to be an ogre. Not a word about my offer of Short Furlong. Not a word about the field being landlocked and access to it out of the question. Bloody cheek! Why don't these people get their facts right? Rashleigh's work, I suppose. God, I'd like to . . .'

'But you won't.' Diane smiled grimly and turned to him. 'You can't. People can say anything they like and we can do nothing.'

John stormed out of the kitchen, leaving her to muse on his words. '*They make me out to be an orgre.*' If only they knew.

'Hi, Terry. Isn't it great? We're throwing a bottle party to celebrate.'

Thinking her sister sounded as though she had just come from one, Terry removed an earring and held the receiver closer to her ear. 'What news? What are you talking about?'

'Oh, Lord, isn't that just like you folks down on the farm? Don't you read newspapers or listen to the news? We've done it! Well, BOAC has. The Comet has. Pan Am were so convinced they'd be the first jet service across the Atlantic but we've beaten them to it. So it's a good excuse for a party, especially since I'm on that service starting next week.'

Her sister's high spirits were infectious and Terry laughed.

'Marvellous news! Of course we heard but . . . well, our minds got bogged down with other things.'

'Such as what, for God's sake? Not the Dame Edith, surely? How's it going anyway? Have you finally learned that there's a more exciting world out there?'

'I like teaching and I think I'm good at it. What's all this about a bottle party?'

'Next Saturday at our flat. Be here. You've yet to meet my cabin crew colleagues. It means bunking down on the floor overnight but you won't mind that, and on Sunday we'll take a walk in Kensington Gardens. If we're not too hungover.'

She certainly was in a good mood, thought Terry. It wasn't often she found herself invited to one of Marisa's parties. 'I'll be there late-afternoonish. How long will it take crossing the Atlantic on the Comet?'

Pausing before answering Marisa said, 'About eight hours out because we'll have head winds and a stop at Gander for refuelling, but less on the return journey because we'll have tail winds then. Fantastic, isn't it?'

A frowning Diane appeared and snatched the receiver from Terry's hand. 'What's this about the Comet?' After listening and saying that of course she was pleased, Diane replaced the receiver then turned to Terry with alarmed eyes. 'The Comet! All those crashes.'

'That was years ago. This, according to Marisa, is the Comet 4 and it's as safe as houses.'

Diane sighed. 'Not that many years ago. I'll be relieved when she gets married and gives up flying.'

'When she's found a rich man, she will.'

'Amen to that.' Diane returned to the kitchen.

It was Saturday afternoon. Having just returned from school, Terry changed her clothes, saddled up Dauphine and cantered her across the edge of ploughed fields until she reached the boundaries of Fenton land. There she drew rein, stroked the mare's gleaming neck and stared across the gentle landscape.

The day was sunny with a cool east wind; the white windmill stood out against a pale blue sky, contrasting with dark soil and burnished woodland. How she had always loved this time of year, loved the smell of damp earth and woodsmoke, the brilliant golds and browns, the mists of evening and the blaze of a fire in the hearth at night. She had loved the sensuality of it and felt nothing of its melancholy, until now, when Paul Verlaine's words summed up her feelings:

> The long weeping of autumn violins, wounds my
> heart with a monotonous languor

If only she had never met Alastair. If only she didn't feel so sick at heart.

Then there was the article which no one at school had mentioned either yesterday or today. Dimplomacy, she thought, not ignorance. Of course they knew; everyone knew. Teachers and pupils alike would have been whispering about it behind her back. How many Fentons lived in Thornley, for goodness' sake? Yes, she was sick at heart, for never in her life had she or her parents done anything to make people dislike them. Yet now everyone did.

A figure appeared on horseback, galloping towards her from the Rashleigh fields. Recognising the black gelding, Terry waved to Fiona and trotted forward to meet her.

Halting beside Terry, Fiona looked surprised. 'I didn't think you rode these days.' She paused, swallowed and tried to regain her breath. 'I'm glad we have met though because I want you to know how appalled we all are at that dreadful piece in the *Chronicle*. When Daddy saw it I thought he was going to have a stroke. You should have seen his colour. But it was after ten and far too late to phone your parents. He was up all night, poor old love, absolutely sure you would think he was behind it. But you must know he would never do such a thing?'

'Well, of course he wouldn't, we all know that. Anyway he saw Dad this morning about it and there's no animosity between them . . . on that matter at least.'

Fiona dismounted, hair falling in wisps below her riding hat, her round face wearing an expression of deep worry. 'You wont let this business of the memorial affect our friendship, I hope?'

'Of course not,' said Terry, dismounting as well.

As they led their horses to the stream, Fiona went on, 'Father wants to set the record straight with the *Chronicle* but your father's dead against it. Let sleeping dogs lie, and all that. He's wrong, you know. Without a letter from my father the paper won't print an apology and everyone will go on believing the silly nonsense – and it simply isn't fair.'

'I know but . . .' Terry's eyes opened wide. 'Oh, my Lord! Mrs Shotley. She'll have read the article or someone will have told her and . . . I must visit her and explain. Goodness knows what she must be thinking. Poor old thing, she'll be so upset.'

Fiona caught the reins of her grazing horse and started leading him back. 'By the way, did you enjoy your day at Snetterton? I haven't seen you to ask.'

The question came like a bolt from the blue. 'Yes,' said Terry, hoping she sounded casual. 'It was certainly different.'

Fiona laughed. 'Sooner you than me! Nice old thing, though, Alastair. His father had a heart attack, did you know? He's out of hospital now but it's left Alastair holding the fort, so I shouldn't think he's too happy.' She climbed back into the saddle and turned her horse. 'Well, nice seeing you. Take care. 'Byeee.'

Terry stood beside Dauphine watching Fiona cantering back across the fields and felt her heart lift. With so much on his mind how was Alastair expected to think of her as well? When things settled down he would phone. Surely he would phone? Just as suddenly her spirits started falling. Supposing he did not? In friendship and ignorance Fiona had brought hope, but if that hope proved false then anger and hurt would return in even greater measure. Better perhaps not to have known about Sir Angus Hammond's heart attack at all.

Chapter Five

Painted in old Suffolk Pink, Mrs Shotley's sixteenth-century timber-framed cottage stood at the far end of Thornley's High Street. Its interior was so small and dark that every time she entered the house, Terry marvelled at the way generations of people could raise large families in such cramped conditions; generations of births, generations of deaths, all here in a tiny two-bedroomed cottage.

Once married to a schoolteacher who was killed on the Somme, Mrs Shotely had been forced to make ends meet by accepting Arthur Fenton's offer of a post as his daily housekeeper, which sounded better than the chilly 'charwoman'. Now in her seventies, she was upright, alert and strong. She tended her own garden, baked bread and cakes, still kept the place sparkling clean and, once a week, took the bus to Lowdham to spend the day with her sister and stock up on goods that could not be bought in the village. Her grey hair was combed back and knotted into a neat bun, as it always had been; her face, now fuller than it used to be, still remarkably free from lines.

To Terry she was a surrogate grandmother since staying on after Arthur Fenton's death to help at the farmhouse three days a week. Mrs Shotley had also looked after Terry and Marisa when their parents were busy with the farm. How many times had this old lady cooked their meals, put them to bed and read them stories?

Thanking Terry for bringing her some fresh farm eggs, Mrs Shotely led her to the rear of the house and out into her long cottage garden where she cut Michaelmas daisies for Diane, saying, 'I know why you've come, dear, and I know how your mother must be feeling. Perhaps these will help to cheer her up?'

Terry took the flowers then followed the old lady along the garden path, admiring tall clumps of chrysanthemums, smelling the few remaining roses and remembering what a blaze of glory the garden had been in June and July. A heavy, lazy bee hovered about the asters and the smell of a bonfire was proof enough that Mrs Shotley had been pruning and burning. Fallen apples scattered the ground close to the vegetable plot. John Fenton or one of his two farmhands did the main digging each year for the old lady, but she took over from then on, planting and weeding, tending and nursing, defying old age.

At last they returned to the small living room where a fire burned in the black range and the aroma of baking filled Terry's nostrils. A kettle steamed on the range. Mrs Shotely picked it up, made a pot of tea, then poured it out and handed a cup to Terry.

Avoiding the upright fireside chair which the old lady favoured, Terry settled herself in the lower one and stirred her tea thoughtfully. 'So you've read the article then? I was rather hoping you hadn't. Mother's worried sick and asks you not to believe all that you read. You see ... what was said isn't true. Well, not as they've put it.'

'I know that.' The old lady sat down, a look of anger on her face. 'It's what I've been telling people. Ignorant fools! I don't know what's got into them. Why must they take sides anyway? Nothing better to do, I suppose. As for that Tom Steel, I'd rather go without than enter his shop again.'

Silence followed, broken only by the ticking of the grandfather clock. Terry sipped her tea and said, 'Dad's feeling so awful about it. They both are. It's a terrible thing to know that people are talking about you, disliking you, yet saying nothing to your face so you can't put your point of view to them.'

'But your father could. All he has to do is write to the Editor of the *Lowdham Chronicle* explaining everything. Surely it would be printed?'

'He won't,' said Terry. 'And you know how he can be once his mind is made up.'

'That I do. He and Marisa ... two of a kind. That's why they've never got on, I suppose.' Mrs Shotely smiled and faint lines fanned out from her eyes as she recalled a small Terry helping with the harvest or running towards her father with a bunch of wild flowers, and her delighted squeals as he would lift her high and swing her around. Marisa, however, was a different story. She neither ran to him any more than he took notice of her. Sad little girl.

'Funny how sisters can be so different,' she said now. 'But you always were, even from the first when you all arrived at the farm from Guernsey. And what a storm there was that night! The heavens just opened. Imagine how worried I was, knowing your father was having to drive through all that and him in a car he'd never driven before, in a place he'd never been before, and after such a long and tiring journey. Poor man.'

Terry looked surprised. 'But we came by ferry and train so whose car was he driving?'

'Why, Arthur Fenton's Riley, of course. His solicitor instructed me to arrange for the local garage owner to drive it to the station and leave it in the forecourt with the keys inside the glove compartment. How your father ever found his way here late at night along that maze of lanes I'll never know. But when you all arrived, well . . .' she paused and shook her head, smiling '. . . your parents looked as if they'd fallen into a lake. Soaked to the skin they were and their shoes all muddy. It seems they had to keep getting out of the car to knock on cottage doors and ask the way here.' She smiled at the memory. 'They must have been popular, knocking folk up at that late hour.'

Mrs Shotley sipped her tea and said, 'But it's Marisa I always remember from that night. She was so frightened, poor little mite. Well, two and a half is old enough to know you're in a strange place. Overtired too. She kept kicking and screaming, pushing away from your mother. I was the only one allowed to comfort her. Shuddering with sobs she was, poor little love. I thought she'd be all right within a few hours, but it took a lot longer than that for her to settle . . . days . . . weeks. You, on the other hand, slept like a log and that seemed to set the pattern of your different personalities. You the calm one, Marisa the tempestuous one. Even later when you would curl up in my arms for a bedtime story, I can remember Marisa banging her doll's head against the wall and screaming in temper.'

Mrs Shotley put her cup down on the table. 'In those days I also worked at Lowdham Hall, which was taken over by the Americans during the war so I was kept pretty busy. But when your mother went down with 'flu, I moved in to take care of you full-time until she was better. That was when I realised how disturbed Marisa truly was. Night after night she would wake up screaming. If she wasn't running up and down the landing in terror, she'd be curled up in a corner of the bedroom sucking her thumb and silent, or else sleepwalking. No wonder your mother always looked so washed out in those days. Unhappy too, I could sense that. Not surprising really. What with Marisa, homesickness, and the torment of knowing that her old home was occupied by the German army. Poor woman! I felt really sorry for her at times. Sorry for both your parents.'

She paused as if wondering if she should go on. 'As for Marisa, it reached a point where I felt there was something very wrong . . . you know, wrong in the head. It seemed to ease off at last, but then she became troublesome again when she was about six years old.'

'Why?' asked Terry.

Shrugging, Mrs Shotley offered cake, then sighed. 'God knows. Still, it's all in the past and Marisa's done well for herself, you have to hand it to her. She's a lovely-looking woman now.'

But a troubled one, thought Terry, suddenly realising that her sister was still mentally banging that doll against the wall.

It dawned on her then that there was so much she didn't know about her past. It seemed to be forbidden territory so far as her parents were concerned. They never spoke of their days in Guernsey, fielding her questions with vague unsatisfactory answers. Arthur Fenton too was a taboo subject.

'What was my father's cousin like?' she asked.

Looking a shade surprised at this unexpected turn to the conversation, Mrs Shotley frowned thoughtfully then said, 'I've some old photographs of him somewhere in here.' She moved to the sideboard and, opening a cupboard door, fumbled among a host of miscellaneous things until she found a worn cardboard box which had once, in the late-twenties, held chocolates.

Sitting down once more, she searched through the box for the appropriate photographs and held out a sepia one to Terry. 'That would be before his father died. His elder brother had been killed in the war. The Great War that was to end all wars.'

Terry looked at photo after photo in growing amazement. Arthur Fenton, whom she had imagined to be old and rough-looking, was in fact clear-eyed and handsome, even in the later photos. There were pictures too of farm hands with plough horses, stooks of corn in Five Acre Field, and the farmhouse with its walls clear of creeper.

'Of course, the farm was even smaller then,' Mrs Shotley was saying. 'When the Rashleighs had to sell some of their land, Arthur Fenton bought more acres. He had met someone, you see.' She handed across one last photograph. 'I suspect she had money.'

Terry looked at a thin plain woman, not in the first flush of youth, standing beside an older and thicker-set Arthur. The picture seemed to have been taken outside the front door. 'So this was his wife? I heard that she died in childbirth. Is that true?'

The old lady nodded, her face clouding. 'Such a nice lady. She came from Lavenham. Weakly, though, always had that taint of illness about her. Too old to have a first baby, if you ask me. It came early, you see, and the midwife wasn't up to handling the complications that set in. The doctor was on another case so she called an ambulance to the farm but Mrs Fenton died twenty-four hours later. The baby too.'

Mrs Shotley paused, as she relived the pain of that terrible time. 'Then . . . well . . . poor Mr Fenton simply wasn't the same man any more. I don't think he knew what he was doing half the time. The accident would never have happened if he'd been his old self.'

Terry said nothing about suspicions of suicide but wondered if Mrs Shotley had them also. 'There now, I've upset you. I am sorry, I didn't think. Stupid of me.'

'Nonsense. It was all a long time ago.'

Even so, thought Terry, she had been thoughtless. Life had not been kind to Mrs Shotley. Losing her only child to measles then widowed, she had kept grief to herself and worked very hard ever since. Now she was entitled to peace and tranquility.

'No, Angela, Boadicea did not marry Prince Albert.' Terry sighed, made notes on the exercise book and gave a low mark before going on to the next. At length she paused, rubbed the back of her neck and stretched. The bedroom was just warming up, the one-bar fire pushed out little heat and she longed to be through the endless marking so that she could sleep. Her throat was sore. Perhaps she had a cold coming.

Returning to the marking she proceeded for another twenty minutes then heard the telephone ringing in the hall. It stopped as someone answered it. Tensing she waited, then heard her father calling up to her and rushed from the room.

John's tight-lipped expression told her who it was. Heart racing, she took the receiver, waited until she was alone, then spoke softly into the mouthpiece. 'Hello.'

'Hi, Terry,' Alastair whispered. 'Your father didn't sound too happy to hear my voice.'

'Nonsense,' she replied, aware that the sitting-room door had been left ajar. 'Just one moment.' Deliberately, she put down the receiver, closed the door, and returned to the telephone. Heart still pounding, she kept her voice calm and matter-of-fact. 'I was just marking. Did you know that king Canute pushed back the waves and discovered America?'

'Must have been a bloody long walk!'

Terry laughed. 'Anyway, how are you?

'I'm in Coventry for one thing and trying to run Hammond Motors for another. Dad was taken ill and I've been holding the reins for him. He's on the mend, but I can't say when he'll be back in harness. I'm sick at having to miss the Three Hours at Snetterton. God knows when I'll get back on the circuit again. Look, I'm in London tomorrow, and wondered if you'd come out on the town with me? Could be weeks before I get back. I'm off to drum up exports abroad. So, what do you say?'

'Tomorrow?' Damn! There was no way she could contact Marisa beforehand to warn her. If she failed to turn up, the gulf between them would become greater. 'I'm already going to a party.' Even as she said it, she realised he would take it as a brush off and, thinking quickly, retrieved the situation. 'In London, as it happens.' Did she sound as casual as she hoped? 'Nothing formal, just a bottle party.' She paused again, sensed he was waiting for her to make the next move, and plucked up courage. 'Come along, why don't you? It might be fun.'

'Fine,' he said quickly. 'No chance of lunching first, I suppose?'

'I was intending to shop.'

'Good. I'll meet you outside Harrods then.'

She laughed. 'Are you mad? How much do you think teachers are paid? I'll be in Oxford Street.'

'Selfridge's then. Dead on twelve-forty-five. I won't be able to park so can you be there on time for me?' When she promised she would be, he paused and murmured, 'I've missed you, Terry. Can't wait until Saturday.'

Replacing the receiver, she felt she had acquitted herself well enough. Running to London when Alastair snapped his fingers would have looked pathetic and undignified. This way she could meet him and keep her pride. Marisa could not have picked a more perfect weekend.

Arriving thirty minutes late on a rain-swept afternoon, Alastair swept Terry from Selfridges to a French restaurant in South Kensington where over Lamb Provençal he spoke non-stop of the designs for the Mk8. 'Dad's illness couldn't have come at a worse moment. Still, the project's under way and that's the main thing.'

Blinding her with auto technology, and oblivious to her increasingly vacant stare, he ate and spoke enthusiastically, his boyish energy finally winning her over to the point where she wanted the project to succeed as much as he did. Even so warning bells sounded in her head. His father's close shave with death seemingly came a poor second to Alastair Hammond's own interests. Perhaps everything did; everything and everyone.

Although Marisa gave her address as West Kensington, the Victorian villa which she shared with two BOAC colleagues was really in Shepherds Bush.

Climbing from the car, Terry glanced up at the bleak-looking house and knew that the coldwater flat with its ancient bathroom, small kitchen, three bedrooms and one large sitting room, would be like ice. Even when the temperature rose outside, the house in Holland Road remained cold. She turned now to Alastair and thanked him for lunch.

'Well, thanks for listening to all my car talk. Not many women like that. You're different. Have to press on, though, masses to do. What time is this bash tonight?'

'Eight-thirty.'

Settling himself back behind the wheel, Alastair grinned then winked at her. 'I'll be there on the dot.'

He arrived just after eleven, when the party was in full swing and Terry had quite given up on him.

'Sorry,' he said, as she led him up the stairs to the noise of voices and music. 'Dined with some racing friends. And when we drivers get together . . . well, you know how it is.'

Yes, she was beginning to know exactly how it was. Racing drivers, it seemed, belong in a world of their own, a boys' club of eating, drinking, womanising, and non-stop talk of cars. They met each other on different circuits, all over Europe, and there was an *ésprit de corps* among them. Alastair had told her all this, so why was she hurt and surprised that he had chosen to be with them rather than her?

'Anyway,' he said, pulling two bottles of Bordeaux out of a brown bag, 'better late than never. And experience has taught me to beware of bottle parties . . . too much cheap plonk. Make sure you drink this if you know what's good for you. No beer by any chance, is there?'

She fought down a desire to say 'get lost' and told herself that since he had left his chums to be here that must mean something. Did he think she looked chic in the black chiffon dress Marisa had passed on to her when she'd found it too small for her expanding waist?

'There's beer,' said Terry, frowning as she glanced about her at the couples sitting on the landing looking very much the worse for wear. 'We made punch as well. Marisa put a bottle of gin in, and Helen, not realising, added half a bottle of vodka to give it a kick. The party's certainly gone with a swing.'

Somewhere in the thick press of humanity bundled into the small noisy room, Terry found Marisa dancing with a thin man who was looking into those green eyes as if scarcely able to believe his luck. Clad in deep sea-green *faille* and wearing the colour as though born to it, the boredom on Marisa's face changed to surprise as Alastair was introduced to her and her friends.

Later she took Terry to one side, whispering, 'Well, you're a dark horse! When you said you were bringing a friend I assumed you meant another female. And we need them like we need a hole in the head. Hmmm. Good-looking too.'

Aware that two glasses of punch were beginning to have their effect on her, Terry now sipped Bordeaux and watched Alastair dancing with the fair and lovely Helen. A pang of jealousy shot through her.

'Helen's three sheets to the wind,' she snapped.

'She's met her Paris, though,' murmured Marisa. 'How did you meet him?'

Terry put down her glass and found a cold vol-au-vent. 'We ran into each other, literally. Unfortunately we were in our cars at the time.

'What does he do?' Marisa wanted to know.

The record had stopped, Alastair was moving towards Terry. 'He's in car manufacturing.'

Manufacturing! Marisa lost interest at once. As Alastair swept Terry into the throng to the strains of 'Some Enchanted Evening', she watched him, thinking that looks meant nothing. She might have known anyone interested in her sister would be dull, with the dull prospects of any pen pusher in a dreary factory office. Later, when Alastair led her around the floor, she remained politely remote, leaving him at a loss to know how he had offended her. Gladly he returned to Terry.

It was that quiet hour somewhere between midnight and dawn, the smooching hour Marisa called it, and Alastair was holding Terry close. She rested her head on his shoulder and wished he would kiss her. Others were kissing but they just moved to the music. Then suddenly he kissed her on the back of her neck. A small electric shock coursed through her, his lips found hers and she felt her body responding as desire flared.

'Oh, Terry,' he whispered, 'I think I'm falling in love with you . . . oh, God.' He led her towards the door, lips brushing her hair. 'If we don't hurry there won't be a spare bedroom left.'

She wasn't that drunk and pulled back from him slightly.

'No.'

'No?' He frowned at her, then smiled. 'Sorry.' They danced on and he spoke again. 'You know . . .' He paused awkwardly in mid-sentence. Terry looked into his eyes, waiting for words of love.

'You know, your sister's rather icy. Was it something I said?'

By four in the morning the party was breaking up. Among the last to leave, Alastair pulled on his jacket and Terry walked with him to the top of the stairs. But it was too late for a quiet goodbye. Other revellers joined them and he was swept away on a wave of laughter and raised voices that could have wakened half London.

Diane looked through the sitting-room window and sighed. 'Oh, no. Guess who's just arrived?' Watching as the Brigadier marched along the drive, his walking cane more ornament than use, she turned to John. 'What on earth can he want at this hour?'

Frowning, John glanced up from the Davenport where he was going through farm accounts and looked at the clock on the mantel. It was five minutes to seven and he could smell dinner cooking. 'Don't tell me,' he groaned. 'Rashleigh?' When Diane nodded, he sighed. It was time for a drink, but he was in no mood to offer Rashleigh one and would wait until the man had left.

The doorbell rang. Diane walked into the hall and John could hear the feigned surprise in her voice as she invited the unexpected visitor in. Rashleigh entered the room, which seemed instantly diminished by his sheer size. Under his left arm he carried a set of neatly rolled plans.

'Sorry to burst in on you like this but that unpleasant business with the press has been on my mind and I'm determined it shan't happen again. So I've wracked my brains to find some other solution.' He smiled and patted the plans. 'Think I've found the answer.'

Glancing uneasily at John, Diane asked her visitor to sit down and explain what he had in mind.

Settling himself in the armchair beside the fire, Rashleigh handed the plans across to John. 'I had these drawn up a few days back. Thought we should discuss it first, iron out any problems before we go any further. Instead of going through your woods they go across my land. As you know, the big stumbling block was the large paddock. I've damned good bloodstock in there. Stud horses. Couldn't possibly have the public walking anywhere near it. Came to me the other night how I could re-locate the paddock using part of Long Meadow. Means cutting back on my output a little, but stud fees will offset that. So, take a look and tell me what you think.'

John unravelled the plans and scrutinised them cautiously. 'Well, yes, but I don't quite see . . .'

'I know it's a hell of a long way round but if it means we can go ahead then it's worth it. I mean to drive a path from Windmill Lane, edging around my fields and past the present paddock. Of course, as you can see, it means cutting through a small portion of your wood, but it's at the field's edge and you don't shoot there. So, good enough?'

Sensing John's hesitation, Diane smiled and said, 'It makes all the difference in the world. Don't you think so, John?'

He rolled up the plans and glanced at her. Stupid bitch! If she thought this would exonerate him then she should think again. Everyone would say the old man had been driven to these measures because he, John Fenton, would not give up his wood. He was still in the dog-house whichever way he jumped. Yet if it meant the memorial could go ahead and the wood remain untouched then he must accept it gratefully, as a dog is grateful for a stale bone. Smiling, he handed the plans back to the Brigadier and nodded.

'It's a good plan and I'm in full agreement. Let's drink to it.'

'Scotch, please. Neat.' The old man looked relieved. 'I feel a great weight lifted off me, I don't mind telling you. It was the last hope to give those boys a decent memorial. We'll set up a committee and get started. There's masses to do and we need to have it all ready by August next year on the anniversary of the crash.'

John handed a glass to the Brigadier and together they drank to the enterprise. 'So, where do we start?'

Sipping his whisky, the Brigadier said, 'First we need to find out from the Air Ministry the names of the pilots, their squadron and base. All we think we know is that their airfield was somewhere in Norfolk. I'm reliably informed that the Air Ministry won't hand out names of the bereaved or their families. It's classified information, apparently. But I think they'll intercede for us in this case. Then there's the memorial itself – which stone mason to use, what kind of monument and so forth. Then of course the site.'

'Oh, something simple, natural and beautiful,' said Diane feeling immensely relieved. 'A place of tranquility. Seven men died, so why not plant seven oak trees in their memory? We could involve the local schoolchildren by having them plant daffodil bulbs for spring and rose bushes for summer. But the keynote must be simplicity. After all, this will be the work and thought of a small farming village and should reflect that.'

The Brigadier drank his whisky and said, 'I think, Mrs Fenton, that we should co-opt you on to the memorial committee.'

'If you do then I shall be only too happy to accept,' said Diane, in a tone so full of passion that John turned his head to look at her.

*

Smart in her dark blue uniform, Marisa stood on the steps of the Comet, watching as passengers headed across the windswept tarmac of London Airport to the waiting jet, then took up her position in the First Class cabin. Glancing at her passenger list she noted among them one American film actress with her fourth husband, two peers of the realm and three industrialists.

The senior stewardess walked up to her and murmured, 'There's been a change to the list. Sir Angus Hammond's place has been taken by a *Mr* A. Hammond. I believe that may be his son. So far he hasn't checked in. Marvellous! Guess who'll have to tell the Captain?'

Marisa smiled sympathetically. Today's flight crew did not suffer fools gladly. Before she could say anything the passengers started entering the cabin and she helped to show them their seats and store hand luggage overhead. When all were settled and the engines whined on the tarmac, there was a ten-minute delay until the late one appeared.

Red-faced and breathless from rushing, Alastair was all apologies as doors were closed and steps removed. 'Sorry, sorry, sorry. Got caught in traffic.' When he saw Marisa, her expression sent him into peals of laughter.

'Good God,' he said, sliding into his seat. 'Terry said you were an Air Stewardess but I hardly thought I'd have the pleasure of meeting you like this. My father wasn't up to a flight to New York so I'm standing in for him.' He glanced around him with an air of amazement. 'Looks different somehow. Smaller windows, surely?'

Still trying to hide her shocked surprise behind a smile, Marisa whispered, 'You're in a jet, Mr Hammond, not a turbo prop. Will you fasten your seat belt, please?'

Calmly she carried on with her duties in her usual professional manner but her mind was racing. Hammond's son? Her sister truly was a dark horse and no mistake. Or was Terry in ignorance? That would hardly surprise her. But no. Even she must know the truth after going out with Alastair. Yet she had said nothing during that party and kept the secret to herself. Well, well. How she had underrated her. Having checked that all seat belts were fastened for take off, Marisa finally settled in her own seat and fastened hers.

The Comet had finished taxi-ing and its powerful engines

now roared into life. In shocked exhilaration, Alastair gripped the arms of his seat as the BOAC jet sped along the runway, lifted off, and London slowly disappeared under a veil of low-lying cloud.

Chapter Six

On a murky November afternoon, Terry was back in London and heading along Oxford Street to Marble Arch. Light drizzle fell on the shoulders of her beige mohair coat and the smell of impending fog warned her not to delay too long if she wished to return to Suffolk before the trains were halted.

Diane had thought her mad to journey to London when the weather forecast was so bad, but Terry had an appointment and nothing on God's earth would have prevented her from keeping it.

'I suppose it's that Alastair? Put if off. He shouldn't expect you to go running just because he's called.'

But it wasn't Alastair and her heart sank every time she thought about that night at the party when he had promised to telephone her as often as he could, no matter where he was. But he, being he, had not kept that promise. She should have known better. Even so she still made excuses for him, telling herself that travelling here, there and everywhere as well as running Hammond Motors hardly gave the man a minute to himself.

She was approaching her destination now. If only she didn't feel so nervous. But Meg had sounded surprised and decidedly unfriendly when Terry had phoned her from the public telephone booth in Lowdham to introduce herself and suggest a meeting.

'Very well. I'm on night duty as it happens. Lyon's Corner House, Marble Arch, at three o'clock on Saturday? I'm auburn-haired and will wear a green coat. Can't stop now. Goodbye.'

Standing outside the Corner House, Terry glanced at her watch. Why was she always on time when others were not? People jostled past her on their way into the building and, realising how busy it was going to be, she wondered if they would get a table.

Suddenly she saw a splash of green among the throng; the rest of the figure was lost under a large black umbrella. When it was lowered, a crop of short thick curly auburn hair could be seen above a plump freckled face. The grey eyes were unsmiling as they finally settled on their quarry.

'Terry Fenton?' The voice had a no-nonsense tone to it.

'Meg.' Terry smiled, and held out a gloved hand in friendship. It was shaken lightly. 'I'm so glad to meet you. Come on, let's get inside out of this dirty weather.'

Inside the famous Corner House, Terry and Meg elected for afternoon tea, found the large restaurant packed but were directed to a small corner table where they were served by a young waitress dressed in black with a white cap and apron.

Meg let her coat fall over the back of her chair and removed her woollen scarf. Short and overweight, her plump face pink with cold, hair damp from the drizzle, she met Terry's eyes without smiling.

Feeling a little desperate, Terry settled for, 'I know you've only been in London a short while, but how are you liking it?'

'Not much at the moment. I'm at Guy's Hospital and working my feet off. I've been to London before, of course, but only on brief holidays. And you? You work here, I suppose?'

Terry shook her head. 'I teach in Suffolk. Started last September.' Was that all it was, last September? It seemed a world away. Tea arrived and she poured. 'I realise this is a strange situation but I'm glad we've met at last. It wouldn't have happened at all if . . . well . . . I don't normally read other people's letters, but when I saw the stamp and post mark I was too curious for words. So, here we are.'

Meg frowned. 'You mentioned that on the phone, but I still don't understand the need for such clandestine nonsense. Why didn't your mother tell you about the letter?'

How could Terry bring herself to say it? Better to take things one step at a time. 'Look . . . we've so much to talk about and years to catch up on that . . .'

'No, you look,' said Meg, leaning forward in an almost threatening manner. 'I must tell you here and now that if your parents are condescending to invite me to Suffolk, they can forget it. After all they've put my poor mother through, I really don't want to have anything to do with the Fentons. Why Mum keeps bothering with relations who simply don't give a damn about her is beyond me. I told her not to write. But she would do it. All these years she's wondered if the worst had happened . . . you know, the air-raids . . . but when she tried to find out, she just drew a blank. Yet she kept on writing, and always put her own address on the back of the envelope, but the letters were never returned so we knew they'd found their mark. I don't understand it and neither does she. It was too cruel of your parents. You've no idea how cruel.'

Terry shook her head. 'But that's just it! My parents aren't a bit cruel. It's just not in their nature to hurt people. There has to be some explanation. I was hoping you could tell me what you think it might be?'

'And I was hoping *you* could tell *me*.'

Terry bit her bottom lip thoughtfully and stirred her tea. 'Only one thing. In your mother's letter she said something about a misunderstanding . . . to do with the occupation. Did she ever mention it to you?'

'No.' Meg buttered a toasted tea cake and went on, 'Even when Dad was alive I never heard my parents discuss the occupation at all. I think they wanted to draw a veil over it all. I remember it, though. After all, I was almost eleven when the war ended.'

Terry stared at her. 'Yes, of course. What was it like?'

'Odd question.' Meg looked thoughtful then sighed. 'I suppose it's difficult for you to understand just what it could be like to be occupied by the enemy. I don't remember how it began, only how they turned the whole island into a concrete fortress. How they brought in slave labour to build for them and how the food we grew was sent to France. The island's too small for wheatfields so we had no flour to make bread. By the end of the war most of us were on the edge of starvation. Being out of town and having our own market garden we were luckier in that respect, but I remember people sneaking out at night to steal swedes or turnips from the fields, anything they could find to feed their families. They faced severe penalties if they were caught. Only when the Red Cross parcels arrived at the end of the war did we know what it was to have real food. Perhaps that's why I eat so much now.'

'I'd no idea,' murmured Terry.

'Don't suppose you would have. You or your parents. You must tell them on your return. I believe Mum wrote, just before the invasion, asking if you would have us. Gran was unwell and we couldn't just evacuate without a destination. Anyway, Mum heard nothing so we were forced to stay.' Meg lit a cigarette, sat back in her chair and scrutinised her cousin with hostile eyes.

Terry frowned. 'They couldn't have got the letter.'

'It's possible, I suppose, with all the chaos of those days. Personally we believe your parents simply forgot about us, just as England forgot about us. Ask them yourself.'

Terry hesitated before she said. 'They don't know of this meeting. I thought it best to wait until I'd seen you. You see, until I read the letter I didn't even know of your existence.'

Meg looked incredulous. 'That's appalling ... unbelievable. Particularly when my mother and grandmother helped to raise Diane after her parents died.' Anger took the place of incredulity. 'Not to know of our existence? Why, it's ... it's ... I can't find a suitable word to describe ...'

'There isn't one. It's all so senseless.' Terry sat back in her chair, a sense of deep shame overcoming her. What a bleak meeting this was. After a long silence she murmured, 'Perhaps I did the wrong thing in phoning you. It certainly hasn't made things better.'

Meg's hostility began to evaporate at this and she let out a long sigh. 'It isn't your fault. I'm glad you did ring. At least I can tell Mum you're all alive, and that one of you cares.'

'I would like to meet your mother,' said Terry, thinking what a good person Grace had seemed from her letter, the one that had vanished from the drawer when Terry had wanted to read it again. 'Does she ever come to England?'

Grace shook her head. 'I doubt she ever will. Some old friends of hers from the island have moved to Finchley and they keep asking her to visit them, but so far she's stayed put. Now that I'm here she might come over.'

'Pity,' said Terry. 'I was thinking that once here, she and my parents could be reunited.'

Meg gave a hollow laugh. 'If your parents had wanted that they only had to answer one of her letters. But they never did. I think it broke her heart. Dad couldn't understand it either. He kept her spirits up, but when he died she sank again. It had been my ambition to come to London when I got my SRN but I waited for her sake. Now I'm about to start my Part One Midwifery, and wanted to do it at Guy's. I feel a heel, though, for leaving her. Hopefully I'll get home for Easter, if they'll let me have time off.'

Terry glanced at her watch. 'Well, I can't leave it too late. Fog warnings and all that. But we must meet up again. You're the only cousin I have . . . well, you and your mother. What does that make you, second cousin once removed or what?'

Stubbing out her cigarette in the ash tray, Meg shook her head then shrugged. 'God knows. But I'm glad we met just the same. Look, if I do get leave to go home for Easter, why not come with me?'

'I wonder what your mother would feel about that after the way she's been treated? I really don't think she would want me.'

Meg shook her head. 'I think she'll be moved by the thought that the baby she once helped to care for has returned to visit her.'

Go to Guernsey, to the place where she was born, to meet a woman she wasn't supposed to know existed? Terry pulled on her gloves in thoughtful silence.

Sensing her hesitation, Meg went on, 'She's shown me endless photos of you as a baby, Marisa as a toddler and your parents helping in the greenhouses. Pathetic really that she should have kept them. Anyway, think about it and let me know later.'

Terry was trying to think how she would explain such a visit to her parents. For some reason the very thought of it sent a chill through her. 'I want to go very much, but only if you explain everything to your mother first. When she hears it, I doubt she'll want me anyway. Will you promise to do that?'

Meg promised. 'So now it's back to work. I never used to like being on night duty. People always seem to die in the early hours but they get born at that time too, so now that I'm on Maternity I like it.'

Fog was settling over London as Terry said goodbye to her newfound cousin and headed for the Underground.

December had arrived and with it the usual rush to be ready for Christmas. It made things no easier for Terry to have the London train arrive late at Woodbridge. Doors opened and slammed shut then Marisa appeared, elegant and smiling as she stepped along the platform, small leather suitcase in one hand, matching cosmetics case in the other. She greeted her sister with the usual cool kiss on the cheek, handed her the cosmetics case and adjusted the slipping strap of her shoulder bag.

On their way to Thornley, she waxed lyrical about the sheer vitality of a city like New York and answered Terry's many questions as well as she could. 'You can't explain about the place. You have to have lived there to understand.'

Sensing tension in her sister's voice, Terry put it down to long flights and too many late nights and dreaded being asked if she had seen Alastair again. She had not. At full month had passed since the party. He was back in England and had not phoned. It was hard to accept that he no longer thought or cared about her. She had lost weight and found sleep impossible.

Tempted to avoid the subject by telling Marisa of the Guernsey letter and her meeting with Meg, she hesitated. Was that wise? Could Marisa be trusted with anything so sensitive? Better say nothing. There was one subject she could not avoid.

'Didn't say anything the last time we met, it was hardly the place or time, but things have been pretty bad here. Our name got into the local paper – vilifying Dad because of his refusal to let a path go through the wood.' Seeing the confusion on her sister's face, she sighed. 'The memorial, remember? Anyway the worst is over. Dad and Brigadier Rashleigh have reached an agreement and the memorial committee have swung into action at last. Just thought I'd put you in the picture so that you'll be on your guard. Poor Mother's borne the real brunt, though, with people spurning her.' She smiled grimly. 'We Fentons are treated like Martians these days.'

Unable to equate this piece of nonsense with the hustle and bustle of flying to a city like New York, Marisa frowned.

'Village gossip and Mother being spurned? Ye Gods, I'd honestly go out of my mind living in a place like this. How can you bear it?' She sighed and glanced out of the window as they passed the church and headed up the hill. 'So, all is doom and gloom here. Which rather puts the damper on my news.'

'What news?' Terry pulled into the drive and stopped the car.

'Let's walk a bit and I'll tell you.' With that Marisa got out and, turning away from the house, headed along the rough track, heedless of her elegant suede court shoes and straight-skirted suit.

Puzzled, Terry followed her. 'They'll wonder what's going on. We should go in first.'

'Really? I don't see any welcome committee, do you?'

'They're busy, for goodness' sake.'

'Then they won't miss us.' Removing a kid glove, Marisa opened her black leather handbag and took out a silver cigarette case. Seeing Terry staring at it surprise, she said, 'It's a present . . . an engagement present.'

Surprise shone in Terry's eyes, then she laughed with affectionate joy. 'Now who's the dark horse? Who is he? A pilot? A steward . . . who?'

Marisa took out a cigarette, lit it then inhaled deeply. She looked away from her sister as smoke left her mouth and vapourised in the dank air. 'It's Alastair. Alastair Hammond.'

In the stunned silence that followed Terry felt the blood drain from her face. At last she found her voice, thin and shaky though it was. 'If this is your idea of a joke then I don't think it's very funny.' But Marisa didn't make jokes any more than she understood them.

Removing the other glove, she is a stretched out her hand. Even in the fading light the large diamond on the third finger dazzled. 'See. He bought it yesterday. It cost the earth, I don't mind telling you, but it's the one I wanted. You're wondering if we started going out after the party, aren't you? The answer is no. It was a strange coincidence, I'll admit, but we met again en route to New York, went out with each other during my time there and carried on seeing each other back home. It all happened rather quickly . . . you know how these things are and . . . well, he asked me to marry him and I said yes.' She looked up and frowned. 'Oh, don't stare at me like that. There was nothing to your relationship with Alastair. He told me so himself. If there had been he wouldn't have looked twice at me.'

Every word cut like a knife. Turning her eyes to the wood, grey now in the gloom of the darkening afternoon, Terry wondered if this was really happening. The hell of it was that Marisa was right. Alastair may have muttered sweet nothings in Terry's ear and kissed her, but it had been the drink talking and meant little to him. There was nothing to their relationship, he had said as much to Marisa. How could he have known how she felt about him? But that it should be her sister, of all people, who had stolen him away, was too much.

'Surely you knew, surely you could see, how I felt about him?'

'What difference does that make, if he feels nothing for you?' With an air of impatience, Marisa threw the cigarette on to the ground and stamped on it. 'Oh, this is ridiculous. Clearly you read too much into what, to Alastair, was just a friendship.'

'And what is it to you?'

Sighing, Marisa folded her arms. 'Oh, Lord. I can see you mean to harbour a grudge against me. Please don't, Terry. I couldn't bear that.'

Terry flashed her a dark look. 'Oh, I think you could.' With that she turned and strode towards the house, leaving Marisa fumbling for another cigarette.

Not for the world would Terry let anyone know the terrible desolation she felt; not for the world would she have people whisper, 'Poor girl.' And so, in the days and weeks that followed, she smiled, concentrated on her teaching and tried to accept what must be accepted. It was a cruel trick of nature that she cared for a man who loved her sister and would soon become her brother-in-law.

Rejection. God, how it hurt. And all for someone who had once admitted she was incapable of love and would marry for wealth and no other reason. What a fool Alastair was not to see it. But a fool in love would heed no well-meaning advice, so she offered none and avoided meeting him.

After their intial surprise and reservations, John and Diane came to accept that they were going to have Alastair Hammond as a son-in-law. Only Diane could guess at Terry's feelings and wondered at Marisa's hardness. Not that it surprised her. Nothing about Marisa had ever surprised her. But to see Terry hurt like this, and trying to hide it behind brittle gaiety, was too much. To make matters worse, Marisa wanted an early wedding, before Christmas if possible. 'Out of the question,' had been the answer to that. 'Such unseemly haste would cause gossip.'

'New Year then,' snapped Marisa. 'No later or we'll have a London wedding, which I'd prefer anyway.'

'You'll bloody well pay for it yourself then,' snapped John.

'All right. January,' said Marisa. 'But there will be an awful lot of people on his side, so it's been suggested by Mrs Rashleigh that we hold the reception at the Hall.'

John glared at her. 'She's suggested *what*? I'm not made of money but I have my pride and no Rashleigh is going to patronise me. You'll be married from this house, at the local church, and the reception will be held at the Swan Hotel. Now go and do whatever you women have to do to organise it but don't bother me again. And don't even think of looking down on us, Marisa, just because you're marrying into money.'

Doors slammed, and she bristled off on her way to a Christmas spent with the Hammonds at their large Warwickshire house, much to the relief of Terry and her parents.

Feeling that it would have been better all round if Marisa and Alastair had married in London after all, Terry turned down her sister's tactless request that she be chief bridesmaid and asked herself how she could even attend the wedding. To make matters worse, the Swan could not accommodate a large reception until February when the hotel would be practically empty.

What had to be endured was borne with as much dignity as Terry could muster, but for all that was happening, her thoughts were still on Grace, Meg, and all the lies her parents had told to conceal their very existence.

There was a stranger in the village. Terry saw him through the window of Mrs Shotley's cottage: a tall, dark-haired figure, huddled into a sheepskin jacket, hands in pockets as he made his way through virgin snow. He stopped in the deserted High Street, looked this way and that, and seemed utterly lost.

In the very act of leaving, Terry pulled on her coat and gloves then wrapped a woollen scarf about her head before saying goodbye to Mrs Shotley and heading out into the bitter cold day. The snow that had fallen overnight now muffled any sound and, on this Sunday morning, only the man's footsteps ahead of her showed that a living creature was about in Thornley. The church bell had rung earlier for Matins and she wondered if the Vicar had stood alone in a cold nave, waiting for a congregation who wouldn't dare venture out. So who was he then, this stranger who had turned and was now staring at her? Another reporter looking for a story about two feuding land owners?

'Excuse me,' he called. 'Is this Thornley?'

'Yes,' she answered warily.

He approached her, intense brown eyes in a swarthy face, snow flakes covering the dark straight hair. 'Thank God! I've been driving around for two hours. Some of the lanes are becoming impassable. I'm told Thornley is only a few miles from Lowdham. You wouldn't think so. Not a sign to be seen.'

'Have you driven far in this?'

'London. But I came down last night. There was no snow then . . . certainly not in London. I didn't listen to the weather forecast.'

'What brought you here?' As if she didn't know.

'I'm looking for the site where a bomber crashed during the war. Can you help me?'

A reporter, and from one of the nationals as well. Had their fame travelled that far? Terry's eyes were guarded, her tone of voice as cold as the day. 'There's no public access as yet. It's on private land.'

He smiled grimly. 'So I understand. And the owner of the land is against the memorial.'

'Oh? Who told you that?'

'I stayed at the Bear in Lowdham last night. It made quite a topic of conversation in the bar when they knew why I'd come here.'

'Did it indeed?' she snapped. 'And just what angle are you after for your story?'

The brown eyes looked bewildered. 'Sorry, I'm not with you?'

She stared at him icily. 'My God, you reporters have thick skins. Can't you see the harm you do?'

'What makes you think I'm a reporter?'

'Because they're the only people who come snooping around the village asking questions, that's why.'

'Well, you're mistaken.' He looked angry. 'I would be glad if you can tell me where the site is and where I may contact this Mr Fenton. From what I've heard he's unlikely to let me walk on his land. But I've come a very long way, so we must just pray he doesn't set the dogs on me when I approach his front door.'

Terry glared at him in mounting rage. 'There are no dogs and Mr Fenton has been unjustly maligned by ignorant people who like to spread gossip. So go back to your editor and tell him there's no story here. As for the site, work hasn't started yet, so there's nothing to see but a ploughed field.' She turned and started trudging her way through the snow.

He caught up with her, saying, 'Why do you insist I'm from the press?'

She stopped walking, turned and squared up to him. 'Why else would you be so interested?'

For one angry moment he almost snapped back, 'That's my bloody business!' But there was no one else about to ask and time was running out so he swallowed his fury and said calmly, The Air Ministry sent a letter, explaining about the memorial. I just wanted to see the place for myself. We never knew exactly where it had happened. My parents were told East Anglia. That was all.'

Wishing the earth would open up and swallow her, Terry flushed a bright pink. 'Oh . . . I see. I'm sorry. I didn't mean . . . you see, life here has been made intolerable by reporters. It started with the *Lowdham Chronicle* and spread to other East Anglian papers. So I thought . . .'

'I understand perfectly,' he said, with no softening of his expression. 'If you would just point me in the right direction, I shall trouble you no longer.'

'Well, then, it's . . .' She sighed and shrugged. 'Look, it's better if I take you. I'm going that way. Where's your car?'

'At the back of the pub.' He pointed towards the Plough Inn which stood at the far end of the High Street.

'Leave it there,' she said. 'The roads haven't been gritted. Anyway it isn't far.'

They made their way carefully through the watersplash, then struggled up the hill, trying to prevent each other from slipping. It relaxed their mood and the conversation became easier as they walked. His brother, she learned, had been twenty three when he was killed in the crash. No one in the family had ever been told the circumstances or location of his death.

The wood was dark against the white snow. At the gate Terry paused, telling herself she didn't know this man and only had his word to go on that he was who he said he was. Then she decided he seemed decent and safe enough, if a touch taciturn. Opening the gate, she gestured for him to follow. But he paused and frowned.

'Through here? We can't. We haven't the owner's permission. The last thing I want is to be prosecuted for trespass.'

'Mr Fenton won't mind in the least.' She swallowed hard and said, 'He's my father.'

He took a sharp breath, then let it out in a long sigh. 'I'm sorry. Really, Miss Fenton, you should have said something long before this.'

'Would it have made any difference, Mr . . .?'

'Kenway,' he answered. 'Of course. What kind of person do you think I am?'

She wondered, and then guessed at his age as they walked on in silence. Thirtyish, she decided. Apart from their feet crunching in the snow there was no other sound and the woods looked depressingly hostile and cold without the sun to set the snow sparkling.

'You know, my father isn't the monster you've decided he is. There've been a lot of misunderstandings over this business. The papers made out he wouldn't give up any land for the memorial. That was a lie. He's giving up part of the cornfield. It was this wood that proved the stumbling block. He just couldn't have people wandering will-nilly in here in the winter months when there might be shooting.' She looked up at him and smiled.' Oh, don't worry. He won't be shooting today. But you can see it was simply out of the question. So a new way has been found for public access to the memorial site and now everything's going ahead. But the newspapers have printed their lies and there's no changing them, even if they printed an apology.'

'And have they? Have they printed an apology?'

Terry shook her head. 'My father preferred to let the matter drop. I think he was wrong.'

He said nothing to this which bothered her. They walked on through the wood in silence and she began to feel the tension grow. This was no time for words, she thought, no time to prattle on about her own family problems.

At last they reached the snow-covered field where Terry pointed out the site of the crash. For some time he stood in silence as snow settled on their heads and shoulders, the bitter east wind coursing the expanse of the field and cutting through them. As she watched him, Terry felt the passage of time. The war had seemed a lifetime away until this moment. Did grief last so long?

After a time she spoke, her voice low and a little husky. 'It happened on a warm summer evening. They were working late on the harvest. My mother saw the aircraft. She thought it would hit the house but then the wing tipped and the plane went down. The field workers, mostly women from the Land Army, rushed across and did what they could. My father joined them and organised things, but . . . the crew had died instantly. People say the pilot saved the lives of the villagers by deliberately banking the plane into the field.'

'Yes,' he murmured at last. 'It's exactly what he would have done. Paul was my brother.'

'I see.' Terry's eyes softened. Paul, she thought. Knowing his name suddenly made him real. 'They told you then that he died a hero?'

He shook his head slowly. 'Letters bearing that kind of news always speak of gallantry, but no – we weren't told that.' The voice was choked as he murmured, 'My parents would have drawn a measure of comfort from it, I daresay.'

Grim-faced, he stared out across the still whiteness and she wondered at his thoughts, feelings and memories. But the wind was strengthening, driving snow across the field to lay in drifts on the side.

'This weather's getting worse. Come back to the house and have some lunch with us. My parents will be pleased to meet you, Mr Kenway.'

As if shaken from a deep reverie he looked up with an air of surprise. 'Thank you but no. I must be getting back. And it's Dr, by the way. I haven't reached the dizzy heights of Mr yet.'

She led him along the edge of the field towards the barn and outbuildings. 'At least come in and have a warm drink. We pass right by the house.'

'Kind of you but I must get back to the hospital. I'm on call first thing tomorrow. If I don't make a move I'll never get out of these lanes to the main road.'

'Look, if you do run into trouble try to make your way back to us.' Leading him down the drive towards the gate she asked if he would be coming to the service and unveiling ceremony.

He nodded. 'Be sure of that. Thank you for your time, Miss Fenton.' With that he turned and walked away, leaving her with the strong impression that he still believed the terrible things that had been said about her father.

She closed the gate and watched him walk back down the hill with a slow and heavy tread. He was a stranger with a grudge against her and her family; a stranger filled with grief. Suddenly, her heart went out to him.

Chapter Seven

When wedding bells rang out on a raw February day, half the inhabitants of Thornley stood watching as a host of famous names from the world of motor racing entered a church bedecked with flowers and awash with Hammonds and Rashleighs.

'Makes our side look a bit thin,' whispered Mrs Shotley to Eliot as they were ushered to their seats.

Wearing a green felt hat with a new dark blue suit, she glanced behind her curiously to see a small group of young men and women and was reliably informed by Eliot that they were Marisa's colleagues from BOAC. Later three of Terry's college friends arrived, and the Fentons' solicitor whom Mrs Shotley recognised from the days when he had served Arthur Fenton. They nodded to each other in greeting. That was it. No relations, no close friends of the family. Sad, she thought, for Mr and Mrs Fenton to have no one. It was almost as though they had no past.

Having timed her arrival carefully to avoid meeting Alastair whom she had not seen since the night of the party, Terry stepped through the lychgate in green velvet, only to find her plan had misfired. With sinking heart she saw the groom, with his best man, standing at the church door talking to guests as they arrived. Damn him, she thought. Why wasn't he sitting in that front pew by now?

Forcing a dignified smile, she greeted him lightly and was about to walk on inside when she heard him whisper.

'Terry, you look beautiful.'

She turned then, and seeing the haunted look in his eyes knew that he sensed he was about to make the mistake of his life. For a moment it seemed he wanted to say more to her but an usher moved between them, insisting that it was time he took his place since the bridesmaids were arriving. Alastair Hammond turned and entered the church, his boyish, happy-go-lucky life now over. He had been catapulted into maturity; a maturity that told him it was too late to do anything about his disastrous error of judgement.

It had been the worst moment in a day she had dreaded but another ordeal would soon follow and Terry wondered how she would cope when it came. Yet at the moment when Marisa, draped in fine lace and duchess satin, had extended her hand to receive Alastair's ring, Terry's mind suddenly filled with the image of a dark-haired man, snow falling on his head and shoulders as he walked with heavy tread down the hill and away from her.

'I'm going to Guernsey for Easter.'

Looking as though she had just received a hard slap in the face, Diane turned to Terry and demanded to know why. 'It's a ridiculous idea. Whatever put it into your head?'

Deliberately testing the water, she went on, 'I'm going with a friend from college and I'd like the address of the old house where we used to live.'

Diane walked into the utility room. A minute or so later she returned with a bowl containing chicken feed. 'The house was sold years ago. There's no one in Guernsey with any connection to us.' She eyed Terry suspiciously. 'You gave no hint you would be away for Easter. So what's brought this on so suddenly?'

'It isn't sudden, I've been thinking about it for some time. As I said, I'm going with a college friend. She was at the wedding and that's when she came up with the idea. We'll be staying with distant relations of hers.' Amazed that she could lie as skilfully as her parents, Terry kept her gaze steady but noticed Diane's fingers tightening on the bowl.

'You're mad. It's the wrong time of year. Stay here with us, please, dear. Easter won't be the same without you. Stay and forget this silly idea.'

'I need to get away,' said Terry firmly.

Diane glared at her. 'Need to get away indeed! From what, I'd like to know?' With that she left the kitchen and walked quickly to the hen house where she proceeded to scatter feed, aware that Terry had followed on her heels. With her face averted and hens all about her feet, she listened to another request for the name of the village and snapped nervously.

'You'd never find it, never in a million years. I doubt I would now. Those lanes are small and twisting. Without a detailed explanation you'd be lost. And for what? For a house that someone else is living in?' She continued her task and tried one last ploy. 'Poor Eliot. He'll be so disappointed. He's hoping you'll take him sailing.'

'I'm committed now. Please, just give me the name of the village where I was born. It's only natural I should want to see it.'

'Well . . . to be honest it's just a group of houses in the middle of nowhere. It's a district rather than a village. It won't help you, believe me.'

How pale she is, thought Terry, with a sense of guilt. Suddenly it dawned on her that her mother was afraid.

When Terry went back into the house, Diane found John in the barn working on the tractor which was causing trouble again. Dreading to tell him what he had to know, she said in a shaky voice, 'She's going to Guernsey. Terry's going to Guernsey for Easter. What are we to do?'

John paused, looked up at her in astonishment then climbed to his feet. 'Stop her.'

'I've tried, don't you think I have?

'Why the hell does she want to go there?'

When Diane told him, John stood thoughtfully for a few moments before speaking. 'If it's gone this far we can't stop her. So long as she never learns the address, and she won't from us, then . . . well . . . what are the chances of her running across them? Practically nil, I'd say.'

'On a small island?' Diane shook her head.

John turned back to the tractor. 'Of all the things I thought might happen, this wasn't one of them.'

The end of March was hardly the best time of year to be standing on the deck of a British Rail ferry. The night was cold, but the sea was calm with a skein of silver moonlight skimming its surface.

Terry shivered in the keen air, glad to be alone, glad to be out on deck away from the smell of stale beer and the sight of passengers trying to sleep on uncomfortable seats because they, like she and Meg, had been unable to secure a cabin. She had left her snoring cousin curled up happily among them, in the manner of one used to interminable Channel crossings.

How bright the stars were. She had never seen them so bright. Positioned at the stern and sheltered from the wind, she felt the vessel lifting gently on the swell and thought about the last time she had made this journey. Then she had been a baby, going the other way, to England. Now she was returning to the island of her birth to meddle in something that was not her business.

It was wrong, surely, to cause distress to her parents? But then, being lied to was wrong also. She recalled the look in her mother's eyes, one that had reminded her of a hunted deer. How could she live with that and not try to find out what was hurting her parents so much? She could not. The answer must lie in Guernsey. It must.

She needed this break anyway, needed to get away from the pain of the last few months and the sense of rejection which had sent her sense of self-esteem to an all time low. It was not just Alastair's rejection either. As she gazed down at the frothing white wake of the ship, her mind turned to Dr Kenway. His terse manner had implied dislike and his insistence on the formal 'Miss Fenton' surely confirmed that.

She told herself that it didn't bother her in the least what some strange man thought, but it did. She had no idea why. It just did. With a great effort she pushed the thought from her and continued her star-gazing. Out here under the bright heavens, Thornley and everything connected with it might just as well not exist.

In grey dawn the ferry passed Alderney and the outcrops of rocks that made this part of the world such a hazard to shipping. Later came the islands of Sark and Herm, then St Peter Port was ahead of them. The town straddled a steep hill, its houses a mixture of eighteenth-century French and English architecture. Soon the ferry passed the ancient fortress of Castle Cornet at the harbour entrance and, struggling with cases, Meg and Terry headed for the exit.

Waiting as those before them made their way down the gang-plank, Meg turned anxiously and said, 'I should have told you before this, but when I wrote to Mum I just said I was bringing a friend.' At Terry's startled look, she went on quickly, 'Well, how could I tell her the truth and leave her sitting there alone, worrying, fretting, crying even? I don't know. So I decided we'd tell her gently, or rather you would. At least I'd be there.'

She was right, of course, but Terry hardly relished the thought of delivering such a blow. Meg had promised, she had definitely promised that all would be well, and so Terry had packed her case quietly, said goodbye on Maundy Thursday and headed for Southampton, confident she was expected. Now she faced the prospect of meeting a cousin who was totally unprepared.

At last they were off the ferry and on the busy quayside. A tall, gangling man was strolling towards them: grey receding hair above a weatherbeaten face, and wearing an old friend of a Guernsey sweater which had seen better days.

Terry judged him to be about sixty years of age as Meg introduced him as Mike, 'a family friend and neighbour'. He shook Terry's hand, picked up the cases and walked with them to a battered old truck. Later, with all three of them squeezed into the front, Mike eased the truck away from the harbour, past the clock tower and town church, along the tree-lined promenade and started climbing the twisting wooded hill towards St Martin.

Gazing at the sea below to her left, Terry wondered about the house where she had been born. Her very roots were in this island, and her eyes tried to take in everything at once.

'This your first visit to Guernsey?' asked Mike, sensing her keen interest.

Before she could answer, Terry felt a warning jab on her hip from Meg. 'Yes.'

'Very quiet at this time of year,' he went on. 'Not like summer when the world and his wife arrive. Pretty place. Surely you must miss it, Meg?'

'Of course.'

He laughed. 'But limiting after London, is that it? You'll end up married to a doctor and living in a London suburb. I can see it all now. Then you'll be sorry, my girl.'

'Doctors!' she sniffed. 'The ones I meet are all married, and God preserve me from the medical students. Some of them are wet behind the ears still.' She turned to Terry and smiled. 'I've known Mike all my life. He owns the neighbouring land to ours and bought our greenhouses after Dad died. Mum couldn't keep the business going.' She smiled and added quietly, 'And he has a boat.'

'Ah, hints, sly little hints,' said Mike, grinning. 'All right then.

If the weather holds good tomorrow, I'll take you out for a short trip. The forecast sounds promising but we've heard that one before. We'll go out on the high tide so be at the cove by eleven unless you hear from me. Oh, and try to persuade your mother to come also. I know she's not much of a sailor, but she's been very down in the dumps of late. A trip out will do her good.'

'Sailing?' Terry looked surprised. 'Dad has a small dinghy which I take out from time to time, but that's just on a river.'

Mike shook his head. 'Not sailing. All I have is a small fishing boat with a dodgy engine. I used to own a yawl but I'm too lazy and too busy to fiddle around with sails these days so I sold it.'

'Mike used to take me sailing when I was still at school,' said Meg. 'And he taught me to fish.'

After St Martin, Mike turned off the main route and eased his way along narrow winding roads, stopping and reversing into a private drive to let the local bus pass by. They drove through a hamlet dominated by high stone walls and on past fields where Guernsey cows grazed then finally came to a smallholding with three large greenhouses. The truck turned in through a gateway and stopped outside a substantial stone house with the date 1795 carved over the doorway. Terry stepped out and found herself in a courtyard which had once been very much part of a farm but was now dominated by a willow tree, a small pond with ducks, and a rusting wheelbarrow. Beside this a black cat lay curled up in the sunshine, while two mallards waddled their way from the pond to inspect the newcomers. Like many of the dwellings on this island, the house was French in style.

As Mike hoisted cases from the truck, a woman appeared from the direction of the rear garden. Small and thin, with salt and pepper hair, she wore a woollen jumper over a grey pleated skirt and smiled happily as she approached Terry, saying, 'I thought I heard the truck. You must be Meg's friend. I'm her mother, but do call me Grace, everyone else does. I'm sorry but I don't believe I know your name?'

'Terry.'

'Welcome, Terry, to the Collinette abode.' Grace turned to Meg, hugged her warmly with tears of joy in her eyes, then thanked Mike who waved goodbye and drove the truck out through the gate. 'Well,' she said, turning back to Terry. 'This is nice. Are you a nurse too?'

'No,' said Terry, glancing uneasily at Meg. 'I'm a teacher.'

'Have you been to the island before?' asked Grace.

It had to be done, and postponing it would only mean she would have to start lying to Grace from this moment on. 'I was born here. I'm Terry Fenton, Diane's daughter.' For one horrible moment she saw the happy smile fade and eyes stare at her in stunned disbelief.

Meg took the bull by the horns. 'I wanted to tell you but I didn't know how. I just thought this was the best way. Perhaps I was wrong. We met a short while ago in London.'

Grace was still unable to take it in. 'Terry? Diane's girl . . . that bonny little baby? Good God.' Then her face lightened, as though the sun had driven away the shadows. 'Your parents . . . they're well? They've sent word with you, a letter perhaps?'

Terry avoided the question. 'I hope you don't mind my being here without an invitation? It's a cheek, I know that, and I can understand your surprise . . . or perhaps shock is the best word for it. It's just that . . . I so wanted to meet you.'

Grace kissed her gently on the cheek and smiled. 'And you can have no idea what it means for me to meet you after all these years.' The smile faded suddenly and alarm filled her grey eyes. 'But you didn't answer my question. I asked if your parents were well and . . . you didn't answer. Oh, God, something's happened, hasn't it? I knew it. I've always known it. Tell me at once . . .'

'They're fine, just fine. Healthy and thriving.' Terry paused, feeling the woman's relief and pain at these words. They said it all, yet how else could she have put it? 'There's so much we have to talk about and you'll want answers which I can't give, I'm afraid.' Grace was exactly as her letter had indicated, a kind, warm, motherly woman. What possible crime could she have committed to have earned such treatment from the Fentons?

Making a concerted effort to regain her composure, Grace placed her arms about the young women and walked with them towards the back door of the old house. 'No matter. You're here and that's everything. Come on in and you can tell me how you and Meg got together while I cook you some breakfast.'

The kitchen was large, with rush mats covering the flagstoned floor. In an alcove which had once housed a cooking range, the small gas cooker looked sadly out of place. On it Grace prepared scrambled eggs on toast, eschewing all meat on Good Friday.

The little black cat had entered the kitchen and now sat curled up at Terry's feet as she ate her breakfast. Grace settled down with them and drank her fourth coffee of the morning, asking about the journey and generally making polite small talk until breakfast was over. Then she led them into the small sitting room, walked straight to the hearth and stirred the coals with a large poker. The fire sparked into life once more and all three sat down on the uncomfortable three-piece suite which had been there since the early thirties and needed re-covering.

Leaning towards Terry, hands clasped nervously before her, Grace asked, 'You have a letter for me from your mother?'

Terry wanted to shrivel up as she whispered, 'No, I'm afraid not.' And could hardly bear to look into those disappointed eyes.

'But she knew you were coming, She must have some word for me surely, after all these years?'

'Terry's parents don't know she's here,' said Meg bluntly. 'Terry herself wasn't even aware of our existence until she found your last letter and read it.'

Meg's harsh words were too much and Terry tried to soften the blow for Grace. 'It's just we were never told anything other than that we were born in Guernsey and that mother's aunt was dead. Then I read your last letter, contacted Meg and here I am.' The look on the older woman's face was such that Terry felt forced to go on. 'I couldn't ask my parents because I shouldn't have read the letter. Now I wonder why my sister and I have been kept in the dark about you all these years. I wish I knew the reason. I wondered if you and Mother had quarrelled and then were parted by war, leaving the bitterness of that quarrel unresolved? It does happen in families.'

Grey eyebrows lifted. 'We were very close. Your mother was like a younger sister to me. She came to live with us at the age of thirteen, her father having died when she was two and her mother eleven years later. So this became Diane's home. She was married from this house.' Grace sat back in her chair, eyes taking on a distant look. 'She was seventeen when she met John Fenton, who came here to work on a building site. He was older than Diane. They fell in love so he stayed on, taking any job he could. After they married they both stayed in this house and John helped us with the market garden. He knew something about the land, being raised in the country. Cambridgeshire, I think. That was all he ever really said about his past. He had no brothers or sisters and his parents too had died.'

Grace smiled fondly at the memory. 'Two orphans of the storm, I suppose, which probably accounted for their mutual attraction. Then, just before the war, John inherited the farm. Diane didn't want to leave Guernsey and cried and cried. But ... well ... a farm. How could they look such a gift horse in the mouth?

Tears filled her eyes as she went on, 'And so they left and Diane wept on my shoulder at the dockside, promising to write and to keep in touch. It broke my heart to see them leave, and to see you two little ones go out of my life. Marisa was about two and a half, I think, and you about seven or eight months ... I can't remember ... but you were both such darlings, I don't think I ever got over losing you all.'

'And from that day to this you've had no word from her?' Terry was now thoroughly perplexed. 'I don't understand it. Mother would never do anything to hurt anyone.'

'So I used to believe,' said Grace. The pale grey eyes turned to the fire. 'My husband was younger than me, and when war came he felt it his duty to join up. I told him his duty was here, looking after the business, but no, he would have it his way. Anyway, after Dunkirk it was clear these islands would be invaded, so the Government arranged a mass evacuation. Many left but there were others who couldn't just up and leave their farms and livestock. Then were those like us, with frail relatives.'

'Gran was ill,' said Meg. 'Cancer.'

Grace bit her bottom lip and paused before going on, 'I wanted to leave with Meg, but we couldn't go without my mother, and couldn't just take her without knowing that we had a proper home to go to. She was too ill for that. So I sent a cable to your parents asking them to take us in. I heard nothing. Maybe they didn't get it. Things were pretty chaotic at the time. The evacuation was well under way when I cabled again, but still I heard nothing. In the end Meg and I stayed with my mother and waited for the German army to arrive. That was the worst time of all, that waiting, that feeling of having been abandoned.

Grace gave the unwilling fire another poke. 'It wasn't so bad at first. The soldiers behaved themselves on the whole, and we kept out of their way.' She replaced the poker and rubbed her hands. 'Of course, it was altogether a different matter for the Poles and

Slavs they had brought in as slave labourers. As for us, things took a turn for the worse later, when it was clear that the war wasn't going Hitler's way. Mike had hidden his wireless set under floorboards and that way we kept in touch with events. When it was discovered he was deported. I thought we should never see him again. He never talks about that time. But I had no way of knowing what was going on in the world. Then all those who were not born on this island were rounded up and deported to camps in Germany.' She turned to Terry. 'Your father would have been among that lot, so too would his wife and children. I thanked God then for the gift of that farm. At least you were all safe in England.'

The very thought of what might have been sent a chill through Terry and she glanced at the flames as though trying to draw in their warmth. 'I'd no idea. Maybe that's why my parents never spoke of Guernsey, perhaps it was all too ... I don't know ... unsettling for them? Clearly they didn't receive your cable. You should have gone to them anyway. They would have willingly taken you in.'

Grace gave a wry smile. 'I thought that. I kept telling myself that all through those terrible years and blaming myself for not just taking a chance, but when the war was over and I wrote letter after letter, without receiving an answer, I came to two conclusions. One, that you might have perished during the war. Or two, you had all survived but sold the farm and moved on. But after making enquiries through the Red Cross and learning that you were all alive and still living in Suffolk, I could only think that your parents did not want to renew their relationship with me.'

'But why?' asked Terry.

There was a long pause, as though Grace was still trying to come to terms with the vagaries of human nature. 'After the war, when the islanders returned, there were some among them who thought we had been too acquiescent, even friendly to the Germans.' She sniffed in contempt. 'They had been in England with no notion of what it was like to live in an occupied country. We kept our heads down, got on with our lives as best we could, did not go out of our way to upset the occupying forces any more than we went out of our way to be friendly to them. But there were those who thought we should have made life harder for the Germans. Just how we were to achieve this without help was a mystery. I believe your parents must have felt some such thing or why else did they ignore me? Why did they never try to find out how we were after the war? They didn't seem to care whether we were alive or dead.'

Terry shook her head. 'I can't believe that.'

'Not of your mother perhaps, but what of your father?' Grace stared at Terry, her eyes hardening. 'We knew very little about him, even though he lived among us and we all got along well enough.'

For some moments Terry pondered this. Her father had never spoken of his background before Guernsey. Even so, if she too knew nothing about that, she was sure she knew him. Such a man as John could never be so cruel or unjust.

'When I return,' she said, 'I'll tell them we met, tell them what you believe and give them a chance to answer for themselves.'

Grace got up and walked to the window where she stood staring out on the greenhouses. 'No. Having you fall out with your parents is the last thing I want. What purpose would it serve? I wouldn't have written last year but for Meg going to London.' She turned and smiled at Terry. 'I'm glad I did though because it's brought you two together and back to me. But, given the circumstances, I see no reason why your parents should know. Now then, tell me what Marisa is doing these days.'

Terry told her, fumbled in her handbag and produced a few black and white photographs of the wedding.

Grace stared at photograph after photograph then said, 'She's turned out a beauty and no mistake. And she's going to be a rich one. Well done, Marisa.' She frowned, staring back at the pictures. 'Your mother looks very elegant. What a pity about that large brim. It shadows her face. I can't see her clearly. Has she gone grey?'

'No.'

'She looks grey here,' said Grace.

Terry let this go, thinking that to say her mother still had her naturally blonde hair might be seen as a rebuff when Grace was iron grey. Maybe she wouldn't take kindly to being reminded that she was Diane's senior.

'Your father's put on weight, I see.' Grace was peering at the photo. Wish he would look at the camera, but in each shot he's looking down. Who's that?' She pointed to Eliot.

'Our brother,' said Terry. 'Of course, you wouldn't know. Eliot's thirteen now.'

'Brother?' Grace looked at her in surprise. 'Well, that's a turn up for the book. Of course, she always wanted a boy but I didn't think she would adopt.'

Now it was Terry's turn to look surprised. 'Eliot isn't adopted. Whatever made you think he was?'

'But . . .' Grace stopped suddenly and closed her eyes. 'I'm such a fool at times. Sorry . . . must be getting confused in my dotage.'

Meg was bored and started yawning. 'Oh, do let's go out. The sun's shining and we only have a few days. Think I'll show Terry the cliff walk.'

'Then be careful,' said Grace, handing back the photographs to a mystified Terry. 'Some of it's in a dangerous state.'

The sunny day was cooled by gusting winds as Meg led Terry through the hamlet and down a narrow wooded hill until they came to a small cove. From there they climbed the pathway up the primrose-strewn cliff which, soon, would be covered in bluebells, campions, wild garlic and foxgloves. After a while they paused and looked along the coastline then out across a blue sea to the islands of Sark and Herm. Beyond that was the outline of Jersey. The light was sharp and bright. Terry wished she had worn sunglasses.

'You don't believe Mum, do you?' said Meg sharply. 'You think there's more to it all than she's letting on.'

Her sudden animosity left Terry at a loss to answer. Feeling that Meg could bore into her innermost thoughts, she turned her head away. 'I don't know what you mean.'

'Oh, I think you do, just as Mum does. We both saw what happened after the war – the recriminations, the women with their heads shaved. Public humiliation for sleeping with the enemy. It's what you're thinking, isn't it? That Mum must have been one of them.'

Terry stood nonplussed. Such a thought had briefly crossed her mind. Trust Meg to have picked it up. But it seemed the only explanation she could think of. If her parents had cause to think it, too, then that would explain everything. Yet she could never say so to Grace. That was the nature of suspicion as she had good cause to know. No one voiced it aloud and so the suspect, guilty or innocent, never had the chance to plead his or her case. As it had been with her own father, so it was now with poor Grace.

'Such a thought never entered my head,' she lied.

'Of course it did. Get rid of it at once. I have a very good memory and, believe me, no German soldier ever entered our house. Mum had nothing to do with them, nor was she ever bothered by them either. I think you should mention that to your parents, and to hell with the consequences. Either way it makes no odds now. Apart from you, the Fentons might as well be on the moon for all we care.'

Feeling she had just been firmly put in her place by this second cousin who probably made the wards tremble, Terry followed her in silence, her mind dwelling on another worrying thought. What on earth had Grace meant about Eliot's being adopted? It was a curious thing to say, and then try to cover up.

The following morning was fair and the winds had died down. True to his word, Mike telephoned at nine saying the boat trip was on for eleven and that he hoped Grace would go with them.

She dismissed the suggestion at once. 'I haven't been on a boat for years. Anyway I've far too much to do here.'

'You've nothing to do here. And if you don't go, I shan't and neither will Terry, and that will be a shame,' said Meg. 'We don't have long, and want to spend our time with you.'

And so Grace relented. In old slacks, a fisherman's knit sweater and her late husband's windcheater, she climbed into Mike's small boat which was moored at the cove. 'I'm not as nimble as I used to be. I hope you're not fishing, Mike. I like the boat to keep moving otherwise I'll be sea sick.'

When they were all in, he started the engine, the boat slid forward and eased out to sea, past Castle Cornet towards the small island of Herm. Terry could see why it had been necessary to wait for high tide. Herm was surrounded by rocks and steering a channel through them took skill and knowledge of these waters. She caught him glancing at her curiously from time to time and knew that Grace had informed him of her identity. He must be wondering why the Fentons had treated his childhood friend so abominably.

As he eased the boat round the tiny island, she could see the dazzling white Shell Beach on the far side and the verdant cliffs beyond that. It was a slow, enjoyable trip. As they came around the tip of the island, a gaff-rigged yacht crossed their path.

Mike waved to the occupant. 'That's Bill Stoker in the *Nicolette*. Do you remember, Grace?'

Grace frowned. 'The *Nicolette*?'

'Went on the rocks.' He looked at Terry. 'It was that last summer, before you left for England. Your father helped me rescue the yachtsman who had chartered it. Bill was able to get the gash in the hull partly repaired so that it didn't sink when the tide changed. Eventually we managed to float her off and tow her to the boat yard.' He laughed at the memory. 'Poor old Bill. He was bloody angry, I can tell you. His beloved *Nicolette*. That was the last time he chartered her out.'

'Yes, I do remember now.' said Grace, 'but I thought he'd sold her?'

'He did, to some rich tax exile in Jersey. Made quite a bit on her. Missed her too much, though, and managed to get her back about four years ago.'

Grace was scratching her chin thoughtfully. 'That yachtsman stayed with us for a short while. What was his name? Nice young man, English, very public school. My husband didn't like him, though.' She smiled at Terry. 'Too good-looking, I reckon. Your mother was quite taken with him.'

Mike grinned at the memory. 'That's it! Having wrecked the yacht he'd nowhere to live so John invited him to stay with you while Bill Stoker was all for feeding him to the fish.'

Gazing back at Herm, Terry could happily visualise her father rushing to the rescue, but not his willingness to play host, especially in a house that wasn't his. They never had people to stay at the farm, but then her parents didn't know anyone outside the village. Odd, though, that he could be so kind to a stranger and so cruel to poor Grace.

In the late-afternoon sun Grace showed her where the old market garden had been. A stone wall now divided the greenhouses from her small rear garden but to the side of her property remained a portion of the old orchard.

They were walking back to the house when Terry plucked up the nerve to address the worry in her mind. 'Yesterday you spoke of Eliot and seemed to think he was adopted. Why?'

Grace stopped walking. 'I shouldn't have said anything. If he was adopted, you'd know.'

'He isn't. What made you think he might be?'

'It was nothing. A silly mistake, that's all.'

If Grace didn't wish to pursue the matter, Terry had the good sense to drop it. She turned to the house, her eyes softening.

'Under the date was written the word "Beaulieu". 'Doesn't that mean beautiful place?'

Grace nodded. 'The Collinettes took it over in the middle of the nineteenth century and kept the original name. After all, it was the most perfect name, certainly in those days, before the modern world encroached on all that beauty. Sad. But I do love it still.'

'And I was born here.'

Frowning at this, Grace looked at her. 'In Guernsey, yes, but not in this house if that's what you mean?' Seeing the puzzled look on Terry's face, she went on, 'Both you and Marisa were born in hospital.'

Terry shook her head. 'Mother always said we were born in this house.'

'I can't think why she would say that. You and Marisa were both born, by Caesarean operation.' Seeing the surprised look on Terry's face, she added, 'Because of your mother's terrible accident.'

'What accident?'

Grace sighed. 'Oh, dear, she really doesn't communicate with you two girls, does she? Come with me.'

Leading Terry to the orchard, she pointed to one of the trees just coming into bud. 'That's where she fell. In her eighth month with Marisa, she still insisted on climbing the ladder to help us pick apples. I told her not to, that it was stupid and dangerous, and didn't realise she had until I heard the crash. When I turned and saw her lying on the ground with the ladder across her, my heart stopped. She was rushed to hospital where an emergency Caesarean was performed. By some miracle, Marisa was just fine. Your mother, however, had a broken thigh, a hip injury and a fractured pelvis. She was in hospital for some time and when she came out she was in a wheelchair before graduating to crutches. Then you were conceived. Her doctor was furious that she had become pregnant again so soon. It meant a second operation; there were certain complications, she was very ill and was then told she couldn't have any more children.'

Terry frowned. 'I didn't know. She never said. I thought I was born in this house, Marisa too. Mother always told us that.'

Grace sighed and shook her head. 'Well, perhaps she thought it better to have you hear of a normal birth in the old family home. Anyway, that's why I assumed Eliot was adopted.'

'But ... I can vaguely remember when she returned from London with the baby.'

Grace shrugged. 'Ah, well then, that settles it.'

'Settles what?' They turned to see Meg standing behind them. 'I've put the potatoes on, but what shall I do about the fish?'

'I'll attend to it,' said Grace, heading for the house.

'What was all that about?' asked Meg.

Wondering why she had crept up so quietly, Terry explained all that Grace had told her. 'Apparently the doctor said she could have no more children, but she had Eliot so he was wrong.'

Meg frowned. 'Even so, having Caesars in those days was a different matter. If she had two consecutive sections, then a third child could be life-threatening.' She paused and stared at Terry. 'And given the injuries your mother sustained in the accident, I'm surprised she didn't heed the advice. Still, I doubt it was her fault. A midwifery course teaches you a lot about life. What some women have to go through is unbelievable. If my husband treated me the way theirs treat them, I'd castrate the devil.'

'Dad isn't like that,' said Terry defensively. 'My parents love each other. Given that Mother gave birth without problems later, I'd say your mother just misunderstood.'

'Given that the mortality rate in those days was much higher anyway, I'd say yours was very lucky,' came the terse response.

Later that evening Grace found some old snapshots taken with her Box Brownie and showed them to Terry. 'I only have these to remember you all by. Your parents took their photos to England when they went.'

'No.' Terry shook her head. 'They forgot them, so they're here somewhere.' She glanced without recognition at the two people sitting on a beach with a toddler playing beside them. 'Goodness, how different they look here!'

Grace was frowning as she rummaged through the box seeking other photos. 'I'm quite sure they took their album. Could have sworn it. Still, it might be in the attic.'

As Terry handed back the photos, it crossed her mind to ask if she could keep them, but that would deprive Grace and her parents would want to know how she'd come by them. 'It's so strange to see my parents in their youth. They don't even have their wedding photos. Left those here too.'

Grace scratched her chin and looked perplexed. 'I was so convinced they had taken them. They kept the album in their bedroom, and the framed photos. I would have stored such treasures away very carefully. You must remember, I was heartbroken when they left. No, dear, they're not here. If you look around your house, you'll probably find they've mislaid them.'

'I will,' said Terry. 'You can bank on it.'

Arriving at Woodbridge station on Tuesday evening, Terry saw her mother waiting with the Morris and remembered Grace's words of warning. She was right. Why fall out with the parents she loved over something that was in the past and done with now she had given her word to Grace and would keep it?

Diane seemed extremely tense as she kissed Terry. 'Did you have a good time, dear?'

'Marvellous.' She put her case in the boot of the car then settled into the passenger seat. 'Weather was kind and we managed to see quite a bit of the island.'

'Good.' Easing the car out of the forecourt and through the narrow Woodbridge lanes. Diane glanced nervously at Terry from time to time before asking, 'Where exactly did you stay?'

'St Peter Port. In a road close to Elizabeth College.'

'And where did you visit?' The edge to her voice was not lost on Terry.

'Oh, Castle Cornet. This bay and that. Saw where Victor Hugo lived although we didn't go into the house. Took a boat trip across to Herm.' Terry paused, wondering if her mother would now speak out, but Diane remained silent. 'How have things been at home?'

The relief in her voice was almost audible. 'Eliot's been down with the 'flu. Apparently he was in the sick bay last week and no one bothered to inform us. He looked very ragged when I collected him, so I'm damned if I'm taking him back to that school until he's completely fit again.'

'Poor old Eliot,' said Terry. 'What rotten luck during the holidays. We've had seven cases at school, two from my class alone.'

'There's a letter for you,' said Diane, turning on to the main road. 'It came the afternoon you left.'

'And what a panic that was! What caused the car to break down like that?'

'Oh, something mechanical which I don't understand. But you caught the train so all was well in the end.'

'By the skin of my teeth.'

Terry still harboured the suspicion that the breakdown of the Morris was fortuitous for her mother who had been driving her to the station. They had stopped at crossroads and been unable to start again. Her mother had used too much choke and flooded the engine. In sheer panic, Terry had rushed to a public telephone and called Fiona, who'd saved the day by speeding to her in the Land Rover and delivering her to Woodbridge station just as the guard was blowing the whistle. Even before Terry had time to sit down the train was moving. Had she missed that, she would have missed the boat train also and not gone to Guernsey.

Could that have been her mother's intention? Would she really have gone to such extremes to prevent her daughter from finding the Collinettes? It was a terrible thought and Terry told herself that since her mother knew nothing about cars she would hardly be able to put on such a charade. Yet once the suspicion had taken root, it remained firmly planted and she was now more resolved than ever to move into a place of her own, away from parental interference and lies.

'You must miss Guernsey dreadfully,' she said cautiously.

'Not as much as I used to,' Diane replied.

'Why don't you and Dad have a holiday there?'

Diane flinched slightly. 'I think it would be rather painful now. You know what they say: Never go back.'

'Perhaps they're right,' said Terry sharply. 'After all, you never know what you may find.'

Chapter Eight

Terry lay in a hot bath soaking off the exhaustion of the long journey, her mind still on the letter she had read earlier and the man who'd written it. It had been on the hall table since the day she had left for Guernsey, the bold handwriting on the envelope unknown to her. Aware of family curiosity, she took the letter upstairs to her room, sat on her bed and opened it.

Dear Miss Fenton,
I feel I owe you an apology for my behaviour when we met a few weeks ago.

If I was abrupt, to the point of rudeness, then please be kind enough to put it down to emotion at seeing the place where my brother and his crew died.

You were most kind and I wish you to know how much I appreciated that even though I may have given the opposite impression at the time.

Since that day, however, the matter has weighed on my mind and I wondered if we could meet and have a drink together? At the end of Easter Week I shall be staying with friends at Bury St Edmunds and, since Suffolk is as rich in pubs as it is in painters, it seems too good an opportunity to miss.

I shall telephone you when I arrive in Bury and trust we might meet again this time under happier circumstances.

Sincerely,
Grant Kenway

Thinking of the taciturn man walking away from her in the snow, Terry was still trying to come to terms with the surprise of it all.

She had not expected to see him again until the memorial service and even then hardly thought he would take any notice of her. But, now it seemed she had been in his thoughts as he had been in hers. Should she meet him. The thought of it made her nervous. Sponging her body lazily, she told herself it was just a drink, nothing more; a way of apologising; a matter of good manners – that was all. It would be churlish of her to refuse.

She lay back, allowing her mind to switch wavelengths. In an attempt to apologise for implying that John Fenton had behaved badly to his wife, Meg had tried to make amends by hinting that Eliot could well be adopted, given her mother's medical history.

Responding with growing exasperation, Terry had repeated what she had already said to Grace. 'Eliot's my blood brother. I remember sending a card to the clinic when he was born.' When Meg had asked which clinic, Terry had to admit she didn't know. 'It was in London. Dad visited alone.'

'But why a London clinic and not a Suffolk hospital?' Meg had asked. 'The top notch clinics are good but very expensive. I shouldn't have thought your parents would want to pay the fees. Many don't even have the facilities to treat complications. They whisk such patients off to the nearest hospital. Given your mother's history, no doctor would countenance her going to such a place.'

Terry had frowned at this. 'I don't know very much . . . I was too young at the time. But I still believe Eliot is my natural blood brother. So could we please forget about it?'

Nevertheless, it was a problem she couldn't get out of her mind and wanted solved. How, though? Having lied to her and Marisa about the place of their birth and the fact that they had relatives still living, it seemed quite probable that her parents had lied about Eliot as well and would go on lying. Why?

She dried herself with a soft pink towel, walked to her bedroom and slipped into her shortie nightgown before sitting at her dressing table to brush her tangled hair. Staring in despair at the weatherbeaten face in the mirror, it dawned on her that Marisa might know more about Eliot. She was older and remembered different things. On the other hand, Marisa was hardly discreet and would probably have screamed out any such secret to the world during one of her tantrums. Terry put down the brush decisively. Meg was just wrong. So, obviously, was the doctor who had told Diane she could not have a third child.

She climbed into bed, settled under the covers and switched out her lamp, murmuring, 'And that is that.'

Far from being on his death bed, Eliot was up and about, bored and peevish. Taking pity on her brother, Terry drove him to Lowdham the following day to buy new shoes and thence to Lucy's Tea Rooms where he devoured a cream tea, two toasted buns and a large strawberry ice-cream.

As they returned to the car, she glanced at him quizzically. 'I'm glad to see you're well on the road to recovery.'

Eliot assumed a pained expression as he climbed into the Austin. 'Still a bit groggy. Rough on the chest and aching all over. I reckon it'll be quite some time before I'm ready to return to school.'

Smiling, she switched on the ignition. 'Better not tell Mother about the tea then.'

'She says I have to keep my strength up.'

'By which she means hot stews, cabbage, carrots and potatoes.'

Eliot's nose wrinkled in disgust. 'I won't tell if you won't.'

'Cross my heart, etcetera, etcetera.' As she drove up the hill towards the Green, Terry frowned. 'You are happy at school, aren't you?'

After a pause her brother said quietly, 'I'm getting used to it now. I've made friends and there's plenty of sport. I like History best but Latin's a bore and Major Whitehouse is always going on at me. What's the point of it anyway if Dad wants me to take on the farm one day? He told me at Easter that's what he wanted.'

Terry had always assumed that Eliot would inherit Lynwood, but for his whole life to be mapped out without his consent seemed wrong. 'At least with a good education behind you there are choices you can make. Without it, there are none.' She fell silent when he made no reply to this. What he really meant was that he was homesick and not as happy as his letters made him out to be. She glanced at him and smiled. 'Still, there's no point in sending you back until you're completely well.'

With a sense of relief Eliot sank back in his seat. It had been a close call, but he knew he could rely on Terry even though she was a teacher herself. He hoped her pupils knew how lucky they were to have her.

Terry drove home thinking of Grant but, on turning through the gate to the farm, suddenly found herself steering a nerve-jangling course between a lorry and a bulldozer. Work on the memorial site had begun and the only access to the ploughed field was via their drive and rear trackway.

Diane was in the kitchen, looking tetchy. 'Didn't hear you arrive because of all that damned noise!' Aware suddenly of blissful silence, she turned to the window. 'Ah, it's stopped. They're finished for the night, please God.'

'I've just been playing dodgems with them,' said Terry, removing her jacket. 'They were parking their equipment as I arrived. What exactly are they doing?'

'Preparing the site. Noisy business, the whole thing. When they've done that they'll start on the path. I'm told that will involve a mechanical digger. Dear God! Still, at least it should be well away from us.'

'When will the site area be completed?'

'They say probably Friday, but won't commit themselves, so it could go on. Don't know how I'll bear it! My head's about to burst and this is only the first day. Even when they've prepared the ground they'll be laying down hardcore, then heaps of gravel.'

'Sounds like it will go on then,' said Terry. 'I'll fetch you a couple of Aspirin and make some tea. Eliot, would you put the kettle on, please?' Carrying the jacket up to her bedroom, she put it away tidily then returned to the kitchen with the pills which she handed to her mother with a glass of water.

Having swallowed the Aspirin, Diane settled herself in the fireside chair, frowning. 'Sorry I had to get you to buy the shoes, but I had so much to do and your father doesn't seem too well. He has a sore throat. Hope he hasn't caught Eliot's 'flu. That's all we need right now.'

At this, Eliot suddenly declared himself to be 'weak and exhausted' after his outing, and took himself off to the sitting room to watch television while Diane voiced her concern for him.

'Oh, he's not so bad,' said Terry. 'Tough little nut. Needs to be completely well, though, before returning to Kingsmead.' For a moment she busied herself with cups and saucers then found herself thinking of Meg's words once more.

Turning to her mother, she said cautiously, 'You know, I can remember the day you brought him home, when Dad said that the midwives called him Desperate Dan because he was so big. I also remember painting a card and sending it to you. A primrose, I think. It had something to do with the clinic . . .'

Diane's eyes were closed and her head hurt too much for her to think straight. 'What? Oh, yes, Primrose Ward.'

'Not the name of the clinic then?'

No . . . no, dear. That was the Westlake. I still have that card somewhere among Eliot's baby things.'

'Why was he born in London and not Suffolk?' Seeing the blue eyes open at this, Terry turned away and made the tea.

'Complications. I needed specialist attention.'

'What kind of complications?'

'Blood pressure. They took me in before Eliot was due and kept me very quiet.'

'Blood pressure? Terry tensed. There were hospitals enough in Suffolk able to deal with blood pressure, surely. This was clearly a lie and she had no intention of letting her mother off the hook. 'So Dr Tranmer sent you all the way to London?'

'He had nothing to do with it. I chose the clinic because I knew it was a very good one.'

'Was Eliot born in the normal manner then?'

Diane stared at her in surprise. 'Yes, luckily.'

'Really?' Terry turned to her. 'What about us, Marisa and I? Were there complications when we were born?'

'No.' Diane regarded her with growing suspicion. 'Goodness, why all these questions? I told you a long time ago that you were both born in the house I grew up in after my parents died.'

Lies! All lies! Terry tried to disguise her anger by pouring tea and managed to slop most of it in the saucers. Why did her mother not mention the accident and the Caesarean sections? What was so secret about it, for God's sake? It made no sense.

Later, however, as she tried to prepare lessons in her bedroom, it dawned on Terry that perhaps it did make sense after all. If Meg was right about her adoption theory and such pains had been taken to make people believe Eliot was a true Fenton, then all else must be kept secret also, including the existence of one who would have known the truth. Yet Grace was a reasonable woman and if asked to say nothing would have honoured such a request.

She got up and walked to the window, thinking this was not reason enough to treat the Collinettes as though they didn't exist.

There must be some other explanation for that particular form of cruelty.

The sun was low behind the wood now and a blackbird trilled his territorial song from the rooftop above her room. Spring was here and Terry's spirits began to lift. Soon the swallows and martins would be back nesting under the eaves but for now there was the wonderful sound of this truly English bird.

Returning to her desk, her spirits sank once more. Why so much mystery and so many lies? She loved her parents, but if she couldn't trust them then who could she trust? It left her with a feeling of isolation and insecurity for how could she ever believe a word they said again?

The sore throat which had plagued John Fenton for the past two days had turned to influenza and on Thursday afternoon he took himself off to bed, feeling like death.

Just before dinner the telephone rang and, as Terry walked into the hall to answer it, mild panic set in. Her hand paused momentarily over the receiver before she picked it up and said in a calm voice, 'Lynwood Farm.'

'May I speak to Miss Fenton, please?' The deep voice sounded strained.

'Speaking.'

'Ah . . . hello there. It's Grant Kenway. Did you receive my letter?'

'Yes.' She paused, hoping he would speak, but he was clearly waiting for her. 'It's kind of you to be so concerned, but really you've nothing to apologise for. After all, I was pretty rude to you in the first place.'

'Which was understandable, given the circumstances.'

Another awkward pause. Terry began to flounder. 'Anyway, how are you?'

'I hardly know. It's been all go at the hospital as usual and I've been studying like mad as well, so I'm looking forward to a couple of days off. Look, I've only just arrived in Bury and wondered if you'd care to have that drink with me tomorrow?'

Now it was her turn to pause and nerves got the better of her. 'Well, I've just returned from Guernsey and have lesson plans to prepare for when school starts. I teach, you see . . .' Why was she saying this?

'I'm sorry. It was just a thought.'

Clearly he was the straightforward type who would take no for no and not ask a second time. Thinking quickly, she rescued the situation. 'Wait, I would like to accept, but there's something you must know. My brother and father have 'flu. As a doctor the last thing you want is to be exposed to their germs.'

'It's you I want to take out, not your father and brother!' His voice relaxed, tone becoming lighter. 'Have pity on me! I'm lost in a strange country and need a friendly guide. Remember how long it took me to get from Lowdham to Thornley the last time?'

She laughed. 'I do, and I worried about you getting back to London. How did you get on?'

'I arrived home at nine-thirty, I seem to recall. The rest is a horrible blank.'

'Well, I'd certainly have it on my conscience if you disappeared into the darkness of Suffolk, never to be seen again.'

'Supposing I pick you up around eleven tomorrow morning?'

'Very well. Eleven.'

Her face was burning as she put down the receiver. How different he seemed from the surly man she had met on that cold snowy day, which seemed so far away now. Knowing little about him was intriguing too. Was that why he had remained in her thoughts since then?

Diane looked up from her dinner plate with a surprised expression. 'You met this man in the winter and didn't say anything? The brother of the bomber pilot? Goodness, dear, you might have asked him in.'

'I did, but he's a doctor in a London hospital and had to get back before the weather closed in.'

Diane's eyes opened wide. 'A doctor! Really?' John could have no objection to him then, she thought. Things were looking up. Still, it would be foolish to pin all their hopes on a brief encounter.

'Perhaps this time you'll make it clear that we should like to meet the brother of Squadron Leader Paul Kenway?' Seeing the surprised look on Terry's face, she said, 'Oh, yes. We now have the names of the crew, their squadron, and where they were stationed in Norfolk. The Air Ministry have been very helpful.'

'But we can't invite him in. He'd feel compelled to accept out of politeness and then he might get 'flu too.'

'I wonder how many sick patients pass their germs on to him.

Still, perhaps you're right.' Pushing away her plate of chicken pie half eaten Diane lit a cigarette. She had given up smoking but her nerves had been on edge from the moment Terry had taken off for Guernsey.

What had really happened there? Was it all as innocent as she'd been meant to believe? Terry had always been filled with curiosity about her birthplace and they had managed to satisfy her questions one way or another until they stopped. Then, out of the blue, she was off with some unknown friend to the one place they'd never wanted her to visit and asking very odd questions about the manner of her birth as well as that of Marisa and Eliot. Too much of a coincidence, surely? No, there was something fishy about that holiday, she was certain of it. Glancing at her son, she snapped, 'Eliot, for goodness' sake, stop goggling at Terry and eat your dinner.'

Grant arrived the following morning in a twenty-year-old green MG. Under a cloudless pale blue sky, with sunlight glinting on the large headlamps, it purred its way along country lanes and through picturesque villages towards Dedham.

'It used to belong to my brother,' he explained. 'After he was killed, one of his fellow officers drove it back to us and I've cherished it ever since. Couldn't imagine driving anything else.'

Terry could only begin to guess at the heart-rending scene when the Kenways saw the car arrive at their home with another young RAF officer at the wheel where Paul should have been. She tried to think of something to say, but nothing seemed appropriate and so she pushed her wind-tossed hair back from her face and remained silent.

He noticed the gesture and frowned. 'Not too cold for you, is it? I can put the top up, if you like?'

'No, I like the open air.' She observed his large hands on the wheel, as she had observed his serious expression and manner. He drove with care along the twisting narrow lanes and Terry found herself comparing him with Alastair. But there was no comparison. Alastair had been an overgrown boy whereas Grant was a mature man. And that, she sensed, was where the danger lay. The chances were that he already had a woman tucked away, someone of his own age and sophistication who understood about his career. She resolved to keep it foremost in her mind. Once bitten, twice shy.

The day was mild and sunny with the countryside awakening after the long dreary winter months. Terry's eyes feasted on shining daffodils, catkins and horse chestnut buds. In the region of the River Stour cornfields gave way to meadows and she smiled to see frisking lambs beside grazing ewes.

Grant stopped the car at a small village pub, where they settled beside a log fire, he with a pint of brown ale and she with a dry sherry. The only other occupants at that early hour were two elderly men chatting with broad Suffolk accents. They sat on a wooden bench with their backs to the window and sunlight on their grey heads.

Observing them, Terry murmured, 'They probably sit in that same spot every day and no one else in this village would dare to occupy it.'

The grin that spread across Grant's face changed his stern countenance completely. His dark eyes warmed, fixed on happier days. 'But they're thoroughly contented. I was raised in a Hampshire village about the size of Thornley. My father was a country doctor.'

'And, unlike your brother, you followed him into the medical profession.'

The grin faded slowly. 'It's what he wanted for Paul as well, but my brother joined the RAF instead. At twenty-one he had flown Wellingtons and Whitely bombers before going on to Lancasters. God, how I envied him during those early war years! He was having one hell of a time, I thought, while I was stuck in a dreary classroom. At twenty three he was dead. We had the telegram which was followed by a letter and his personal effects. My parents never got over it. I'm not sure I have either. He was a marvellous brother to me and I was so proud of him.

'Anyway, that's when I knew I would take up medicine, not just to please my father but because it seemed the natural thing to do. A calling, if you like. I've never regretted it.'

'Are your parents still in Hampshire?'

He shook his head. 'Father sold the practice and bought a house in Richmond so that they could be near my elder sister. 'Then she married an Australian and went off with him to Sydney. Three years ago my father died, so Mother let the house and moved in with my sister down under.' He smiled wistfully. 'One moment you have a family and the next you don't. All I have of the old life is the car.'

'No wonder you treat it with such care,' said Terry, suddenly and surprisingly aware of his vulnerability. She had always thought that to be her own particular Achilles heel. As he spoke on, she found his gaze disconcerting. One moment it seemed slightly amused and the next serious to the point of intensity. 'Which hospital are you at?'

'St Thomas's'

'That's a teaching hospital, isn't it?'

'One of the best, if not *the* best. It's where I trained. I seem to have been there for years, working and studying.'

'But now you're a doctor at least the studying is finished.'

This time he laughed out loud. 'Don't I just wish! I've never stopped. I take my FRCS in a couple of weeks, so I'm still burning the midnight oil.'

She sipped her sherry and frowned. 'FRCS?'

'Fellow of the Royal College of Surgeons.'

Aware of her appalling ignorance about his life and work, she hestitated before saying, 'And when you get your Fellowship?'

'I become a Mr again.' He lit a cigarette and smiled. 'Funny old world. It took years of training to become a doctor. I'll never forget the first time anyone called me that. After many more years of training I've no doubt at all that I'll be over the moon when I finally achieve the accolade of Mr Kenway.'

He then wanted to know about her and, unlike Alastair, agreed she should have gone for a degree course. As they spoke of their backgrounds she found herself telling him how the family had come from Guernsey just before the war.

'So there you have it. Fate smiled on us by causing a tragic accident. As you say, funny old world.'

When they left the pub she decided that Grant was handsome. Not in the conventional way that Alastair was, but in some inner, deeper way. When they reached Dedham, she knew that she already cared for him and dreaded the thought that this was likely to be just a one off interlude.

They wandered around Dedham looking at the old church with its heraldic shields, including those of Dedham, Massachusetts, since many people from Dedham emigrated with the Pilgrim Fathers in 1620. All this being news to Grant, Terry felt her confidence growing as she told him of the past, then showed him the Grammar School where Constable had once been a pupil. She spoke of the Flemish who came to this area when it became a prosperous centre for the cloth industry during the fourteenth century, and pointed out their timber houses. Grant listened with intense interest, asked many questions, then realised she must be hungry.

They found a hotel for lunch and as Terry looked at the menu she wondered whether a young surgeon, not yet a Fellow, could afford such prices. He seemed unconcerned however as they enjoyed soup, lamb with rosemary, followed by apple pie and cream with a good wine to accompany the meal.

'You're staying with friends at Bury, I believe you said?' Terry stirred her coffee, wondering how long he would be with them.

'Tomorrow I'm best man to my closest colleague. We trained together. Now I have to get the poor devil through his stag night in one piece and make sure he's upright in time for the wedding.'

As they talked she learned of his long hours. That 'on call' meant operating all day and often during the night as well, with two weekends on and one off. In all a working week of over a hundred hours. On top of that came the studying. But, hard as it was, he loved it and couldn't imagine doing anything else.

She heard him with mounting dismay. Nothing could come of this, she realised. Even if there was no other woman, they were so far apart and his days so full that this might well be the only one they would have to themselves. She would see him at the ceremony, and then maybe never again.

After lunch they found their way across meadows to the tranquil Stour, and followed the river towards Flatford Mill. Along the banks, wintry branches of ash and willow swayed lightly in the wind that swept across the vale. Grazing cows stared blankly and, in the diamond sharp light, Dedham church could be seen on the skyline.

Grant stopped, ran a hand through his straight black hair and gazed back the way they had come. 'It's just like stepping into a bloody painting. Nothing's changed since Constable's day. His large skies ... and the colours ... it's all still here and I didn't think it would be somehow.'

After twenty minutes they came to the lock then stood looking across at the large red brick mill, where the famous painter was raised, before making their way over the bridge and along the lane towards Willy Lott's cottage. Banks of willow were reflected in the water as the river wound its way past the old house. All too aware of the silent man beside her, Terry felt a strange sensation somewhere in the pit of her stomach and remained as silent as he did. He took a photograph of her at this point and she assumed he needed her as foreground for the cottage.

They ambled back towards the mill and hired a rowing boat. Fixing the oars into the rollocks, Grant pulled the vessel slowly along the shallow river, unable to take his eyes off Terry who, aware of his gaze, stared resolutely at her hand as it trailed in the water.

How quiet and still she is, he thought, knowing it was this stillness that had been the principal cause of his interest in her. The spring sunlight lifted her hair to a honey colour. He liked the way it turned under slightly at jaw level, a blue bandana keeping it back from her face, heart-shaped and lightly tanned by wind and sun with fine eyebrows over grey eyes and full lips. Not pretty, he thought, but something more, something bordering on beauty with looks that would last the years. But those eyes were troubled.

'Are you staying at Bury all weekend?' she was asking.

Realising that he had stopped rowing and that the boat was drifting towards the bank, Grant pulled on one oar, set it midstream again and carried on until it was time to row back.

'I have to return to London on Sunday morning.'

Of course! After leaving the boat they walked to a small tea garden beside the river and sat surrounded by birds and ducks, before returning back along the meadows to Dedham. There, Grant bought two Constable prints, one of Dedham Vale and the other of wide dramatic skies above the Stour.

He handed one to her, saying, 'To remind us of a lovely day.'

On the way to Thornley they stopped at a remote little pub and had a drink before Grant finally headed through the village High Street, across the watersplash and up the hill. It was dark when the MG turned through the gates of Lynwood; the light from the sitting room shone its welcoming glow.

Allowing no awkward pause, Grant climbed out, opened the

passenger door and helped Terry to her feet. As he did so, she felt a sudden chill. A brief stay of execution was better than parting. To hell with the 'flu! 'Won't you come in this time and say hello? My father will be in bed, of course, but Mother would like to meet the brother of the pilot who saved this village.'

Diane greeted them inside the hall, said how pleased she was to meet him and asked if he would care to stay to dinner.

Grant thank her for the invitation but said his hosts at Bury were expecting him, then stayed chatting for ten minutes. 'What you and the villagers are doing here is a wonderful thing. It means a great deal to me and my family, and I'm sure to all the other families. Would you please convey my feelings to your husband and tell him that I hope he'll be better soon?'

Terry walked back to the MG with him and murmured, 'I'm glad you said that. It'll mean a lot to my parents after the hassle they've received.'

'I meant every word.' He stared into her eyes and murmured, 'This has been one of the best days I've had in years. Goodbye, Terry.'

With that he returned to the car and was soon driving out through the gates. Watching until the tail lights disappeared she started walked back to the house. 'Goodbye, Terry' sounded so horribly final, just as 'To remind us of a lovely day' had sounded in the picture gallery at Dedham.

Only then did she realise that the two prints were still in his car.

The following day Terry rose early and spent the morning in her room, determined to make up for lost time on her class preparation. Her father stayed in bed; Eliot was happily making a galleon from the plywood model kit she had bought for him on their visit to Lowdham, and outside the noise of machinery could be heard in the distance. She sighed as the sound of it intruded on her concentration.

By noon the clatter from the workmen seemed louder. Terry looked out of her window but the source of the noise was out of sight. Deciding it was time to check on her father, she found his room in darkness while from beneath the heap of bedclothes came the sound of snoring. Suddenly the snoring stopped and John's hoarse voice murmured, 'Whoever's there, for God's sake get them to stop that bloody row! What's going on anyway?'

Noticing the window was up, Terry pushed it down and the

noise level faded a little. Returning to the bed, she looked down at her father's red watery eyes, and asked if he would like a hot drink and more Aspirin.

'No,' came the gruff reply. 'I just want some peace.'

Terry went down to the kitchen. There was no one about. Bored with his own company, Eliot had wandered off somewhere, leaving his kit strewn across the kitchen table. Lunch seemed a thousand years away and since the Morris was not in its usual parking spot, she guessed her mother was either delivering eggs to customers or shopping. Looking in the refrigerator to see what could be gathered together for a quick meal, she turned at the sound of her brother's voice.

'No lunch? I'm starving.'

Her thoughts still very much on yesterday and the man she so desperately wanted to see again, Terry said, 'I can rustle up an omelette or eggs and bacon. The galleon's looking good. I'd no idea it was going to be so complicated.'

'The rigging's the worst. I'm not sure whether to paint the model before I do that or afterwards.' Eliot sat back at the table and pondered the problem. 'I've just been in the wood. What's going on? I thought Dad said the path wasn't going through there? Wasn't that what all the fuss was about?'

'He did and it was,' said Terry, taking two eggs from the refrigerator. 'Why?'

'Well, there's a man with some kind of digging equipment churning the place up.'

Terry's hands froze on the eggs, almost crushing them. 'What?'

'Didn't you know?'

'No.' Her hands relaxed after a moment. 'Ah, I know what it is. We expected the path to be started from the other end. You see, the new plans are for it to skirt the top end of the wood then go on across Rashleigh land to Windmill Lane.'

For some time Eliot was silent then he said, 'So why is he digging right down along the old track?'

'Oh, no! I don't believe it.' Terry put down the eggs and raced towards the kitchen door, telling Eliot to inform their mother on her return. 'I'll go on and stop him.'

But Eliot followed her, saying, 'You won't know where he is. I'll show you.'

As they entered the wood the noise that had assailed them all morning stopped and only the sound of nesting birds and twigs underfoot broke the silence. At last they came to the scene of devastation. The workman had done his work well, leaving a trail of muddy chaos to right and left of the mechanical digger. Now he was just standing and staring down at a heap of newly turned earth.

'What on earth do you think you're doing?' cried Terry. 'You're not supposed to be in here. The path goes from Windmill Lane, not through our wood.'

The man looked up, his jacket and well-worn trousers both mud-spattered, and stared at Terry curiously before speaking in an infuriating slow manner. 'Not according to the plans it don't. Look 'ere.'

In stupified rage, she heard herself shouting, 'Then you've got the wrong plans. How did this come about?'

Scratching his jaw casually, he answered, 'Boss told me last night e'd left the plans in 'is office and would I get them and start things going? So I did.'

'Well, you can stop. Right now,' she said.

'I 'ave.' He looked down at the pile of earth. 'I 'ad to 'cos of that.'

Terry followed his gaze. It fell on an object which, at first, resembled a muddy football. Only when she saw the sockets where eyes used to be did she glance to the right of the skull. There, protruding from the earth in obscene fashion, were the long bony fingers of a skeletal hand.

Chapter Nine

The Morris Traveller was just turning in through the gate as Terry and Eliot reached the house. Having told her brother to say nothing yet, Terry opened the car door, took a shopping bag from her mother and hoped the shock she had just received was not evident on her face. But her mind could not dispel the sickening sight of those empty sockets and the hand reaching from the earth like a corpse trying to climb from a grave.

Diane's antennae clicked into action. 'What's wrong? Is your father worse?'

'No . . . no.' Terry bit her bottom lip. 'But there is something wrong. Come on. Let's go inside and I'll tell you all about it.'

In the kitchen Terry spoke first of the excavator's accidental progress through the wood before mentioning the unearthed human remains. 'All I saw was a skull and a hand but . . .' She stopped and stared at her mother in alarm.

Her face draining of blood, Diane emitted a low groan and sank down onto the sofa. Fearing her mother was about to faint, Terry sent Eliot for a glass of cold water, persuaded her to drink then went on. 'Look, I know it's a shock but the area of excavation isn't too wide and the damage is limited. No trees have been felled and by mid-summer the ferns will have grown back . . . and things will look much the same as they did before. It's just a pity about . . .' She paused. 'I think you might have caught the 'flu, Mother. Go to bed and leave this to me. I'll phone the police house. I hope Lily's in.'

Eliot looked surprised. 'The police! Why? They'll only come and destroy everything. An archeologist is what we need, not people who don't know what they're doing.'

Terry glanced at her mother, who was staring at the wall with a strange expression on her face. 'Eliot's convinced we've uncovered an ancient chieftain's grave, no less.'

'Why not? How do we know it isn't another important find?' he said, feeling he was being ridiculed. 'If it is then it must be handled in the proper manner.'

'A chieftain, surrounded by treasure?' Terry shrugged. 'He would be in a barrow not in a shallow woodland grave.'

Eliot remained unfazed, however. 'But the grave would be much older than the wood and that could mean . . .'

'Oh, stop it! Do stop it,' cried Diane. 'All this talk of graves . . . can't you see how horrible it is?'

Terry put her arms about her mother and apologised. 'Of course. Go to bed and leave everything to me. I must ring the police. That man operating the excavator won't leave the site until we do. He's none too happy about being there alone, I can tell you.'

In the hall, she turned to Eliot who had followed her and whispered, 'Look, I want nothing more said about this, not here, not anywhere. Do you understand? Keep it under your hat for now. The last thing we want are gawping sightseers.'

Grudgingly he agreed and waited beside his sister as she made her call to the police house.

Diane meanwhile stared at the neglected fire in the grate. It offered little of the warmth she craved. Like one who was sleep walking she put on more coal then sat down in the armchair, pulling her grey woollen cardigan closer about her.

When Terry returned to the sitting room she stood looking down at her mother. Anger she had expected, shock of course, but this long silence was disturbing. It must be 'flu, yet her mother's forehead felt cool. Worry caused anger and she found herself snapping where she should have been soothing.

'Mother? Please, Mother, for goodness' sake, snap out of it. We have a problem and much as I hate to tell him when he's so unwell, Dad has to know. So does Brigadier Rashleigh. Believe me, I'm no happier than you are about it, but since we do have a situation to deal with, it would be nice if I could have some reaction and support from you.'

Diane slowly turned and looked up at Terry as though awakening from a dream. 'Of course.' The words seemed to come hollowly from somewhere deep inside her. 'We'll go and tell your father now.'

'I take to my bed for two days and the result is chaos.' John Fenton stood in his woollen dressing gown, eyes heavy with influenza fixed angrily on his wife. 'Where the hell were you to let this happen?'

Starting at this loud reproof, she gave him a cold, hard stare. 'Ah, so now it's all my fault?'

'But you must have heard the machinery. I just don't understand why you didn't check. How much damage has been done?'

Terry said, 'He's dug halfway through the wood, starting first on the old track then moving across to the eastern boundary, according to the original plans.' She swallowed hard. 'But, look, it's not too bad . . .'

'They've found a skeleton.'

The long silence which followed Diane's stark announcement even affected Eliot who realised, from the expression on his father's face, that this was no time to be speaking of chieftains.

Terry broke the silence at last, saying, 'Goodness, how dramatic that sounds! They've unearthed a skull and a hand so far. Ancient bones, of course, but I've phoned the police house and Lily's going to tell her husband as soon as he returns. The man who was operating the excavator is sitting in the barn until the police arrive. Can't say I blame him, poor thing. He's had quite a shock. Shouldn't we ask him in?'

'No, we blasted well should not!' shouted John, without taking his eyes off Diane. 'Otherwise I won't be held responsible for my actions. Where the devil is Rashleigh?' His voice fell quiet with simmering rage. 'I want him here this instant. I want to know how his last plan was so *conveniently* mislaid.

Terry's eyes widened in astonishment. 'I don't believe you said that. Come on now, it's the 'flu talking. Perhaps you should go back to bed and let me handle everything?'

'Not until I've seen Rashleigh. Get him here at once.'

'Very well,' she murmured uncertainly.

Diane looked at her husband anxiously. 'It isn't his fault. Be careful what you say.'

John shot her a black look. 'It's a bit bloody late for being careful now, don't you think? Meanwhile I'll dress and go to the wood.'

'It's nonsense even to think of such a thing,' chided Terry. 'You must go straight back to bed, and let me handle things. I'll phone the Rashleighs right away.'

It was Lydia who took the call at Thornley Hall. 'Oh, dear. I knew something would go wrong. What a mess people make of everything.' Her tone implied that only the tiresome Fentons could be so accident-prone. 'Well, it has nothing to do with me, Terry. I shall inform the Brigadier as soon as he returns for luncheon.'

Feeling she had just been dismissed, Terry replaced the receiver and wondered how anyone as cold as Lydia Rashleigh could produce kind, disorganised, friendly Fiona. Small wonder mother and daughter had never seen eye to eye.

It was just past one o'clock when Rashleigh's Land Rover overtook PC Kimber who was pedalling slowly up the hill. At the front door, Terry explained to the Brigadier all that had happened then added that her father had been out to the wood already. 'I tried to stop him. He has 'flu and should be in bed . . .'

Taken aback at this, Rashleigh entered the house nervously. Influenza, for God's sake! At his age that was the last thing he needed. Two years earlier the Asian Flu epidemic had almost carried him off. Had that made him more vulnerable or given him immunity against the wretched virus? Drat Fenton for calling him to the house when he could quite as easily have discussed this over the telephone! Inside the sitting room he found his old adversary, dressed in a fisherman's knit sweater and leaning against the mantel, his pasty-looking face covered in sweat, watchful eyes watery and nose red.

Settling himself in the chair farthest away, which happened to be a hard upright beside the desk, the Brigadier asked for a Scotch, hoping it might ward off germs.

'Well, this is a pretty kettle of fish,' he said, taking the whisky tumbler from Terry. 'Came as soon as I heard. Can't these people do anything right? How the devil did they get hold of the wrong plans? Did they say? Have you been in touch with the contractors? Marshall's the man you want.'

John just glared at him. 'Terry's tried phoning,' he said in a dangerously quiet voice. 'But, surprise, surprise, everyone's gone home for the weekend. It seems that, in his haste to get away, Marshall took the original plan from the cupboard instead of the revised one and, failing to check it, left the damn' thing on his desk to be collected this morning by one of his workers. And that's another thing – since it's Saturday and the firm has closed down, I'm surprised to find anyone working on the job.'

'I asked them to continue,' said Rashleigh unhappily. 'It was cheaper to pay overtime than have hired plant standing idle for the weekend.'

John smiled thinly. 'Cheaper? Christ! Ironically, Marshall might have realised his mistake on Monday and prevented all this but for your zeal to save money. I'll make damned sure he puts things right *and* pays us compensation.'

'Of course,' said Rashleigh, feeling wrong-footed. 'Why on earth didn't he destroy the original plan? You could sue, of course, but that would mean suspending the work and we'd never find another firm who could get the job finished in time if we were forced to cancel Marshall's contract now.'

'There's more,' said Terry. 'Human remains have been unearthed.'

She glanced at her father who had turned his face towards the fire. Fearing his silence was anger which might explode at any moment, she looked back at the shocked Brigadier and went on, 'I've called the police house.'

'Good God!' Another long swig of whisky followed the first. 'What next? I saw Kimber cycling up the hill. On his way here, I suppose. His first brush with anything remotely gruesome, I daresay, apart from the odd traffic accident. Money for old rope, being a country policeman.'

'I think we've uncovered a plague victim,' said Terry.

Eliot screwed up his face in disgust. 'Plague?'

Terry nodded. 'I've been thinking about it. In 1666 plague wiped out half the population of Norwich. A merchant fled the city and settled his family here in Thornley, thinking they would be safe. But they brought the pestilence with them and it spread through the village and surrounding areas. There's a plague pit between Thornley and Boxham.'

'I've seen it,' said her brother. 'So why would we have a plague victim in our wood?'

'Because we're some way outside the village and maybe the

people living here were too ill themselves to let anyone know. I'm certain there was an earlier dwelling on this site.'

Rashleigh nodded. 'There was. Sounds logical to me.'

But Eliot would have none of it. 'I still say it's ancient.'

'My brother's hoping for another Sutton Hoo.' Hearing the doorbell, Terry jumped to her feet thankfully. 'That'll be Constable Kimber. He'll have to be taken to the scene.'

'I'll come with you,' said Eliot, glad to get away from the heavy brooding atmosphere his parents had generated. Even the boring old Brigadier was livelier just now, he thought.

Rashleigh drained his glass and stood up. 'I'd better go along too and see what's happened for myself. 'Don't worry, Fenton. Everything will be sorted out and the damage made good. You have my word on it. So go back to bed and get well. Flu isn't to be taken lightly, believe me.'

After they left, John walked into the kitchen and watched through the window as the three of them joined the village policeman and started toward the woods. He stood there for some time, his dark thoughts racing! When at last he turned away it was to see a grey-faced Diane standing in the doorway, arms tightly crossed over herself in an effort to fight off the terrible chill which racked her body.

Eliot lay on his bed, his mind a whirl of excitement still. He longed to telephone his friends and tell them he had been helping the police, just like in the films, but not now, though. Not now when he had promised Terry, and his parents were in such a black mood. Suddenly realising how hungry he was, since dinner, like lunch, had vanished into the ether, he slipped down to the kitchen and made himself a large doorstep of a cheese and tomato sandwich.

Terry saw him heading up the stairs, plate in hand, and felt a sudden twinge of guilt. 'Sorry. What with one thing and another food has been the last thing on my mind. In any case, I couldn't eat a thing after seeing . . . well . . . after what we saw in the wood.'

Eliot turned and frowned. 'Well, I'm starving.' He took a large bite and chewed quickly, staring at Terry all the time. 'What's taking so long? It's twenty past eight, for goodness' sake.'

'Don't speak with your mouth full. The Lowdham Police had to be called in and they've a team still digging around.'

'Oh, great. That's all we need. They'll ruin everything.'

At that moment the doorbell rang. Terry glanced at her brother. 'Either go up to your room or eat that sandwich in the kitchen. I don't want visitors seeing you standing like that on the stairs.' When she opened the door, Fiona was standing in the light of the porch lantern. Surprised and glad to see her friend, Terry led her into the sitting room where Diane was seated beside the fire. She looked up and forced a smile of welcome which clearly said, 'Now what?'

'Dad's in bed,' Terry was saying as Fiona flopped down heavily on the sofa and stared from one to the other with ill-concealed excitement in her eyes.

'I hope he's better soon. But what a turn up for the book! A body in the wood, eh? It's pure Agatha Christie. What a hoot!' Aware that Terry's mother did not look as though she found it at all amusing, Fiona turned to Terry who was settling down in the other armchair. 'There's a policeman standing outside your gate. Did you know? At first he wouldn't let me through, then David Kimber came along, told him who I was and so here I am. You saw the bones, I gather. Pretty gruesome.'

'Yes,' murmured Terry, not wishing to be reminded of the sight, or her father's face as he'd returned from the wood, paler than ever. 'What do you know about the dwelling that used to be on this site?'

A little surprised at the question, Fiona shrugged. 'Not much. It was the original home farm and built at the same time as the Hall. That's sixteenth-century although it's been given a Georgian façade. Anyway I do know that the old farm here burnt down around the early part of the nineteenth century so my great-grandfather put up this house. Why?'

Terry explained her plague victim theory then, seeing her brother standing on the threshold of the room, smiled and added. 'Eliot's of the opinion that the bones are ancient, which is also possible. I can't wait to hear some news. They're taking so long.'

Fiona frowned. 'Dad went back to the wood. They've got the area cordoned off and won't let anyone through, but he's learned this much. It isn't one skeleton they've uncovered but two.'

'Two! said Terry Well, that surely upholds my theory about plague victims. There might be a whole family out there for all we know.' Her expression changed as she realised what she had said and a shudder coursed through her. The thought was too horrible to dwell on.

Fiona was looking appalled. 'A whole family? Oh, surely not . . . you don't really think . . . a whole family?'

Diane spoke now for the first time since her arrival. 'Tell me, Fiona, does your father say what is to happen now? Only we seem to be denied the information he's able to obtain so freely.'

The sarcasm went way over Fiona's head as she shrugged. 'No, he didn't say anything else. Still, from what Terry says it seems it's either a matter for the archeologists or the church.'

Sensing that Fiona was not helping matters, Terry led her into the kitchen where they sat chatting over coffee until the late hours, finding comfort in general gossip which had nothing to do with death.

Throughout the night the police continued their grisly task, cordoning off the entire area of the farm and bringing in lights. Eliot looked out from his bedroom window on to a wood made eerrie by the greenish glow in its midst. Everything had changed suddenly. His hope of another Sutton Hoo was fading into something sinister and he hated it.

Later he stirred in sleep, dreaming of the Deben glowing in the setting sun. Suddenly a grey mist rose from its banks and through it loomed the giant figure of a warrior, the eyeslits of his terrifying battle mask like the sockets of a skull. On came Raedwald, striding across the river, on and on over the countryside towards Thornley, towards the farm, towards his bedroom . . .. With a cry, Eliot shot up in bed, heart racing, his body covered in sweat.

For a moment he sat there, rigid with terror, then suddenly his room was flooded with light. Terry stood in the doorway, still tying the belt around her blue dressing gown.

'Did you cry out?'

Eliot just stared at his sister as she walked towards him and sat on his bed. How long had it been since he had been plagued by that dream? True, it always had frightened him, but not in the way it had just now. This time was different; this time he was left with a terrible foreboding.

'I'm all right,' he murmured. 'A nightmare, that's all.'

'All that cheese before bedtime. What do you expect?'

Terry stretched out a gentle hand, felt his brow and frowned.

‘Goodness, you’re burning up. Not over the ‘flu after all. I’ll fetch you some water and an Aspirin.’

‘No. Don’t go . . . don’t go . . . not yet.’

Anxious to calm him, she agreed to stay awhile. ‘I wasn’t exactly sleeping myself.’ She walked to the window, saw the eerie light in the wood, and knew now why Eliot was troubled. ‘It’s odd, isn’t it, that what seems acceptable in daylight becomes something else in the middle of the night? But you mustn’t worry. By tomorrow they’ll all be gone and then we’ll be back to normal.’ She looked down at his alarmed expression and added, ‘There’s nothing out there now that hasn’t been there all our lives, Eliot. Certainly nothing to be afraid of. Now lie down and go to sleep.’

Settling back on his pillow, he murmured, ‘I’ve decided to go back to school.’

Terry raised her eyebrows. ‘Well, that’s a sudden sea-change.’

He sat up once more. ‘I don’t want to miss too many lessons.’ How could he tell her that he would feel safer sleeping in a cold school dormitory with his friends than here, where the wood could be seen from his window and Raedwald entered his dreams bringing a portent of something so terrible he just wanted to run away . . .

Terry felt his forehead again and was relieved to find it cool. But she was sad for him. Only a short while ago he had been filled with excitement. Now his eyes were shadowed with fear and it worried her. She kissed him on the forehead and left the room, keeping the bedroom door ajar and leaving hers wide open in case he needed her again.

Immediately, Eliot climbed from his bed, looked through his window and saw the glow once more. Battle mask and skull had become as one in the dream, as though Raedwald was death coming to Lynwood. For some time he stared at the wood then, too afraid to go to sleep, switched on the light and decided to sit up until dawn.

At four in the morning, he was the only one asleep.

In the kitchen Terry made tea, took it up to her parents then returned to the kitchen and prepared toast. The moment she settled at the table there was a gentle knock on the kitchen door. Slightly apprehensive, she got up and opened it. Standing in the dark, his helmet and cape now rainsoaked, PC David Kimber smiled at her.

'Saw the light. Just thought I'd look in on you to check you're all right. I'm on duty guarding the rear of the house. They've another chap on the front entrance.'

'Guarding?' Terry stared at him open-mouthed. 'Why?'

'Word gets around. You know how it is. We don't want people troubling you. Anyway, I'm out here should you need me.'

'Well, look, I've just made some tea. Come in out of the rain.'

He shook his head. 'Daren't do that, but I won't say no to that cuppa.' A man in his early-thirties, he had come to Thornley from Dagenham with his wife and two children six years earlier and knew every man, woman and child in the village and most of the surrounding area. He liked the Fentons, and felt they had been given a raw deal by the local newspaper. Now there was all this, and again the family would find themselves plastered over the front page. It seemed unfair.

Terry handed him a mug of good strong tea, and then offered to make him some toast. He was glad of both and stood in the doorway, the light from the kitchen giving him a clear view of the area he was guarding.

'How are they getting on? Any news?'

He shook his head. 'No more human remains, so far as I know, but the County Police are on the job now. They'll tell you what's what, which is more than I've been told.'

'County Police?' Terry frowned.

Kimber finished his tea and toast, answered her polite queries about Lily and his two children, handed back the beaker and plate and thanked her. 'Must get back to my post.' He paused and added, 'I know it's hard, all this, but don't let it get to you. Give your parents my regards.'

Terry shut the door then stood like stone. County Police! What on earth was going on out there? She felt cold suddenly and, moving to the fireside chair, huddled into it, wondering why her stomach was twisting itself into knots. Eliot's fear, it seemed, was becoming hers.

With the coming of daylight, Terry felt her spirits lift once more. By nine o'clock the sun was shining and she decided to cook a huge breakfast for herself and both her parents who were wandering about the house, heavy-eyed and vague.

Fifteen minutes later, David Kimber entered the kitchen to say he was going off duty and that another officer would be taking his place. 'There'll be one on the front gate also and one at the gateway to the wood, sir. Just to keep the curious at bay.'

'Thank you,' said John in a quiet, courteous voice. 'You must be very tired, cold and hungry, standing out there all night. Terry told me about it this morning. Please, do stay for some breakfast.'

Thinking that John Fenton looked even worse today than he had yesterday, Kimber smiled but shook his head. 'Thanks, but I'd best be off home. It's my youngest's birthday. Presents and cards to open – you know how it is. Still, if you need me, don't hesitate to call. I'll be up here in a flash.'

'That's kind of you,' said John. 'What day is it? I've quite lost count.'

'Sunday, sir.'

He smiled and let out a sigh. 'Somehow I don't think we'll be going to church.'

'Best not to, sir, under the circumstances.' The smell of grilling bacon caused Kimber's empty stomach to rumble. 'In fact, you should be in bed. You don't look at all well.'

'Too much work to do,' said John. 'I take it I'll be told when I can go back into my wood? There's a devil of a mess to sort out.'

'You will, sir. But they're extending the search.'

John stiffened. 'Why, for God's sake?'

'They've found remnants of clothing apparently. Perhaps they think they've uncovered a crime.'

Turning quickly to her parents, Terry thought they looked like a still frame from a film. Even the kitchen seemed to be part of this strange frozen moment. Then life flickered back as her mother moved forward, thanked David Kimber for keeping them informed and bade him good morning.

It was almost ten-thirty when Terry set out for the Sunday papers which should have been delivered but today had not. She closed the front door, felt a fresh breeze wipe the tiredness from her, lifted her face to the spring sunshine and listened to church bells pealing out across the fields. The earth smelled so fresh after the overnight rain. How wonderful life was suddenly, when the night had been so focussed on death.

As she approached the closed gate her steps faltered. A large group of people stood in the lane beyond, their way to the house barred by a lone policeman from Lowdham. There were the curious, who slowly drifted away with disappointment plain on their faces, and there were inevitably the others, the men with notebooks and cameras. Shocked at the scene, Terry was about to return to the house when a car pulled up outside the gate, causing much interest. It was a green MG. She felt her shoulders sag with relief and walked forward to see Grant arguing with the policeman.

'It's all right, he's a friend.'

The gate remained open just long enough for Grant to ease the MG on to the short drive. It shut again quickly before reporters could follow. 'What is it? What the hell has happened?' he asked, practically leaping from the car.

Never so glad to see anyone in her entire life, Terry led him out of sight of the curious onlookers. Reaching the rear of the house she walked on, past the kitchen door towards the barn, and there told him all that had happened.

Grant listened intently then sighed with relief. 'Is that all.'

She raised her eyebrows in surprise at this mild reaction. 'Isn't it enough?'

He took her hands in his and looked down at her pale, tired face with a grim expression on his. 'When I saw the police and that crowd outside your gate, I was sure you'd all been murdered in your beds! A couple of old skeletons comes as quite a relief in the circumstances.'

Feeling the warmth of large hands on hers, she took comfort from his quiet presence and knew then that she didn't want him to leave her. Not now, not ever. Aware that she was hardly looking her best, she just wished he had telephoned first, to give her a chance to cover the ravages of a long stressful night. Well, it was too late for that. She looked up at him curiously. 'I'm so glad you're here. But why are you? I thought you were returning to London this morning.'

'You left your print in the car. I came to return it.'

The print. Her heart sank with disappointment at this prosaic explanation when she had hoped for a deeper one. 'Oh, yes, of course. I missed it after you'd left. It's very kind of you to come miles out of your way to return it.'

'I would have come anyway.' His hands tightened on hers. 'I'm glad I did now.'

Terry felt a stirring within her and, thrown into confusion, said the first thing that came into her mind. 'How was the wedding?' How stupid and trite it sounded, she thought dismally.

'Stag party was the killer,' he said, releasing her hands. 'Even so I carried out my duties to the letter. Still have a head, though. What I need now is some very strong coffee.'

'Which you shall have at once,' she laughed, suddenly at ease again. 'I'm glad you came today. It's been horrible. I can't tell you how it feels to learn that there are bodies buried on your property.'

'I almost missed you. You seemed to be on your way out as I approached the gate.'

'I was going to get the Sunday papers.'

He smiled. 'With the local press on your heels? What on earth were you thinking of? I'll run you down in the car.'

After Terry had made him strong black coffee and he had chatted amiably with her parents, asking how John was feeling and showing concern for their unhappy situation, Grant put the car top up and slowly eased his way out through the gate. Both he and Terry heard the click of a camera as a reporter pushed forward and started shouting questions at them. The shouts died away as a grim-faced Grant drove past the crowd and down the hill to the village.

'Say nothing to them,' he said firmly. 'It's a police matter and has nothing to do with you or your family.'

The newsagent stood behind the counter of his empty shop. When Terry and Grant walked in his elderly face lightened with surprise and anticipation.

'Good morning, Terry. Sorry about the delivery boy, but he turned back when he saw the police. Must have been quite a night. I've heard about the skeletons. Four, I understand. I'm told the police are still up there looking for more, is that so?'

She sighed with exasperation. 'Two not four, and they're probably plague victims.'

The elderly face fell with disappointment, and a wrinkled hand held out the Fentons' usual Sunday paper. Before he could ask any more questions, Terry walked quickly out of the shop.

Smiling, she returned to a waiting Grant and climbed back into the car. 'Body count's going up with every minute that passes, but that's Thornley for you.'

'How many?' When she told him, he laughed. 'And the day's only just started!'

In the drive to the farmhouse stood a black police car with a uniformed PC standing beside it. The crowd by the gate was larger than ever and excitement was mounting.

'What the devil . . .?' Grant helped her out of the MG, handed her the print and said, 'Time I made myself scarce.'

'No, please stay. You've stacks of time.'

To her crushing disappointment he decided that the Fentons had enough on their plate without him hanging around like a spare sock. Aware of the crowd at the gate, she did not argue, but took his hand and felt his gentle squeeze of hers.

'Don't worry,' he whispered. 'It'll all be forgotten in a few days' time.'

Then he returned to the car, gave her a last look and drove out into the lane, leaving her suddenly bereft. Was he truly being sensitive to her parent's feelings, or had he found it a convenient excuse to make his getaway?

Standing beside the sitting-room desk, Eliot was distinctly unimpressed with Detective Sergeant Hopwood. He simply was not the thing. Detectives in films were not short and plump with slight Suffolk accents and hand-knitted pullovers beneath crumpled grey suits. They had sharp eyes, smart suits, wore raincoats and trilbys and spoke in the cultured tones of Scotland Yard authority. No, he was not the thing, not the thing at all.

When Terry entered the room, the sergeant was seated on the sofa but rose awkwardly to his feet as John introduced her to him. She shook the extended hand, noticed the receding hairline and put an extra ten years on a man who was not yet forty.

Hopwood sat down again and took from his pocket a notebook and pen, saying, 'I won't keep you long, but there are a few things I need to get clear in my head.'

She glanced at her mother's anxious face, smiled reassuringly and settled herself on the desk chair beside Eliot.

Hopwood turned to John. 'You're not from these parts, are you, Mr Fenton?'

John paused before speaking as though surprised that the police knew this much about him. 'No,' he whispered hoarsely. 'We came here from Guernsey. I inherited the farm after my cousin's death, you see.'

'Ah, yes. A shooting accident, I gather.'

The watery eyes were guarded as John nodded. 'Yes. Very tragic. Although we never knew him.'

'You're both islanders then?'

'No,' said John. I'm from England originally. Mrs Fenton is the true islander.'

'I had a holiday there once. Charming place.' Hopwood turned to Diane. 'And which part of the island do you come from, Mrs Fenton?'

'The St Martin area.'

Terry was growing impatient. 'Can you tell us how old the skeletons are? How long have they been in the ground?'

Hopwood shrugged. 'We've yet to establish that, Miss Fenton.' He turned back to Diane and asked, 'Would you mind if I smoked?'

'For my part, no,' she said. 'But my husband does have the 'flu and I daresay it would affect his chest.'

Hopwood put the cigarette packet back in his pocket and looked sympathetic. 'I'm sorry to hear that. Thought you didn't sound too good. Don't want to set you coughing. This 'flu is really going the rounds. My wife had a bad bout recently, but so far I've escaped.' He hoped to God he would escape again but Fenton did look rough. If he could light up, the smoke might kill off the germs, he told himself.

Wishing his head would stop throbbing, John pulled out his handkerchief, wiped his moist nose and whispered, 'Sorry about all this.'

'No, I'm the one who must apologise for bothering you at such a time. But, unfortunately, such matters cannot wait. I gather the remains came to light because of a misunderstanding. Could you explain that? Something to do with a memorial, I believe.'

'A bomber crashed here during the war,' said Terry, wishing this man would tell them the one thing they all wanted to know instead of asking a lot of totally irrelevant questions. 'All the crew were killed and now the village wishes to mark the spot with a memorial.'

Hopwood nodded and wrote in his notebook before turning to John. 'And there was some problem earlier concerning a pathway to the site? You didn't want it to go through the wood, is that right?'

Sensing John's growing anger, Diane stepped in quickly. 'We couldn't have people wandering at will through a wood where shooting takes place in the autumn and winter months. Anyway, that was all sorted out and new plans drawn up. The contractor made a mistake and the next we knew a mechanical digger was churning the place up. But obviously you know this already.' Her voice ended on a slightly hysterical note..

'More or less,' said Hopwood. 'The Lowdham police were able to fill me in.'

'Were they?' said John tetchily. 'I didn't know they were so *au fait* with our affairs. You seem to know a great deal about our private lives.'

Diane shot her husband a warning look. 'Dearest, the police must be allowed to do their job.'

'If such knowledge is relevant,' he snapped.

Ignoring all this, Hopwood went on. 'So, had all gone to plan, the grave would never have been uncovered. You could call it fate, I suppose.'

John glared at him. 'I call it a bloody nuisance! My wood's a shambles and after the bad publicity about the path, I don't need to see my name plastered all over the goddamn' papers again.'

Terry put a stop to the gathering atmosphere of rancour by asking what information the police could give them. 'We've been on tenterhooks. Have you no idea at all as to the age of these skeletons?' She smiled at him. 'Tell me, then I'll leave you in peace and make us all some coffee.'

Hopwood warmed to her and smiled back. 'Well, their age is properly speaking a matter for the pathologist. Shallow graves are often disturbed by foxes who do a lot of damage and make off with a bone or two.' Seeing the appalled expressions on their faces, he cleared his throat. 'Forensics will give us data on the clothing, though.'

Terry shook her head in disbelief. 'After so many years, there's still clothing? That's incredible.'

Hopwood turned and looked at her questioningly. 'I'm sorry. After how many years?'

'Almost three hundred.' Seeing his look of confusion, she added, 'The plague. It was here in 1666. They're obviously victims.'

Hopwood smiled wryly. 'I'm afraid you're wrong. Seventeenth-century people didn't wear twentieth-century shoes.'

After a shocked silence, Terry was the only one to find a voice. 'We thought . . . well . . . we thought . . . are you certain the shoes were of this century?'

Hopwood nodded. 'Your plague victims were murdered, Miss Fenton. At a very rough guess, we would say their bodies, a man's and a woman's, went into the ground about thirty years ago.'

Chapter Ten

Earlier on that same Sunday, Alastair locked his case, pulled on his sheepskin jacket and, entering the drawing room, eyed his wife angrily.

'Oh, for God's sake, stop this sulking. You knew I'd be busy this weekend.'

'As you are every weekend,' Marisa retorted. She stared through the tall Georgian windows that faced on to Cadogan Place and took no pleasure in the April sunshine. 'You only arrived back in the country last night. There's nothing to stop you returning to Coventry tomorrow.'

Alastair smiled wryly. 'There's nothing to stop you returning with me. We do have a house there though it might have escaped your notice.

She gave a brittle laugh. 'A depressing Victorian museum! And when we do have people in to liven it up, they're either your speed-loving, beer-swilling, racing buddies or people from the motor industry.'

'They're my friends and I've a business to run,' he snapped. 'You know how hectic things are at the moment.'

Marisa swung round, green eyes blazing. 'That's all fine and dandy for you, but what is there for me in that Godforsaken hole?'

'Very well, stay here with your party-loving friends.'

'I didn't marry my friends, I married you!' she shouted. Sighing, she let the anger seep from her and tried a softer approach, which usually worked. 'Somehow, I thought it would all be so different. I thought we would spend our lives together, as other married people do.' When he said nothing to this, she stiffened slightly. 'Next week you *must* be here. It's all been arranged.' His baffled look made her despair and she spoke to him as she would to a difficult child. 'Covent Garden? Remember?'

Alastair frowned. 'Christ, I'd completely forgotten. It's no use. We'll have to do it some other time.'

'You promised faithfully.' Marisa folded her arms and glared at him angrily. 'The Huntley-Reeds arranged it. We're sharing their box and dining with them afterwards. I can hardly ring them to say we're pulling out now.'

He shrugged. 'You must, or else join them on your own. Sorry but there it is. Anyway I hate opera, you know that.'

'It's ballet.'

'Even worse.' He sighed with exasperation. 'Look, you know we're about to test the new car at Silverstone. Do understand that I can't make social engagements at this time. Work must come first.'

'And all your other pursuits,' she hissed. 'So much for your promises.'

He gave her a long measured look then said, 'We're worlds apart, aren't we?'

'Whose fault is that?' she snapped. 'I thought I was marrying a man, not a bloody racing car.'

But Alastair was already out of the drawing room and heading for the front door. 'I'll ring you later,' he shouted.

'Don't bother!' she shouted back.

Alastair shut the door behind him and heaved a sigh of relief that his work took him away from Marisa. God, what a mess he had made of his life! A few heady days in New York had made him believe he was in love with a woman who had been so hot in bed and yet presented a cool, polished image to the world. Madness! He had known it before his wedding, yet even so it had taken these few months of tempestuous quarrels to make him realise just how disastrous a marriage he had made. Unworldly as she was, it should have been Terry and not Marisa he'd chosen. Too late, he knew now he had married the wrong sister.

Still in her cream silk nightgown and négligée, Marisa heard his car pulling away and walked back to the drawing room where two large gold brocade-covered sofas faced each other across a walnut coffee table. She sat on one, leaned back against the soft cushions and stared angrily at the empty grate. Mrs Mount had laid a fire there first thing that morning before taking her day off, but Marisa hadn't bothered putting a match to it, cold as the morning was.

Feeling abandoned, she glanced about her with a brooding eye. Above the marble mantel hung a gilt mirror and on the walls oil paintings chosen many years since by Alastair's parents and maternal grandparents. The furniture had also been in the house for years, a mixture of Hepplewhite, which Marisa liked, and French, which she loathed. As for the fine porcelain ornaments, only a few were to her taste and she took no interest in their make or origin.

Had this been her home she would make sweeping changes, but while Sir Angus had passed not just the company to his eldest son and heir but also the Warwickshire house, before taking himself and his wife to the tax haven of Jersey, Cadogan Place remained the property of Lady Hammond and she intended to keep it that way. Perhaps she sensed this marriage would fail.

Divorce, however, was the last thing on Marisa's mind. She'd wanted what she now had: a house in a fashionable area of London and a country house in Warwickshire, even if it needed modernising. What she no longer had was a husband to share them with her. Ironic though it was, Alastair's sudden change in status and fortune, owing to his father's poor health and determination to avoid death duties, had placed a heavy burden on his shoulders before he had rid his system of the racing bug. It irked him to see another driver pushing the Hammond around a circuit while feeling he could do better himself. But his promise to his ailing father must be kept.

Between this passion and the day-to-day business of manufacturing cars for the market, Marisa felt he had no time for her. Time and again she turned up at parties unescorted, wearing a couture gown and making excuses for her husband's absence. As a result she found herself constantly fending off men who saw her as a spare woman looking for an affair.

She smiled to herself now, remembering the many occasions when she had argued with Alastair, saying that he had enough on his plate with Hammond's and must give up the racing scene. Talking to a brick wall would have made more sense. His love for motor sport would always come before her; before anything if they were not careful. Meanwhile it was his brother, the quiet and capable Sean, who was keeping a sharp eye on the welfare of the company while Alastair lived out his dream of building a racing car that would leave the others at the grid. How much longer could that continue before Sir Angus got to know about it?

After her third cup of black coffee, Marisa's thoughts turned to her mother-in-law. She missed Annabel more than she'd thought possible, for Lady Hammond had been warm and affectionate to her from the first moment they had met. It was she who had brought real wealth into the Hammond family and she who had financed her husband when times had been rough. It was she who had shown Marisa the way, given advice and introduced her to many of her old friends. Some of those old friends had offspring in their twenties, so that Marisa's social diary was soon full.

Then had come the parties when Alastair had drunk too much and behaved like an overgrown schoolboy. Unable to understand why he was so unhappy, she read him the riot act before guests arrived at their home, which always culminated in a blazing row after the guests had left. Then there were the long nights when Alastair made fumbling love while she lay passive and bored. In New York she had given him the impression that she found him exciting as a lover.

Marisa smiled to herself now as she thought of it. Men were such children, and so easy to deceive. At their first party back in London, Alastair had been pretty drunk when he'd asked her to marry him. She had said yes and immediately told everyone else they were now engaged. The congratulations flowed along with the champagne. After that, how could he go back on his rash proposal? As for bed ... She smiled at the thought. If he had thought of himself as a speed-loving Casanova, by now, he was sadly disillusioned.

At length Marisa stood up, stretched and wondered what to do with her day. Most of her friends would have made plans and she had too much pride to ring them saying she was at a loose end.

Having bathed in the cold tiled bathroom that had not been changed since the early thirties, she put on a cream woollen dress, piled her dark hair into a chignon and made up her face carefully. Then, standing by the window once more with her fourth cup of coffee and a cigarette, she looked down at her own car parked outside, the one Alastair had bought for her when she passed her driving test. Thinking her too inexperienced to drive a powerful

Hammond sports car, he had opted for a Hillman Convertible instead.

On a bitterly cold morning, he had led her blindfold to the door, removed the scarf from her eyes and she had found herself staring at a car wrapped in ribbons with a large card saying CONGRATULATIONS. The memory touched her, despite her current mood. There had been times when Alastair was wonderful, as if trying to make a real go of the marriage. But that was then. Today was more typical.

Only now did she notice the spring sunshine and suddenly her mind was made up. Instead of wasting this lovely day indoors she would go home. It would take hours to drive to Suffolk and she had never driven further than Virginia Water but there had to be a first time for everything. She would stay the night, of course, and would not be here when Alastair rang. That would worry him. Good! Let him stew in his own juice. In any case, it would be good just to see the look on Terry's face when her sister arrived at Lynwood behind the wheel of her very own brand new car.

The shocked silence which followed the Detective Sergeant's words would stay with Terry forever. She busied herself in the kitchen, wishing the feeling of stomach-churning depression would lift from her. Murdered! Shot in the head, both of them. Her mind turned to all those occasions in her life when she and Marisa had played or roamed in the wood, sometimes apprehensive about the ghost of Arthur Fenton but never dreaming of the two unfortunates buried beneath their feet.

She peeled another onion, then sliced carrots, wishing she could run away from the house, run to London, to Grant who would make her feel secure, to Marisa who would share her horror, or even to Meg whose no-nonsense attitude would stop her feeling sorry for herself at the very least. As it was, her parents had taken the whole thing very badly, and she had escaped only as far as the kitchen.

Eliot entered and flung himself down at the table. 'I feel such a prat now, going on about ancient chieftains.'

Terry turned. 'Join the club with me and my plague victims. But how could we have known? Anyway, it's over now. The bodies have gone. You heard what the Detective Sergeant said.'

'He said they were keeping a cordon around the grave for a

while. And that the police would still be here.' Eliot stared at her with an anxious expression. 'So it's not over.'

'Well, they have to search for clues. Anyway, it's none of our business. Are you hungry?'

He shook his head.

'Wait until you smell the soup I'm about to make.'

'I'll never go into the wood again. It's all changed now.'

Desperate to lift his mood, Terry smiled. 'I'll crisp up those rolls Mother bought yesterday to have with the soup. Then, if you like, I'll take you to the cinema this evening.' One look at his face told her she was wasting her time.

Eliot hovered about the kitchen, casting gloom and doom into the atmosphere. Terry switched on the radio and filled the room with light music. Suddenly, the sound of the outside world coming into the house brought back a sense of balance and normality. She took comfort in it.

'Where's Mother?'

'In the hen house.' Terry turned to Eliot and said chidingly, 'And you should be out there helping her. We're all at sixes and sevens so an extra pair of hands would be very welcome. Off you go.'

He left but returned a few minutes later, his eyes wide and solemn. 'I think you'd better go to her, Terry. I think she's crying.'

Rushing out of the kitchen, she found her mother leaning against the chicken run, empty basket hanging from one hand, the other covering her face. Her body was shaking with sobs.

'Oh, come now,' Terry murmured, placing her arms about Diane. 'There's no need for this. You're overwrought and should rest. Leave this to me and go back.'

Diane removed the hand from her tearstained face and whispered, 'Oh, God, it's terrible ... it's all so terrible. Poor people. Poor, poor souls. I feel so sorry, so very, very sorry ...' She fell to weeping again. 'Horrible, horrible.'

Alarmed, Terry led her away towards the house, told Eliot to collect the eggs then settled her mother beside the sitting-room fire and gave her a small glass of brandy.

Slowly Diane recovered enough to ask routine questions about lunch and such, while Terry told her everything was being taken care of and that she must just rest.

At four o'clock Grant rang, his voice reassuring to Terry who'd suddenly felt very alone. At length he said, 'I know it's a shock but it happened years ago and has nothing to do with you. It's now you should be thinking about. Look, I've been called to the hospital early. We've an emergency on our hands. Remember, Terry, it's now that matters, not the past. So get on with your life. Must go. I'll be in touch.'

She replaced the receiver with a sense of dismay. 'Get on with your life, Terry' seemed horribly final. And wasn't, 'I'll be in touch,' just another way of saying goodbye?

Once free of the endless London suburbs, Marisa drove fast, too fast, anger at Alastair forcing her foot down on the accelerator. Even so the journey seemed to take forever, and by the time she had reached Thornley, the spring sunshine had changed to dark clouds and a steady downpour.

The rhythm of the windscreen wipers made her feel tired as she drove through the watersplash then turned up the hill towards the house she had not entered since her wedding. Now anxiety broke through the tiredness. How would Terry react to her sudden arrival? What were her feelings after all these weeks? Did she still truly believe Alastair had been stolen from her? Perhaps this spur of the moment decision was a mistake after all.

She frowned through the windscreen at the knot of people outside the gate. In their midst stood a policeman. Her heart missed a beat. Frantic, she stopped the car, opened the door and said, 'What is it? What's happened?'

'Sorry, miss,' said the police constable from Lowdham. 'No one is allowed inside.'

'But I live here!' shrieked Marisa. 'My name's Hammond . . . no, that's my married name . . . I'm Marisa Fenton and my family . . . what's happened to them?'

'Nothing.' The gates were opened, Marisa accelerated and screeched to a stop outside the front door. Even before she had managed to climb out, Terry appeared on the porch, surprise written all over her face.

'Marisa! What on earth . . . did Mother phone you then?'

'What's going on?' she cried. 'What's happened? Why are all those people here and the police . . .what's wrong?'

'Don't looked so alarmed.' Terry took her sister firmly by the arm and led her out of the rain to the porch, whispering, 'Calm down. We're all fine. But there's been a mix up. A path was dug through the wood and . . .' she swallowed hard '. . . two skeletons have been uncovered.'

Marisa blinked in astonishment. Then, relief claiming her, she burst into peals of laughter. 'What? Oh, come on, you're kidding?'

'Shhh, they'll all hear you and there are reporters out there. It's no laughing matter. It seems they are murder victims and have been there for years. I find it horrendous, not funny.'

The laughter left Marisa's face at once. 'You really mean it? Bodies? In our wood? Unbelievable. When did all this happen and why didn't you let me know?'

'We've been up all night and it's been a terrible time, so do be careful what you say. Dad's ill with 'flu and this coming on top of everything else has been an awful shock.' Suddenly she stopped talking as realisation dawned. 'Good heavens! You're driving.'

'How the devil do you think I got here?' said Marisa. 'That was why I came. Well, it all seems pretty unimportant now. Where is everyone?'

'In the sitting room. They'll be glad to see you, but please . . . be careful what you say.'

Marisa smiled. 'Don't worry. I'll be the soul of tact.' She entered the house, walked directly into the sitting room and glanced at her parents' surprised faces. 'Well then, what's all this I hear about grisly goings-on in our wood?'

'Well, how did I know they'd react like that?' Marisa sat at her old dressing table, putting on fresh lipstick. 'Can't anyone around here take a joke? As for being glad to see me, no one's bothered to say so. I rather wish I'd stayed in London.' She turned accusing eyes on Terry. 'No doubt you do as well. Am I never to be forgiven?'

Terry sighed and shook her head. 'Marisa, this is hardly the time.'

Disgruntled, she glanced about the room with its old single bed and dark oak headboard, the 1930s dressing table which Diane had shifted from the master bedroom years ago, and the Victorian iron grate with the small still life above it.

'Do you know, I never realised how utterly depressing this

room was. It's high time all this was thrown out. Tell me more about these murders. What did the police say?'

Terry sat on the bed and plucked at the beige quilted eiderdown thoughtfully. 'Not much they can say at the moment. We had a detective here, a dear man, who told us that the bodies, a man and a woman, had been shot in the head then buried in the same grave, one on top of the other.'

Wide-eyed now, Marisa shuddered. 'And you call him a dear man?'

Terry nodded. 'He's been very kind and friendly. Somehow it's important. Dad doubts they'll catch the killer after all these years, but Sergeant Hopwood tried to sound more confident.' She smiled wryly. 'When he said it meant checking through their lists of missing persons going back thirty years, even the biggest optimist would see they had an impossible task on their hands.'

Marisa lit a cigarette thoughtfully. 'I suppose they're checking the list for East Anglia only, but these people could have been murdered anywhere and disposed of as far from the scene as possible. It'll probably end up as a nationwide search and nothing will come of it.'

'Exactly.'

Standing up, cigarette in one hand, Marisa turned to check that her stocking seams were straight. 'I agree, it's a pretty horrible business, but that's no reason why the entire family should be cast into such despair. It's nothing to do with us. The gruesome remains have been removed, you say, so what's the problem?'

Terry looked surprised. 'You didn't see it as you arrived at the gate? We Fentons are suddenly in the news again and it isn't very pleasant.'

Sighing, Marisa glanced around for her old ash tray, found it missing and stubbed out the cigarette in a crystal bowl which stood on the dressing table. 'I certainly chose the wrong day to show off my new car. But, since I did, you might as well have a look at it.'

'Why did you come alone?' asked Terry. 'Why isn't Alastair with you?'

Marisa turned her face away from that keen stare. 'You'd have liked that, wouldn't you?' she said and, before her sister could remark on this barbed accusation, went on, 'He's in Coventry. Up to his eyes in work since his father handed things over to him.'

At that moment a faint knock on the door was followed by Eliot's low voice. 'May I come in?'

'Yes,' said Terry, relieved at the interuption.

The door opened. He stood there murmuring, 'I don't want to muscle in on girl talk or anything but the atmosphere down there could be cut with a knife and I wondered if . . .'

'Of course,' said Terry. 'Marisa was just about to show me her new car. Come and see it.'

'I've seen it,' he said. 'Why haven't you got the latest Hammond?'

'Because I like the Hillman.'

'When did you learn to drive?' asked Terry.

'I started before Christmas with a good driving school and passed my test first time.' Marisa threw her a triumphant smile. 'Alastair bought me the car as a present. He's always buying me expensive things. Spoils me rotten. Come and see it.'

Following his sisters down the stairs, Eliot kept up his usual flow of non-stop chatter. 'I had 'flu all over Easter, you know. Dad caught it from me. Mother tried ringing you but you were out and didn't ring us back. Why not? And where's Alastair? Why isn't he with you? And when is he going to take me to a race meeting, like he promised?'

'He's too busy at the moment,' Marisa said, opening the front door. 'It seemed a good opportunity to come and visit you.'

'And about time too!' came her brother's disgruntled reply.

Dinner that evening was a strained affair. Having been warned to say nothing of the discovery in the wood, Marisa spoke endlessly of her new life, wealth and friends, adding: 'Lady Hammond is coming to London for the Season and wants to take me to her box at Ascot. Unlike her husband and sons, the only races she cares about are run on four legs.'

She cut into her roast lamb and eyed everyone carefully to test their reactions to her words. Her parents didn't seem to be listening at all. What on earth was the matter with everyone?

She turned to Terry, saying, 'You must come to our next party. It'll do you good to have a proper social life. I realise you've nothing to wear, of course, but we can find something at Harrods and put it on my account. I have friends with unattached brothers, so you could get lucky. I'm sure Alastair would be delighted to see you fixed up with someone.'

Terry listened with mounting anger. How dare she! How dare she be so patronising? Too choked to speak, she was grateful when her mother came to her rescue.

'I'm sure Terry will try to get around to visiting you soon. She's been very busy lately. Was that Grant I heard you speaking to on the phone earlier, my dear?'

'Yes.' Terry ignored the surprised expression on Marisa's face. 'But he was rushing to the hospital because of an emergency.' She paused. 'He said we're not to worry about all this, because it happened long ago and it's what's happening today that counts.'

There was a long silence then John murmured, 'Sounds like a man of integrity.' He toyed with his roast, wishing Marisa had chosen some other time to pay them a surprise visit.

'Hospital? Grant?' Marisa looked at Terry agog. 'Well?'

'Oh, just someone I met,' she said casually.

'He's a doctor and the brother of the pilot of the Lancaster that crashed,' Eliot explained.

'He's a surgeon and about to take his Fellowship exams,' Diane added.

Marisa could find no words. How was it that here, in the heart of rural Suffolk, Terry had not only met the Hammond heir but a young surgeon too? How could that happen?

John pushed his untouched plate of food away from him and asked her why she was not in Coventry with her husband. Before she could answer he went on to make it quite obvious that he thought Alastair incapable of running a company like Hammond's.

'Hope he has good reliable staff around him. Still, Jersey's near enough if his father does feel the need to step in.'

'He won't need to do any such thing.' Marisa's voice was tense.

'You are happy, both of you?' asked Diane, more to focus on something other than the horror in the wood than from any real anxiety for the marriage.

After an awkward pause, Marisa smiled a shade too brightly and said without conviction, 'Ecstatic.'

Eliot was in no mood to speak or think about anything but the murders. 'I suppose it'll be in the *Lowdham Chronicle*. Thank goodness I'll be back at school where no one will see it!'

Seeing her parents freeze up once more, Marisa, in a rare attempt at tact, turned to Terry. 'I gather you went to Guernsey for Easter. What was it like?'

Guernsey, thought Terry, keeping her eyes firmly on her plate. She had only returned when . . . a week ago? Yet so much had happened in that short time. 'Interesting and . . . enlightening.' She saw her mother's fingers tighten on her knife and fork.

'Enlightening?' Marisa frowned. 'That's an odd word to choose.'

'Historically, I meant.'

'Did you find the house we were born in?'

She allowed a long pause, sensed the tension increasing and decided she was being unfair to lay this on her parents at such a time. 'No, we only had a few days and spent most of it exploring the island.'

'We?'

'A college friend of mine.'

Marisa lost interest at once. 'After the South of France, there simply isn't anywhere else I'd want to go for a holiday.'

At eight o'clock, John took himself back to bed and at nine-thirty Diane decided to end a terrible day by taking sleeping tablets and turning in herself. Eliot went to his room to finish off packing, leaving Terry and Marisa alone beside a dying fire.

Poking the coals back into life, Terry spoke of their brother and how badly affected he had been by all this. 'He can't wait to leave.'

'Why?' said Marisa. 'Most boys of his age would be thrilled at it. I hope he isn't turning into one of those spineless creatures who runs from his own shadow?'

'Of course not. He's just very sensitive, that's all. Perhaps, had you been here, you would have been a little upset yourself. It was all rather creepy.' She paused and looked thoughtful. 'He has these dreams, these nightmares. He won't tell me what they're about, but it terrifies him. You used to be the same.'

'What do you mean, used to? I still have them,' said Marisa quickly. 'And always the same dream.'

'I didn't know.' Terry leaned forward with growing interest. 'What's it about? Can you recall it well?'

'All too clearly,' murmured her sister, eyes on the fire, hands gripping the edge of the chair. 'It's not like other dreams, it's . . .

it's more somehow.' There was a long pause and then, for the first time, she spoke of the nightmare that had plagued her for as long as she could remember.

'It starts with a pinpoint of light in the darkness. The light comes nearer and grows larger and . . . and I know there's something behind it, something dark and terrible. It frightens me. I want to run away but I can't. And then . . .' She stopped speaking.

'Then you wake up screaming,' Terry murmured, remembering what Mrs Shotley had told her. Suddenly she realised how pale her sister had become. 'Are you all right?'

After a long pause Marisa murmured, 'Would you get me a large Scotch and soda?' She leaned forward in the armchair. 'A very large one.'

'Whisky?' Terry moved to the drinks table. 'When did you go on to the hard stuff?' There was no reply. Thoughtfully she lifted the crystal decanter and said, 'As for Eliot . . .'

'The lily-livered one?' Marisa's mouth curled in disdain. 'Just like Dad, refusing to stand up for himself. Weak and cowardly, that's what they are. Two of a kind.'

Terry turned to her in surprise. 'What on earth . . .? That's an awful thing to say.'

'Well, I'm in a bloody awful mood.'

'Then it's time to snap out of it. Eliot's a fine boy. And as for Dad, well, all this business is very upsetting for him. For all of us. Don't be so harsh.'

Pouring whisky into the glass, Terry reached for the soda syphon and said, 'Did you know that Mother had high blood pressure when she was expecting Eliot?'

'No, but it doesn't surprise me. She was as big as a house. Great with child, as they used to say. All those terrible maternity smocks! Eliot was a big baby. Used to kick a lot too.'

'Did you ever feel him kick?'

'Once. And decided there and then that I would never have children battering my insides like that.'

Terry frowned, her hand still on the soda syphon. 'You're sure you felt him kicking?'

'Of course. Children never forget things like that.' Marisa turned impatiently. 'Hey, where's my drink?'

So much for Meg and her preaching, thought Terry with a sense of relief. But that still begged the question of why Meg and Grace had been cut out of their lives. She had gone full circle and her head ached with it all. Suddenly she felt desperately tired and handed the glass to Marisa who now wanted to know about Grant.

'Oh, he came one day to see where his brother's plane crashed. We went out for a drink together. That's all. End of story.' And it was too, she told herself. 'I'd better go up myself. I was up all last night and still have my lessons to prepare. Yesterday and today I couldn't think at all. But I have "promises to keep and miles to go before I sleep".'

Marisa frowned. 'Promises? What promises?'

'I was quoting Robert Frost.'

'Who?' Marisa delved into her leather handbag and brought out two theatre tickets. 'Here, you might as well have these. They're for June. Theatre Royal, Drury Lane. Alastair can't go and since I don't want to without him, I'm giving them to you.'

Terry looked surprised. 'Thanks.'

'It's for *My Fair Lady*. Dress Circle. Do use them. Perhaps you can get a friend to accompany you? I'd go with you myself but I prefer a man on my arm. Parties are one thing, the theatre's different.'

'*My Fair Lady*! I've longed to see that. Thanks again.' Taking the tickets, Terry murmured, 'Marisa, is everything all right between you and Alastair?'

'Why shouldn't it be?' The brittle smile was followed by a nervous laugh. 'Why on earth not? I think I can safely say that my life is perfect.'

Knowing she would be the last person Marisa would open her heart to, Terry glanced at the tickets in her hand which said everything that her sister had not. At the door she turned.

'Well, see you in the morning.' She paused, aware suddenly that all animosity for Marisa was over. Why was that? Sisterly love overcoming anger or growing feelings for Grant overcoming the hurt she had suffered? Whatever it was, she found herself saying, 'I'm glad you came today.'

Marisa looked at her warily at first, then sensed that her sister truly meant what she said. 'I'm glad too.' It was something she had never expected to hear from her own mouth.

In the middle of the night Terry was awakened by the distant sound of the telephone. She switched on her light, squinting in its brightness, and then made her way down the stairs, wondering who on earth was ringing at this hour.

'Is she there?' The voice at the other end of the line was filled with anger.

'Alastair?' Terry frowned. 'Marisa's here, yes. Didn't you know?'

'No, I bloody well didn't! I've been telephoning the house and . . . well, at least she's with you.'

'Yes. I take it you don't want me to wake her up?'

'No.' After a pause. 'Terry?'

'Yes.'

'Terry, I . . .' There was a long pause. 'No . . . no sense in saying it now. Goodnight. Sorry I got you out of bed.'

Knowing in her heart what he had been about to say she agreed. No sense in saying it now. She replaced the receiver and wearily took herself off to bed. He was unhappy, that much was obvious and, in spite of everything she still cared enough to feel sad for him.

Living up to the Fentons' fears, the *Lowdham Chronicle*, along with other East Anglian papers, made the story their lead item. The *Chronicle* went on to say:

> Although the police are receiving co-operation from all over East Anglia in their search for a man and a woman listed as missing around thirty years ago, their hopes of tracing the identity of the victims are hampered by the length of time that has passed between crime and discovery.
>
> The wood in question belongs to Mr John Fenton of Lynwood Farm who last year was involved in a row over the route for a memorial site being raised in memory of the crew of a Lancaster bomber which crashed in 1943. A new route was found but, by an oversight, digging took place in his wood and the bodies were discovered.
>
> Mr Fenton's eldest daughter is married to Mr Alastair Hammond, the sports car manufacturer.

Lydia Rashleigh found her husband in his study and threw the newspaper down on his desk.

'Have you seen this? Well, have you?' Without waiting for an answer she went on, 'This rag goes further downhill with each passing week. Every time I pick it up these days all I seem to read about is the Fentons. Now they've even dragged poor Alastair into it. Why? What on earth has it to do with him? If they have to mention any member of the family, why not you? After all, you're the Chairman of the Parish Council and the Lancaster Memorial Committee, but you're never mentioned or consulted on anything.'

Confused at her thinking, Gerald frowned. 'What on earth should they be consulting me about? I didn't put those bodies there.'

'We simply don't need this sort of publicity a few months before the memorial ceremony. It's tasteless and bad for Thornley at a time when the entire village is pulling together to do something good.'

'For goodness' sake, woman, two bodies found in a wood is bound to be news.' He picked up the paper, read the column and sniffed. 'No need to mention Alastair, I agree. Should have left Fenton out of it too. Can't say I like the man, but damn it all, there's no need for this. Poor Diane. What she must be going through.'

Diane! Lydia's eyes blazed. Snatching the newspaper from his hand she marched out of the study, leaving her surprised husband sitting like a stone.

'Ah, Miss Fenton. Take a seat, would you?' Miss Yeats looked up from a report she was writing and removed her glasses thoughtfully. 'Sorry to call you in during the break but I'm sure you must know the reason.' She reached into a drawer, brought out a copy of the *Lowdham Chronicle* and sighed.

Terry sat down nervously. 'Ah, yes . . . well . . .'

'Your family do seem to have a penchant for getting into the news, Miss Fenton. First there was all that fuss over the memorial route, then the wedding, and now this. I do realise that such reports are not your fault but it is difficult to keep discipline among the girls when one member of the staff is constantly in the news.'

'With respect, Miss Yeats, I have not been in the news once.'

'But your father has.'

'It's hardly our fault that two skeletons were unearthed on our land, Miss Yeats. We had hoped the press would leave our name out of it. They had no reason to print it or rake over old coals. My parents are very angry, as you can imagine.'

'Yes, yes, but I have to think of my girls. They're all agog at the news of bodies being found outside Miss Fenton's home. How are you supposed to teach under such circumstances?'

Terry's hands clenched with anger and suspense. She was going to be dismissed. How unfair, how ridiculously unfair!

'When I took you on I had my doubts,' Miss Yeats mused. 'But I took a chance ...' Suddenly her stern features relaxed into a smile. 'I have to say I'm very pleased I did. So far you've exceeded my expectations. The girls not only like you, they respect you, and that's very important. Their work has improved dramatically since you arrived. Those you persuaded me to allow the benefit of extra tuition have progressed well. But how about that girl . . . Margaret . . .?'

With a sense of deep relief, Terry answered, 'Temple. Margaret Temple has more problems than the other girls with certain words. She does try very hard, however, and the time spent after school is paying off.'

'Good,' said Miss Yeats. 'I'm glad that class is sorting itself out at last.' Her face lightened. 'Nevertheless, this is a fee-paying school and any kind of notoriety surrounding a member of the staff can cause parents to have second thoughts about sending their girls here.'

Terry sat like stone. Having just been praised to the roof, was she about to be dismissed after all?

'So I want you to be very careful. Say nothing to any of your pupils concerning this case, which could take months, maybe years even, to clear up. I want to be certain that your family's name will not be mentioned in the press again. Will your father extract such a promise from the editor of the *Chronicle*?'

'Well, he certainly doesn't enjoy finding his name in it. Last time he thought it best not to make matters worse by getting involved, and he was right. This time is different, however. I think he will act. If not I'll contact the editor myself and put a stop to it.'

Miss Yeats shook her head dismissively. 'No, no. You're too young and have no clout. If your father gets nowhere then I'll do it myself. Anyway, break is nearly over so I'll keep you no longer. Good morning, Miss Fenton. Think about what I've said.'

Terry walked out, closed the door and stood wondering how on earth she could stop the girls whispering and twittering behind their hands when she was not there to confront them. All morning she had felt their eyes following her wherever she went. One girl alone, clearly pressed by the others, had raised her hand and asked about the skeletons.

Terry had given a firm reply. 'That is purely a matter for the police and has nothing to do with us. It has nothing to do with you either, so forget about it and concentrate on your lesson.'

God, it was all so unfair, and just when everything was finally getting back on to an even keel. Her father was almost recovered and both parents had picked up the threads of their normal busy lives. Terry had found a strange solace in teaching, immersing herself so much in her subjects and pupils that when she did pause to think about recent events it all began to seem unreal, as though she had dreamed it. Now this! Last night her parents had read the newspaper and despaired.

In the Staff Room those who had not seen her earlier that day now came up to ask about the discovery and to commiserate over what must have been a terrible ordeal. Thanking them politely, Terry decided to skip coffee and slipped out quickly into the morning sunlight just as the pupils were heading back into the building.

There she breathed in fresh clean air, counted to fifty slowly and felt her body relax. Then it was time to return to the classroom and start reading *Silas Marner*.

On her way home that afternoon Terry stopped the Austin outside Mrs Shotley's cottage, knowing she would have seen the article and been upset over it. She found that Diane had visited the old lady on Monday, warning her of the discovery before she heard of it from other villagers.

'She needn't have bothered,' Mrs Shotley said now, as she carried on with her ironing. 'I'd already heard on the Sunday. Mrs Godwin couldn't wait to come and tell me. Silly woman! She's on cloud nine, that one. Being privy to what goes on in your home gets her a lot of attention these days. So you be careful what you say in front of her. Never did like the woman. Shall I make some tea? I've made a delicious rum cake.'

Much as she loved rum cake, Terry had to decline. 'I'm so

behind hand at the moment. I just thought I'd look in . . .'

'Because of the *Chronicle*, I know.' Mrs Shotley put down the iron and sighed. 'Wicked to bring your father's name into it. All they had to do was say the remains were found in a wood near Thornley. That's all. But no, they have to go raking up old dirt. Wicked! Your poor parents. Anyway the *Chronicle* got it wrong.'

'Got what wrong?'

'They said thirty years . . . well, that can't be right, now can it?'

Terry looked lost. 'Can't it?'

The white head shook slowly from side to side. 'You forget that Arthur Fenton had two Labradors. They followed him every time he went shooting in the woods. Now come on. Two bodies freshly buried would have been discovered by those dogs at once. Pity you never knew them. Lovely creatures they were. Gone before you arrived, though. Old age.'

For a moment there was a long silence then Terry said, 'It's possible the dogs missed them. The grave was over by the Rashleigh boundary, by that old oak, the one I used to climb.'

'And fell and broke your arm?'

'Yes. Fancy you remembering that.'

Mrs Shotley closed her eyes as if concentrating, then looked at Terry, unplugged the iron and set it to cool on the ironing board stand. 'Would you drive me up there now, before it gets too dark?' It was the last thing she'd expected the old lady to say. She had been prepared for sadness, tears even, anything but this determined manner which now bordered on the ghoulish.

'I don't think that's a good idea. It would only upset you.'

'Upset me? I'm no stranger to shock, Terry. I was the one who found Mr Fenton that day. A heap of mud and an empty hole in the ground won't cap that, I can assure you.'

She made for a cupboard which stood between the kitchen and tiny sitting room. From it she brought a grey woollen coat and black felt hat which she secured to her hair with a large pin. 'I have my reasons for wanting to go to the wood, so be a good girl now and pop me up there.'

'What reasons?'

'I'll tell you when we get there. Right, let's waste no more time. You've lots to do, I know that. Park where your parents won't see me or they'll only start fussing.'

Utterly bewildered, Terry ran the old lady up to the farm,

parked at the front of the house, knowing her parents would be at the rear, and straightaway started leading Mrs Shotley across rough ground to the wood. 'Careful now. Don't stumble.'

'I know, I know, don't fuss. I've walked this way a hundred times and more.'

The sun which had shone all day was low in the sky; shadows had lengthened and the wood was darkening as they entered. Terry shuddered involuntarily.

'Stop that,' said Mrs Shotley firmly. 'It's just a wood when all's said and done. Have the police gone now?'

'Yes,' she said, wishing they were still here. 'It was over there. They've removed the excavator now . . .'

'And there's your oak tree,' said Mrs Shotley. 'It withstood the storm, you see. It must be the oldest tree in the wood. Some say four hundred years old. The two next to it were torn out by their roots. Take me closer, Terry.'

'What storm?' she asked as they walked to where the grave had been. It was filled in now and the cordon removed. All about, though, was devastation and mud, just as it had been when the skull had been uncovered.

For a moment Mrs Shotley looked at the spot then lifted her head and gazed about her. 'Yes. It was here all right. In the autumn of 38 we had a terrible gale. I've never known such strong winds. It hit Thornley badly. Tiles came off our roof. I thought the chimney would crash down on me. The following day, I came here with Mr Fenton to see if any damage had been done and that's when we saw it: two great oaks crashed to the ground as though a giant hand had plucked them from the earth. The roots were completely exposed. You've never seen anything like it. We both wept at the sight. If this one is four hundred years old, then they must have been around the same age. Anyway, by February Mr Fenton had had the entire site cleared. Then he had his accident, and you came in the summer.'

Terry listened to all this, wondering what it had to do with anything, then realised what the old lady was trying to say.

'Oh, I see. The bodies had to have been placed here *after* that storm or they would have been exposed when the trees fell. So it's more like twenty years, not thirty?'

'I suppose whoever did it found the ground was still soft enough to dig,' said Mrs Shotley thoughtfully.

Terry led her away. 'Which could mean that the killer knew the wood? Knew the clearing had been made?'

Mrs Shotley frowned. 'No. That would mean someone local, and that's quite out of the question. Will there be time for me to see your parents before you have to drive me home?'

'Of course,' said Terry, her mind twisting and turning over all the new possibilities which this little conversation had suddenly opened up. The police would have to be informed. It might help in their interminable search for missing persons.

John Fenton had been checking the fencing around the mare's paddock and was walking towards the house when he saw his daughter and their former housekeeper walking from the wood in the thickening twilight. His anxious frown did not change as he glared at them both. 'What on earth were you two doing in there?'

When Mrs Shotley explained and Terry added that she was going to ring Sergeant Hopwood at once, John smiled and shook his head.

'I'll contact him first thing tomorrow. It's better that I deal with these matters.'

Terry looked at him. 'I didn't think . . . well . . . of course, I wasn't trying to . . .'

'Of course not.' He placed an affectionate arm about her and turned to Mrs Shotley. 'I'm grateful to you. Although I should think the police pathologist has the time pinned down by now. But I'll call Sergeant Hopwood anyway. You never know. It might just help.'

Since Mrs Shotley wanted to get home before dark, Terry led her back to the car, leaving John standing there, watching, as the Austin pulled out of the gate and out of sight.

Chapter Eleven

Although confined to the inner pages, news of the discovery found its way to the editors of the national press. Most newspapers merely mentioned a Suffolk wood near the market town of Lowdham Market and spoke of a thirty-year-old murder mystery.

'Thirty!' Terry looked up from the breakfast table and frowned at her father. 'Why don't they get their facts right? They only have to check with the police. You did tell the Detective Sergeant, didn't you?'

Looking a shade hesitant, John put down his coffee cup and shook his head. 'Not personally, no. Someone took my message and said they would pass it on.'

'Perhaps he forgot?'

'I doubt it.' John pushed back his chair and stood up. 'Twenty years or thirty, what the hell does it matter after all this time? Meanwhile there are some of us who have no time to linger over papers.' Smiling, he walked to her side of the table, kissed her on the head and said, 'I've a mind to go to church today, pet, and I want you there, too. So does your mother. You know, put on a united front for the benefit of the villagers. Let them see we can take it on the chin and aren't unduly disturbed.'

Terry looked up at him. 'We're not. Are we?'

At the door he turned, his lips working as they always did when he was fighting inner demons. 'The Vicar came to see us during the week and kept on about "our time of trouble". I did point out it was someone else's trouble, but it shows how people are thinking.'

Terry saw her father smile then and thought him almost

handsome. He seemed almost his old self again and that sent a wave of relief through her.

'Anyway,' he said, 'old Clements will be expecting us today, so don't let's disappoint him. Although what he'll say in his sermon doesn't bear thinking about.'

Terry frowned. Church? With everyone staring at them as though they were a musical turn? No. She couldn't do it, not even for the father she loved. 'I was going to ride Dauphine.'

John raised one eyebrow as a sailor would raise a storm cone. 'Very well. But be back in time for church. We don't want to make an entrance, now do we?'

But even as Terry was heading for the paddock she heard her mother calling her back to the house. Diane's eyes were alive with anticipation. 'There's a phone call for you. I think it's him.'

Saying nothing, Terry felt her heart pounding as she entered the hallway and picked up the receiver. 'Hello?'

'Terry?' Grant sounded relieved. 'Good. Your mother said you'd gone riding.'

'I was just about to.' She hoped she didn't sound breathless.

'I don't know whether you've seen the Sunday papers?' When she said she had, he said firmly, 'Don't let them upset you.'

Terry paused for a moment, not knowing what to say. 'I suppose it was only to be expected.'

'If it's any comfort to you, I bought four and only one mentioned the name Thornley.'

There was another awkward pause. 'Have you taken that exam yet?' she asked.

'No, that particular pleasure is reserved for next week. Then I have a weekend off and only have to deal with my nerves until I hear the result. They'll take the strain better if we could meet on that Saturday? These past days have been horrendous. A car accident involving six people, all in serious condition, plus five other emergencies. We had to pull out all the stops and reschedule the routine surgery. All of which has put me well behind with my exam work. I'm on call now, so can't speak for long.'

Terry slowly sank on to the chair beside the telephone table and concentrated on seven words that had almost been lost among the crash victims and the sudden emergencies. 'Did you say, meet you on Saturday?'

'The one after next. After my exam. I think we could

both do with a break. Do you like classical music?'

'That depends. I like Wagner but couldn't sit through The Ring.'

'How about Brahms?'

'Love Brahms. The last concert I went to was the Proms and . . .'

'You heard it twice?' He laughed. 'You'll find the Festival Hall a very different kettle of fish. I have tickets. Will you come with me?'

'Yes,' she said, suddenly floating on a cloud. 'Saturday week then. So you won't know the result by then?'

'No. I'll have to sweat it out. Brahms will help, but you have to be with me or it won't work.'

When at last Terry replaced the receiver, a flush of nervous excitement set her face burning. Seeing her mother's enquiring eyes as she entered the kitchen, she said, 'Festival Hall, Saturday week.'

'With Grant?'

'Yes.'

Diane looked delighted. 'Then ring Marisa at once and ask if you can stay the night with her.'

Terry just stared at her. How insensitive could her mother be? Staying under the same roof as Alastair was completely out of the question. Both of them would be highly embarrassed and Marisa would take full advantage of the situation to crow in triumph.

'Later. I'm taking Dauphine for some exercise.' Terry turned, back at the door. 'Tell Dad I might be too late for church now.'

Diane's expression turned to one of disapproval. 'His heart is set on it. A united front is what we need to present or people will think we're skulking in our lair because of the newspapers.'

'Skulking?' Terry flushed with anger. 'I'll give them skulking!' Glancing at her watch, she murmured, 'I'll leave the ride until after church.'

In her bedroom she made up her face carefully, put on a navy jersey wool suit and topped this with a cream Breton-shaped hat. She loathed hats but her parents would hit the roof if she went to church without one. Wondering at the morality of attending for the sake of appearances when, for some time now, she had felt there was no one listening to her prayers, she stood up and prepared for the battle to come.

At that moment the door opened and her mother stood there, looking put out. 'It seems we're never to have any peace today. Another call for you. This time it's someone called Margaret. Don't be long or we'll be late.'

Terry's look of bemusement mirrored Diane's perfectly as she walked down the stairs and picked up the receiver. 'Hello?'

'Terry?' came the whisper. 'It's Meg.'

The shock sent her swinging round to see her mother hovering by the kitchen door. Waving a dismissive hand, Terry smiled at her. 'It's the friend I went to Guernsey with.' Diane nodded and went into the kitchen. Only when she heard the back door open and close again did Terry speak.

'Why are you ringing me here? You know what we agreed?'

'Of course I know,' whispered Meg. 'That's why I gave my full name. We agreed your college friend would be called Margaret, isn't that so? Can you speek freely? Is the coast clear?' When Terry assured her it was, she went on in her normal voice, 'I saw the paper today. Thornley, I thought. Sounds familiar. It's your Thornley where these murders took place, I assume?'

'It is,' Terry replied with a sense of growing despair. Trust Meg and her friends to buy the one paper that mentioned the village itself. 'And the bodies were found in our wood. That's right, *our* wood.'

It was some moments before Meg took this in. At last she said. 'Your wood? How ghastly for you.'

'Meg . . . please. Can we talk about something else?'

Disappointment in her voice, she said, 'Well, that wasn't my reason for ringing to be honest. I've had a letter from Mum. She's at her wit's end, poor thing, and wishes now that she hadn't said anything about the accident and the Caesareans. She's certain you've probably had a flaming row with your mother and blames herself entirely. Have you, Terry? Have you told them?'

'Of course not. So you can set her mind at rest. Hold on a moment.' She put down the receiver, checked the kitchen to be sure the coast was clear for her to speak openly, then went on. 'I did quiz Mother about our births but she insists we were born normally at your house and that Eliot was born, without complications, at a London clinic.'

In the silence that followed Terry wondered if the line had gone dead, then a quiet voice said, 'I know Mum's no spring chicken but neither is she in her dotage. Her memory is excellent and what she says is the truth, so you'd better believe it. It's your mother who's not being truthful. You said a London clinic. Any idea which one?'

'The Westlake. Do you know it?'

'I've heard of it. South of the river, unfashionable, not very good. Just an ordinary maternity home which is about to close. At one time it was run by nuns – as a charity for poor women – then the nuns left and it became private in the thirties. But even today it has no special care facilities. Their problems usually wind up with us. Strange place for your mother to go with her history. No doctor would ever have sent her there.'

Terry frowned. 'Eliot's our blood brother, there's no mistake. His birth presented no problems whatsoever, apparently.'

'Then your mother was very lucky, as I said before.'

Terry sighed. 'Well, it's all in the past and frankly, after what's just happened here, suddenly doesn't seem so important.'

'I daresay you're right,' said Meg. 'Just thought I'd like to put Mum's mind at rest, that's all.'

A sudden thought occurred to Terry. 'Look, I have to go now but I'll be in London on Saturday week. Any chance of me bunking down in your place for the night? Then we can have a longer chat. Do they allow you to have a visitor at the nurses' home?'

'I've left there anyway. I'm sharing a rather grotty flat with three other nurses now. It's fairly close to the hospital. Since two of us are usually on nights when the other two are on day duty, it works out pretty well. I'm on nights at the moment so you can have my bed. You'd better take down the address and telephone number.'

Terry did this then smiled to herself as she put down the receiver. Although she could never think of her as a friend, and had to admit to herself that she didn't really like her, Meg was a good sort nevertheless and right now would provide the means of avoiding a possibly embarrassing night at Cadogan Place.

Thornley's ancient church was full at Christmas and Easter but, for the rest of the year, only twenty people turned up regularly, most of them elderly or, like the Rashleighs, out of a sense of duty.

And some, like the Fentons, out of a desire to be accepted into the community they had adopted.

Today, even the Vicar seemed a shade taken aback as he found himself facing an exceptionally large congregation. He smiled wryly as he opened his prayer book. There was nothing like drama or a scandal to bring his flock safely back to the pen.

Feeling all eyes upon them, the three Fentons stared directly ahead during prayers and hymns then, with a twinge of anxiety, sat back and waited for the much-dreaded sermon.

As the Reverend Clements climbed the pulpit Terry's heart started beating a shade faster. She felt her father's hand on hers as if to say, 'I know, pet, but we'll see it through.'

As it was, to their utter relief and the rest of the congregation's disappointment, the sermon rambled on in its usual manner, the text implying that nothing untoward had happened in Thornley since the Great Plague.

After the service more people stood chatting outside the church than usual. There was a general sense of letdown at their Vicar's inability to mention the village's moment of fame and drama. But since Reverend Clements had, in his opinion, already brought comfort to the Fentons by speaking of their 'rather distressing event', he could see no reason for upsetting them further by mentioning sensational occurrences which had little to do with God.

After he and his wife had spoken briefly with the Rashleighs and accepted an invitation to pre-lunch sherry at the Hall, the Vicar watched as they walked down the stone steps to their car and drove away. Realising this would be a signal for the rest of the church goers to move in on the Fentons, he chatted quietly to them for some time, hoping the others would leave. Yet still they hovered until he had no choice but to return to the Vicarage.

As John led Diane and Terry towards the steps they found themselves surrounded. Question tumbled over question to which John replied with remarkable calm.

'We know nothing more than you, I'm afraid. It's a police matter.'

It was Mrs Shotley who turned on her neighbours in the end. 'Let them be, can't you? You've all read about it so what is there to add? Stop pestering folk and go home to your Sunday roasts.'

At last the Fentons made their way to the Morris Traveller and climbed inside. John started the ignition and headed through the watersplash while Terry, tense with anger, could not hold her tongue.

'I'm afraid you disappointed the ghouls, Dad. They wanted all the gruesome details.'

Smiling grimly, he turned the car up the hill. 'Well, we're over the worst. They'll leave us alone now.'

Terry glanced at her mother for some reaction but Diane said nothing, just stared through the window as the three then drove home in silence.

Late in the afternoon she entered Terry's room with a cup of tea and looking a shade put out. 'I thought you were going to ring Marisa? As it is she's just rung us to tell us what's in the papers. As if we didn't know! She lives in another world that one. Anyway, since you didn't ring I've asked her about Saturday week and she says you're to stay with her.'

Terry sighed and looked up from her marking. 'Does she? I wish you hadn't interfered. I've already made other arrangements.'

Diane's eyes glinted. 'Oh? Who else do you know in London but Marisa?'

'Margaret. When she was on the phone she offered to put me up at her flat. I accepted.'

'In preference to your own sister?' Diane's lips tightened. 'If it's because of Alastair then you have to get over it. He's now your brother-in-law and the sooner you accept that the better. Hiding away won't help. I want you to stay with Marisa when you're in London. Promise me you'll do that?'

Realising that her mother thought she was going to stay with Grant overnight, Terry felt her patience snap. 'Oh, for goodness' sake, stop treating me like a child!'

'We're doing no such thing.'

Terry glared up at her. 'I think it was your lack of trust and understanding that made Alastair back away from me. He found Marisa was living independently, no longer under the thumb of her parents and doing as she pleased. As for Margaret, I've already accepted her offer of a place for the night. But if it will make you feel any better, I'll look in on Marisa before returning home on Sunday.'

Diane hovered uncertainly for a moment, still suspicious, still fearful that once away from the strictures of her family, her daughter could just be fool enough to kick over the traces. Hadn't she been foolish herself at that age, falling under the spell of a man, afraid she would lose him if she didn't do as he wished? And living to regret it. John was still good-looking in her eyes and was charm itself to those who didn't know him as she did. That was the problem. Only she knew what he could really be: a man she had learned to fear, one she should and did hate, and yet, in spite of it all, someone to whom she felt bound by a strange love. How was that possible? Was it purely sex or was it a form of madness to hate and love at the same time? If only she could say all this to Terry, but there were things that could never be said between them.

'Don't let your tea get cold.' With that Diane left the room, a deeply troubled woman.

Picking up the cup and saucer, Terry drank the tea feeling dismal. Just when it seemed that her mother was almost her old self again, she had smacked her down. 'Oh, hell.' The worst of it was that, having given her word to call on Marisa, she would now have to keep it.

As the train pulled in at Liverpool Street station, Terry buttoned the woollen swing-back dusky pink coat which she was wearing over a soft jersey cream dress, and stepped on to the platform. It felt cold as she took in the noise and smell of the terminus, and she was apprehensive, more so than she had ever been with Alastair. But then Grant was not Alastair. For one thing he was an older man with more depth, she suspected, than he allowed anyone to see. She sensed also that he didn't think of women as conquests, and once deeply attracted would remain true. But such a man would be very careful over making his choice. No wonder she felt apprehensive.

He was waiting for her by the platform gate, looking formal in a dark grey suit, so different from the man in the sheepskin jacket she had seen wandering forlornly through the snow.

The roof of the MG was down against a sharp east wind and made their proximity seem closer as he eased out into the London traffic and headed directly for the South Bank. For a while it seemed they could find nothing to say except bland references to the journey but suddenly there was ease in their silence as though just being together was enough and Terry asked herself why. Why did the apprehension vanish once she was with him?

Over dinner at the Festival Hall restaurant they glanced at the lights across the Thames and spoke first of his final exam then the event at Thornley.

'Has it caused you and your family many problems?'

'A few, but we're weathering it all. School was the worst. Not only did I have pop-eyed girls to contend with, I also had a dressing down from the Head. You know . . . don't let it happen again.' Her eyes twinkled with mirth which he found infectious and both of them left the restaurant laughing.

After the concert they wandered slowly along the South Bank. The wind had dropped and the evening now seemed mild. Lights from the Embankment were reflected in the dark river as they leaned on the parapet and gazed across.

'Grant is unusual for a first name, surely?' observed Terry.

He gave a short laugh. 'I'm named after an American Civil War general. My father was an enthusiast. Since the General's first name was Ulysses, I consider it a close-run thing.' He turned and looked into her upturned face, fighting down a strong desire to touch it. 'There were only two kinds of books in our house. Medical and those about the American Civil War. His one dream was to go to the States and find the battlefields he had read so much about. The nearest he ever got was to sit through *Gone With The Wind.* When he retired he planned the trip but while he was preparing his itinerary for the greatest adventure of his life, he died of a heart attack.'

Terry's face shadowed. 'I'm sorry. That's so sad.'

'Yes.' Grant's voice had thickened. After a pause, he went on, 'There was no warning, you see, no previous attack, nothing.' Another brief moment and he took her by the arm and said, 'Come on, let's find a pub before they close.'

Later, as they drove towards Southwark, he said, 'Do you have special plans for tomorrow? Only I have to look at a desk. The owner of an antiques shop promised to keep a look out for one and now has a Victorian kneehole for me to view. If I don't go tomorrow he'll be forced to put it on sale. Would it bore you very much to come with me? I'd value your advice.'

'On antiques?' Terry laughed. 'Although I do know woodworm when I see it.'

He grinned. 'Ah, well, I wouldn't, you see.'

They approached the address Meg had given and drove along a road of terraced houses searching for numbers in the dim light from outdated street lamps.

'That's it,' said Terry. 'Thirty-seven. Meg's on nights but one of her flatmates will let me in. 'She glanced at her watch anxiously. 'We are rather late. Hope she hasn't turned in for the night.'

He grinned and said, 'Then you'd have no choice but to come back to my flat instead.'

Why was it, she thought then, that nothing he said ever made her feel uncomfortable? Even his long silences no longer filled her with unease. She saw his expression change and knew he wanted to kiss her but suddenly a light shone from the house as the shabby front door opened.

'Is that Terry?' a voice said. 'Terry Fenton?'

Quickly she left the car and moved towards the woman in a dressing gown standing on the doorstep. 'I'm afraid I'm horribly late. Please forgive me.'

'No problem. I saw the car headlights and thought you might have difficulty reading the house number.' She turned as Grant approached and said, 'Good evening. I'm Celia Horley.'

'Grant Kenway.' The large hand went out and was taken politely, then the dark-haired woman stepped back for Terry to enter. It was the signal for Grant to leave and let her get to bed.

'Tomorrow then,' he whispered to Terry. 'Ten o'clock.'

Sadly, and more than a little miffed that a precious moment had been so effectively destroyed, Terry watched as he walked quickly back to the car and drove away. Turning, she entered a long narrow hallway and followed Celia up a staircase covered by a threadbare carpet.

'I'm afraid it's a bit of a mess,' Celia was saying as they entered the sitting room of the flat. 'But we had friends in and haven't had a chance to clear up. Janet's gone to bed but she'll help me do the necessary before we go on duty tomorrow. We're both early risers.'

Terry cast an appalled eye over the detritus left by Janet and Celia and their friends. Glasses still smelling of spirits were standing on any surface that was available, ashtrays filled with stale dogends were everywhere and plates containing the remnants of food lay on the large coffee table.

'Meanwhile,' said Celia, with a sigh, 'I'll transfer this lot into the kitchen. Come on, and I'll show you Meg's bedroom. She shares with Pam but since neither of them will be home until nine, and both then have a hearty meal which of course will be their dinner, you don't have to jump out of bed at the crack of dawn. She's put clean sheets on for you, by the way.'

The bedroom was tidy, and Terry thanked God for it. She was too awake and alert to fall into used crumpled sheets or stare at clothes scattered everywhere. Slowly she undressed, put on her lemon nylon nightgown and matching short négligée, searched into her small overnight case for make-up remover then took herself off to the bathroom, which was freezing. Stockings and undies hung from a drying rack over the bath beside which was an old, suspicious-looking geyser which provided the only hot water. For a quick wash at the sink a hot kettle would be required. Terry washed quickly in ice cold water, cleaned her teeth, sprinted back along the narrow landing to Meg's room, and climbed into bed, pulling the crisp laundered sheets up to her chin and feeling the weight of two blankets and an eiderdown upon her.

Curling into a foetal position for warmth, she lay there looking into darkness, thinking of Grant and wondering what his embrace would have been like. Maybe now she would never know. Just as well, she told herself. She had given her heart too readily before and paid the price. The same thing could happen again. Even so, she wondered how she would get through the long hours until morning, until ten o'clock when she would be with him again. Wakeful until dawn, she finally drifted into a fitful sleep.

From somewhere a car door slammed. Terry's eyes opened and, for a brief moment, she wondered where she was. As the fog of sleep cleared she saw sunlight through the curtains, glanced at her watch and saw it was almost seven thirty. For some minutes she lay there, unwilling to push back the bed covers to the cold air, but eventually she climbed out, put on the cotton wrap which was worse than useless in such a flat, then made her way to the kitchen, hoping for a cup of tea.

There she stopped and looked around her in dismay at the dirty dishes, glasses, cups and saucers which had been transferred from the sitting room the night before. At that moment Celia appeared, dressed in her uniform and struggling to pin a white nurse's cap to her hair.

'Oh, Lord, we meant to get up early to sort this lot out! As it is we're both late. Must be the booze. Janet's waiting downstairs.' She swung a cape about her shoulders. 'Tell Meg I'm sorry. Must dash.'

Terry called after her, 'Where are the clean sheets so that I can make Meg's bed?'

Celia glanced back and laughed. 'She has two sets. One's at the laundry and the clean ones are on the bed already. Bye. Nice meeting you.' With that she rushed down the stairs and out through the front door.

Left alone in a cold silent house Terry took one look at the dishes and got to work. When Meg and Pam came up the stairs, chatting noisily, they entered the kitchen to see clean cups, saucers, glasses and plates all neatly stacked and Terry standing there in her nightclothes.

'I don't know where they all go, I'm afraid. Thanks for letting me stay the night, Meg.'

'Good God,' she said, looking at the crockery on the table. 'It's a fairy come to deliver us from Celia and Janet. Don't tell me you've been cleaning up after them?'

'Well, they were late and I'm in no rush.'

'You should move in,' said Pam, before disappearing for a hot bath.

Meg took off her cape, flung it on her bed then returned to the kitchen. She sat down and removed the white cap from her hair. Freed at last her red curls bounced once more as a long sigh escaped her. 'What a night! Have you had any breakfast?'

Terry shook her head and smiled. 'A cup of tea is all I crave.'

'Rubbish! I was going to cook pork chops but since you're here I'll do a big breakfast instead and you'll eat it or I'll want to know the reason why.' She looked at Terry and smiled. 'Don't forget, this is our dinnertime. Anyway it isn't fair that you're a sylph while I'm now a size 14. Did you enjoy your concert? Who did you go with?'

Terry sat down at the table. 'Someone I met back in the winter.'

'Really? What does he do?'

On learning he was a doctor at St Thomas's, Meg stared at her open-mouthed. 'Isn't that just typical? Country school teacher meets London doctor, while London nurse meets sweet bugger all!' She rose from her chair and filled the kettle for the long-awaited tea. 'Tell me about him?'

'I don't know very much. This is only the second time we've been out together.'

'Yet you met him back in the winter?'

As the frying pan sizzled away, Terry explained. When she had finished, Meg shrugged and asked, 'Two eggs or one?'

During breakfast, Terry asked how Grace was, adding that she hoped to see her again.

Buttering a round of toast Meg said. 'She hopes to come some time in August to stay with those friends of hers, the ones who left Guernsey to live in Finchley.' After a pause she added quietly. 'At least they kept in touch.'

At this barbed comment Terry frowned. 'Well, that's just the point. If she comes to London then I'm going to do my best to reunite her with my parents.'

'Except that Mum no longer wants to meet them. I thought she'd made that quite plain? Forget the whole thing.'

'If only I could.' Terry put down her knife and fork sighing. 'And yet I promised her I'd say nothing.'

'And so we'll let sleeping dogs lie,' said Meg firmly. With all her being, though, she wanted to kick those dogs awake so that many questions could be answered.

At that moment Pam returned, candlewick dressing gown tied about her waist. Stifling a yawn, she took her plate from the oven, sat down and joined the others. The three of them chatted happily until Terry glanced at her watch and blinked in astonishment. 'Good Lord, he'll be here at ten. It's almost that now. We're to look at a desk.'

'Then get your skates on,' said Meg, starting to clear away. 'I'll use the bathroom after you've finished. Don't worry. If he's on time, I'll let him in. What's his name?'

'Grant Kenway. But I doubt he'll be on time,' said Terry as she raced out of the kitchen.

Grant was five minutes early. Terry heard the doorbell just as she was stepping into the bath. Damn! She had wanted to look her best, spending ages on make up and fiddling with her hair. Now she would have to rush and look rather as she had that awful Sunday when he had arrived at Lynwood so unexpectedly.

Meg apologised to Dr Kenway for the mess in the kitchen, said

Terry would not be long, and asked if he would like a cup of tea or coffee.

'Coffee, please. Black, no sugar. And there's no need to apologise. I do know what it's like returning home from a long stint. That's the best of being on call. At least I eat at the hospital.'

As it was warmer in the kitchen, Meg kept him there and after a few pleasantries Pam left them alone. After pouring more coffee, Meg asked if he had met Terry's parents and when he said yes, wanted to know what he thought of them.

Surprised at the question, he answered, 'Charming couple, even though her father had 'flu at the time.'

Meg just stared at him. 'Charming? I've never met them myself but charming is hardly the word *I* would choose.' Seeing his reaction to this outburst, she let out a long breath and said, 'Sorry. I dare say I shouldn't have said that, but the fact is that John and Diane Fenton are extremely odd, believe me. Did Terry tell you I was her cousin from Guernsey? No? Well I suppose she's afraid you'll blurt something out in front of her parents. You see, I'm not supposed to exist.'

Grant was nonplussed as he saw the anger in her eyes, a volcanic simmering anger that almost unleashed itself in one unguarded moment. But Meg took a hold on herself and said.

'That was unforgivable of me . . . but I have a bad feeling about them. They lie to Terry.' As Grant listened, she explained everything then sat back and lit up a cigarette. 'Dear God, to have such parents . . . I'd rather be an orphan.'

Feeling uncomfortably as if he was being dragged into a family row, Grant just smiled and said nothing as he drank his coffee. He didn't like Meg and thought she must be one tile short of a roof to go on like this in front of a total stranger. Wishing to God Terry would finish getting ready and take him out of here, he hoped the tirade was over. But Meg was only just getting warmed up.

'There's something else, and it's the reason I'm telling you all this. I need to clarify a problem in my mind.'

He stared at her warily. 'And what's that?'

'Well, back in the thirties Diane had a very bad accident in her eighth month of pregnancy. She sustained a broken femur, a fractured pelvis and some damage to her hip, though I'm not sure what. Anyway she was delivered of her first child by section and was pretty well crippled for months. Then Terry came along and was delivered by section also. Doctor, furious with husband and so forth, told Diane she couldn't have any more children.'

Grant waited then asked. 'Couldn't or shouldn't? There is a difference.' Meg frowned. 'My mother said couldn't.'

Grant looked thoughtful. 'Two consecutive sections in those days would make a third child high risk. The deep incision across the uterus would have left a weakness which could be fatal and she would have been strongly advised against a third pregnancy.' He shrugged. 'Even so, there must have been women who did have a third child. I don't know. It was before my time. As you know, things have changed.'

Meg looked at him. 'Hmmm. Diane did have a third child in spite of being high risk and, to cap it all, had a normal delivery at the Westlake Clinic. Why London? And why that clinic of all places? We get their emergencies because they have no facilities, so why would her doctor send her there?'

Grant thought it strange but kept his silence. 'We're speaking of Eliot, I take it?' When Meg nodded, he said. 'But that would be about six years after Terry's birth. So it's just feasible. Her injuries would have mended – but not knowing her medical history makes it impossible to comment. Anyway it's really no business of ours. We have no right to be discussing it.'

'I realise that, but it's so strange that Diane should lie to her daughters, telling them they were born in our Guernsey house when they were born in hospital by section. You see what I mean? So many lies . . . so much deception. Charming you thought them?' She smiled wryly.

Grant stared at her for some time wondering why she had chosen to unburden her thoughts to him. 'I really don't feel comfortable discussing it, frankly.'

Glancing at him, Meg suddenly felt embarrassed by her outburst. Why had she done it? 'You're quite right,' she said quickly. 'I know you'll say nothing of this discussion to Terry. Please forgive me if I overstepped the mark in telling you.'

For all her apology, he sensed she had acted not just from curiosity but from revenge. He was close to Terry, and Meg thought somehow that through him she could strike at Diane and John for the wrong done to her own mother. Well, she would have to think again.

At that moment Terry entered the kitchen, her softly gathered moss green skirt topped by its matching blouse and a heavy wool cardigan flung over her shoulders. Her blonde hair was combed loose and fell softly to her jawline; her face, in spite of the sleepless night, looking bright and softly made up.

To Grant she was manna from Heaven and the relief must have shown on his face. He wanted to sweep her into his arms and kiss her passionately.

She flashed him a radiant smile. 'Sorry I kept you waiting.' Not as sorry as I am, he thought.

Meg laughed. 'Don't worry! We've had a very interesting chat. And you're only late because you were kind enough to wash all those dishes. Lovely seeing you again, Terry. Don't make it too long before your next visit.' She turned to Grant. 'So nice meeting you. Enjoy yourselves.' Waving as they walked down the stairs, she heard Terry call up to her.

'Thanks for having me.'

The front door opened and closed. Meg stood on the landing for a moment, hoping Grant would keep all she had said not only to himself but in the forefront of his mind. He would do both, she told herself. She had calculated it just right.

Chapter Twelve

Standing in an unprepossessing Greenwich side street, the antiques shop was hardly fashionable with its tables of bric-a-brac and a collection of furniture which in many cases could only be rated second to jumble. Yet amongst it all were one or two treasures which only a sharp and knowledgeable eye could detect. It was Grant's favourite place to browse.

The owner, a tall, thin middle-aged man, recognised Grant immediately, greeted him then led him to the rear of the shop, where, in the corner of another room, stood a large mahogany kneehole desk.

'It was made around 1875 so can't be called antique just yet,' the owner said. 'But I think it's rather what you had in mind, Dr Kenway.'

Grant examined the desk thoroughly, testing each of the six deep drawers for ease of movement then running an appreciative hand across the green and gold leather top which had seen much use over the years. It was exactly what he'd had in mind. With Terry beside him, both looked for any tell-tale sign of woodworm.

The owner smiled. 'It's in perfect condition. I've checked it out very carefully. Well made too. Came from Brandon House up on Blackheath. House and contents were auctioned last week after Sir Hugh Pennythorne died. He was in his late-nineties.'

Grant looked even more interested. 'Pennythorne? Good Lord.' Turning to Terry, he said, 'Another sawbones. Started his career in the old hold 'em down, blood and sawdust days. Became something of a pioneer in surgical techniques.' After some careful thought, he asked the owner how much he was asking.

When the deal was done and a date and time set for the desk to be delivered to Grant's flat, Terry settled back in the car, wondering how large this flat was to take such a solid piece of Victoriana.

'Fifteen pounds?' She glanced at Grant questioningly. 'That seems a lot for a non-antique, and no-one likes old furniture these days.'

He shook his head. 'I've always had a hankering to own a piece like that, and now I've got old Pennythorne's I feel it must be a good omen.' Starting the ignition, he sniffed the air appreciatively. 'God, what a marvellous day! Let's get out of these dreary streets.'

Greenwich Park was popular with families on that bright Sunday morning as she and Grant wandered there, talking and laughing, totally at ease with each other. On the hill they stood looking down at the Queen's House in the distance and beyond that the grand Palladian buildings of Wren's Royal Naval College. Then Grant led her to the Royal Observatory and the building which straddled the meridian line. Placing herself directly before the plaque which marked the line itself, Terry said, 'I suppose this means I'm neither here nor there?'

She turned to him and their eyes held before Grant cleared his throat and said, in a strange voice, 'Time, as well as longitude, is marked from this point.' He shaded his eyes from the sun and pointed to the roof of the Meridian Building. 'If you look up, you'll see the red marker at the masthead? I gather it's lowered each day at 1300 hours so that vessels passing on the Thames can check the correct time.' Placing his hands firmly on her shoulders he turned her slightly so that she could look up at the marker. 'Do you see?'

Yes, she could see. Here, where east met west and pips and red markers heralded the true hour, she was suddenly no longer neither here nor there, but as grounded in certainty as Greenwich Meantime itself. With his hands still on her, warm and secure, her feelings were growing for this man, one she hardly knew. Yet she had the strangest sensation that she had always known him and that, for good or ill, he would change her life. They left the park at noon, and drove through narrow streets of old warehouses until they came to the the Angel at Rotherhithe. The popular pub was crowded and they had to wait with drinks in their hands before finding somewhere to sit.

Staring out on the Thames, Terry's eyes strayed to the outline of Tower Bridge, trying to come to terms with her discovery. She was in love again only this time it was a love far deeper than anything she had felt for Alastair. So why was it that, in spite of this, there was a disturbing undertaste to this love which left her at a loss? Was it fear of rejection, or a foreshadowing of something worse? He would change her life, but now?

Having no appetite after Meg's huge breakfast, she settled for a glass of light ale, pushed unpleasant thoughts away and gave herself up to the moment. Today was today and he was here. That was everything.

Having tried without success to encourage Terry to eat, Grant settled for beer and sandwiches, then lit a cigarette, leaned back and studied the young woman seated opposite him. Meg had said Terry was troubled but right now she looked radiant, her soft eyes belying any tension. It begged the question why any mother should lie to such a daughter. Yet Diane, it seemed, had lied. So too had John Fenton, a man Grant had come to admire because of the memorial. Damn that nurse for unloading her worries on to him so that now he found himself concerned! Concerned about what, though? That was the devil of it. It was unsettling knowing there was a problem, yet not knowing what it was.

All he did know was that his feelings for Terry were growing. Odd that. He would never have thought her his type. Maybe it had something to do with her stillness and those grave eyes. Whatever it was, he didn't want this, not yet, not after the heartbreak of two years ago when love had not worked out. He could never go through that hell again.

Even so, until he had met Terry his feelings for Louise had not really changed. They had been together a long time but he was too poor and up to his neck in work and study even to think of marriage then, and so she had tired of her hard-working doctor and found someone richer with more time for her. When that relationship petered out, she had rung him at the start of this year, hoping to renew their relationship. Remembering the pain, he was too cautious to get burned again, but Louise was persistent.

Then had come that snowbound day at Thornley and everything changed. Louise had not given up, however, and throughout these past weeks, when he should have been concentrating hard for his Fellowship exam, he had been emotionally torn. It wasn't easy casting aside someone he'd once expected to marry, but now there was Terry. She'd been fixed in his thoughts long before the snow had melted. What about the age difference, though? Ten years was a long time. Ten! Terry had been that age when he was doing his National Service, for goodness' sake. What did she know of the world? Was he being selfish wanting this relationship with a very young woman who should be out partying with men her own age? Grant's hell-raising days were over. Work, study, golf and cricket had become his lot. She probably saw him as middle-aged. In a very short time she would become bored with him, and then the pain would start all over again. Better to cut out the source right now and allow this patient to recover. But how could he cut out his own heart?

Later they drove in silence towards Sloane Square, then Grant turned into Cadogan Place and stopped outside the Hammonds' London home. For some time neither of them moved but sat staring ahead, each dreading to say goodbye.

'Why the devil do you live so far away?' he said at last.

Terry heard the tension in his voice, felt tears welling up and blinked them back. When he said nothing about their meeting again, she became desperate. Afraid she would frighten him off if he knew her true feelings, she spoke of the tickets Marisa had given her, trying to sound casual and failing dismally. It was fate, thought Grant, fate in the shape of theatre tickets bringing them together once more. Well, perhaps he would let fate take the helm and pray their ship avoided the rocks.

'I'll check my hours on call and let you know.' He smiled, then winked. 'I'll swing it somehow, believe me.' At that moment he knew that neither hell nor high water would keep him away.

Terry wanted to stay with him until the last possible moment and was on the verge of asking him inside to meet her sister. But the thought died even as it was born. Marisa could never be trusted in that respect again.

Neither saw the slight movement of a curtain at a window above them.

Still trying to recall the events of last night's party through an alchoholic haze, Alastair had been struggling to work at his desk before returning to Coventry. All about him were pictures of motors old and new, signed photos of racing drivers and silver models of earlier Hammond sports cars. His hangover was taking a long time to go and he vowed he would never touch a drop again. For one thing it kept him here when he could have been on his way to Coventry. As it was, he had taken sanctuary in the one room his wife knew better than to enter. She, meanwhile, was curled up on the sofa with the Sunday papers, only leaving it to answer the telephone which had rung five times today.

Hearing a car draw up outside the house, Alastair went to the window, his shoulder catching the curtain as he looked down on the street below. Seeing Terry, his heart stopped momentarily. Then he saw a man climb out of the MG and walk round to open the passenger door. The man held Terry's hand for some time, talking to her while she looked up at him with eyes that said everything.

His world turning to sudden frost, Alastair turned away. He waited in suspense for the car to drive off and the doorbell to ring. The seconds ticked by slowly and his eyes stared unseeing at the far wall, now dominated by a large photograph of himself racing at Snetterton.

Finally the moment came. He heard Marisa's voice as she greeted her sister.

For all her slight hangover, Marisa looked as lovely as ever as her eyes scanned the square in disappointment. 'Where is he? Didn't you invite him in?'

'He had to get back to the hospital,' said Terry, entering the hall and hoping with all her heart that Alastair was in Coventry or on a circuit somewhere.

Marisa was not fooled. Aware that her sister was keeping the new man in her life from her, she beckoned Terry into the house, saying tartly, 'I was disappointed enough when you phoned this morning to say you wouldn't be here before three o'clock. Well, it's way past that and you haven't brought him either! You won't have much time to see the place now. It's Sunday, remember. You'll have to hang around for ages at Ipswich for that Woodbridge train. You should have come earlier.'

'I'll phone Dad and ask him to pick me up at Ipswich.'

'Oh, I daresay he'll put himself out for you,' said Marisa dryly.

Coat over her arm and still carrying her overnight case, Terry entered the drawing room for the first time. She stood for a moment, looked around and said how lovely the room was. 'So light and elegant. Did you arrange the flowers yourself?'

'You're joking! Mrs Mount is my particular angel. She cooks, cleans and arranges flowers too. She took a course apparently. Marvellous woman. Can't imagine how I'd manage without her. So you like this room, do you? I'm not sure I do. The furniture's horribly old-fashioned. I'd have it changed tomorrow if I could.'

'No, you mustn't,' said Terry, frowning.

'Well said.'

The voice from behind made her swivel round. Alastair was leaning casually against the door frame. His expression was grim. 'What's this then? Surprise visit?'

Terry fought down the unwelcome lurch her heart had given, and knew suddenly that she could face this man at last. 'Hardly a surprise.' Her voice was deliberately light and casual.

With an accusing glance at his wife, he said, 'You didn't tell me Terry was expected?'

Marisa shrugged. 'I would have done had you not been hiding away in your study all day. As it was, I didn't think you'd still be here at this hour, so there seemed no point.' She turned to her sister. 'You could have stayed here last night as Mother wanted. We were out but Mrs Mount would have let you in. She has Sundays off but is here until breakfast, so you wouldn't have been alone.' Her eyes narrowed. 'Where exactly did you stay?'

'Let me take your coat and suitcase,' said Alastair quickly. 'I'll put them in the bedroom.'

'Thank you.' Relieved that this long-dreaded meeting was not the traumatic event she had feared it would be, Terry pushed the sleeves of her cardigan up to her elbows. 'I must look a mess but we've walked a long way today. How's work going on the new car, Alastair?'

Trying to fight anger and jealousy, he blinked at the unexpected question. 'You remember that, do you?' His eyes softened as he looked at her. 'It was going like a dream but cornering is still a problem and . . .'

'Oh, Alastair, don't be such a bore!' said Marisa, lighting a cigarette. 'My sister doesn't want to hear all that nonsense. Now then, Terry, tell me what you've been up to and I'll make some tea.'

Seeing Alastair's eyes glint dangerously at this put down, Terry knew then that her suspicions about this marriage were all too true. Only someone as insensitive as Marisa could be unaware of that. Alastair stood for some moments then slowly walked out of the room, carrying the coat and case. She saw no more of him until after her tour of the house when Marisa was preparing tea in the kitchen.

Settling herself on one of the sofas before the blazing fire, Terry stiffened as he returned to the room and sat opposite, staring at her. If he didn't find it embarrassing then she did. At last she forced a smile. 'Do tell me more about the car? I am interested, truly.'

He leaned forward, hands clasped loosely together between his legs. 'I don't want to talk about the bloody car! This is the first time we've been alone since the wedding and I've things to say to you.'

'You've nothing to say to me,' she said quickly.

'God, you know I have. From the moment you walked into the church that day, I realised what a bloody fool I'd been. I don't know what happened. It's you . . . it's always been you, only I just didn't realise it until . . . I mean, you did have some feelings for me too, surely?'

'Madeira cake and smoked salmon sandwiches, Will that be all right?'

Marisa was wheeling a trolley into the room, her eyes on the silver teapot which seemed a shade unsteady as one wheel refused to glide as easily as the others. Looking up, she saw Alastair's eyes fixed on Terry. The expression in them shook her to the core. That her sister had cared for Alastair had never been in doubt but that he could ever have felt anything for Terry had never crossed her mind. In that brief moment her world fell apart.

For Terry, tea was horrendous. She found herself chatting in a strained voice while Alastair never took his eyes off her and Marisa sat smoking in sullen silence. Finding it an impossible situation and wishing she had stayed until the last with Grant, she finally stood up to go.

'I really must get moving if I'm to catch that train.'

Alastair was on his feet at once. 'I'll run you to the station.'

Marisa glared at him. 'You can't. You've work to do before returning to Coventry. I'll drive Terry.'

'No. I've done as much work as I can today,' he said.

'I'll take it with me and go straight on to Coventry after I drop her off.'

Feeling a sense of panic, Terry said quickly, 'There's no need. I can take a taxi.'

'Nonesense!' said Alastair, rushing into the bedroom. He returned with Terry's coat and suitcase then shot into the study to collect his bulging briefcase. Slipping on his jacket and ignoring Marisa's furious expression, he moved to the door, telling her he would ring when he arrived at the Coventry house. 'Don't forget to lock up carefully.' After that he looked at Terry and said, 'Well, let's go.'

London was quiet and free from traffic on that sunny Sunday afternoon as the Hammond moved slowly towards Liverpool Street station. For some moments Alastair said nothing, and Terry glanced at her watch anxiously, wondering why the speed king next to her was keeping to exactly twenty-seven miles an hour. Oh, if only he was Grant . . . if only . . .

'Where exactly did you stay last night?' Alastair asked quietly.

'With a friend.' She shot him a dark glance. 'What's this, brotherly concern?'

For a while there was silence then Alastair sighed and shook his head. 'You didn't answer my question.'

'I don't intend to,' she retorted.

After a moment he murmured, 'I can't imagine what you must think of me.'

Terry shot him a dark look. 'I think of you as my brother-in-law.'

'Don't. Please don't. At the wedding your eyes said everything and I knew how much I'd hurt you. But I'm paying for it now. My life with Marisa is hopeless. It's you I want.'

'You've taken a wrong turning,' she said sharply. 'In more ways than one, I think.' Alastair cursed loudly, did a fast U-turn, causing the car behind him to hit the horn, and headed back on course as Terry went on. 'Yes, I felt pain when you left Marisa to flash her engagement ring at me. A word from you might have helped. However, you broke no rules save that of good manners. But you're breaking them now.' She glanced at her watch and cried, 'For goodness' sake, get out of third gear or I'll miss my train!'

At the station forecourt she was climbing out of the car before Alastair had time to bring it to a stop. He called after her to remember the suitcase. Snatching it from him, she ran into the station and, waving her ticket at the gate inspector, rushed on to the platform. With just thirty seconds to spare she climbed on board the Ipswich train and sank breathlessly into a corner seat.

As the whistle blew, Terry gazed through the window, thinking of Alastair alone in his car with the long drive to Coventry ahead of him. The train started and her thoughts whirled round and round. What sort of man would confess to wanting his wife's sister? Dear God!

Grant's face swam before her, wonderful, gentle Grant who was going to change the pattern of her life for the better. She was free of Alastair at last.

The final scheduled operation of the morning was over. Hoping he would have time for lunch and to catch up on his reports before tackling the gall bladders awaiting him that afternoon, Grant pulled off his gloves, threw them into the bin, then allowed the theatre sister to remove his mask and untie his gown.

The morning's surgery had gone smoothly in spite of his mind constantly wandering back to Meg's words. 'They tell her lies . . .' The words were still with him as he stood in the ward office with the Sister, checking the notes of patients listed for afternoon theatre. When she left him there, his mind returned to Meg. Four days ago he had sat in that dreary kitchen listening to her strange ramblings and ever since then hadn't been able to drive them from his mind.

Trying to focus his thoughts on the work in hand, he wrote up two sets of notes then paused, pen tapping the table top. Yet it had to be said that she was right. No way would Diane have been sent to the Westlake Clinic with her medical history. That must be a mistake. Yet it was one he could easily check up on. Reaching out for the telephone beside him, he asked the hospital switchboard operator to put him through to the Westlake.

During the thirty minutes it took for the clinic to seek the information he required, Grant continued checking notes and asking himself what right he had to pry into someone else's life. Diane Fenton was not his patient, even though he had told the clinic she was. He had no right, no right at all, and yet this woman was lying to her daughter, and he loved that girl. By the time he rang back, he had convinced himself that he did have the right. For Terry's sake.

Listening to the report of Eliot's birth Grant frowned in disbelief. 'Primigravida? My understanding is that Mrs Fenton had had two previous babies delivered by section.' The slightly miffed female voice replied, 'Diane Alice Fenton, Lynwood Farm, Thornley in Suffolk? The date, May 1945.'

'Yes, that's correct.'

'According to her notes she was thirty-five and this was her first child. Mrs Fenton was admitted two days before labour began. Labour was twenty-six hours. NVD. No complications. Baby weighed 9lbs 7oz at birth and was healthy. No post-natal problems. Mother and baby went home after four days.'

It took Grant some time to register this then he pulled himself together and said, 'I see. Does the report mention a bad accident sustained by Mrs Fenton some years ealier?'

'No. Nothing here. All it says, I've told you.' She paused and said in icy tones, 'This is the second time this week I've had this file out so I know it's the right one, Dr Kenway. But do you have the right patient?'

'Wait . . . did you say you'd had this file out earlier. Why?'

'There was another query, much the same as yours. Only this was from Guy's Hospital.'

'Guy's?' Grant sighed. Meg. Who else? 'No, no. It's a case that seems to have involved two hospitals. Maybe that's where the confusion has arisen. You're absolutely sure the information on that file hasn't in some way got mixed up with that of another woman with the same name?'

The tone softened. 'Ninety-nine per cent sure, but I will cross check, just in case. It may take some time, though.'

Grant thought about this then said, 'No. The confusion seems to be at this end. Forget about it for now. If I have to get back to you, I will. Meanwhile, thank you for all your help.'

Walking to the Doctors' Mess he tried to make sense of everything. There was only one explanation. Eliot had to be the result of an illegal adoption and the woman posing as Diane Fenton at the clinic was probably a friend of hers who, after a love affair with a serviceman, had found herself pregnant. How many illegitimate children had been born during the war? he wondered. And so Diane had adopted the son she had wanted. Even so this explanation posed further questions. Was Diane's local doctor in on the whole thing? If not, how could she get away with a fake pregnancy in such a small community?

During lunch Grant's mind worked away. Why, at a time when there must have been many unwanted babies needing adoption, did two women go through all this cloak and dagger stuff when the Fentons could legally have adopted the son they wanted and the woman could have put her own child up for adoption through an agency? As it was both women were now tied into a lie. Crazy! He sipped his coffee, frowning as he stared ahead, ignoring his colleagues eating and chatting around him. Meg! Damn it, she knew too. Would she say anything to Terry?

Meg was just about to go on night duty when the telephone rang in the untidy sitting room. She rushed to answer it and heard Grant's voice.

'Look, this is difficult but I'm asking you a great favour. Whatever you know about Terry's mother, I want you to keep to yourself.'

'Oh?' On full alert, she said, 'What do I know then?'

'What we both know and from the same source. You've surely drawn the same conclusion.'

'There's only one conclusion. That boy is adopted.'

'I don't want this to get back to Terry.'

'What we know we don't talk about. That's a breach of trust. And, as I said before, it's none of our business.'

'I've no intention of saying anything,' came the stiff reply. 'As a qualified nurse I do know about ethics.'

'Of course. I'm sorry. Goodnight, Meg.'

Grant replaced the receiver, not liking the way she had sounded. She was eaten up with a palpable sense of injustice and there was no telling what she would do next.

Work on the memorial site was almost finished and seven newly planted oaks now stood among the bright green winter wheat of Five Acre Field. In front of them was a horseshoe of low stepped flower beds where the children of Thornley's primary school had planted shrubs that would bring colour for each season. All that was needed now was for the memorial stone itself to be laid in place.

Things were not going so well on the murder investigation, however, and Sergeant Hopwood despaired. If promotion rested on the solving of this case, then he could kiss it goodbye. At forty and once passed over he knew the Chief Detective Inspector had handed the file to him because it seemed a hopeless case from the start. What clues there ever had been would have disappeared years ago, along with the gun used to kill the victims. They had searched the woods and found nothing. As for missing persons, those in East Anglia did not fit into the case or had been accounted for years later. The search would now be widened.

There had been one brief ray of sunlight, though, when it was discovered that a man, missing from Ipswich for twenty-five years, matched the height and build of one skeleton. Dental records soon ruled him out, however, and Hopwood was back to square one.

Naturally, the whole sorry tale was printed in the *Lowdham and District Chronicle*.

When Terry read it she frowned, searched the drawer of the hall table for Sergeant Hopwood's number, then dialled and asked to be put through to him. He was out, she was told, and so left a message explaining about Mrs Shotley and the storm-felled trees.

'Mr Fenton did ring about this before but clearly the message didn't get through. So could you make sure that Sergeant Hopwood gets it? What's that? Mrs Shotley's address? Yes, of course. It's Laurel Cottage, High Street, Thornley. No, she doesn't own a telephone, but if you need her in a hurry you can always contact us and we'll get in touch with her.'

Diane's nerves were at breaking point as she watched John pacing the kitchen like a caged lion. When his fist came down on the table top, she almost jumped out of her skin.

'Why in God's name does Terry do these things?' he bellowed. 'I told her to leave it to me.'

'She did,' snapped Diane. 'And you did nothing. Now we shall have the Sergeant back again.'

It had been just after eight-fifteen when Terry, leaving for school, had paused on the threshold and dropped this little bombshell into her mother's lap before beating a hasty retreat. It had fallen to Diane to pass the news to John, his reaction all too predictable.

Now he stared through the kitchen window and slowly his anger slipped away. 'Perhaps he'll leave us alone. What difference can a few years make? Trees or no trees, they haven't a hope in hell of solving this one and Hopwood knows it.' He sighed and looked at the sky. 'Looks like heavy weather coming up.'

It was during the morning break, that dark skies sent down a hail storm which had girls racing across Dame Edith's lawns for shelter inside the school. In an effort to help one pupil from her own class to pick up the books she had dropped, Terry ran out of the main building and down a flight of stone steps, not realising the hail had made them slippery. Suddenly her feet shot out before her and she fell to the ground in a crumpled heap, right leg buckled beneath her and hail beating down relentlessly.

The girl ran for help. It was Terry's misfortune to be driven home by Miss Yeats herself.

'Your parents will have to fetch your car,' the Head told her tersely. 'Miss Beddoes will take your English lesson and I, no doubt, will have to take History. It's all very unfortunate with Mrs. Burton off sick as well. Get a doctor to look at that ankle as soon as possible. Shouldn't think it's more than a sprain, but it will need resting. We can count ourselves lucky you didn't break your leg.'

At the door, a startled Diane helped her hobbling daughter into the house, then thanked Miss Yeats, who was anxious to return to the school.

'How on earth did you do it?' Diane asked. She listened to the explanation as she settled Terry on the sofa in the sitting room and set the cushions at her back. 'Pity you didn't leave the girl to pick up her own books. Comfortable? I'll call Dr Tranmer right away, then bring you some painkillers.'

Wincing with pain as the ankle was examined, Terry heard their family doctor pronounce that it was badly sprained and she must stay off it for a week at least.

'But I can't!' wailed Terry. 'They're short-staffed and . . .'

'Now they'll be even shorter,' said Dr Tranmer. 'Be good, Terry. Do as I tell you, just as you did when you broke your arm that time. If you like, I'll bring you some crutches for later on.'

When John's work on the farm ended for the day, Diane caught him at the kitchen door as he took off his boots. 'Don't you dare take out your anger on her now. She's in terrible pain, poor thing, and all because she ran to help one of the girls.'

John washed his hands. 'I daresay I can be trusted to say hello to our invalid. Pour me a beer, will you, and watch the head on it this time.' He paused at the doorway. 'And don't worry, I shan't bite her ears off.'

'Don't mention the subject at all,' said Diane with obvious misgiving.

It was almost nine o'clock in the evening when the telephone rang. Terry could only sit and listen as her mother's voice drifted through from the hall.

'I'm afraid not. She's sprained her ankle. Had a fall at school and can't walk.' There was a long pause during which Terry became agitated. Who was it? Grant? Marisa perhaps? Not Meg, please God. No, Grant . . . she just knew it was him and her mother had taken charge. 'Yes . . . oh, I see. I'll tell her. How are you? Oh, dear . . . yes, well, I'm not surprised'.

Eventually Diane re-entered the room to see her daughter's worried expression. 'Grant, dear. He's sorry to hear about your ankle.'

'And?' Terry's eyes were wide.

'And what?'

'Well . . . what else did he say?'

Diane switched on the television. 'Nothing much.' She frowned and picked up the *Radio Times*. 'Except to tell you that he's a Mr again and you'd understand. Oh, good, there's a Gary Cooper film on soon.'

Terry's elation was followed by sinking despair. He had wanted to tell her his wonderful news while she, like Prometheus bound to a rock, had been a mere few feet away, unable to congratulate him and share in his joy.

Settling herself in an armchair, Diane turned to Terry and frowned. 'This one's important to you, isn't he?' The question was answered by a slight nod. 'He seems a decent man and we both like him but he is older than you so be careful.' She sighed and added, 'Life has a way of not turning out as you expect.' With that, she picked up her sewing and fell silent.

Terry was staring at her in surprise. 'You and Dad . . . you're happy, aren't you?' When Diane made no reply, she repeated, 'Aren't you?'

'My dear, we make the best of things as many others do.' She wanted to add that they were bound to each other, come what may, but turned instead to Terry and said, 'And your interference in things that don't concern you doesn't make life any easier between us.'

'What do you mean?'

'You shouldn't have rung the police. Your father told you to leave matters to him.' She glanced at the clock. 'Do you need more painkillers? It's over four hours since your last lot.'

It wasn't just the pain in her ankle that kept Terry awake that night, but those strange words of warning. Marisa had always said their mother had thrown herself away on a man who didn't love her. It seemed now she had been right.

Terry sat up slowly and drank from the tumbler on her bedside table. How could she have been so unaware of her mother's unhappiness? Why had she had stumbled blindly through life filled with her own worries, not seeing what should have been so obvious? But then, her parents never rowed unless Marisa had been the cause. Most of the time they sat in silence, one she had assumed to be one of contentment, not contempt.

In the middle of the night Diane awakened suddenly and, looking across to John's bed, saw it was empty. At that moment she heard footsteps beneath her window and, glancing out, saw his dark figure on the moonlit track. She knew then he was heading towards the windmill. She also knew what it was he carried so carefully.

The following morning, Diane helped Terry to bathe and dress, and told her to stay on the bed. But Terry insisted on making a slow and painful progress down the stairs, trying not to put pressure on her ankle.

Having some trouble with the sitting-room fire, Mrs Godwin was holding a sheet of newspaper in front of it to draw up the flames. Just as it seemed the whole thing would catch alight, she crumpled it quickly and stood back with a frown.

'Chimney needs sweeping, that's the trouble. You can smell the soot in ere.' With that she watched vacantly as Diane helped her daughter back to the sofa, then sniffed. 'Painful, is it? Well, it'll give you a long weekend at least. Wouldn't mind a rest myself.'

'I'm about to make coffee so you can have one now,' said Diane testily.

At ten minutes past eleven, Terry had drifted into sleep at last. She did not hear the car entering the drive or the doorbell ring. She did not hear her mother's surprised voice or see Grant enter the sitting room and look down at her, concern written on his face.

'She's had a bad night,' whispered Diane. 'I think the painkillers have probably made her drowsy too.'

'Then don't wake her,' he whispered back. 'I'll go, and return later.'

'Go where?' Diane smiled and shook her head. 'Come into the kitchen. I'll put the kettle on. John's out and about on the farm at the moment but he usually comes in around this time for a break. I'll wake Terry up in a while. You've come a very long way. I'm sure she'll be pleased to see you.'

Grant sat down at the kitchen table. 'How did the accident happen?'

Diane told him, bustling about with cups and saucers as she talked, and he found himself looking at her with new eyes. But it was difficult to equate this good-looking, kind woman with the Diane Meg had conjured up. Had she really set out to deceive her own children? He found it hard to believe as they chatted over coffee and biscuits like two old friends. In that moment he might have thought the whole thing a figment of mad Meg's imagination, had it not been for the medical report from the Westlake.

Later, in the stillness of the sitting room, he sat on a chair beside the sofa watching Terry as she slept. With her pale face free of make up she looked so achingly young and so at peace that he hadn't the heart to wake her as Diane had urged that he should before resuming her many chores. It was an hour later when Grant saw Terry stir. He longed to take her in his arms but contented himself with taking her small hand in his. At last she opened her eyes and looked into his.

'The prognosis is not good,' he said solemnly. 'In fact, I'd say the case was hopeless. I let you out of my sight and look at the result.'

Blinking in disbelief, she raised her head from the cushions and laughed. 'Good God. When did you arrive?'

'I left soon after seven with one day's grace only before I'm on call again for the weekend. And you, dear lady, are sleeping it away.'

Struggling back to wakefulness, Terry squeezed his hand. 'I'm sorry. You should have hit me or something. The exam!' She beamed at him, her whole face lighting up. 'Congratulations, Mr Grant Kenway, FRCS. Did you celebrate with your friends?'

He laughed. 'We had a small but riotous party.' Glancing down at her foot, he saw the crêpe bandage had worked loose. Carefully he unbound it then slid his fingers gently across the ankle, placing pressure here, moving the joint this way and that, testing her reaction before binding it firmly once more. 'Slight sprain, some swelling and bad bruising. Time and rest are the only healers. Are you warm enough? Shall I fetch a blanket for you?'

She found his concern touching and his touch concerning. 'I'm fine now that the fire's finally going. But I can't believe you drove all this way to see me. I'm glad you did, though,' she whispered. 'So glad.'

Grant touched her face gently then let his fingers slide along her cheek to her neck. Her hand closed on his quickly. He moved closer, lifted her chin and kissed her warmly on the lips. She raised her hands to his neck then sat up as his arms went about her. His kiss was hot and swept her away on a cloud of emotion and desire. She wanted the moment to last longer but the sound of footsteps cut it short. Releasing her, Grant sat back on his chair as Diane entered the room.

'Ah, awake at last. This poor man's been sitting here forever.' Frowning, she looked through the window. 'Thought I heard a car. I did. Now who on earth . . .?' Her shoulders sagged as she saw who was walking towards the door. 'Oh, no.'

Terry forced her eyes from Grant's face and glanced up. 'Who is it?'

'That Detective Sergeant . . . what's his name?

'Hopwood.'

'And he's brought Mrs Shotley with him.' Darting an accusing glance at Terry, Diane went to the door.

She let out a long sigh and whispered, 'Oh, Lord, I didn't expect him to come back here. I shouldn't have rung, but Dad's message didn't get through.'

'I haven't the faintest idea what you're talking about,' said Grant, exasperated at this unwelcome intrusion and feeling he would now be expected to make himself scarce.

'Stay with me whatever happens,' whispered Terry as footsteps sounded in the hallway. 'Please stay with me.'

Surprised and worried by the intensity of her voice, he squeezed her hand and whispered, 'I'll stay.'

Diane ushered Sergeant Hopwood and Mrs Shotley into the sitting room, introduced them to Mr Kenway, a family friend, bade them sit down but remained standing herself. 'Clearly you received my daughter's message. And presumably Mrs Shotley has told you about the storm?'

As she spoke, Grant thought her smile a shade too brittle and noticed her hands clenching and unclenching at her sides.

Hopwood sat down and placed his trilby on his lap. 'Indeed, Mrs Shotley has been most helpful, but I would like to talk to your husband, Mrs Fenton.'

'But why?' asked Diane. 'I really don't see that he can add anything to what Mrs Shotley has told you. The storm happened before we came here.'

'Even so, I think Mr Fenton should be here.'

Diane looked hesitant. 'Yes . . . of course. He's somewhere on the farm at the moment so you must bear with me while I find him.'

With that, she entered the kitchen, pulled on her boots, then leaving through the rear door, stepped along the track now muddy from early-morning rain. She saw John heading towards her from the direction of Five Acre Field.

When they met her face was grim. 'He's back and wants to see you,' she said in a terse voice. 'It seems Mrs Shotley's information is of importance to him after all because he's brought her with him. Oh, and we have a guest. Grant has driven all the way from London to see Terry, so you can't throw him out any more than you can banish me to the hen house.'

John stopped dead in his tracks and glared at her. 'Hopwood, Kenway, Mrs Shotley and Mrs Godwin? Why don't we just invite the whole bloody village?' With that he turned and strode towards the house, leaving Diane following slowly and reluctantly behind him.

Having changed into shoes and washed, John entered the sitting room, greeted Hopwood and Grant affably then settled on the chair beside the desk. 'So, you received my daughter's message?'

'Yes, sir. I understand you phoned also. When exactly was that?'

John frowned, then shrugged. 'Can't say for certain, but I think it must have been the day after I heard about the storm, whenever that was. Couldn't get hold of you so I left a message.'

Asking permission to light a cigarette and receiving it, Hopwood took his time over his task then replaced the lighter in his pocket, and stared at John curiously. 'Strange. It's standard practice to log all messages. Yours, it seems, was not entered.'

John's lips worked and a thin smile took the place of affability. 'Someone forgot.'

'If he did he's in serious trouble. All police messages are logged, Mr Fenton.' The voice was calm but firm. 'They could be used in evidence.'

Anger now got the better of John. 'Well, clearly the system broke down. Can't say I'm surprised. Anyone listening to me going on about fallen oaks might well have thought me a half wit and just not bothered to log it. I don't see that your coming all the way here helps in any way at all. This old story about a storm can't be of any real consequence.'

Hopwood smiled in a practised manner that said he was not smiling at all deep down. 'On the contrary, it could be of great consequence.'

Pull the other one, thought John grimly. Who did this man think he was kidding? 'In what way?'

With a sense of discomfort at sitting in on this embarrassing conversation, Grant's eyes were fixed on John Fenton. The man had lied about that call, he thought, and nothing he said could conceal that.

Mrs Shotley stood up and looked impatient. 'Are we going to the wood or not? Only I always go to see my sister on Fridays and she'll wonder where I am.'

Diane frowned. 'Stay here by the fire, Mrs Shotley, and let the men go.'

'Can't think why you've got a fire,' the old lady retorted. 'It's warm outside, warmer out than in.'

'You ask why it's of consequence, Mr Fenton,' Hopwood was saying. 'Mrs Shotley will explain.'

The old lady looked thoughtful, then light dawned. 'Oh, yes, that. Well, it was Terry who said it. Do you remember, dear, when I showed you the place?'

Mystified, she looked up at the old lady. 'Said what?'

Hopwood bent to an ashtray and stubbed out his cigarette. 'Something about soft earth, I believe.'

'Oh.' Terry cast her mind back. 'It was the ground, you see, the ground where the trees were uprooted. that made a clearing and the earth would have been soft at that time for digging. Since the grave was in that spot it must mean the murders took place soon after the ground was cleared and before the earth hardened again. That would pinpoint the time more accurately.' In the silence that followed she felt certain she had just made a complete fool of herself and, biting her bottom lip nervously, asked, 'Well, wouldn't it?'

Hopwood said quietly, 'Yes. It would. It would also point to a local man or someone who had access to the wood.' He looked at John. 'But you don't allow people on your property.'

He smiled wryly. 'I don't, but I can't speak for my predecessor. All this happened in his time, remember. In any case, notices threatening prosecution don't mean a damned thing to some people if they're hell-bent on taking a short cut across private property. Farmers can't be everywhere at once.'

'What about poachers?'

'A couple,' John told him. 'They lay traps, which angers me, but otherwise they're harmless old souls. And you can rule out a local man. In a community of this size, everyone knows everyone else and their business too. Believe me, half the village knows you're here by now. They would certainly have noticed if any of their number had gone missing, or in this case two. "To lose one may be regarded as a misfortune, to lose both looks like carelessness".'

Grant winced and Hopwood grimaced.

Terry shifted uncomfortably and said, 'It was just a passing thought . . .'

'And a pretty stupid one too,' snapped her father. 'Let the detectives do the detecting, pet.'

Hopwood smiled across at Terry. 'Not so stupid. If the date is correct we can now narrow things not just to within twenty years but to within weeks of the ground being cleared. Good thinking, Miss Fenton. Sorry about your ankle. I hope you'll be up and about again soon. Well, I just want to see the site, that's all, then I'll be off.' He turned to Mrs Shotley and asked her to accompany him. 'You are certain about the date of the storm? It was a long time ago after all.'

Her grey eyebrows arched indignantly. 'Of course I'm certain. I might be getting old but that doesn't mean I'm senile. I've an excellent memory. In any case, a gale like that, which brought tiles off roofs and trees crashing down around our ears, has to be on record.'

'Sergeant, the woods will be very muddy.' Diane looked from him to their former housekeeper. 'Mrs Shotley can wear my boots, and you'll have to make do with a pair of my husband's. He takes size ten.'

'Nine and a half,' said Hopwood. 'Close enough. Thanks.'

She turned to John. 'Come and tell me which ones would be best for the sergeant.'

As he followed her into the kitchen she rounded on him like a whip lash. 'Must you antagonise the man?' she hissed. 'For God's sake, keep a hold on yourself and watch that temper.' 'Just find the bloody boots and get about your own business,' he snapped.

'Watch your temper, that's all I'm saying.' She led him to the vestibule where she chose two pairs of clean boots. 'Here, they can use these. Lead them out the front way. Keep hold of Mrs Shotley's arm or she'll go flying over a root.'

When at last the three of them had set off for the woods, Diane gave Terry a strange look then shook her head and sighed deeply. 'And just when we were beginning to get over it all.' Aware of Grant's presence once more and the fact that her domestic help was probably listening to every word, she forced a smile and said in a rather loud voice, 'Well, I'll go up and see how Mrs Godwin is getting on in the bedrooms.'

When she left, Grant moved from his place near the fireplace and walked over to Terry. Knowing she would be on the receiving end of her father's anger later, he decided to remove her from the house. 'It's a beautiful day out there, and you'll be better in the sunshine than stuck in this smoky overheated room.'

'But I can't walk.'

'Did I say we were going on a hike?' He walked to the doorway and called up the stairs, 'Mrs Fenton? Could I have Terry's coat, a warm blanket and a pillow.' When Diane frowned at him over the banister, he laughed. 'The pillow's to be doubled over to make a rest for her ankle and the blanket is to go over her legs to keep her warm.'

'You're taking her out?' Diane looked at him as though he was mad. 'But the doctor said . . .'

'I'm a doctor too, remember. And I say it'll do her the world of good. Don't worry, I won't let her put any weight on that foot. We'll have lunch somewhere. I won't keep her out too long. That's a promise.'

At the front door Diane stood watching as Grant carried a laughing Terry out to the car and settled her in the passenger seat, foot on pillow, blanket snugly about her waist, silk scarf over her head. They both waved back as he drove the open-topped MG out through the gates and into the lane.

Terry shook her head, still laughing at the ridiculousness of it all. 'Poor Mother. She'll be having a fit.'

Grant grinned as they headed down to the water splash. 'On a day such as this, only the dead should be incarcerated.'

After yesterday's sudden chill and hailstones, today felt like the start of summer. In a cloudless sky the sun shone, blossom was in every garden, and hawthorn flowered on the hedgerows. A light haze of green lifted trees from their winter slumber as new leaves broke through the buds.

Terry looked at the awakening countryside and felt a deep sense of happiness. April, the 'cruellest month', was on its way out and May was coming in on a kinder note. Suddenly life was wonderful and all things were possible. She hardly knew or cared where they were driving. Grant had arrived like a shining knight and gathered her up. The memory of being held close in his arms was fresh and wonderful, so wonderful that she had already forgotten about the wood and her father's anger.

Chapter Thirteen

The pub garden was not well tended. The borders had a few clumps of dead daffodils, the lawn was patchy and the shabby old rabbit hutch in the far corner had no inhabitant, but celandines and daisies growing in wild abandon gave a sense of nature reclaiming her own.

Terry thought it beautiful as she watched bullfinches flying among the branches of apple trees now thick with blossom. As she watched she smiled at the memory of the astonished faces in the public bar when Grant had carried her through it and out into the sunshine. He had then placed her on this wooden garden seat with a pillow beneath her ankle and his folded jacket at her back for support. She lifted her face to the warm sun and closed her eyes, murmuring, 'This is heaven. I could stay all day.'

'They'll throw us out at two,' Grant said.

He sat on the far side of the wooden table which held his pint of beer, her shandy and two plates of cheese and egg sandwiches. They were no longer alone. At a table nearby sat an elderly man and his wife, eating the same dubious sandwiches in a silence that told the world they had nothing left to say to each other. From time to time they glanced with curiosity at the lame woman on the bench seat, their expressions mirroring those of the few people in the pub.

Grant sipped his beer, reached out for a sandwich and examined it suspiciously. 'I wanted to take you to a decent restaurant, but you wouldn't have it.'

'Impossible! Think of the stir we would have made, you carrying me inside like an accident case.'

'Which is exactly what you are.'

'Even so, a pub garden is less public. Anyway, there are no restaurants in this area, unless you count the Mill House at Houghton and that only opens in the evenings.' She frowned suddenly as it dawned on her she was depriving him of a meal. Men in flats didn't cook. 'You will stay with us for dinner before driving back to London?'

He pulled a face. 'I can't. I've surgery first thing tomorrow.' And a showdown with Louise later on, he thought. The prospect was appalling. Just how was he to tell a woman of such persistence that it was all over? That he now loved a quiet young woman who was still inexperienced and too trusting? It was a moment he dreaded.

Terry drank her shandy, saw his troubled expression and told herself that it couldn't have been easy for such a busy man, who had been under so much strain of late, to drive many miles to be with her of just a few hours. He must care, she thought, he must care a great deal, for all that he says nothing of his feelings. But honeyed words of romance were not in his character, she knew that. She sipped more shandy and felt a shadow cloud her happiness. Had that troubled look something to do with witnessing her father's loss of temper? Why not? It hadn't been pleasant to witness. Not so long ago it had sent Alastair packing. Who could say what Grant was making of it?

'I'm sorry for what happened this morning,' she said cautiously. 'It was unlike Dad. He's always been so calm and relaxed, but since those newspaper articles and the hostility he and Mother encountered as a result, he's changed and Sergeant Hopwood seems to set him on a short fuse, I'm afraid. I don't know why. I like the sergeant. He's kind and considerate . . .'

'But not to be underestimated,' said Grant.

She picked up his meaning at once. 'Poor Dad. He's had so much on his plate lately, I think he forgot to make that call and was too embarrassed to say so in front of everyone. He felt caught out and that didn't help his temper one little bit.'

Grant drank his beer in silence, and thought that here, in this badly tended yet strangely beautiful garden on such a day, the last thing he wanted to talk about was John Fenton. He changed the subject quickly. But as they chatted idly he saw how Terry's eyes kept clouding.

'Your ankle hurting?' he asked anxiously. 'Perhaps I was wrong to bring you out after all.'

'No,' she said quickly. 'It's not that.' Frowning, she put the unappetising sandwich back on the plate and looked at him for some time before saying, 'If I ask you a silly question, will you promise not to laugh?'

'That depends.' he answered with mock gravity. 'There are degrees of silliness that can amuse or irritate. Which is yours?'

Picking up her glass, Terry absently ran a forefinger around the rim and murmured, 'It won't have you rolling in the aisles. You'll think it stupid. In fact I never dreamed I would ever think such a thing . . . but . . . well . . . here it is. Do you believe that a place can be evil? Of itself, I mean? Evil in the sense that it draws disaster to it? Please . . . please don't laugh.'

Grant was not laughing. He knew she meant the wood and said quickly, 'No, I don't believe that. Pinning the blame on a place for the evil men do may answer some deep primeval fear buried in all of us, but it's nonsense of course.' He lit a cigarette and looked thoughtful. 'Something to do with sacred groves and the Green Man, I daresay. Odd really, in this day and age, but it's still with us one way or another. Like the dark at the top of the stairs.'

'And strange forebodings?' After a short pause, she stared at him with solemn grey eyes. 'Would that explain the one which keeps pressing on me? Eliot has it too, I know he does. We received a letter from him this morning saying he wanted to spend his next half term with a friend. He's afraid to come home, you see, he's afraid of the wood. Think about it. My father's cousin was accidentally killed in there while shooting, then two people are murdered and buried there, and then the plane crashed within yards of it. So doesn't that mean . . .?' Her voice trailed off.

Grant reached out for her hand and gave it a gentle squeeze. 'The plane was shot to pieces by Germans and crashed in the cornfield, not the wood. As for your father's cousin – well, many people have accidents with shotguns. I should know, I've patched up a few in my time. So, all right, two people were murdered . . . somewhere . . . and buried in the wood.' He paused and smiled wryly. 'But look on the bright side, Terry. At least you don't have plague victims.'

For one moment she stared at him, then her eyes softened. 'It's so good to have you here to force some common sense into my addled brain. You must think me a fool.'

'No, I'm the fool for letting you talk me into eating these sandwiches which are as bad as the beer. I vote we head off to Aldeburgh. I want to see where Benjamin Britten lives and composes. Is it far?'

The day stayed fine for them, only clouding over as they left Aldeburgh and took the fastest road back to Thornley. As they turned into the High Street the church clock was striking the quarter hour. Terry glanced at her watch. 'It's gone five.' Suddenly she stiffened at the sight of a black Riley Saloon outside the newsagent's.

'Oh, hell. That's our doctor's car. Keep going, keep going. Too late.' Dr Tranmer emerged from the shop and stared straight at her in obvious surprise. 'We'll have to stop, I'm afraid.'

As Grant pulled the car into the kerb she grinned up at the plump, grey-haired man who was walking towards them.

'It's all right,' Terry said, smiling. 'Believe me, I'm in very good hands. Mr Kenway is a surgeon. I'll swear he hasn't allowed this foot to touch the ground.' She turned to Grant. 'This is Dr Tranmer who gave me specific orders to stay in and now finds me junketing around Suffolk.'

'Blame me, Doctor. I thought fresh air and sunshine would do more for her than sitting in a stuffy room.'

Tranmer's stern expression lifted into a beaming smile. 'And I'm sure you were right. Which hospital are you at?'

'St Thomas's.'

'Really? Are you staying here for a while?'

Grant shook his head. 'Sadly, no. I'm just about to return.'

'Pity. Nice meeting you, Mr Kenway. Have a safe journey back to London. And, Terry, look after that ankle.'

Grant started the car once more, headed through the water-splash and up the hill towards the farm. Diane came out and bustled around as he carried Terry back inside and placed her on the sofa. He had wanted to hold her longer, kiss her goodbye, but that was impossible and so he chatted politely to her mother, gave Terry a lingering look and left.

Trying to peer through the window she could just see him climbing into the MG then felt her heart sink as the car disappeared from her sight. Suddenly her world had turned to winter once more.

Five minutes later, a grey Morris Minor turned into the drive from which a woman emerged carrying a large bunch of flowers.

'It's Miss Beddoes,' said Terry in surprise.

Miss Beddoes was plump, middle-aged, happy-go-lucky, and one of the most popular teachers in the school. Always ready with a smile, she wore it now like a beacon as she walked into the sitting room and saw Terry.

'And how is the invalid today?'

Hardly able to say that the invalid had just returned from Aldeburgh, Terry thanked her lucky stars that she had arrived back on the sofa before Miss Beddoes found out the truth. She reached out for the flowers, a riot of freesias, jonquils, mimosa and harebells.

'Oh, how lovely!' she gasped. 'Thank you. Thank you very much.'

'They're from the Lower Second. They decided among themselves to bring in their pocket money, have a whip round and detail me to purchase the flowers on their behalf. There's a card and a brief letter too.'

For one moment, Terry was speechless with surprise. 'The girls did this?' She looked at the card, then read the letter which said they were very sorry she had hurt herself and wanted her to get better as soon as possible. Meanwhile they hoped the flowers would cheer her up. Each girl had then signed the letter.

Deeply moved, Terry felt tears come to her eyes. 'What a marvellous thing for them to do.'

Miss Beddoes looked at Diane saying. 'Your daughter is very well liked at the school. Her girls can't wait to ditch me and have her back.' She turned to Terry, smiling. 'From what I've heard you make History and Literature live for them, no mean achievement I can tell you. As for the stragglers, they've improved immensely.' Her smile faded into a slight frown. 'Of course there's still Margaret Temple. She has a long way to go. There's something wrong there. Why should a girl of her intelligence have such difficulty in reading? Anyway, you'll be pleased to know I've persuaded Miss Yeats to agree to your request for one to one sessions with the girl. It's what she needs. In fact I'd like to discuss Margaret with you some time. Meanwhile, I'll leave you in peace. Now rest up and get well.'

Taking the flowers, which had brought the smell of spring into the house, Diane said she would put them in water and make some tea. As she walked into the kitchen she wondered just how many cups of tea and coffee she had made for the bewildering number of people who had visited her home that day.

Heading out on the Lowdham road, Grant drove past field after field, wishing the ache in his heart would vanish. It was getting harder and harder to leave Terry but he asked himself how he could go on facing her until he had put right the the mess in his private life. Louise! Why couldn't she leave him alone and take no for an answer? Instead he faced tears and accusations and being made to feel a heel.

Suddenly he spotted a black Riley parked by the side of the road. The bonnet was up, masking the top half of Dr Tranmer who was staring in bewilderment at the engine.

Pulling over, Grant stopped and walked towards him. 'Having a spot of trouble?'

The grey head emerged from the bonnet and looked up. 'Oh . . . it's you again. Well, how very kind of you to stop. Yes, it's trouble right enough. Car just came to a jerky halt. I'm no mechanic, I'm afraid. Petrol's fine. Last time it was a fuel pump blockage, the time before that it was . . . something else. As you see, I know nothing about cars except that it's time to buy a new one.'

Grant looked under the bonnet and frowned. 'Engine's very hot.' He peered under the car and saw what he had suspected. 'Radiator. You're losing water and the engine's conked out. You'll need a garage mechanic to have it towed back. Where would you like me to drop you?'

Tranmer opened his car door and took out his black bag. 'I was on my way to a case. It's a child. I'm very afraid it could be meningitis.'

'Hop in,' said Grant, opening the passenger door of the MG. 'I'll take you. Do they have a phone?'

'Yes, thank God. I may have to call an ambulance. Goodness, what a relief! This is very kind of you, Mr Kenway. I'm so worried about that child. Go left at the crossroads, then first right.'

As Grant eased the MG through a maze of narrow country lanes, hoping he wouldn't meet anything coming the other way, he wondered if this was the same doctor who must have 'treated' Diane during her non-existent pregnancy.

'This takes me back a bit,' he said. 'My father was a village GP. I learned a lot from him.'

Tranmer smiled wryly. 'I'd hoped my son would follow me into the profession but he had no interest in medicine at all. I'm not as disappointed now as I was then. As a Chartered Accountant he earns twice my salary. Turn right just here, and it's that house set back on the left.'

Grant found himself on a long track heading towards a small red brick farm cottage. 'I'll wait and take you home afterwards.'

'That's very decent of you. My wife has a car, so I can steal that for the rest of the day. But I don't like to keep you since you've a long journey ahead.

'Nonsense. Look, if it is meningitis, let me take the child straight to hospital. Every minute counts.'

Dr Tranmer took his ample frame into the house and fifteen minutes later returned to the MG. 'Not what I feared, thank God. Touch of 'flu, not helped by an ear infection.'

'Thank God for that!' Grant started the car and followed Tranmer's directions to his surgery. 'Have you been practising here long?'

'Almost thirty years.' Tranmer smiled. 'I brought most of Thornley's younger generation into the world.'

Grant looked at him quickly. 'Eliot Fenton too, I daresay?'

'Eliot?' Doctor Tranmer shook his head. 'No, strangely enough, he's the odd one out. Born in a London maternity clinic.'

'Oh? Why was that?'

'Wish I knew.' Tranmer sounded a little peeved. 'Mrs Fenton didn't consult me about her pregnancy. With the exception of that time I was called to the farm. She had slipped on a muddy path. Nothing serious, but dear old Mrs Shotley panicked and phoned me, so I turned up expecting just a twisted ankle, only to discover my patient was into the eighth month of a pregnancy I knew nothing about.' He laughed. 'I can't imagine what the expression on my face was like. I hadn't seen Mrs Fenton for a long time. Mind you, it was only the children I really attended, the parents had sound health.'

'And you examined her after the fall?'

Tranmer shot him a curious glance. 'I checked the foetal heartbeat. They were both sound, mother and baby in fine fettle. It was all rather embarrassing for both of us. I was their family doctor yet she went to an Ipswich GP and decided on a London maternity home. Couldn't make out why. I did point out that third labours could be pretty quick and that she had better be close to that clinic when contractions started, otherwise she'd have to put up with yours truly bringing her child into the world.'

Completely baffled, Grant somehow managed normal conversation as he made his way to Tranmer's home and surgery which was just outside Thornley. But as he set off for London once more his mind was in turmoil. Just when he'd thought he had found a solution, the whole thing was falling apart. There was no adoption, no unmarried woman handing over her baby illegally, there was only the mysterious and secretive Diane who seemed so normal while the world she created about her was all confusion and lies.

He drove through Lowdham, then pulled into a lay-by to collect his thoughts. He was all at sea. Lighting a cigarette, he sat back and tried to make sense of it all. The medical notes had to be wrong. If not, it meant that Diane Fenton could not possibly be the mother of Terry and Marisa.

If that was the truth of the matter, then who the hell was?

Three weeks later, when Terry had almost despaired of meeting Grant again, she stepped from the train on to the platform at Liverpool Street and heard the incoherent tones of the station announcer over the tannoy. Three long weeks, she thought, during which he had phoned but not returned to Suffolk.

In the end she had been forced to remind him about the theatre tickets for this Saturday, expecting him to say he would be on call and unable to meet her. To her surprise he had kept his word, switched duty hours and would now be at the station waiting for her. They would dine early in order to be at the theatre in time for curtain up. Since then she had counted the hours.

As she walked towards the gate, her ankle started hurting, the low sensible footwear of the past fortnight having given way to high-heeled court shoes to go with her black chiffon dress. But what was she to do? Meet Grant looking like a frump?

She approached the ticket collector and heard the voice over the tannoy once more. This time it was clearer. Terry stopped dead in her tracks.

'Would Miss Fenton from the Ipswich train please call at the Station Master's office where a message awaits her?'

Three times the message rang out over the concourse then the announcer returned to giving out train information, leaving Terry stunned. Heart thumping, she asked the ticket collector where the Station Master's office was, found it and was handed a piece of paper by a sympathetic-looking clerk.

'You're to ring this number.' He cleared his throat and murmured, 'It's St Thomas's Hospital.' His expression was one of concern touched with sympathy but he said nothing and returned to his duties. Someone she knew had probably been in an accident, but he could hardly ask.

'Thank you,' said Terry weakly. He wasn't coming; Grant wasn't going to make it after all. In dismay, she walked towards the public telephone box, saw a man inside speaking into a receiver and glanced at her watch. It was ten to six. He should have been here, but he wasn't. He wasn't coming, that's what the message would say.

After six precious minutes, the man came out of the box and she entered. The operator told her to put coins in the slot, the ringing tone stopped and Terry pressed button A.

'St Thomas's Hospital.'

'Hello. I believe there's a message for me? My name is Fenton.'

The hospital switchboard operator asked her to hold on, then came back, saying, 'Miss Fenton, the message is from Mr Kenway. He's dealing with an emergency and asks you to meet him later at the theatre. He suggests you leave his ticket at the box office so he can join you if he's late.'

Heart lifting at this news, Terry thanked her, replaced the receiver and left the telephone box. She had counted the days, hours and minutes to this moment. Ah well, he was a doctor after all. What to do? Where to go meanwhile? Supposing he didn't make it? But she wouldn't think of that, not now. He must make it. He must.

Her thoughts turned to Marisa. There had been no communication between them since their last meeting at Cadogan Place. Calls from Terry were always answered by Mrs Mount who said that

Mrs Hammond was out and would phone back. Marisa had not done so yet. This was an opportunity to find out why. In any case, it would be good to see her sister and rest until it was time to go to the theatre.

Her hand paused on the receiver. If Alastair was there, the whole thing was impossible. She decided to give it a try and hang up if he answered.

'Marisa?' Her shoulders fell with relief. 'Hi. It's Terry. I'm in London. Alastair isn't with you, I take it?'

'Why?'

Thinking her sister sounded odd, Terry said quickly, 'Because if he isn't, I wonder if I could come to you for an hour?' She went on to explain. 'Quickly, Marisa, before the money runs out. I've no more change. Is it all right? How do I get there?'

'He's not here,' said her sister. 'And we need to talk. Take the tube to Sloane Square and turn right off Sloane Street for Cadogan Place.' With that there was a click followed by the dialling tone. Terry replaced the receiver, wondering what her sister had meant by 'we need to talk'.

The evening was still sunny as she left the underground station and wandered along Sloane Street. By the time she reached Cadogan Place, with its elegant terrace of white Georgian houses, her foot was hurting badly but her spirits were high. Grant could well be waiting at the theatre when she arrived and maybe Marisa would give her a lift to Drury Lane.

Mrs Mount answered the doorbell and led her to the drawing room, where Marisa was standing by the window, arms folded, her dark hair pulled back into a chignon, her oatmeal-coloured dress figure-hugging and elegant. She could have been on the front cover of *Vogue*, thought Terry.

'So then, he stood you up?' The voice was sardonic. Making no attempt to greet her sister, Marisa kept her stance by the window. Seeing Terry's small overnight case, she asked, 'Where do you propose staying the night?'

Surprised by her sister's tone, Terry pulled off her coat and placed it on a chair before smoothing the skirt of her dress and settling down on the sofa. Something told her she would not be welcome here overnight. 'I've arranged to stay with a friend, the nurse, the one I stayed with last time.'

Marisa moved towards the desk, opened a silver box, took out a cigarette and lit it thoughtfully. 'Ah, yes, in some grotty part of London, as I recall.' She exhaled slowly. 'Why did you want to know if Alastair was here or not?'

Perplexed by such questions and her sister's hostile manner, Terry searched for a suitable answer but could only come up with the feeble, 'I don't like to muscle in on anything and . . .'

'You couldn't meet Alastair in front of me. That's it, surely?' The green eyes narrowed. 'Too embarrassing for words. Well, you won't have to. He's at Silverstone again. More trials on that damned car of his.' She paused and drew on her cigarette in a vain attempt to calm her nerves. 'But then, you surely know all this? Tell me, how long has it been going on?'

Terry stared at her blankly. Had Alastair been indiscreet? Had these two quarrelled and he, in anger, given Marisa the wrong impression? 'Has what been going on?'

'Your affair with my husband, your own brother-in-law.'

Terry was on her feet instantly, eyes blazing. 'I find that remark stupid and insulting.'

'And I find your behaviour a dead give away.' Marisa stubbed out the cigarette and, as her anger rose, so did her voice. 'Don't tell me you aren't seeing him because that's an insult to my intelligence. I saw how he looked at you! No doubt when you left here you were all over each other'. Her voice had now become a scream of hysteria. 'It's disgusting, an abomination. And you stand there, innocence personified. God, do you take me for a fool?'

Badly shaken, Terry slipped on her coat. 'You should have told me on the phone you just wanted a row. I'd have saved myself the journey. I don't understand, how can you think such a thing? You yourself said he didn't care a jot for me, that had he loved me he wouldn't have wanted you.' She paused, saw her sister's unrelenting expression and sighed with despair. 'Marisa, I happen to love someone else. Alastair means nothing to me.' It was clearly useless. 'I'll go. It's obvious there's no reasoning with someone who allows their imagination to run riot as you seem bent on doing.'

'Yes, go!' screamed Marisa. 'Clear off and leave my husband alone.'

Picking up her case, Terry walked to the door then turned back. 'You know, you would have a happier marriage if you took more interest in his world.'

Marisa's lip curled into a vicious sneer. 'As you pretend to do, you mean? I'm not such a hypocrite.'

'Well then,' Terry murmured sadly, 'I'm sorry for you both. It's what comes of marrying without love.'

Marisa gave a mirthless laugh. 'Don't be so bloody sanctimonious. What do you know when love is all you've ever had? Yes, you, the loved one Mother meant to save the night the bomber crashed. Not me . . . never me, you see. I was expendable. She grabbed you and left me to die.'

For one moment Terry looked at those wild green eyes, the head thrown back so that the long neck bones showed, and thought her sister was like a deer held at bay by hounds. Shocked to the core, she left the house and limped back along Cadogan Place. After a lifetime of quarrels this was the mother of them all. Angry and deeply hurt, she could hardly comprehend what she had just heard and found it hard to keep tears from streaming down her face.

Somewhere around Sloane Square she found a coffee bar and sat drinking cappuccino after cappuccino in a vain attempt to calm her nerves and give her ankle a chance to recover. What on earth was all that nonsense about the bomber crash? Had Marisa really had such a thought going round and round her head all these years?

Making her way to the powder room, Terry splashed cold water on her face to hide the tell-tale signs of crying, touched up her make-up then made her way back to the underground, worrying about Marisa all through the journey.

The foyer of the Theatre Royal was crowded as she stood at the entrance watching theatre goers arriving. Her eyes looked to left and right along Drury Lane but of Grant there was no sign. If he didn't turn up before the show started, she decided to leave both tickets and return home.

The foyer began to empty as the audience took their seats for curtain up. Dismayed, Terry took one last look along the Lane. Suddenly she saw a figure running towards her. Jacket undone, tie askew, Grant caused a slight commotion as he bounded into the foyer and grabbed her by the hand, gasping,

'Thank God! Almost didn't make it. Did you manage to eat?'

The surprise and joy on her face were beautiful to him as he took her coat and case and handed them to the cloakroom attendant. Leading her up to the Dress Circle, he explained he had been called in that afternoon since a lorry had crashed into a bus queue and the hospital was inundated with casualties, leaving them short of surgeons.

'Were many people hurt?' she asked, forgetting her own troubles. 'In the bus queue?'

'Six seriously. A good number of walking wounded. Didn't get away until ten to seven. No time to change, and couldn't park any closer. I ran all the way from Covent Garden.' As he led her to her seat, he added, 'I had this sinking feeling that you wouldn't wait for me.' They found their seats and sat down. He looked at her. 'Well, would you have done?'

She avoided answering by pointing out a programme seller hovering beside them.

Grant bought a programme and glanced at it. 'So then, what's this *My Fair Lady* all about?'

'It's based on Shaw's *Pygmalion*,' she whispered.

'*Pygmalion*?' Grant frowned. 'A musical version of *Pygmalion*? What a Godawful idea! I'll give it two weeks.'

She laughed. 'It's been running since last year.'

The overture started and Grant's thoughts fled to the traumatic evening when Louise had rushed weeping from his flat. It was over. Thank God it was all over at last and now he was sitting with the woman he truly loved. And how trusting she had been. Suddenly he felt bad. Terry had been lied to enough. Wasn't keeping quiet about a past love a form of lying too? He took her hand and squeezed it gently. She had never asked, but he wondered now if she had guessed.

With music still ringing in their ears and memories of thunderous applause as curtain call followed curtain call, they left the theatre and made their way slowly through the streets of Covent Garden, nostrils filling with the smell of flowers and vegetables from that day's market.

Terry smiled. 'Odd feeling to walk out of the theatre and straight into the set.'

'Hmm.' Grant stood with car keys in hand, trying to recall where he had parked his precious MG. 'I just rushed away from it without thinking. Now where the devil . . .?'

They found it eventually in Floral Street, looking sadly

abandoned under a street lamp. As Grant held open the door for Terry to settle into the passenger seat, he glanced at her shoes and frowned. 'How the hell are you walking in those heels with that ankle?'

'With considerable difficulty.'

'Is it painful?'

'No,' she lied. 'Not too bad.'

He knew she was lying and smiled. 'There's a place in Wardour Street which still serves at this hour. Not fashionable, I'm afraid, but the food's pretty good so long as you like pasta. Used to go there in my student days. There'd be about six of us, blowing our meagre salary on one meal and generally making a nuisance of ourselves into the small hours.'

'Sounds perfect,' said Terry, thinking how quickly things changed. Only a few hours ago she had been shocked and desolate. Now she felt happy, safe and secure, as she always did when he was with her. Glad that the car top was up against the chilly night air, she saw him place the small case behind them before getting into the driver's seat.

He started the ignition. 'Where did you go after you got my message?'

She paused before answering, 'To Marisa's place.'

'Why didn't you leave your case with her?'

'Because I'm not staying there. I'm going to Meg's again.'

A sense of unease crept over Grant. Meg might talk. She probably would talk if hurting Terry meant she could strike out at the Fentons. He drove in silence, his mind turning once again to the mystery of Diane. Something was cockeyed somewhere. Meg must be kept at arm's length. If she spoke of the Westlake's notes while Terry and her family doctor knew for a fact that Eliot was Diane Fenton's son, what would that do to Terry?

'When did you last speak to Meg?' he asked sharply.

Surprised at his tone, she frowned. 'Not for some time. She was out when I phoned, but left a message saying it was fine for me to stay when I rang back. You don't mind driving me to Southwark, do you?'

'That's not the point,' he said, turning into the Strand. 'I don't want you to go to Meg's.'

If this was a line he was shooting, then it wasn't his style, not his style at all. Wondering at the tension in his voice, Terry glanced at him warily. 'She's expecting me.'

'Call her from the restaurant and say you're not going.'

She smiled to herself. 'Oh? Why?'

'I don't like her.'

Blinking with astonishment, she said, 'But . . . but you hardly know her. How can you say such a thing when you know she's my friend?'

'She's your cousin. But she's not your friend.'

'Did I tell you she was my cousin?' Terry was trying to recall.

Brought up sharply by the fact that he had put his foot right in it, Grant recovered the situation quickly enough. 'I'm not sure. Maybe, or maybe she did.'

Frowning, Terry glanced at him warily. The lights from shop windows and lamps lit his grim expression. 'What else did she tell you?'

'What should she tell me?' If only he didn't have to lie, if only he could get Terry to speak of it herself, if only he could make her understand that Meg was a hotbed of resentment and could hurt her.

After a long pause, Terry said, 'She shouldn't have mentioned we were cousins. Please don't pass that information on to anyone, Grant. Especially not to any member of my family.'

He promised he would keep the secret. 'Although it seems a strange request. Meanwhile, I'd be happier if you gave her a wide berth.'

This was no line he was shooting, she realised, this was genuine anxiety. But why? What had poor Meg done to merit such character assassination?

'I'll take you to your sister's house after dinner.'

'Oh, no, you won't! We've just had an almighty bust up. I hardly think I'm welcome there just now.'

The Italian restaurant was small and as busy as it always had been. Two waiters were being worked off their feet as young men and women ate, drank and laughed together, reminding Grant of days gone by. Leading them to a corner table, a waiter lit the candle with exaggerated aplomb, before handing them menus.

Gazing at Terry across the flame, Grant smiled. 'It's just like the old days, only we drank beer then, not wine. Even so, it's hardly what I had in mind for you this evening.'

But his thoughts were miles from his words and, reaching out for her hand, he said once again, 'Don't go to Southwark. Please, Terry.'

His touch sent a quiver through her. 'You're so strange tonight. All right, it's true I could never choose Meg for a close friend, but she's been kind to me, and you hardly know her.'

Grant sighed with growing despair. The happiness that had been evident in her eyes had faded. He had made her anxious when he so wanted to give her peace of mind. 'All I can say is that I sense anger and hostility in her. That's it, nothing more dramatic than that. I'd rather you had as little to do with her as possible.' How bewildered she looked, he thought. The flame flickered, his grip on her hand tightened and his dark eyes became intense. 'If you can't go to your sister's then come home with me.' She remained silent. 'Come home with me, Terry.'

Her mind and emotions were all over the place. A night, she thought, a whole, wonderful night together? The very idea made her head spin, even as she asked herself was this wise? When she finally found her voice, it sounded as weak as she felt. 'But . . . but I'm expected and . . .'

'Telephone now.'

Something in his voice and manner made it impossible to go against him. Whatever was wrong, she must accept it because it was his wish. But it was all so unlike him. What on earth had Meg said to make him feel this way?

'Trust me,' said Grant.

She would; she did. 'I . . . I think I'd better telephone the flat or someone will be waiting up to let me in.'

Both of them were quiet in the car as they drove towards Westminster, then followed the line of the Thames past Millbank towards Chelsea. Grant turned into a maze of small streets until he finally pulled up outside a large Victorian house. Like Meg, he lived on the top floor; unlike Meg he lived alone, and in comfortable surroundings.

Terry found herself in a large room where sage green velvet curtains hung at tall windows; upholstered in dark gold velvet the armchairs and sofa stood on an Axminster carpet. In front of the window stood the desk and she realised now why he had chosen it. The fireplace had long since given up its hearth to an electric fire but the polished mahogany surround was original. On the wall hung the framed Constable print he had bought at Dedham, and in it were a thousand memories of a day in April when they had slowly come to know each other.

Having put her coat away, Grant walked back into the room and saw her staring up at the print. How often had he done the same thing, thinking of her, wondering what she was doing, wondering if he was in her thoughts as much as she was in his.

'Sorry about the mess,' he said, glancing at the desk which had books and papers strewn across it. 'But I was working when the hospital called. I had to leave everything and go.'

Terry laughed. 'I was just thinking how tidy everything was for a bachelor pad.'

'The landlord lives downstairs, a retired Colonel and his wife. Their domestic cleans for me twice a week, otherwise I'd be knee deep in chaos. Guess I'm lucky to have found this place. A quick drive over the bridge and, depending on the traffic, I can usually make the hospital within fifteen minutes. It's quiet after sharing with students, but I needed quiet in order to study.' He had also needed to find somewhere else after Louise left him.

Bending to the fire, he switched it on, saying, 'You must be cold.' As the bars began to glow he stood up, saw her radiant face and thought how much he wanted her. Not just for a night, but for life. 'I'll make some coffee. Put a record on, if you like.'

How quiet she was and how unreadable. He walked into the kitchen, put coffee and water into the percolator and found himself wondering again about the mystery of her background. All those lies. And who was her mother if not Diane? The whole damned thing was a mess. He would do better to forget it than turn it into a Gordian Knot that could never be untied, unless like Alexander he severed it with a sword.

Terry meanwhile was floating and wanted fate to take charge tonight rather than propriety. Seeing a framed photograph on the desk, she picked it up and found it was the picture of her, smiling pensively in front of Willy Lott's cottage. How odd that she should have forgotten him taking it. Yet he kept it on this desk, where he worked and could see her. Her eyes misted with tears.

Turning she saw a portable record player on a small table. In a cabinet beside it she found the records. Mostly classical, but finally she came across an old favourite of hers.

Switching on the player, she set the needle on the first groove of the record and Ella Fitzgerald's voice rang out across the room singing 'Everytime We Say Goodbye'. Suddenly an ice cold finger slithered around her heart. She knelt before the electric fire and crossed her arms over her shoulders in a hugging gesture, not for warmth but in an unconscious urge to protect herself.

Grant found her like that when he walked into the room with a tray of coffee and two glasses of brandy. 'You really are cold.' Placing the tray on the table he looked worried and knelt beside her. 'Sorry it isn't a blazing log fire.'

Terry recovered. The cold receded. Ella's voice sang on.

Thinking how pale she looked, Grant touched her forehead and found it cool, then his fingers stroked her face and moved down to the back of her neck. He let his hand run through her soft shining hair. She caught at the hand and held it for a moment, then he pulled her towards him and kissed her on the mouth. Gently at first, then more firmly as she responded. Bending her back, his fingers stroked her long white throat and his hand moved down to the small firm breasts. She shuddered involuntarily. Gently he let her go and stood up.

'I almost forgot why I persuaded you here. It wasn't to take advantage,' he murmured in a shaky voice.

Oh, don't spoil it, she thought wildly, her body burning for him. Don't be a gentleman, not now.

He saw her eyes and suddenly she was the most beautiful creature he had ever known. 'Coffee and brandy?' The words seemed strangled at the back of his throat.

'Coffee, yes,' she murmured. 'I've never had brandy.' She slipped off her shoes but stayed where she was, curled up beside the fire. 'Perhaps I'll try a little.'

He shook his head. 'Perhaps not, under the circumstances. I wasn't thinking.'

She didn't want him to think, she wanted him just to be, but he was going to be responsible and treat her like a child when she wanted to be treated like a grown woman who knew exactly what she was doing.

Handing her the cup and saucer, Grant found himself asking what she had thought of the show, admitting that it was a whole lot better than he had anticipated. After a while they fell silent. He sank down on to the floor beside her, leaned against the armchair and tried to keep his mind off his yearning while he drank coffee and asked her why she didn't want her parents to know about her cousin.

Terry frowned. This was the last thing she wanted to talk about. 'What did Meg tell you?'

'Only that you once lived with her mother in Guernsey.'

After a long silence Terry was unburdening herself of the strange gulf created between her parents and the Collinettes. She spoke of the letter and her subsequent visit to Guernsey where she'd found her roots and more besides. She spoke of her secrecy about this, feeling guilty that she had deceived her parents as much as they had deceived her.

Glad now that it was Terry who was telling him what he already knew, Grant felt relieved that he could speak to her without having to watch his tongue.

'Why don't you just ask your parents why they feel this way about Grace? he asked.

She shook her head. 'If only you knew how I've longed to ask. But I can't. It's hard for you to understand ... but I just can't. Stupid, I know, but you saw my father that day. You know how things are with him just now. With both of them. They're under such strain, I couldn't put this on them as well. Not yet anyway.' She sighed. 'They have their reasons, even though I can't imagine what they could be.'

Grant was quiet. He had always prided himself on solving difficult puzzles and completing *The Times* crossword in twenty minutes, but this had him completely beaten. If only he could rid himself of the feeling that there was something sinister about it. But he could not.

His concern for Terry mounted with his love. He wanted to take the worry out of her eyes and drag her from shadows to sunlit uplands. As it was he felt helpless. Watching her now, he thought her beautiful as she sat there, legs curled beneath her like Penelope on a stone, her dress contrasting with her pale, perfect skin.

He put down his coffee, reached out for her and pulled her back into his arms. She nestled her head against his shoulder; he put his lips to her neck, lingering there before lifting her face to his and bringing his mouth down on hers, his kisses becoming fervent as his passion grew.

Terry responded to his kisses with a feeling she never knew was in her. Then she was being lifted and carried into the bedroom. He laid her on the bed, began undressing her then kissed and caressed her lithe white body.

She ran her hands through his dark hair and silently gave herself up to him.

He awoke first and, raising himself up on his elbow, looked down at her. She lay with eyes closed, morning sunlight kissing her hair which fanned out in disarray on the pillow. Grant watched her tenderly for a long time. This had been her first time, so shouldn't she have looked different, more worldly wise perhaps, not like a sleeping angel?

He had no sense of guilt, he was too happy for that and felt that all that happened last night was so right, so marvellous, there could be no guilt in it. However many times they made love from now on, last night would be a night to remember. But as he watched her, he began to fear she might think differently.

Terry stirred slightly, and he kissed her on the forehead; she opened her eyes; he touched her cheek with his finger; she looked up at him as if wondering what he thought of her now. He kissed her lightly on the mouth and told her how much he loved her. Terry smiled, and they made love again. Afterwards, she lay curled in his arms and slept.

After a leisurely lunch they went boating on the lake in Regent's Park, thoroughly at ease and happy, then all too soon it was time to say goodbye.

He stood on the station platform holding her hand as she leaned out of the carriage window. 'God, how far Suffolk seems now. Come to London? Everyone should be in London. We can't go on being so far apart.'

Throat too constricted to speak, she nodded and gripped his hand tightly. Her eyes were filling up. The guard's whistle blew; the train shunted forward, and finally their hands parted. She leaned out, watching until his still figure receded into the distance and was lost from view.

Tears streaming down her face, she sank down in a corner seat and stared through the window, bereft yet happy all at the same time.

But as she sat back and closed her eyes she felt that icy cold descend on her again and saw how transient a thing happiness was. Granted one day, snatched away the next. Their happiness had been built on a terrible tragedy after all. If seven young men had not lost their lives, she and Grant would never have met.

Chapter Fourteen

The school day had ended. Pupils who had stayed later were now mingling with staff as they headed towards the wrought-iron gates.

Walking to her car, Terry saw Margaret Temple heading out towards the bus stop and recalled with anger the bleak fifteen minutes when she had defended the girl to Miss Yeats. Of the backward pupils she had brought up to scratch only Margaret still had a long way to go. Miss Yeats wanted to know why and in her office, during morning break, Terry had met those stern eyes with a steady gaze and said, 'No, Miss Yeats. Margaret isn't lazy. She works hard and has improved immensely after her extra tuition.'

It was true. From stuttering and stammering through simple sentences, Margaret had now progressed to reading more confidently, but still there was something wrong. 'However, she's thrown by certain words, especially those with silent letters, such as in might, high, or bough.'

'Then it's time she put her thinking cap on and tried harder.'

Terry leaned forward, her eyes eager to convey how she felt. 'Oh, but she does. If only you could see how hard she tries, and how frustrating it is for her to be bright and intelligent yet not read as her peers do. She has to work twice as hard to keep up with them and it tires her so. At first she was afraid to read aloud in class, so I stopped it and let her read only to me. Slowly her confidence grew. During our extra tuition we worked on the problem and she has responded to that. I believe that more lessons on a one to one basis would help her enormously. She has a keen talent for art, not shared by her classmates. Her mental arithmetic is also good, she loves drama and dancing, there's so much life in that mind of hers, I would never call her backward.'

'Of course she's backward!' Miss Yeats sighed with exasperation.' She can't read properly, her writing is all over the place and as for her spelling . . . She shook her head. 'Quite frankly, I think she belongs in a council school for the educationally subnormal.'

Terry heard this in horror. 'Oh, no, please! That would be the worst thing for her. How can we know whether anyone would care for her there or give her the help she's getting now? What more could they do that isn't already being done? She would just lose all her confidence and fall by the wayside along with the rest of the pupils from such establishments.'

Miss Yeats sighed. 'I admire the way you stand up for her, Miss Fenton, but you must understand that a girl like that is only fit for menial work, as a waitress or shop assistant perhaps. Dame Edith girls do not go into such low-grade jobs. Goodness, what on earth would that do for our reputation?'

Biting her lip, as if trying to decide whether to speak her mind or not, Terry plucked up courage and chose the former.

'I did discuss the problem with Miss Beddoes when she took the Lower Second after I hurt my ankle. Miss Beddoes has a friend who teaches in Copenhagen. There, it seems, they believe that some children have a mental block when it comes to reading. So far as I can understand, it's . . . well, it's like a word blindness. Some have it so badly they can't read at all, but there are others who can read some words but remain stumped by others. I wonder if Margaret suffers from this . . .'

'Word blindness?' Thin grey eyebrows were arched sceptically. 'What absolute nonesense! Trust the Scandanavians to come up with such a crackpot idea. If Margaret doesn't pull her socks up then she will have to leave the school. I've put her back a year already. She can't stay in the Lower Second all her school life, and she won't be ready to go up.'

With a boldness born of anger, Terry stood her ground. 'If Margaret leaves the school then she will slip right back and that would be tragic for her.'

The room was filled with an angry silence as Miss Yeats tapped her pen on the table top and stared at Terry like an eagle about to attack its prey. 'You are very outspoken for a junior teacher, Miss Fenton. You are young and you are keen but you are still very inexperienced, so don't try to tell senior staff how to educate.'

Terry tensed. 'That was never my intention. Forgive me if I gave such an impression, but I do feel that Margaret can make further progress. It won't be quick, and exams are a torment for her, but she's receiving a good education here and that will stay in her mind for the rest of her life. All I ask is that you give her more time.'

The eyes narrowed, the pen tapped a little faster then a reluctant voice conceded, 'Very well. If her father will continue to pay for extra tuition on a one to one basis with you, then I may consider allowing her to return in September. If not, she must go.'

Steering her Austin towards the gate it dawned on Terry that moving to London to be near Grant could ruin Margaret's life. Had Miss Yeats not made it plain enough that the child could only stay if the one to one lessons continued?

Since it was warm, she wound down the window and waved to the Science teacher, cycling along the drive. Soon she would be home; her own home, consisting of one bedroom, bathroom, kitchenette and small sitting room, all furnished in modern style.

Formerly rooms for servants, the flat was on the top floor of a Georgian house overlooking Lowdham Green. Its owner, a nervous middle-aged widow who liked the idea of having someone else in the building and had decided a teacher was just the thing, had lowered the asking rent when she saw Terry hesitating.

Gaining independence had not been easy for her. John and Diane had been quite unable to understand her reasons for wanting to leave a good home to live six miles away. Her explanation that she was a grown woman and that her pupils would expect their teacher to have left the nest by now, had made no impression on them at all.

'Rubbish!' John had stared at her with anxiety in his eyes. 'I think you want your independence for other reasons. Well, you watch yourself, that's all. Watch yourself.'

Angry at these words Terry had stormed up to her room, to be followed by a weeping Diane pleading with her to stay. 'You can't leave . . . please don't leave . . . don't leave me alone!'

Staring at her mother in disbelief, Terry had thrown up her arms in frustration. 'You have Dad, how can you be alone?'

Diane had looked at her strangely. 'You'll never know just how alone I really am.'

At that moment, Terry had come very close to giving in to her mother but common sense hardened her heart. After all, if she couldn't leave home at the age of twenty-one, she would probably still be there at thirty-one.

Anyway, there was Grant. No more would she have to explain where she was going or lie about who she was staying with in London. No more would Grant have to rush away if he came to Suffolk. At his flat or hers, they could relax, make love, laugh and talk with complete ease. But their halcyon days together were rare since he frequently worked when she was at home and she taught when he was off duty. Finding a weekend when both of them were free was increasingly difficult.

Sometimes, at night, she wondered why she hadn't said anything to anyone about their love. Was it fear? Fear that Marisa would find out and do something to damage their relationship, or fear that having told her secret, the spell would break and her happiness be taken from her? Whatever it was, she wanted to keep Grant to herself, as someone of her own who would not have to try pleasing her parents when he should be pleasing her.

Driving slowly through the school gates, she started her turn towards Lowdham and saw a familiar-looking sports car on the far side of the road. Suddenly a head poked through the open window, causing her to jump with fright.

'Alastair!' Slamming on the brakes, she blinked at him in astonishment. 'What are you doing here?'

'I have to see you. We have to talk.'

'Why?' Terry instantly regretted her tone of voice as she saw how tired and drawn he looked. What had happened to all that carefree golden shining youth?

'Please. A few moments is all I ask.'

Parking her Austin at the roadside, Terry climbed out and groaned inwardly as she saw the Head's car come through the gateway. Those eagle eyes were staring at them. 'We can't talk here. Let's walk.'

She led him across the road and along a lane until they came to a small wooden footbridge which straddled a trout stream. The last of the year's bluebells nestled beneath whispering willows which overhung the water; on the river path a woman was helping her small daughter to feed the ducks while in the meadow to their right, sheep grazed beside the ruins of a thirteenth-century priory.

Aware that on this golden afternoon, in this most tranquil of places, her nerves were about to be tested to their limit, Terry stopped walking and watched as he lit a cigarette with trembling hands, inhaling deeply. He looked like a man on the verge of a breakdown. 'Alastair, what's the matter?'

'What the hell do you think? I've hardly slept since we last met, knowing that I've earned your contempt. I'm asking you to forget what I said that day and not cast me out of your life completely.'

Seeing the look on his face, she smiled gently. 'I have forgotten it, and so must you. As for casting you out of my life . . . we're in-laws now.' She paused then said, 'Marisa thinks we're having an affair. Did you know that?'

He stared at her and gave a hollow laugh. 'Bloody marvellous! If I'm to be accused I could at least be guilty of the crime.'

'It was the impression you gave and nothing I can say will stop her thinking it. When I last saw her she was in a terrible state.'

'That doesn't surprise me.' His eyes glinted like steel as he threw down the cigarette and lit another one without being aware of his actions. 'Your sister's half mad, do you realise that?'

Into Terry's mind came a picture of a beautiful woman, eyes darting wildly and head thrown back as she screamed hysterical nonsense. 'That's a dreadful thing to say.' But is it true, she asked herself. Is it true?

'Terry, she's a neurotic mess who gets a bee in her bonnet over the most idiotic things and nothing will move her. I can't make her out. I thought I'd married a sophisticated woman of the world, but she's the most insecure person I've ever known and causes rows at the drop of a hat.' He drew on his cigarette and waved his free hand wildly in the air. 'She's paranoid, I tell you, bloody paranoid, and I can't live with it. I must be free of her.'

'But that's what she fears the most.' Terry stared into the shallow weed-filled water, remembering a childhood filled with traumatic scenes. Had an unhappy marriage brought back those terrible days? 'Marisa's always believed herself to be unloved. Not true, of course, but there it is. It's made her difficult, yes, but it's also given her strength and determination to suceed.'

'Strength?' Alastair smiled wryly. She's as fragile as

porcelain.' He looked at her as one would look at a painting. 'Funnily enough, I used to think that was you.'

Terry was thoughtful for a moment then said, 'When we first met, did you say to yourself . . . Miss Goodie Two Shoes?'

'Why do you ask?' he said warily.

'It's what Marisa always called me.'

He smiled. 'Perhaps I did a little. You seemed extremely reserved, young, inexperienced and very much under the thumb of an over-protective father. I didn't know how to handle that. Marisa's reserve was different. I took it for disdain and that told me she was a woman of experience, in control of her life, and that was . . .'

'More of a challenge?' said Terry with a sardonic smile.

Looking at her, he smiled weakly. 'She isn't the only one who's changed. Something's happened to you.'

'You didn't answer my question?'

He shuffled awkwardly. 'Look, it's how I am, it's why I race cars and race them to win.'

'Trying to capture something that's almost inaccessible? Women aren't cars, Alastair.'

'No. They're schemers. It seems I was the one who was captured.'

'Serves you right for speeding ahead without looking where you were going!' Terry turned away, thanking her lucky stars she hadn't tied herself to anyone as air-headed as the Hammond heir. With all bitterness gone, she only wanted Alastair and Marisa to patch up their marriage and be as happy as she was. When that happened, Marisa would be well again.

'Who was the fellow you were with that Sunday? Anyone special?'

'Yes.'

His face became dark. 'I see. And you don't want to tell me about him?'

'No.' They ambled on in silence for a while and Terry took in the strange fact that, having married for money, Marisa had fallen in love with her husband. Why else would she care what Alastair did with his life?

At last she stopped walking and turned to him. 'I'm worried about my sister. She thinks you don't love her. Make her see you do.'

Alastair looked down at the ground and shook his head. 'I don't honestly know how I feel about her any more. Jesus . . . have you any idea what it's like to live with someone whose moods swing from high to low in less than a minute? When I married Marisa, I had no idea she was mentally unstable. Honest to God, Terry, I really do believe that one day she'll do something terrible.'

At this she turned on him. 'Oh, don't exaggerate. Unstable, indeed. How on earth could she have held down a responsible position if she was unstable? She's just very unhappy and that's your fault. How was she to know you only wanted an ornament on your arm – someone to show off to your racing friends? But you found a flaw in your Galatea. She isn't the perfect woman after all, so now you want to change her for a new model. Women and cars are one and the same to you, Alastair.'

Taken aback at this, he just stared at her in silence, then his eyes softened as he murmured, 'You don't know just how wrong you are about that.'

Understanding his meaning, Terry pointedly glanced at her watch and said in a matter-of-fact tone, 'Where are you heading now?'

Throwing down his cigarette, Alastair stamped on it and started back along the path. 'Can't go to Thornley. Too many damned questions. So it's back to Coventry.'

'Why not London?'

'To my flawed Galatea?' He smiled grimly. 'I'm beginning feel an affinity with poor bloody Rochester. At least he could lock up his mad wife in a tower.'

'Oh, stop it!' snapped Terry.

Alastair stopped walking, waited until his anger had died down then murmured in despair, 'Is it really only nine months since we went to that meeting at Snetterton? Just nine? I was happy and carefree then. *Now* look at me. Marriage up the creek, can't race any more because I run a company, and on top of all this I've earned your contempt. All within nine months. It's unbelievable.'

'You haven't earned my contempt,' she said calmly. 'Just my pity.'

'Christ! Spare me that at least.'

'You wouldn't have it if I didn't care about you. And in spite of everything, I do. We're brother and sister now and should be friends.' She stopped walking, turned to him and stretched out her hand. 'Brother and friend?'

For a long time he stood there as if struggling with himself. Then the fight left him, he gave a sigh of resignation and took her hand, saying, 'Oh, very well. But it won't be easy.'

As June slipped into a changeable July, Terry's life hinged on the precious moments when she and Grant could be together. Things were eased when school broke up for the summer and she could spend more days in London. When he had time off to visit Suffolk, they would return to Dedham Vale and walk across the meadows to Flatford Mill, or head for Southwold or Aldeburgh. On other days they would take the dinghy out on the Deben.

Sometimes Eliot joined them on sailing trips and Grant would take him under his wing, instructing the boy on helming, weather, winds and tides so that Eliot began to think of him as the big brother he always wanted. At least Grant didn't make promises and then forget about them as Alastair had done, getting him all fired up over a race meeting only to forget about it, leaving him waiting eagerly for that all-important phone call.

'Why does he say it if he doesn't mean it?' he had almost wept after the last such disappointment. 'Alastair's a dead loss.'

As August drew nearer, Terry sensed a change in Grant. He still had not asked her to marry him and seemed to grow more withdrawn, leaving her to fear that he was tiring of their relationship and could not find a way to tell her. Something else bothered her too. He had never once accepted an invitation to dine at Lynwood Farm, leaving Terry and her parents wondering why. On the Deben one day, when Eliot was not with them, she asked him.

'You turned them down again today,' she said in a dismayed voice. 'Why? Don't you like them?'

'Of course I like them,' Grant said guardedly.

'Well then, I should have thought . . .'

'But you haven't thought.' He pointed the mainsail into a freshening wind and turned to her with a troubled look on his face. 'If you had, you would know how impossible it is for me to eat a hearty meal so close to the spot where my brother and his crew died.'

Mortified by this answer, Terry cursed herself for being such an insensitive fool.

Seeing the look on her face, Grant's expression relaxed into a smile. 'Paul would be the first to call me a jerk, I daresay. But even so, I just can't do it. Please, darling, try to understand.'

He looked towards the Tide Mill, knowing that his reasons for staying away from Lynwood ran far deeper even than this. Deeper than he cared to admit to himself. Diane! Always it came back to her. Whoever Diane truly was, she seemed to be a loving and much loved mother. But to face her, knowing what he knew now, was a sheer impossibility.

The mystery would not leave his mind and the longer it stayed the deeper it became implanted. The Westlake double-checked their records and said everything was in order. There was no mix-up with Diane Fenton's file. They pointed out also that in those days identity cards and ration books would have been a prerequisite for each patient. In their opinion, there could be no mistake.

One evening Grant sat at his Victorian desk and, pulling a sheet of paper before him, wrote.

Guernsey
Diane Fenton sustains injuries after a fall. Broken femur, fractured pelvis and damage to hip (nature unknown). First baby born by section on day of accident.

Twenty-three months later second baby delivered by section.

London 1945
Diane Fenton gives birth to son in Westlake Clinic.
Primigravida. NVD. Confirmation of this pregnancy given by Dr Tranmer who examined her in her eighth month.

Conclusion
Diane Fenton is *not* the mother of Marisa and Terry.

He sat back and looked at his jottings thoughtfully. So what then had happened to Terry's real mother? And why was Eliot's mother calling herself Diane Fenton? Hell, it was crazy! More than anything he wanted Terry to be his wife, but how could he contemplate even asking her under such circumstances? There was something very wrong. Until he knew what it was he could not accept the Fentons as in-laws. He longed to take Terry away with him, far away from the shadow that cast such a chill over them. But she, not realising how deep that shadow was, would never understand.

He sipped a malt whisky given to him by a friend on his becoming a Fellow and turned his thoughts around and around, trying to find some grain of sanity in an insane situation. Always, though, it came down to the notes. For some time he stared at them then scribbled the whole lot out. If only he could scribble it out of his mind also.

Marisa glanced at her bedroom clock. It was almost nine o'clock. He would be here by now, parked farther along Cadogan Place to avoid arousing suspicion.

She checked her make up, which was as flawless as her complexion, put on pearl earrings set in gold and decided against a necklace. The sea-green chiffon dress set off her green eyes and, with its figure-hugging design and low cleavage, was Julian's favourite along with the Chanel No. 5 which she now dabbed on her wrists.

It had come as something of a shock to learn that she did love Alastair after all, but it came one Sunday afternoon at the same moment she realised she had lost him to her sister. After that she had felt only hurt and rage until she'd thought she was losing her mind.

All that had stopped three weeks ago when she had gone to a party in Knightsbridge and met Julian. They were instantly drawn to each other. A forty-four-year-old widower with two teenage children, he was the Chairman of a City merchant bank, owned a mews flat in Harley Place and a large house in Gloucestershire. His children lived there close to their schools, their mother's role now taken on by a warm-hearted housekeeper and Julian's caring sister.

From then on they had met in secret whenever his nights in London coincided with Alastair's in Coventry, and Marisa had worn a glow of excitement that everyone, except Alastair, had noticed and wondered at. He, finding his wife more affable, had sighed with relief and she had played him like a fish to lull him into a false sense of security.

Now Marisa placed a satin stole about her shoulders, checked through her bedroom window and saw the Jaguar parked two hundred yards from the house. Instantly she felt that quiver of excitement, the lure of a secret affair, a thrill that had shaken her from utter boredom and discontent.

Soon she would be in the mews house with the spiral staircase where they would have supper and champagne before making love. Julian was so tender, so caring and so skilled, she had never known love could be like that. But then, she had never known love.

He told her she was his world and that he couldn't live without her.

She spoke of gaining her freedom to marry him.

At this he would smile and say wistfully, 'If only. But I don't wish to harm your marriage or reputation, I love you too much for that.'

She hung on his words. No one else had ever loved her too much to hurt her. Deep down she sensed that such a man would hate scandal of any kind. Well, she must be certain that securing a divorce from Alastair would not involve Julian in any way. Her husband had been unfaithful to her, and with her own sister too. She would have to box clever on that one and start collating proof. Meanwhile, she would go on enjoying her secret affair and all would come right in the end.

Even the dreams had stopped at last; those terrible, fearful nightmares when the light came closer and closer and the terror behind it had made her scream. But the screaming had stopped long ago, leaving her with a deep inner fear which she didn't understand. Now, at least, it seemed that inner fear had been replaced by inner peace.

She left her room, walked down to the hall and called out to Mrs Mount who looked up from the basement. 'I'm just going out. Another bridge evening. Don't wait up, I have my key.'

Mrs Mount nodded and returned to her small room with a sense of outrage. Why did Mrs Hammond insult her intelligence? Bridge evening indeed! Poor Mr Alastair, working in Coventry unaware that his wife was deceiving him. Having watched him grow up, she longed with all her heart to put him on his guard. But she was still just a paid servant when all was said and done and servants kept their mouths shut. Let things sort themselves out. This affair would end as all affairs ended.

She sat down in her armchair, picked up her knitting once more and carried on watching her favourite quiz show on the television.

*

The weeks leading up to the memorial dedication ceremony had become more and more frenzied. John and the other members of the committee worked long hours arranging everything; relatives of the crew were contacted again with final details, so too were members of the RAF squadron concerned, some still serving, some now civilians.

Talk of converting the Rashleighs' large barn into a reception area for refreshments was quashed by Lydia who reminded her husband that after their long journeys, followed by a church service, the invited guests would need certain facilities more than they needed luncheon. A barn could provide none of these and neither could the farmhouse.

'In any case, as the first family of this area it's only to be expected that we should play host to the Lord Lieutenant and the Air Marshal.'

And so a large marquee was erected on the lawns to the rear of Thornley Hall and the house itself given over to the 'comfort' of the guests. Lydia took upon herself the supervision of flower arrangements and the lay-out of the buffet in the marquee. If the weather were kind, chairs and tables would be set on the lawn.

To Diane she delegated the task of organising the women of the village to provide a luncheon of cooked cold meats, salads and various desserts; then, like a commander in the field, called upon the local publicans to supply liquid refreshment. They lost no time in offering to donate it!

With the names of the crew carved upon the large granite stone, the memorial was now in place and surrounded by flowering shrubs and rose bushes. In the golden cornfield the seven newly planted oaks had established themselves well and John Fenton was pleased as he saw the results of all the planning and hard work.

On the eve of the ceremony, Terry put a photograph of each member of the crew into a large frame and placed it on a table inside the door of the church. Later it would find a permanent place on the wall. As she looked at the photographs, the youth of the seven men gnawed at her heart. Few were older than she was now. To be cut down at her age, be denied the years she expected to have and the life she expected to lead, was unthinkable. Paul was so like Grant, but he had died in his twenties and his face was frozen in time without the maturity of his younger brother.

Grant! As Terry arranged flowers beside the large frame she wondered how he would get through tomorrow. She hadn't seen him for five days. It might as well have been five months.

Because she had finished her chores so late, Terry stayed at the farm that evening. Grant was due to arrive there around ten in the morning. When the telephone rang she raced to it, expecting to hear his voice.

'Terry, can we speak?'

It was Meg. With sinking heart, Terry told her to hang on, checked her parents were not in the kitchen or sitting room then said, 'Yes. Go ahead.'

'I've tried before but your mother said you'd moved. I tried your new number but you must have been out. The thing is, Mum's been in London and wants to see you before returning home. How about tomorrow? Can you come up?'

Terry said how much she wanted to meet Grace again but added, 'Tomorrow's out of the question, I'm afraid. It's the dedication ceremony. How long is she staying?'

'Four more days. She's with her old Guernsey friends. It's better for her than being here. They've a lovely house and can drive her to places.'

Terry was thoughtful then put forward a suggestion she knew would be dismissed at once, but it had to be tried. 'Would they drive her to Suffolk? Not tomorrow, of course, but . . . well . . . this is a heaven-sent opportunity for a reconciliation between your mother and my parents. Perhaps then we can get to the bottom of this mystery.'

'You must be joking! Can you really imagine Mum turning up at the farm just to have the door slammed in her face? So, when can you come to London?'

Terry sighed. At least she had tried. 'I'll get back to you on that one, but I will come, I promise.'

'Fine. You can stay at the flat and we'll take it from there. So tell me about tomorrow?'

Terry explained, adding, 'The church is going to be packed. After the service there's the dedication of the memorial, then the families are to have lunch on the lawn at Thornley Hall, so they can meet each other as well as the villagers. Everyone here has been involved one way or another.' She paused. 'I think it's going to be a very emotional day. Especially for Grant who's the brother of the bomber pilot. Do you remember him? The Doctor from St Thomas's?'

'Yes . . . yes, I do recall him.' Meg said goodbye then replaced the receiver and sat in her kitchen drinking coffee. Slowly an idea began to form in her mind.

Chapter Fifteen

The following day started with threatening clouds as villagers and the families of the crew began to arrive at the church.

Brigadier Rashleigh with his wife, the Fentons and other members of the memorial committee greeted relatives, members of the RAF Squadron in which the seven had served, an Air Marshal and civic dignitaries including the Chief Superintendent of Police and the Lord Lieutenant of the County.

With Grant seated beside her and Eliot, Terry was aware of curious local eyes turned upon them and kept her own firmly ahead as the organist struck the first chords of 'Oh, Valiant Heart'. The Vicar and choir processed along the nave followed by the Squadron Standard party, Standard Bearers of the British Legion and the local Scouts and Girl Guides.

As the clouds began to break up, sunlight slanted through the stained glass windows, casting a colourful pattern on the stone columns of the nave. The congregation were called on to give thanks for the lives of the seven men, whom the Vicar named, and for the sacrifice they had made for their country. Terry felt emotion beginning to overwhelm her and took Grant's hand, wondering at the grief he must be feeling; at the grief all the families must be feeling.

When the deeply moving service had ended the procession made its way out of the church into Windmill Lane and along the newly gravelled pathway, which skirted the wood, until they reached the memorial site for the dedication ceremony.

By the time people were gathered around the flag-draped stone, the dark clouds had drifted away completely, allowing a hot August sun to burn down on ripened corn about to be harvested.

There were those who remembered that the weather had been exactly the same on this very day sixteen years ago.

Into Grant's mind came the memory of a snow-covered field on a bitterly cold winter's day; the day he had first met Terry. But on top of this recollection came another; that of the happy-go-lucky older brother he had loved and admired, one who had taken him to rugby matches, played cricket with him, taught him to sail and helped with his homework. How then could he have dreamed that one day he would be standing in a Suffolk field looking at a carved stone, covered with the Royal Airforce flag, paying final homage to this brother? Once they had been a family of four. Now he alone stood for his dead father and far off mother and sister. Here he had lost someone he loved and found the woman he cherished. One was now inextricably caught up with the other, as if loving Terry brought him closer to Paul.

He heard the Vicar speak of the evening when, fighting for control of the doomed aircraft, the pilot had seen the village ahead and banked the Lancaster away, saving the lives of people on the ground. His eyes dimmed with tears as prayers were said for Paul, Keith, John, Eric, Edward, Robert and Liam. Standards were raised then lowered. A member of the British Legion stepped forward and intoned Binyon's 'For The Fallen'. Then a bugler sounded the 'Last Post' and two minutes' silence followed.

When standards were raised once more the Air Marshal stepped foward, removed the flag from the stone, wreaths were laid and prayers said. Then came a familiar sound as a Lancaster bomber flew over the memorial in a final salute.

Moist-eyed, people walked slowly back along the path towards Thornley Hall. There the families met each other for the first time and talked to men who had served in the squadron, some of whom remembered their dead sons and brothers. Looking on, Gerald Rashleigh and John Fenton felt that all the months of preparation and even trauma had ended on a dignified note and been well worth it.

Drinks were served followed by a buffet luncheon laid out in the large marquee. Small cloth-covered tables stood on the lawns and an army of helpers made sure everyone was comfortable. Lydia thanked her lucky stars that the sun shone, the gardens looked magnificent, and the lake glistened in the sunlight. Her worst nightmare had been wondering how everyone would crowd under the limited amount of shelter had it poured with rain.

Not wanting to push in on people who had so much in common, Terry stood back when Grant was introduced to men from Paul's squadron. When he came face to face with a Group Captain who turned out to be the pilot who had returned Paul's car to the family all those years ago, she knew there was no place for her at such a poignant reunion.

Quietly she stole away, intending to help her mother and other village women who were clearing crockery from tables to the large old-fashioned kitchen inside the house. Suddenly, someone tapped her on the shoulder. Turning she found herself looking at a pretty woman wearing a pert little hat over bottle blonde hair.

'Don't remember me, luv, do you? I'm Elsie. You know, one of the Land Army girls who worked on your father's farm.'

Terry stared at her for a while then light dawned. 'Elsie? Why, yes, of course. Didn't you used to push me around in the wheel-barrow?'

'And drag you off tractors and climb up trees to get you down. You was a right tomboy, and the light of your dad's eye, I remember. But look at you now. I bin talkin' to your mum and dad and they pointed you out to me. Saw your sister just now too. Couldn't believe 'ow lovely she's turned out.'

'My sister?' Terry's heart sank as she glanced around. When on earth had Marisa turned up? Having insisted she was not coming, why had she changed her mind only to arrive after the service and dedication ceremony? At length her eyes fell on Marisa who was chatting to a group of people. She looked relaxed, poised and at her most charming. In short, thought Terry, with a pang of anger, her sister looked stunning in her navy and white Chanel suit and matching Breton hat. Why had she come? Deep down, Terry knew and a sense of panic began to set in.

'Funny coming back 'ere after all these years,' Elsie was saying. 'Place looks the same, yet different some 'ow. In the war the cottages was all run down, and the one I was billeted in 'ad no electricity. But now they've bin newly thatched and given a coat of paint, Thornley looks real pretty.'

With a wrench Terry forced her mind back to Elsie and glancing at the wedding ring on her finger, asked if her husband was here also.

'No. Ted's a bus driver and couldn't get the day off. I came by train all the way from Woolwich. Couldn't miss this day . . . felt I 'ad to come.'

Terry's father joined them, saying, 'Ah, so you two have met up again after all these years. Do you remember Elsie, Terry?'

'I do now,' she answered.

'I don't know how we would have managed without her and the other girls. They kept this farm going during the war.' His smile faded as he whispered, 'They were harvesting that evening and risked their lives rushing to the crashed plane.'

'But it was too late,' whispered Elsie. 'It caught fire straight off and we couldn't do anything. Then we found six of the crew dotted across the fields. They'd baled out but the parachutes didn't open, you see. Too low apparently.' She paused and a sob entered her voice as she struggled to add, 'There was 'ardly a mark on any of them. They could 'ave been sleeping. Just boys . . . that's all they was. Just boys.'

After an emotional silence, John turned the conversation. 'But there were good times too, eh, Elsie? You were never short of young airmen escorts, British or American. What was the name of that GI?'

Elsie's face lightened at once. 'Bill Ryder, do you mean? Oh, yeah. We 'ad good times, me and Bill. Poor sodding devil, never bin out of 'is 'ome town before and suddenly finds 'imself in a strange country going on missions in those great Flying Fortresses. Lots of crashes those things 'ad.' She twiddled an earring thoughtfully and smiled. 'They was nice lads, though, and always giving chocolate bars to the local kids. Candy, they called it, even though it was chocolate. Bill used to get me nylons. Like gold they was.'

John smiled wryly, knowing very well what she had done to earn them. 'Where is he now?'

'Chicago, last I 'eard.' She looked at him wistfully. 'I often wonder what life would 'ave been like if I'd become one of them GI brides and lived in one of the 'ouses with a white picket fence and frilly net curtains, like in a Bette Davis film. As it is, I live in a terraced 'ouse in Woolwich with an outdoor lav.'

She smiled up at John, remembering how interested he used to be in her relationship with Bill. Always asking questions, always teasing her. They used to have long chats and she had always thought him very good-looking. He still was, for all he was greying slightly.

Terry's eyes strayed with dismay towards Grant whose group had now been joined by Rashleigh and the Lord Lieutenant. Five minutes later, people started moving away and Terry breathed a sigh of relief as Grant made a move towards her. At that same moment, Dr Tranmer appeared on the scene, saw him and headed him off with arm extended in greeting.

With a sinking heart Terry turned and then heard her mother approaching, her voice cheerful and relieved.

'Well, we're getting there at last,' she said. 'Mrs Shotley insists on helping to wash the dishes. I wish she wouldn't. She's done enough today, truly she has. Anyway, it all went very well. There was masses of food and everyone had plenty. Now then, Elsie, I realise I've had little time to talk to you, but would you mind if I stole John away? He's needed. I promise we'll have a really good chat in a minute. Terry will look after you until then. I can't imagine what's happened to Eliot. I know he'd love to meet you.'

'Eliot?' Elsie beamed. 'Just a baby when I last saw 'im.'

Terry watched her mother heading back towards the marquee and smiled. 'The baby is that gangling youth fishing in the lake. He won't catch anything. Herons took most of the fish in the spring. But at least it's keeping him amused.'

She chatted on, wondering who best to introduce Elsie to and pass her on that way, but even as she thought it, a deep sense of guilt rushed over her. As her eyes drifted across the groups of people she suddenly saw her mother leading Marisa across to Grant. Dr Tranmer said something then moved away, leaving the two together. Grabbing Elsie by the arm, Terry said, 'Do come and meet the pilot's brother. He's a good friend of mine.'

Elsie hesitated, remembering how they had tried but failed to get the pilot out. Supposing his brother should ask questions?

Marisa could see her sister and Elsie staring towards them and knew they would soon head her way. She had little time but was determined to carry out her resolve, her whole reason for being here today. She found Grant extremely attractive and said how glad she was to meet him.

'It's a pity Terry refused to bring you in to meet us that Sunday. But . . . well . . . it's sad she's never forgiven me for marrying Alastair. Poor girl. I feel sorry for her. It really is time she got over him. Anyway, I don't mean to bore you with family history, it's just that I'd hate you to think you weren't welcome in my house. I hope you weren't too offended?'

He stared at her nonplussed. 'Why . . . no.'

'Alastair will be joining us later at the farmhouse, for dinner. He'll stay the night. He usually does. Can you stay too?' When he said no, she smiled and said, 'Oh dear, I think Terry is bringing that awful cockney woman over. I must away. As you now must realise, my sister and I don't get on too well. Lovely meeting you. Goodbye.'

Something strange happened to Grant's stomach as he slowly took in her meaning. He thought then how hard those green eyes were, as though reflecting a sliver of ice at the heart of this glamorous woman. What on earth did she think she was doing, rushing up to him with such information? Then he turned, saw Terry's expression and knew with sickening certainty that every word Marisa had said was true.

As Marisa took herself off, he tried hard to push the thought away and listened kindly to Elsie who was telling him about the war years while Terry just looked at him with big anxious eyes. A moment of reprieve arrived in the shape of Lydia Rashleigh who took his arm, saying, 'Mr Kenway, I must steal you away for a moment. The Lord Lieutenant is about to leave and would like to say goodbye to you.'

With that she led him towards the house and through it to the front drive where, resplendent in uniform and sword, the Queen's representative was standing beside his Rolls-Royce shaking hands with people and bidding them farewell.

Only when Elsie caught sight of someone she remembered from the 'old days' and rushed across to her, did Terry spot Marisa smiling at her from just a few feet away.

Storming across to her sister, she hissed, 'Why are you here? You missed the service anyway so why did you come?'

Marisa smiled. 'Oh, it is nice to be made to feel so welcome. Mother kept on and on at me to attend, but it's a long drive to Suffolk and I don't get up too early these days. But I had a mind to meet this man of yours. Very good-looking. Mr too . . . I didn't know he'd risen that far.' She sighed and shook her head slowly from side to side. 'You can't be serious, though.'

'What do you mean?'

'Oh, for goodness' sake. You're far too young and gauche for such a man.'

'What have you been saying to Grant?'

Marisa's face gave the answer. Producing the silver cigarette case from her handbag, she lit up and exhaled smoke into the air which evaporated in the sunlight. 'Why? What do you think I might have said to him? Something touching on Alastair perhaps?'

I won't let her goad me, thought Terry. Goading people was Marisa's favourite game and she excelled at it. Deciding not to rise to the bait, she was deeply worried just the same, knowing only too well how her sister worked. Sometimes a hint was all it would take, a hint based on a lie, and sometimes a more direct approach would be employed. Either way it was all part of the game.

'Marisa, if you've done anything to harm my relationship with Grant then I shall never forgive you.'

The green eyes narrowed. 'That I can understand. You harmed my marriage with Alastair and I have never forgiven you.' And she turned on her heel and was soon joining another group of people.

Meanwhile the Lord Lieutenant's Rolls had left the Hall, but as the group began to disperse, the Vicar took Grant's arm and held him in conversation by the porticoed entrance. Smiling as they passed the two men, the Rashleighs returned to the rear lawn.

Suddenly Lydia's eyes fixed on two women she had not seen before. 'Good heavens,' she whispered to her husband. 'Who can they be? I thought all the relatives were accounted for? How terrible, poor things. I'll have to rustle up a very late lunch for them. You go and talk to the Chief Superintendent and the Air Marshal. They look a little lost somehow. Oh, yes, and get hold of Fiona and introduce her to that Mr Kenway. You know, the brother of the pilot. Rescue him from Mr Clements first.'

Gerald sighed. 'Any more orders?'

Ignoring his comment, she wandered across to the two women. Both were hatless; the older one drab in a navy jacket over a grey pleated skirt, the younger looking as overweight as Fiona in a floral full-skirted cotton dress.

Introducing herself, Lydia said how sorry she was that they had missed the ceremony. 'I'm sure it will help you when I say how deeply moving it was and so beautifully done. My husband will show you the memorial as soon as you like, Mrs . . .?'

'Collinette,' murmured Grace, feeling overpowered by the stately Lydia who, in head-to-toe blue, put her in mind of a delphinium.

'Have you come far?' asked Lydia, eyes filled with sympathy.

'Guernsey,' said Grace, ignoring the surprised look on the delphinium's face.

'We're staying in London at the moment,' explained Meg, glancing at her mother who having been bullied into this venture still wanted no part of it. 'And we're not here for the ceremony. We're relatives of Mr and Mrs Fenton but found they weren't at home. Someone told us they were probably here. We're sorry to intrude and hope you'll forgive us?'

It was a lie. In fact Meg knew that this was her one in a million chance to confront John and Diane, knowing they would be forced to receive them in a civilised manner. Thus, with the ice broken, they could speak later in private about the past and learn why they had been ostracised all these years. In Meg's opinion, the Fentons owed her mother that at least. So what if they found the whole thing awkward? It served them right.

'I see. No problem, no problem at all.' Curiosity now had the better of Lydia. After all, how many visitors did the Fentons have? In her opinion they led the most stultifyingly boring lives and knew no one apart from their new son-in-law. Guernsey? Hadn't she once been told that all their relatives there were dead? She glanced around, saying, 'I believe Mrs Fenton is helping the other women. Follow me and I'll find her for you.'

Meg and Grace followed and found themselves inside the marquee where three women were removing plates from the buffet table. Gesturing to where Diane stood, Lydia said, 'There's Mrs Fenton. I'll leave you now, if you don't mind?'

'Where?' asked Grace. 'I don't see her.'

Lydia gestured towards Diane again. 'The lady in the navy blue dress with the bolero jacket.'

Grace shook her head. 'There's been some mistake. I'm looking for my cousin, Mrs Diane Fenton of Lynwood Farm.'

Lydia's eyebrows rose. 'That *is* Diane Fenton.' There was an awkward pause and she frowned. 'Wait one moment.' She walked towards Diane, touched her on the shoulder and whispered, 'You have visitors, my dear.'

Blue eyes looked at her questioningly.

'It's Mrs Collinette and her daughter, all the way from Guernsey.'

Diane's grip on a plate tightened. For one moment she seemed turned to stone, then slowly she turned her head.

Terry was still wondering what had happened to Grant when she heard a familiar voice behind her and turned. Try as she might she could not keep the shock from her voice.

'Meg! Good Lord . . . I mean, I'd hoped you would come but today . . .' She paused anxiously, marvelling that Meg could have been so singularly lacking in sensitivity, then saw Grace hovering uncertainly behind her daughter.

'Grace, lovely to see you again.' The tension in her voice was impossible to hide, and the look in their eyes set warning bells ringing in Terry's head. 'What is it? Oh, don't tell me you and my parents have quarrelled?'

'No,' said Grace. 'We haven't met them yet.'

Terry let out a sigh of relief. 'Thank goodness! We'll go together and find somewhere private. You see, I kept my word to you, Grace, they don't know we've ever met. I'll have to prepare the ground first and . . .'

'You don't understand.' Grace's voice began to crack. 'You don't . . .' Turning away, she left Meg to speak for her.

'I brought Mum here today because I thought it the best way to handle a tricky situation but when she finally came face to face with Diane the whole thing backfired badly.'

Terry was puzzled. 'But you said you hadn't met her just now?'

Grace looked her straight in the eye and said: 'I was taken by Mrs Rashleigh to meet a woman called Diane Fenton. But it wasn't her. Terry, where is your mother?'

Still feeling shaken by Marisa's remarks, Grant was rescued from the Vicar by Gerald Rashleigh, only to find himself stuck with him, Dr Tranmer and the Chief Superintendent of Police as they returned to the rear lawn.

There, Rashleigh held forth on the issue of a by-pass for Lowdham and said he was emphatically opposed to the idea. The

Chief Superintendent was all for it and said the time would come when traffic would take so long to get through the town that such a new road was inevitable. Suddenly, Lydia entered the group and, making polite excuses, pulled her husband aside from his guests.

Looking a shade put out, he moved back a few paces and glared at his wife. 'Now what?'

Scarcely able to contain her excitement she explained what had happened, voice rising as she went on.

'The woman's so odd! Keeps insisting she's Diane's cousin from Guernsey and that Diane . . . well . . . isn't Diane. It's all very strange. Diane looked quite ill and glanced at me as if to say "get her out of here". Well, I tried to mediate . . . you know, calm things a little, but Mrs Collinette became most agitated, demanding to know the whereabouts of her cousin.'

'Good God!' said Gerald. 'What does Diane say to all this?'

'That she has never seen the woman before in her entire life. Then she almost fainted and later left the marquee looking like a ghost.' Lydia paused for breath. 'There's something funny going on. I want you to do something about it.'

Gerald's expression turned to that of a man ordered over the top. 'Do what exactly?'

Lydia's voice rose in desperation. 'I don't know, but do it. We can't have this woman making a scene.'

'Shouldn't John do it? I mean . . . can't just bust in on someone else's business.'

'I tried that, but when Mrs Collinette saw him she said he wasn't Diane's husband.' Lydia took a calming breath then glanced at the small group beside her, hoping no one had heard, before going on. 'Do something about it, for goodness' sake. She's over there by the marquee. Oh, dear, Terry's talking to her. Poor girl, goodness knows what she'll make of it. The ginger-haired woman is the daughter, I understand. She seemed to have more about her so she's the one you'll have to deal with.'

'Deal with?'

'Get them to leave without causing a fuss. It's all too embarrassing for words.'

Looking for all the world as though he was interested in the argument over the by-pass, Grant had managed to overhear the conversation going on behind him. It was hard not to since the voices kept rising and lowering.

Letting his eyes drift towards the marquee, he saw Meg and Terry with a small grey-haired woman and hid his growing concern while replacing his coffee cup and saucer on a table close by. Why on earth had Meg brought her mother here on this day of all days? Had Terry suggested it?

He studied Grace with fascination. The anxiety on her face and the angry pursed lips made her seem unprepossessing somehow. Yet, as the only person who could have identified the cousin who'd left Guernsey in 1939, she had failed to do so and that tied in with his own suspicions about Diane. But failing to recognise John as well was something he had not expected.

Vaguely he was aware of the Chief Superintendent's voice and that a young woman had joined their group, but his mind was elsewhere. Before the war Mrs Collinette had said goodbye to her cousin and her cousin's husband. Now she had come here to find them and found two strangers instead. He felt involved somehow and wanted to do something about the situation, but he could do nothing. And so he stood on an English lawn, on a golden afternoon, polite conversation and good manners smothering growing alarm as he was introduced to Fiona and watched the Brigadier make his way to the three women.

Having despatched her long-suffering husband to sort out the awkward matter, Lydia now joined Grant's group and said breezily, 'I'm so sorry about that. My husband will be back immediately. Well, we have been lucky with the weather. Everything seems to have gone well today, don't you think?'

Everyone murmured that it had, saying the organisation had run like clockwork. Then came a lull in the conversation when Lydia glared at her daughter, willing her to say something that would gain Grant's attention.

Finding him dishy to look at but terse and introspective to the point of not being with them at all, Fiona could find nothing to say. It was embarrassing. Trust her mother to throw her into the path of a bachelor who loved someone else. But how could her mother or anyone be told that when Terry had sworn her to secrecy on the matter? And so Fiona stood there, aware that her silk pleated skirt and jacket did nothing for her ungainly figure, wishing herself elsewhere, anywhere but in this particular group. Her mother was still glaring at her. She would have to say something. Turning to the Chief Superintendent, she asked bluntly, 'Any news yet on those bodies? We've heard absolutely nothing.'

Lydia's eyebrows rose in shock and despair. 'My dear, this is hardly the time or place and the Chief Superintendent is our guest.'

Fiona looked surprised. 'But there must be some developments. Surely we're allowed to know what they are?'

Her mother's eyes blazed.

Beside the marquee meanwhile, Terry was still trying to come to terms with Grace's reaction to meeting her parents. 'But you didn't give it a chance. Of course it's them.'

Grace fumbled in her handbag and brought out a photo. 'Look.

This is the picture taken of your mother and father on their wedding day. I couldn't find it when you were in Guernsey so brought it here to England to give to you. Look at it, Terry. Do these people in any way resemble the two you call your parents?' Taking the photograph in her hands, she stared at it and had to admit to faces that were completely unrecognisable, but still put it down to the years. She shrugged and gave a little laugh. 'How can you expect them to look the same? Of course they're my parents. How could they be anyone else?'

'Ah, Terry.' Gerald Rashleigh moved in on them, beaming at her. 'I don't believe I've met these good ladies?'

Taken by surprise she found herself murmuring, 'Brigadier Rashleigh, this is Mrs Collinette and her daughter Meg.'

After an awkward pause, Gerald stretched out his right hand and murmured, 'How do you do? My wife tells me you are related to Mrs Fenton. Is that so?'

Hoping he was about to shed light on a confused situation, Grace shook his hand, and nodded as she waited. Gerald then glanced at Terry, expecting her to deny the relationship, but when she did not he wondered what all the fuss was about and said, 'Good. Good. Well, er ... if everything's all right and Terry is looking after you, I'll just return to the fold. Would you excuse me?' With that he turned slowly, confusion all over his face, and decided to stay well away from his wife.

Fiona was still goading the Superintendent, ignoring her mother's objections with a curt, 'It's hardly a secret, Mummy. The national press printed the story. Everyone knows and people are wondering what's happening.'

'Nevertheless,' snapped Lydia, 'I don't want any of the families here today to know about it.'

'Well, don't mind me,' said Grant. 'I know all about it anyway.'

Lydia looked at him in surprise. 'You do?'

'Mr Kenway is Terry's friend,' said Fiona in exasperation. 'Of course he knows.'

'So then,' said Dr Tranmer. 'Since it's just this little group, how about it, Chief Superintendent? What progress is being made?'

Feeling thwarted by a twenty-year-old crime which was going nowhere, the Superintendent frowned and said, 'All I can say is that there have been developments, but it's far too early to release any information.'

Developments, my eye! thought Dr Tranmer. This was just police talk for 'we haven't a clue'. They were bored with a crime that could not be solved and had more important things to do than worry about something that had happened so long ago. Time to shake them up a bit. 'I thought the pathologist's report would provide a strong clue as to the identity of one of the victims?'

'The pathologist's report?' Clearly searching his memory the Chief Superintendent murmured, 'Yes, we did too.' Gaining more confidence as details of the case returned to his mind, he added, 'Copies of the report were despatched to hospitals, clinics and surgeries, but . . .' he shrugged . . . 'the response has been limited. It happened a long time ago, after all. Records of missing persons have to be searched and twenty years means a lot of searching. We must be be patient.'

'May I ask what the report said?' asked Grant. 'Or am I treading on classified information?'

'Don't see why,' said Tranmer, sounding a little peeved. 'I had a copy and can see no reason why its contents shouldn't be revealed. The more people who know the better, surely?' He glanced at the Superintendent who nodded as a sign that he could go ahead if he really felt he must. 'They found that both skeletons were in their early-thirties, one male and one female and both had been shot in the head. That much we all know. But here's the thing that I thought would help the case along. The female skeleton showed signs of injuries, probably caused in an accident.'

Fiona's eyes widened. 'Go on.'

'By the way the bones had knitted together, it was judged that her injuries had been sustained some two to three years before her death.'

As Tranmer described in detail the extent of the injuries, Grant stared across at Terry and felt the blood drain from his face. Then he was being dragged through a dark tunnel, Terry's face and Tranmer's voice fading away. The tunnel dissolved into bright daylight again but the moment seemed frozen and unreal, as though everything and everyone about him had turned to stone.

Tranmer's voice broke into his consciousness. 'The woman must have received treatment so unless she came from a far distance, I'm surprised that no one has . . . I say, are you all right?'

Shaking himself into the present, Grant said, 'Yes . . . yes . . . I'm fine.'

'You look the very devil.' The doctor was frowning. 'Still, this has been an emotional day for you. A brandy is what you need. I'm sure Mrs Rashleigh . . .'

'Of course. A brandy,' said Lydia quickly. 'Do come into the house, Mr Kenway, and sit quietly for a moment.'

'That's very kind of you,' murmured Grant. 'But there's nothing wrong, I assure you.' He glanced back at Terry whose anxious eyes met his stricken look. 'Please excuse me.' In a shell-shocked daze he moved away from the others and walked across the lawn towards the house. Hardly knowing what he was doing, he climbed the steps to the terrace and walked through the open doors.

Lydia turned to the local doctor and shrugged. 'One doesn't wish to be a nuisance when he would rather be alone . . . but he does look so ill. Oh, dear, I hope it isn't something he's eaten.' She glared at her daughter as if to say: It's all your fault. We none of us wished to hear such gruesome details. Fiona ignored the look.

Inside the large hallway, Grant paused, heard the sound of women's voices and the clatter of crockery from the kitchen area, then headed up a wide staircase and found the bathroom. Feeling physically sick, he stood still for some moments then stumbled towards the sink and splashed cold water on his face. Looking at his haunted reflection in the mirror he saw only Terry and heard Tranmer's words going round and around inside his head.

'. . . broken femur, fractured pelvis . . .'

It can't be, he told himself. He splashed more cold water on his face and thought: Oh, dear God, don't let it be her.

In the kitchen below him, a white-faced Diane was seated on a wooden chair, her heart racing as she recalled the moment when she had come face to face at last with her Nemesis. The women about her worked and worried. She looked so ill, they said. She really should go home. They could manage.

'Yes . . . yes,' murmured Diane. 'That would be best. Would one of you find my husband and just say he's needed in the kitchen? I want no fuss . . . we mustn't draw attention to ourselves on an occasion such as this. He'll drive me home quietly and no one will be any the wiser.'

Standing with Grace and Meg, Terry was now alarmed. That look . . . that terrible look on Grant's face just now . . . what on earth could have happened? Even Marisa, at her worst, couldn't have been the cause. She would have to go after him.

Grant paced up and down the large hallway, not seeing the antique furniture or the large Delft vase which held the Brigadier's walking sticks, but telling himself he must be mad to think what he was thinking. What could he tell Terry? That the woman buried in a shallow grave in the wood was her mother and the dead man her father? How could he say that to anyone, least of all the woman he loved?

He stopped walking, leaned his hands on the top of a long rosewood table and stared at a painting by Stubbs without even seeing it. Calm down, you stupid bastard, calm down! After all, what do you really know? That Terry's mother sustained injuries which happen to coincide with those of a dead woman?

His hands tightened into fists. No. Too many coincidences. It had to mean that Diane and John were frauds who knew the identity of the bodies found in the wood. Had they put them there? An ice cold shudder went through him. Was it possible that these very ordinary people, were in fact murderers?

'Don't be so bloody stupid,' he murmured, angry at himself for even thinking it. Not only had Diane and John Fenton played a large part in raising a memorial to the seven airmen, they had shown him nothing but kindness and consideration from the moment he had met them. How could he let his imagination run riot like this?

'Grant, are you all right?'

He turned his head and stared at Terry in a dreamlike way, as though she were a stranger. Suddenly shaken into life, he said, 'I'm fine.'

'No, you're not. Something's happened. Why did you look at me like that?'

Floundering for an answer, he said, 'I . . . I felt a bit off colour for the moment. I'm glad you followed me in here. We've had no time together since lunch.'

Nothing in his words could explain his grey pallor. She touched his face gently. 'But you look so ill, darling. Come into the drawing room and sit down for a while.'

His only movement was a shake of the head. 'No, I'm not ill, I promise you. Just tired. Anyway, I must go back out there soon otherwise Mrs Rashleigh will come looking for me.'

Terry saw his knuckles white against the table and knew there was something wrong. What exactly had Marisa told him? Why had he not reacted to her touch? He looked so ill, traumatised even. Maybe this day of highly charged emotions had affected him more than she had realised and Marisa's lies had proved to be the last straw.

Don't leave me, she screamed silently. Please, darling, don't leave me.

In the drawing room she poured him a brandy. Grant took it but refused to sit down, saying, 'Did I see you with Meg?'

Terry nodded. 'She brought Grace. I don't know why she chose today of all days. I asked her not to . . . and now Grace is all upset and I've been told that my parents have gone home because Mother fainted.'

'I warned you about Meg.' Grant set the brandy glass down on a Pembroke table and suddenly wanted to clasp her tightly to him. But she walked over to the window, and he found himself questioning her instead.

'Why is Grace upset?'

Terry was too afraid to turn and look into his eyes, afraid to think of what Grace had said about her parents or what Marisa had done to her relationship with Grant. Staring at the ancient Cedar that dominated the centre of the rear lawn, she murmured, 'She doesn't believe that Mother is her cousin or that Dad is her cousin's husband, if that makes any sense. So far as I can gather she didn't even speak to him. Oh, it's all too ridiculous for words.'

She turned and stared at him with such torment in her eyes that he moved across and held her close. How clean her hair smelled and what was that perfume that seemed so much a part of her? He looked down at her confused, lost expression and felt it pierce his heart. Suddenly it crossed his mind that Meg and Grace might well have put Terry in danger.

Feeling the strength and warmth of him, she thought then that she had been mistaken after all and that he did still love and want her, that Marisa had not touched him one little bit.

'I wanted Grace and Meg to come to the house and talk it out with my parents . . .'

'No,' he said quickly. 'That's the last thing they must do.'

She blinked in surprise. Why would he say such a thing? 'It's too late anyway. They've gone.'

Grant frowned. 'Gone? How long ago?'

'They said they were leaving when I came to you.'

He pulled away from her, saying, 'I must go too. I've stayed too long as it is. Come with me, Terry. Just get in the car and come with me. You can telephone your parents later.' He started towards the door then looked back at her astonished face. 'Come on. There's no time to waste.'

'Why? Where are we going?

'London.'

'London! Grant, you know that's impossible for me just now. What on earth has got into you?'

'Don't ask questions, just do as I say.'

'I can't just do as you say,' she retorted angrily. 'Mother's been taken ill. I must go home. I don't understand what . . .'

He caught her by the shoulders and cried, 'For God's sake, just do one thing I ask of you. If you love me, come with me now. Speak to no one as you leave and don't go home. Just wait for me at the front of the house while I say my farewells then . . .'

'I want nothing more than to be with you but this is madness.' She touched his face lovingly. 'You're overwrought. I think you should stay with us for a while and rest before driving home.'

It was no good. He would have to tell her the truth but even as he started, Grant checked himself just in time. Terry's best chance of safety lay in ignorance. She would never believe him anyway and then he would probably lose her forever. If he couldn't persuade her to go away with him now, then the Fentons must have no hint that she had learned anything from Grace.

As anxious for him as he was for her, Terry repeated, 'Stay here a little longer. You're not on duty until tomorrow morning so you have time.'

The fear in her eyes brought him to his senses. 'I have to leave. But promise me one thing – if Meg and her mother are mentioned in any way then you don't know them. Do you understand? *You don't know them.*'

His manner was such that she could only stare up at him in amazement.

'Do you hear me, Terry?' When she nodded, he saw tears glimmering in her eyes. 'And will you promise me you'll do as I ask?'

Unable to understand why her sorry little tale of family squabbles should be of any consequence to him, she agreed in order to calm him down. 'I promise.'

Grant seemed relieved; his intense gaze softened and he folded his arms about her and kissed her lovingly. At last he pulled back, his eyes lingering on her awhile, then, turning, walked quickly out of the room.

Feeling he had stepped into some surreal scene, Grant went through the motions of taking his leave of the Rashleighs and the Vicar then found himself climbing into his MG.

Weary to the bone suddenly, he longed for time alone to think. There was so much to consider and he didn't know which way to turn or how to handle the information he had acquired. Had he over-reacted and frightened Terry unnecessarily? How could she understand?

Heavy of heart, Terry arrived at the front of the house just in time to see him start the ignition. She prayed he would look back at her, but he eased the car along the drive and out into the lane without turning his head.

'Hmmm. He's certainly a dish.'

Turning, Terry saw Fiona standing behind her, and hoped her friend would fail to notice how upset she was feeling.

But Fiona had noticed. 'What's wrong? You two haven't had words, have you?'

Shaking her head, Terry strolled slowly towards the lake, golden now in the late-afternoon sun. There was a painful lump in her throat and her eyes were blurred with tears. She willed them away but they spilled over and ran down her cheeks just the same.

Walking beside her, Fiona wanted to help but felt she might be intruding on Terry's desire for solitude. Lovers' quarrel, she thought. Was love worth all this pain? Perhaps she was the lucky one after all.

At the lake, Terry turned and looked back at the house. Few people were left now on the green lawn where lengthening shadows spread finger-like from the large Cedar.

'Perhaps you'd rather be alone just now?' said her friend at last.

Finding her voice, Terry murmured, 'No, stay. It's just that . . . Grant's acting so strangely, and looks so ill.'

Fiona nodded. 'Yes, I know. He had a funny turn when he was with us. Although . . . well, maybe it was my fault. Mummy tried to stop me but I would go on. You see, I asked the Chief Superintendent if there had been any news about the bodies found in your wood. Not the thing, of course, on an occasion such as this. One sherry too many, I suppose.'

She fingered the waist of her skirt and murmured, 'Blast this thing! It's cutting into me. Can't wait to get changed.' Anyway, getting back to what I was saying. It appears there was some pathological evidence concerning one of the skeletons. Then Dr Tranmer started explaining to Grant who suddenly looked ill. He stared across at you with the strangest expression then excused himself and walked towards the house.'

Terry frowned, failing to see how this could explain anything. She turned back to the lake. On the far side, Eliot had removed his suit jacket, rolled up his shirt sleeves and was sitting quietly, with one arm around Max and the other holding the fishing rod. Dog and boy seemed blissfully at peace with the world. How she envied them.

'You're not at fault, Fiona.' She saw Marisa heading towards them and said, 'But I know who is.'

Fiona looked puzzled for a few seconds then followed Terry's gaze and decided it might be diplomatic to take herself back to the house.

Marisa was all smiles as she paused to say a word or two to Fiona, then carried on towards the lake. Approaching Terry, she said, 'What's this? Has Grant left you all alone?'

'He had to get back to the hospital,' snapped Terry.

'Really? I did tell him that Alastair was joining us for dinner at the farmhouse and that we hoped he would stay. What a pity.'

Terry looked at her in amazement. 'You told him what? And is it true?'

Marisa shrugged. 'I thought it might be at the time but since then I've learned he won't make it. Well, you know Alastair, all say and no do.'

'He never dines with us and rarely comes to Thornley. You lied to Grant. What else did you make up?'

'Really, Terry, don't be so childish. I didn't have to make anything up, as you well know. Anyway, I'll take my leave of you all now and get back to civilisation. 'Bye.'

With that she turned on her high heels and made her way back to the house, leaving Terry staring after her with dismay and rage. Grant had wanted her to leave with him, and what had she done? Refused. It had been a test and she had failed it. Had she gone with him he would have known that Alastair was very much in the past but she had stayed, leaving Grant struggling with a lie and in that awful state of mind. When she should have been a woman, she had acted more like a schoolgirl.

Grant was driving along the High Street when he saw Meg and her mother strolling ahead of him towards a Morris Minor. He was not too late, thank God.

Pulling up beside them, he said, 'Meg, we need to talk. But not here. The Swan Hotel at Lowdham as soon as possible.'

Understanding at once, she nodded. 'The Swan at Lowdham. We'll be there in about fifteen minutes.'

Diane leaned back in an armchair and sipped the brandy John had poured for her. 'I can't believe I behaved like that.'

Standing by the fireplace, brandy in hand, he looked down into the empty grate and said in a cold voice, 'You handled it badly. I thought you capable of better things.'

He turned and glared at her for some time then added thoughtfully. 'Still, when all's said and done, what happened exactly? Two women gatecrashed the reception and made a nuisance of themselves. Nutters I dare say. You told Lydia yourself that you'd never seen them before.' After a long pause his expression turned grim. 'Did they meet Terry or Marisa?'

Ashen-faced, Diane's eyes widened. 'Oh, John . . .' She fell silent as the back door opened and shut.

Glaring at her, he hissed, 'Pull yourself together and leave the talking to me.'

Terry entered with Eliot in tow and found her parents in the sitting room. 'Are you all right, Mother? I was told you were taken ill.'

Diane managed a weak smile. 'I think the heat of the marquee got to me that's all, dear. Truly, I'm much better now.' She turned her head slightly, looking beyond Eliot. 'Didn't Grant come home with you?'

Terry felt her throat tightening. 'No. He needed to get back to the hospital. Has Marisa gone?'

'Oh, yes,' said John. 'She came, she saw, and she bloody disappeared before we knew what had happened. I don't understand that girl.'

Terry was silent for a moment then felt rage overcome her. 'I do.'

'What's for dinner?' asked Eliot. 'I'm starving.'

Diane looked at him. 'After that huge lunch?'

'That was hours ago and anyway that wasn't proper food.' He left the room and stumped loudly up the stairs, calling back, 'I don't mind egg and chips.'

Seeing that Terry was about to go up to her old room, John spoke to her. 'The day went very well, I thought.' Scanning her face for any tell-tale sign that she might have thought otherwise, he went on, 'Did you manage to meet the families or were you stuck with Elsie for too long?'

'Elsie!' Diane sighed and put a hand to her brow. 'Oh, dear, poor Elsie. She spent hours getting here and we practically ignored her. I meant to return, but then . . . why didn't you ask her back, Terry?'

At that moment the telephone rang. John walked into the hall and picked up the receiver. A tense silence fell on the room as Terry and Diane heard him saying, 'Hello. Yes, she's much better now, thank you.' After a long pause he went on, 'Really? No. Diane hasn't mentioned that. What happened?' He was silent as Lydia explained about the strange Collinettes. 'They sound like a couple of odd-balls to me,' he said at last. 'Relations? That's a nice one. Probably saw our names in the newspaper and used them to gain access to your property. You need to be careful about that. Who knows? They might have been looking for an easy way to break in. You hear of such gangs. I hope they didn't go into the house.'

Curious, Terry walked to the door and stood there. Receiver to his ear and still listening to Lydia, John's jaw tightened then slowly he turned and stared at Terry, eyes glinting like steel. 'Terry? Are you sure? A misunderstanding obviously. Anyway they've gone now, I take it? Good. Well, thanks for enquiring about Diane. Goodbye.'

He replaced the receiver in silence then said in a thin voice, 'That was Mrs Rashleigh. Apparently two gatecrashers turned up this afternoon. You spoke to them, Terry. What did they say to you?'

She just stared at him. Had he not seen Grace after all? But her mother had and still the lies went on. Mindful of her promise to Grant, senseless though it seemed, Terry frowned as if trying to recall. 'There were lots of people there today. How would I know which ones were gatecrashers?'

'The Brigadier's under the impression they're relations of ours. Apparently, when he asked, the woman nodded yet you said nothing.'

A chill swept over Terry, the same chill she had felt on hearing her father's footsteps on the stairs that night after she'd read the letter from Grace. Today Grace had journeyed to Thornley hoping to reach out the hand of friendship to her parents, yet still they were denying her very existence. And why had Grant been so anxious that she must deny all knowledge of Grace?

Meanwhile her father was waiting for an answer.

'Well?'

'Oh, yes, those two,' she said at last.

'What did they say to you?'

'Nothing of significance. I assumed they were guests. Can't remember much about them to be honest.'

As though trying to read what was going on behind those grey eyes, John stared at her for a long time before saying, 'They weren't guests, they were a couple of gatecrashers who had no right there at all.'

Turning away quickly, she said, 'Well, how was I to know? I'd only just heard that Mother was unwell and my mind was very much on that. I can't see why you're so angry with me.'

John's whole demeanour changed at once. 'I'm not angry, pet. I'm just trying to find out who those women were.' With a sense of relief, he smiled at her. 'Well, tomorrow I can finish the harvesting. Please God the weather holds. Meanwhile get Eliot to make himself useful by feeding the hens and housing them for the night. Perhaps you'd help your mother by finding something for us to eat? I don't think she's up to it tonight.'

As she walked away from him Terry felt that old sense of foreboding. What on earth was going on? How could her father and mother lie to the Rashleighs about poor Grace? It was unbelievable. To think she had refused to leave with Grant because she'd felt it her duty to return to the house and check on her mother's health! Now her thoughts were very different. Back in the home where she was being lied to again, she would give anything to have gone with him to London instead of obeying her sense of family duty.

Chapter Sixteen

In the lounge of the Swan Hotel, Meg was still trying to come to terms with all that had happened. Unable to relax, she sat forward on the chintz-covered armchair, sipped a gin and tonic and glared across at Grace. From Diane she had expected a scene, but from her mother . . . never. She winced at the memory. '*Where is my cousin and her husband? I demand to know and won't leave here until I've found them.*' The whole thing had become so embarrassing that, having dragged her mother unwillingly to Thornley, she'd then had to drag her, even more unwillingly, away.

Driving to Lowdham had given Grant time to sort out his thoughts and he was appalled to think that a man of his education and profession could have had them in the first place. He had overreacted and caused Terry needless alarm.

Feeling calmer now, he offered Grace and Meg a cigarette, which only Meg accepted, then sat back hoping light would be shed on this mystery, a light that would show him what an idiot he had been to jump to such wild conclusions. What possible motive after all could John and Diane have for impersonating two dead people?

Meg inhaled and exhaled quickly, her nerves shot to pieces. 'I still can't believe you behaved as you did, Mum. What on earth got into you? You and Diane haven't met for over twenty years, so of course you didn't recognise each other. You hardly saw her face before she ran out of the marquee, so how could you say it wasn't her? You acted hastily and without thought. As for poor Terry . . . well, fancy saying a thing like that to her. What must she be thinking? She and all the others. Mum, you sounded as though you were . . .' She stopped abruptly.

'Crazy?' Grace glared at her daughter. 'Believe me I've never been more sane in my entire life.' She glanced across the coffee table at Grant and was glad that this kind friend of Terry's had joined them. He had calmed her with soothing words and bought her a brandy. The first sip had sent fire coursing through her but the second, and now the third, had relaxed her without befuddling her mind as she had thought it might.

'It was all your idea, Meg,' she went on. 'You wanted us to, go to Norfolk. The Broads are wonderful at this time of year,' you said,' glaring at her daughter. 'How was I to know you would then persuade us on to Suffolk? You planned it all, and . . .'

'Wish to God I hadn't.' Meg flicked ash viciously.

Grace looked through the latticed windows of the old coaching inn to see her friends strolling across Lowdham Green towards the large and ornate wool church. How kind Tim and Marjorie were to leave, enabling the three of them to talk. She told herself that she had good friends and a bad daughter. Sipping more more brandy, she murmured, 'It's impossible to believe that only this morning we were in Norwich Cathedral. It seems so long ago now. If only I had known what you were planning, Meg.'

'How else could I have got you to Thornley?' she snapped. 'And admit it, you were curious. I didn't have to twist your arm too much.'

Grace could not deny this. Curiosity, it was true, had overcome pride. There just had to be a reason for all those long years of silence. Here was her chance to find it out and put matters right she'd believed. But nothing could have prepared her for the shock she had received. Nothing.

Meg turned to Grant. 'Terry wanted me to bring Mum to meet her parents. Not today, though. She explained why and said she needed to prepare the way for such a reunion. But it seemed the perfect opportunity to me. I thought I was doing the right thing.'

Grant looked at the auburn curls framing the chubby face and disingenuous green eyes, wondering now if he had been wrong about Meg after all. Had she meant to stir up trouble or was she really innocently doing what she thought was best for everyone? It was difficult to know. Those eyes were like Marisa's, hard and defiant, yet would Meg willingly have put her mother through the trauma she had experienced today? No. Whatever else she was capable of, she would never do that.

'Meg, did either of Terry's parents see you talking to her?' Grant's hand tightened on his whisky tumbler as he waited for a reply.

'No,' she said. 'Give me credit for having some common sense. Terry wasn't supposed to know of our existence. Anyway, by the time we found her, Diane had rushed away and John had vanished into thin air without speaking to Mum.'

Grant sighed with relief and let his hand relax.

'John?' Grace tightened her lips. 'If he was John Fenton, then I'm Margot Fonteyn!'

Meg sighed. 'Twenty years, Mum. Twenty long years and . . .'

'To you it might as well be fifty, I know, I know,' Grace conceded patiently. 'But twenty is no time at all when you're my age. And, yes, people change as they get older, of course they do, but not into other people. Diane was never pretty. She had an angular face with thin lips and her bottom teeth were too crowded so that they crossed slightly. She did, however, have lovely eyes. They were large and a sort of dark grey-blue. "Like deep pools." John used to say. He wasn't being romantic either, not the type. He was just stating the obvious.' She paused and looked into the distance, her forehead puckered with anxiety. 'The woman I met today had bright blue eyes and a small round face. And her teeth were perfect. The woman I saw today was very good-looking and bore no resemblance whatsoever to Diane Fenton.

Meg sighed impatiently. 'Your memory's playing tricks, that's all.'

But Grace wasn't listening. 'As for that man . . . when Mrs Rashleigh told me he was John Fenton, I knew perfectly well he wasn't. Yet . . . and yet I've seen him before somewhere. And he recognised me too, I'm sure of it. He gave me the strangest look, then walked off towards the house before I could speak to him.'

'You recognised him because he's John Fenton,' snapped Meg.

'He is not,' her mother retorted angrily. She looked towards the church again, eyes focussing not on ornate castellations but on the past. 'Where have I seen him before? It's been worrying me and worrying me – but I just can't recall.'

Grant felt uneasy but said nothing that would interrupt the intense concentration that showed on Grace's face.

After a long silence, she scratched her chin and murmured, 'Boats. I seem to connect him with boats somehow.'

Meg gave a wry laugh. 'Not surprising, since John used to sail with Mike! You told us that yourself, the day you came out in his boat with us. Remember, last Easter? When Terry was with us?'

'Yes, I *do* remember.' Grace's eyes widened. 'The *Nicolette*! That's it, that's who he was. The yachtsman who put the *Nicolette* on the rocks years ago. We saw it that day and I told you then about this fellow who was rescued by Terry's father. He came to stay with us for some days after the accident. Now what was his name?' She closed her eyes and bit her bottom lip in an effort to recall. 'Oh, Lord, what was it? Damn! If Mike were here he'd know. In fact, if Mike were here he'd tell you that I'm right about those two back at Thornley. He knew John and Diane very well. He'd back me up.'

Meg looked at her mother suspiciously. 'But you also told Terry and me that the yachtsman became very friendly with John. Well then, that would surely account for his presence today? He's visiting the Fentons, that's all.'

Stomach muscles knotting, Grant said, 'No. I was at the house this morning before the church service. The Fentons had no guests.'

'And Mrs Rashleigh definitely pointed him out to me as John Fenton,' said Grace stubbornly. In the silence that followed, she turned fearfully to Grant. 'What on earth is going on?'

All his old fears now returned, he tried to sound calmer than he felt. 'Tell me more about this yachtsman? Tell me anything you can remember? You say he stayed with you and became friendly with John?'

Grace nodded. 'That's right. After the *Nicolette* was badly holed, John brought this man back to us.' Her brow furrowed deeply. 'Peter . . . something or other. He was an architect on a sailing holiday.'

'When was this exactly?' asked Grant.

'Let me see,' murmured Grace, staring down at her hands as she concentrated. 'Now I know he was with us when John received that letter from his cousin Arthur, saying that his wife had died . . . that would have been in '38. John didn't know Arthur save for the annual exchange of Christmas cards, although he and Diane did send him a wedding gift. Poor man hadn't been married very long so the letter came as a terrible shock to John because Arthur was the only relation he had, you see. The First World War took most of the others. It's a pity those two never met.'

Grant frowned. 'Meanwhile our shipwrecked yachtsman was in your house at the time and learned all about John's cousin in Suffolk?'

'Why, yes,' said Grace. 'Carlton . . . that was his name. Got it at last! Peter Carlton. He and John got on like a house on fire. He promised to look in on us if he returned to Guernsey.'

'And did he?' asked Grant.

'Yes. He came back the following spring to work on plans for an extension to Elizabeth College. At least, that's what he said at the time. John and Diane were pleased to see him again especially since he was able to advise John, being a professional man. He was very kind. We all liked him.'

Grant looked confused. 'Sorry . . . advise John on what exactly?'

'On the farm. Oh, dear, I'm getting ahead of myself. You see, Arthur had been killed in a shooting accident shortly before, and John received a letter from a solicitor saying that, as Arthur's only living relative, he was the main beneficiary and now owned a farm in Suffolk. Peter made John see how ill advised it would be to sell the farm instead of working it. I think he rather gave John the impression that he and Diane were living on us, but that wasn't true. We really needed their help in the business. Still, perhaps he was right. No man should turn down a chance to be independent and own land.'

Grace sounded choked as she murmured, 'Peter left, and a short while later so did John and Diane. I . . . waved them off at St Peter Port and . . . and never saw them again.'

A strange silence fell between them, one thought now passing through three minds. Only Grant gave voice to it.

'So Peter Carlton knew of the inheritance and now he's here, and you said Mrs Rashleigh called him John Fenton?'

Her face turning grey, Grace stared at him and nodded slowly. Suddenly she started to her feet, voice rising on a note of hysteria, causing others in the lounge to look at her.

'The police. We must tell the police. I'm going to them at once.'

Grant was at her side in an instant and, placing a gentle hand on her arm, bade her sit down. 'Please, Mrs Collinette, I'm sure there is a perfectly reasonable explanation for this.' Knowing there was only one explanation, he was, inwardly no calmer than Grace, but it couldn't be shouted from the rooftops. 'Look, if it makes you any happier, I'll contact the police right now. What they'll need, I think, is some firm proof before they go stomping around Lynwood Farm.'

'Like what, for instance?' demanded Meg.

'Like dental records,' said Grant, trying to sound casual. 'Is it possible to get hold of Diane's and John's old ones, given that the Channel Islands were occupied by the enemy?'

Grace nodded, saying that their family dentist and doctor had remained on the island throughout the war. 'Thank God they did or we'd have been in a pickle. I don't recall mentioning the fact that John and Diane had left for England, though. So if their records weren't sent to a local dentist here later, then they should still be in Guernsey.'

Grant took a small address book and pen from his jacket pocket and asked Grace for details of dental and doctor's surgeries and the name of the hospital where Diane had been treated. Armed with this information, he walked into the foyer of the hotel and, heart pounding, made his way to the public telephone.

Suddenly he felt a hand grab his arm. Turning, he looked into Meg's frightened eyes.

'What are you thinking?' she whispered.

'The unthinkable,' he replied. 'Your mother is right about Diane at least. She isn't Terry's mother. Believe me, I know. As for the rest . . . well, we must leave it to the police. But I need to be certain that I'm right about Diane's injuries?'

Meg frowned. 'Broken femur, fractured pelvis and hip displacement. Why?'

'That's what your mother told you. How sure can you be?'

'Very sure,' said Meg. 'After I mentioned the injuries to you, I thought it best to be certain of my facts, so I asked a nursing colleague of mine in Guernsey to check with the hospital concerned. She did. The notes were still in their archives and she read them out to me. Please don't tell anyone. We'd both get into a lot of trouble. Anyway, that's why I phoned the Westlake Clinic, to check. But why do you need to know this?'

Grant glanced about him, waited as two people walked from the lounge and into the restaurant then whispered, 'I take it you know about the skeletons found on the Fentons' property?' When Meg nodded, he went on, 'The report on the female skeleton showed she had sustained those same injuries some years before her death at around the age of thirty. She's been in the ground for twenty years. Now do you see why we must have those dental and medical records?'

Meg took this in slowly, then her eyes widened and she clasped her hand to her mouth, gagging.

Taking her by the shoulders, he said firmly, 'Say nothing of this to your mother. Nothing, do you understand? Personally I'd rather you gave her another brandy and got her home, but the police will want to interview her. And, Meg, for God's sake say nothing to Terry. Leave that to me. Any interference on your part could put her in danger.'

Nodding and shaking her head at the same time, Meg finally found her voice and groaned, 'Oh, Lord . . . Lord . . . my poor mother. It will kill her.'

Grant turned away, his eyes heavy. 'I fear it may kill Terry.'

Darkness had fallen as Detective Sergeant Hopwood walked across the car park of the Swan Hotel, his mind on all he had learned in that quiet old-fashioned lounge.

Reaching his vehicle, he stopped, fumbled in a pocket for the keys and shook his head in disbelief. Never, in all his years on the force, had he heard anything quite so bizarre. Even so, it was the only clue he had been given throughout these past months. He climbed into the driving seat, started the ignition and sat staring into space, still trying to sift through the strange story just related to him.

Had fate handed him a breakthrough or fool's gold? He was being asked to believe that two very likeable people had killed the real Fentons and taken their place. Even if it were possible to deceive a community for so long, what motive could they have had? The farm? Men had murdered for less but . . . come on . . . the Fentons? That poor sod with flu and his charming wife and daughter? The whole thing was utterly ridiculous. And yet there was that report on the woman's body. Well, maybe, maybe.

He started moving out of the car park and on to the road that circled Lowdham Green. Of course, Mrs Collinette knew nothing about the bodies found in the wood, Mr Kenway had made that clear to him as he'd arrived at the hotel, and so he had only her story of a stranded yachtsman and a disappearing cousin to go on. Kenway was another matter. Although he'd come up with additional interesting facts, out of the hearing of the two women, at no time did he accuse anyone of murder. Yet all that he said implied the folks now living at the farm knew of and were impersonating the people found buried in the wood. In which case they were certainly involved in the murders.

At Lowdham Police Station, Hopwood asked for a call to be put through to the States Police Force at St Peter Port in Guernsey, then sat down and lit a cigarette. He wanted those dental and medical records flown over at once and checked out before even mentioning this to his superiors. Passed over he might be, but no way was he going to become a laughing stock as well.

It was only then that he remembered his promise to take his wife to the cinema that evening and groaned inwardly. Eric Hopwood, you're in the dog-house again. And for what? A wild goose chase.

In the early hours, when it was not yet dawn, Marisa returned to the house in Cadogan Place and crept up the darkened stairs to the bedroom as she had done many times before. She hated these moments – leaving Julian's warm bed to return to her cold one before Mrs Mount was up and about.

It had been a long journey back to London and a slow one so she had gone directly to the flat where he was waiting and, feeling that she had accomplished what she had set out to do, had savoured her moment of triumph during their lovemaking.

Opening the bedroom door quietly, she reached for the switch. Before her hand had found it the room was flooded with light.

Still fully clothed, Alastair lay stretched out on the bed, bottle of whisky and a half-filled tumbler on the bedside table. Next to this was a large ash tray filled with dogends. The table lamp shone out like an interrogator's spotlight.

Marisa turned to stone.

'It's almost four o'clock,' he said thinly. 'When I arrived here yesterday evening, Mrs Mount told me you'd gone to Suffolk. I rang your father and was told that you left Thornley around five and would be home about eight. I've been waiting. What happened?'

'Nothing happened,' she said shakily, still trying to get over the shock of seeing him here. 'I had a very slow journey back, and called in to see some old friends of mine. We got talking well into the night . . . you know how it is.'

'Oh, I know how it is all right,' he snapped. 'Julian Hart and his little love nest! Don't insult my intelligence with lies, Marisa. How long has this been going on?'

Never one to be cowed by any man, she would not stoop to any futile attempt at self-defence. Lifting her chin stubbornly she said, 'Six weeks and four days.'

'You keep a careful count then?'

He was calm, she thought, too calm. 'What does it matter to you? You're never here.'

'Even so,' said Alastair, his voice a shade slurred, 'if I'm to wear cuckold's horns I might as well use them to my own advantage. I want a divorce and now I can get one. I know who your lover is, where and when you meet. It's all on record.'

She stared at him in amazement. 'You mean . . . you actually mean you've had me followed?'

'I mean just that. Somehow I don't think a well-respected banker with a brother in the Government will take too kindly to being cited in a messy divorce, do you?' He let out a long breath and shook his head. 'Can't imagine what'll he think of you when *that* happens.'

Alarmed, Marisa held her ground. 'You're drunk. We'll speak about this, again when you've sobered up. Not that you could possibly understand. What would you know about feelings when you have none?'

'Feelings!' he thundered. 'You speak to me of feelings?' Alastair's rage flared and died, then he smiled sardonically. 'Still, there is another way and you'd better jump at it. I still count myself a gentleman and . . . well . . . a cuckold is a thing of pity after all. So, much as I should enjoy ruining lover boy, I think it would be better for everyone concerned if I allowed you to divorce me. A settlement would be drawn up that both of us could happily accept and you would sign it first. I would then furnish you with grounds. I'm sure I could find some.'

'I daresay you could,' she said bitterly. 'Adultery with my own sister, for instance. God, how people will despise you when they hear of it!'

He sighed. 'That one won't run, I'm afraid. I haven't seen Terry since the day she came here and I drove her to Liverpool Street. What on earth made you think I had? Well, there it is. I haven't committed adultery with anyone but these things can be fixed . . . they always used to be. Brighton it was in the old days. An uncle of mine got a very neat divorce that way.'

When Marisa remained silent, he sighed. 'Let's face it, we both married for the wrong reasons and now it's time to end this farce, once and for all. You have someone else in your life and I want my freedom.'

She gave him a blank stare. Did he mean what he said or was it the alcohol talking? No, it was too good to be true. There had to be a catch. Terry! He still wanted her, that was the truth of it. Was it possible that by destroying Grant's faith in Terry she had handed her sister straight back to Alastair? That had been the last thing Marisa wanted. But her mind leaped ahead to a large house in rolling acres of Cotswold countryside where she would live with the man she loved. That was all that mattered now. Terry and Alastair could go to hell, and probably would.

'I didn't think you would stoop so low as to have me watched.'

Alastair grinned. 'Bridge parties, indeed. You're bloody hilarious!'

'And you're quite a bastard.' Marisa backed to the door, her hand tightening on the knob as she wondered how alarmed Julian would be when she told him that divorce was now a *fait accompli*. 'I agree, though. We must be free of each other.'

'How civilised we're being about it all.' Alastair breathed a sigh of relief. It was over. And without the almighty row he had dreaded and expected.

Marisa opened the door to leave. 'When do you return to Coventry?'

'Not for a few days. Sean needs me in London. Difficult for us both in this house, don't you think? Go home, Marisa. Stay there for a while, that would be best. Oh, that reminds me. Fiona rang earlier. Apparently something strange happened today, after the memorial ceremony. Did you witness it?'

She looked puzzled. 'No.'

'Fiona wanted to talk to you but Lydia took the phone from her and told me that some woman had turned up, declaring that your parents were not your parents. She said she came from Guernsey and was your mother's cousin. Caused quite a scene. Lydia wondered if you could shed any light on it. You weren't here to, of course, but I told her that you had no relatives other than your parents and siblings.'

'Who was this woman?'

'I've just told you. She claimed to be your mother's cousin. According to Lydia, she was distraught. Had a daughter with her. The daughter led her away.' He smiled mischievously. 'I suppose half of Thornley is busy saying "There's no smoke without fire".' At the look on his wife's face, the smile left his. 'Spectre at the feast? Something nasty in the woodshed, Marisa? What is it you've been hiding all these years?'

With that he switched off the light and said, 'Best if you sleep in the spare room. It's all made up for you. Shut the door when you leave.'

Something rushed past his head and smashed against the wall behind him. He knew it could only be the Royal Doulton figurine. that had stood on the dressing table. Then the door slammed shut.

The ward was as neat as a new pin as Grant walked through it checking the patients about to undergo surgery. They sat or lay in newly made beds with sheets and blankets tucked and cornered with the utmost precision, their books and magazines tidily out of sight as the Ward Sister, Staff Nurse and a handful of students accompanied Mr Kenway on his slow progress along the ward. To those he was not operating on he chatted briefly and to those who were about to go under his knife he was reassuring.

No one could have guessed at the turmoil raging in his mind.

He came to the last bed in the ward and stood smiling down at the fifty-four-year-old woman who sat with large anxious eyes waiting to hear him explain her coming ordeal.

'I've never 'ad an operation before. In fact, I've never been in 'ospital before.'

Grant touched her hand gently and smiled. 'Well, I've been in one for a very long time, so take my word for it the food's the only thing you need worry about. This afternoon you'll be wheeled to the theatre, and before you know it – you'll be fast asleep. When you wake up, you'll be back in your bed wondering when you're going to have the operation.'

He was about to leave when she grabbed his hand tightly. 'Will you be operating?'

'I most certainly will, Mrs Grainger.' He smiled and patted her hand to calm her. 'Don't worry. I've performed this operation more times than I've had hot dinners. I'll see you again later.'

The woman's pale and prematurely aged face relaxed into a smile and she watched as he moved on. There was something about Mr Kenway that made her feel less afraid. It wasn't just that he was more friendly than the other doctors wandering through the wards, it was something in his eyes that made her feel her life was in safe hands.

Grant, however, was suffering grave misgivings. Should he be operating on anyone with all this on his mind? Why hadn't he phoned in saying he was sick? No. That would have meant cancelled operations. There was nothing for it but to clear his mind and concentrate only on his work. But it was hard when he kept wondering whether Hopwood had obtained the dental records he sought.

On his way back from Lowdham last night, he had phoned Terry from Ipswich to set his mind at rest that she was all right. Her voice had sounded strained and he had wanted then to rush back to Thornley and snatch her away. But she'd insisted that everything was fine, that her mother had gone to bed early and that her father had been invited to the Hall for a drink with others on the memorial committee. So he had travelled on to London, unable to rid himself of the heavy feeling of dread churning over and over inside him.

It was still with him as he toyed with his lunch and told himself that, for now, Terry was safe only because she was ignorant of the imminent collapse of her world. But he would have to warn her before the police made their move. Then she would turn on him, and hate him with a passion that would remain with her until the end of her days. And how could he live with that agony? Yet what other way could he have taken? Ignore it? Hope it would all disappear overnight? Even without Grace, he couldn't have done that. After listening to her story, there was no way he could have avoided involving the police.

Pushing his lunch away, he glanced at his watch. There was just time to phone Terry at her flat.

'Grant!' The relief in her voice was obvious. 'Thank God you phoned. I've been worrying about you all night.'

'And I've been worrying about you. Are you all right?'

'I'm not sure,' she said, thinking how silly this conversation was when there was so much underlying it. He still sounded odd, like a man falling back on good manners before delivering a severe blow. 'After yesterday, I'm not sure of anything any more. The word's gone crazy all of a sudden. My parents, Marisa and Grace . . . all of them saying strange things.' She paused and said quietly, 'And then there's you.'

'What do you mean?'

'Your very odd behaviour. You seemed afraid . . . afraid to tell me something.'

Something in her voice alarmed him. 'Look, Terry, we have to talk. I'm on call until tomorrow but have work after that. Can you come up?'

She froze. Go to his flat to hear him tell her it was all over? 'I'm taking Eliot to Hampton Court. He's meeting a school chum there and is going to spend a few days with him and his family in Kingston. Then I'm returning home.'

'Why? Why not come to me.'

'I . . . no. I must get back.'

'Very well. I'll come to you at Hampton. Wait for me. I hope to make it at about five and don't know the place well, so stay by the river entrance. If the palace is closed by the time I arrivc, I can always spot you from the bridge and we'll take it from there. But I must see you, Terry.'

After a long pause she said, 'Very well. Five o'clock by the boats.'

He placed one hand to his brow, thought what he must say to her tomorrow and murmured, 'Whatever happens, I want you to know that I love you, Terry.'

He replaced the receiver, walked to his office and pulled a file towards him. As he studied Mrs Grainger's notes he saw again the woman's frightened eyes slowly calming at his soothing words. But her operation promised to be a complex one. Determined to erase all that he must say to Terry from his mind, he made his way to the theatre and started scrubbing up.

It was Eliot's first trip on the Thames and he leaned over the side of the pleasure boat, eyes darting this way and that in eager anticipation of being with his friend for a few days. Anything was better than home where his parents were so quiet and tense. They had hardly said a word to him since the dedication ceremony. Something had happened, he could sense it, but no one ever told him anything. Yesterday he had taken himself off to Terry's flat and stayed the night with her and they had set off early today for Woodbridge Station.

Beside him she gazed at London drifting past: Houses of Parliament, St Thomas's Hospital where Grant was working, even now, Lambeth Palace and Battersea, until the city eventually gave way to Georgian houses at Strand on the Green, then riverboats, islands, banks of willow and green pastures before more riverside houses, towns and old stone bridges. And all the time her mind was fixed on Grant's words.

'Whatever happens, I want you to know that I love you, Terry.'

What terrible thing lay ahead that he must soften the blow like this? In her heart, she knew. For all his endearments, he would take her hand in his, as a lover would, then deliver the *coup de grâce*. And all she could do about it was sit in this boat and sail slowly, oh, so slowly, to that dreadful moment.

Hampton Court was busy with tourists, many of whom were lost in the maze, along with Terry, Eliot, his school friend and the friend's mother. In the end all four admitted defeat and had to be helped out by a kindly German couple. Then they wandered through the great palace and grounds until Eliot was finally swept off to Kingston for a few days.

Standing alone in the Fountain Court, Terry didn't in the least blame her brother for spending most of this summer's holiday away from home rather than inviting friends to stay. Although he no longer spoke of what had been uncovered in the wood, it seemed that being anywhere but Lynwood was his way of handling it.

She wandered alone around the beautiful gardens then sat on a bench looking towards the Great Fountain, took a lipstick and mirror from her black leather handbag and retouched her lips. Hoping no one was watching, she then combed her hair, dabbed a little powder on her face and Chanel No 5 on her wrists. As she did so she remembered a warm June evening when they had wandered along a river path towards a Chiswick pub. The sun was just setting, all London seemed to be outside enjoying the evening and Grant had given her this gift, admitting that Chanel No 5 was the only perfume he had heard of.

At a quarter to five, she made her way towards the West front of the Palace and peered anxiously through the Tudor arch towards the long path ending at the river. The hot day had become more sultry and the river seemed busier than ever. Butterflies fluttered in her stomach. She longed to see Grant yet dreaded it also. Did she look all right? Had her blue cotton dress creased in all this heat? She must look her best, she must be perfect, she must do everything to make him still want her.

She walked down to the quayside and stood watching the boats and bridge as the minutes ticked away.

Having left the hospital earlier than expected and had a good run to Hampton, Grant parked his car and headed towards the river entrance, thinking of what Meg had told him early this morning. After a bad night and before his wake up call, he had phoned her before she went on day duty in case she had been trying to contact him.

'No, but I do have news,' she had said. 'Mum phoned saying Mike had arrived in England. Apparently the dental records have been found. That's all.'

That's all? It was everything. He didn't need to know what the records would reveal, he just wanted to know how in God's name hc could tell Terry?

The garden was quiet. Few visitors had found it, nestling as it did in a corner of the palace, off the beaten track. They sat on a bench, he holding her hand tightly as he spoke, she staring vaguely at a bumble bee hovering about the roses.

When he had told her as much as he felt she could absorb, he stopped, turned her small hand over in his and stroked its palm gently. Her silence worried him.

Have you understood me?' he asked.

His touch sent a small tremor through her body and she stared down at his large hand in bewilderment. This was very different from the 'time to say goodbye' speech she had expected.

'Have you understood?' he repeated gently.

Terry shook her head. 'You speak of some yachtsman . . . and my mother's not being my mother because she's Eliot's mother, and you tell me she was Dad . . . No, I don't understand. Oh, I know quite well what Grace has been saying, but she's wrong.

Why did you listen to her? Why did you take it on yourself to meet her and Meg in Lowdham without asking me along too?'

Grant squeezed his fingers around hers and placed them to his lips. His heart ached for her with each word he said. 'Grace isn't wrong and that's the hell of it. Think back to that evening after she arrived at the Hall. What did your parents say of her?'

Turning her head away, Terry shrugged and lied. 'I . . . I don't recall.'

'You recall very well, so tell me?'

With a long sigh she murmured, 'Oh . . . well . . . they insisted that the Collinettes were strangers to them, gatecrashers, nutters, certainly no relation of ours.'

'Which you know is not true.'

'They were confused. Twenty years is a long time.'

Grant was growing desperate. If she couldn't accept this much then how on earth could she ever be told the rest of it? 'Look, darling, all I ask is that you come with me now to Finchley, see Grace and hear for yourself what she has to say.'

Terry snatched her hand away, and shook her head.

'Well, don't then,' said Grant angrily. 'Bury your head in the sand, why don't you?' With mounting despair, he sighed. 'Last Easter in Guernsey you met a man called Mike? He took you out on a boat trip?'

'Yes. What about him?'

'He's in England. Grace wants him to verify her testimony to the police.'

'Police?' Terry stared at him in disbelief. 'What on earth has it to do with them? How dare Grace go that far? What does the woman think she's doing? All right, so there have been things in the past that all three of them wish to remain secret, I've known that for ages, but to come here causing trouble for my parents is . . .'

'They're *not* your parents,' said Grant in a loud voice. He looked at her confused, frightened face and said more gently, 'They're not your parents.'

Terry was on her feet in an instant, glaring down at him. 'Oh, don't say that again, I'm sick and tired of hearing it. If they're not my parents then tell me where my true parents are? Go on. You're the one insisting I'm in the hands of imposters. Well, where are my real parents?'

This was the moment, but the words stuck in his throat. Instead he stood up and, placing his hands on her shoulders, said thickly, 'Detective Sergeant Hopwood wants dental records to help him establish that. They've been sent over from Guernsey.'

'Dental records?' She stared him in amazement bordering on alarm. 'Why?' When he turned his face away she shook her head in pained confusion. 'Oh, Grant, this can't be happening. Now the Sergeant's going to upset my parents all over again, and for what? For Grace? And you . . . what part are you playing in all this? How can you be involved in such a thing after all the kindness they've shown you?'

When he said nothing to this, Terry searched his eyes and saw in them something that sent ice cold fear through her. She tried to drive it away with anger, hysteria in her voice as she shouted, 'I've had enough of all this. I'm going home, I'm going to tell them what's going on and ask them outright why they've lied about Grace. I'll even tell them my part in deceiving them . . . I'll tell them everything and you can't bloody well stop me!'

'No,' cried Grant, catching her arm and trying to calm her. 'Listen to me . . . please listen to me.' But she twisted from his grasp and fled from the garden in tears. He chased after her and saw her pale blue dress disappearing in the crowd. By the time he had made his way through them she was out of sight.

He ran from garden to garden, court to court, then rushed down to the river, hoping she would be waiting for the next boat. One brief glance at those already gathering for the return journey, was enough to convince him she was making her way home by train.

Home, he thought, where two possible killers were waiting. Terry would blurt out everything and then what?

Rushing back to his car he started off for Liverpool Street station, pretty sure he would find her before her train left. If not, and she was already on her way to Woodbridge, he would have to drive like the wind to reach Thornley before her.

Chapter Seventeen

Emotionally exhausted, Terry finally reached Woodbridge. She had spent the entire journey staring through the train window, trying in vain to choke back tears and drive Grant's words from her mind.

Leaving the station, she headed towards the empty car park where her Austin stood in isolation. Walking on past the car, Terry made her way towards the old Tide Mill and paused by the water's edge with thoughts spinning round and around in her mind.

What had made her run from Grant? Fear? Fear that he could be right? After all, not only had her parents lied about Grace and Meg's very existence, they had denounced both of the women as strangers and possibly thieves. Why would they go to such lengths? And why would Grace go so far as to bring in the police? It was all so horrendous that she desperately wanted the whole thing to be a big mistake. But today Grant had told her it was not and that medical evidence could prove that Diane was not her mother just as Grace could prove that John Fenton was, in truth, a wrecked yachtsman who had stayed in their Guernsey home before the war.

Ludicrous nonsense! It had to be. What logical reason would any man have to take the place of her father? And given that he had, then where *was* her father? And where was her true mother? Grant had been unable to answer these questions but something in his eyes had made her run from him without wishing to hear more. Fool that she was, behaving like an hysterical child at such a moment.

The sultry day had turned to grey, storm-threatened evening.

Light was fading fast, and from somewhere beyond the Deben came a distant rumble of thunder. The tide was out and boats had settled on the mud banks. There was no one around. She was all alone. Sick at heart, she thought how different the scene had been two weeks ago, when she and Grant had sailed along the river in bright sunshine, without a care in the world. Or so she had thought. How could she have known then the suspicions forming in his mind about her parents or the depth of fear which she had seen in his eyes only a few hours ago?

The shadow of his fear lay on her now but she refused to let her mind dwell on that. If only she had stayed, gone with him to see Grace as he had wished, then returned to the flat with him for the comfort of his arms and body during the long and lonely night that now lay ahead. Too late now. She must face the dark hours alone, her mind wandering this way and that. And, as with the maze at Hampton Court, finding no way out.

A flash of lightning across the river was followed by a louder roll of thunder. The storm was coming her way.

Turning swiftly, she headed back to the station car park, her mind made up. It was time to confront two people she loved dearly and ask them for an explanation.

Speeding towards Ipswich, Grant skidded the MG round corners and raced along roads and lanes, praying that either he or the police reached the house before Terry.

How could he have botched things so badly? His only intention had been for Terry to see Grace then spend the night safely with him while the police did their work. Now she was a loose cannon, armed with information which could put her in grave danger.

He blamed himself for not anticipating her reaction. That she should disbelieve him, yes, that she should turn on him, yes, but that she would flee from him and run to the very place he had wanted to keep her from . . . No, he had not foreseen that.

Getting through London's rush hour traffic had been a nightmare and by the time he reached Liverpool Street station the Ipswich train had just left, taking Terry with it. Panic welled up inside him at the lateness of the hour. Suppose the police decided to make their arrests tomorrow and not before?

Pulling up at a public telephone box, he rushed inside and picked up the receiver, intending to get an urgent message through to Lowdham police station. Only then did he see the notice: OUT OF ORDER. Cursing himself aloud for wasting precious moments, he drove off once more, telling himself that Hopwood would surely be at the farm by now. He must be, he had to be! 'Please, God, let Terry's journey be a slow one,' he prayed.

He saw a flash of lightning and heard a thunder clap, but with no time to waste on raising the top he raced on into the gathering darkness.

The storm was moving towards Thornley as Terry turned into the drive and pulled up outside the front door of her home. She sat for some moments, listening to rain beating on the roof while the wipers moved rhythmically across the windscreen. How could a house that had always been so welcoming suddenly feel so threatening?

A curtain moved at the window, then the front door opened and Diane appeared with a black umbrella, shouting, 'For goodness' sake come in out of the storm.'

Or into it, thought Terry, dreading what was to come. Grant had advised caution. 'Say nothing,' he had warned . . . when . . . two days ago? Two days? Was that all it had been, just two days since the dedication ceremony? She climbed from the car and, sheltering under the umbrella her mother was holding over her, walked quickly towards the house.

'Saw the car lights,' Diane was saying. 'I'm so relieved you've come here. I began to worry when there was no answer from your flat. Are you staying the night? I think you should with this storm coming.' She stood the umbrella in a corner of the vestibule where it dripped puddles on to the flagstones. 'Did Eliot meet his friend all right? Did he enjoy Hampton Court?'

How normal she seemed, thought Terry, watching her bustle about the kitchen asking questions that any mother would ask. So normal that her own resolve to confront her parents began to evaporate. Here, in these familiar surroundings, the whole thing seemed like a far-fetched dream.

Diane picked up the kettle and filled it with water. 'When I got no reply from your flat, I wondered if you'd decided to spend the night with Margaret.' She turned and gave Terry a strange look. 'Margaret? Isn't that her name? Isn't that what you told us?'

Shaken from her complacency, Terry's heart took a sudden

leap. That look, that voice. Had they known all along about her association with Meg? Had they realised all along she knew they had been lying? Suddenly she was afraid.

'Margaret?' Why was her voice so weak? 'No, I'd planned to come straight back.'

'I see. I'll make you some tea.' Placing the kettle on the stove, Diane frowned. 'Everything's all right between you and Grant, isn't it?'

'Of course.' Shoulders sagging with relief, Terry quietly berated herself for letting her imagination run away with her. Even so there was an air of Alice Through the Looking Glass about her present situation. What was reality? The terrible world which Grant had painted for her or these homely surroundings with her mother worrying and fussing as she always had done? If only she would stop asking awkward questions.

But Diane was not through with them. 'It's just that you seemed so down the other evening after he had gone. And you're not staying over with . . . Margaret?' She turned and glared at Terry. 'Oh, my dear, do you take us for fools?'

Alert once more, Terry swallowed hard. 'What do you mean?'

'Don't play the innocent. You and Grant, alone in your flat or his. Just ask yourself if you're not making yourself cheap in his eyes.'

This second false shock had set Terry's adrenalin racing once more and, now on her guard, she took shelter in the safe territory of a mother and daughter spat.

'Mother, I'm over twenty-one. And Grant is hardly as you've just painted him.'

Diane's lips tightened in anger. 'You little idiot! Don't you know what men are? Oh, you've a *lot* to learn. Well, don't come weeping to me when the inevitable happens.' Anger spent, she let a sigh escape her lips and said quietly, 'And we liked him so much. That's what makes it feel like a betrayal of our trust.' After taking a moment to calm down, she turned to Terry and asked if she was hungry, signifying the subject was now closed.

To Terry it was suddenly unbearable. How could she sit there as though nothing had happened, deceiving the parents she loved and who loved her too? What possible wrong could they have done? Yet Grant said they had done wrong and he, like Brutus, was 'an honourable man'.

'No, I'm not hungry,' she answered quietly, moving across to Diane who was looking at her anxiously. This was it, this was the moment, she decided. 'Mother, I . . . I must know . . .' Terry swallowed. 'It's all so difficult . . . but I need to understand . . .' It was useless, the words simply would not come. 'I've a terrible headache. Would you mind if I went straight up to bed?'

Diane narrowed her eyes. Lightning flashed, causing her to start. She hated storms, they brought back such terrible memories. 'Stay downstairs with us for a while. I'll give you a couple of Asprin then you drink this tea and . . .'

'No,' said Terry, a shade too quickly. 'And no thunderbolt will strike our chimney, as you always insist it might. It's just that I am so tired. Where's Dad?'

'Taking Dauphine to her stall, out of the storm.'

'Well, say goodnight to him for me, and tell him I'll see him tomorrow.' Tomorrow! Terry paused at the thought then walked into the hallway, aware that her mother had followed and was watching her as she made her way up the stairs to her room.

Alone, and away from those piercing blue eyes that seemed to be searching her mind, Terry looked out at the storm then lay down on the bed and flinched at the next thunder clap.

Tomorrow. What would happen then? Would the police come with their strange accusations? She should warn her parents, so why didn't she? She had come here resolved to ask questions and receive answers, so why hadn't she? Tears flooded her eyes and rolled down her cheeks and soon convulsive sobs wracked her body. Dear God, tomorrow!

Diane was still in the hallway when John entered through the front door. Water dripped from his macintosh and splashed on the floor as he stood, wondering at her expression.

'Terry's here,' she whispered, frowning. 'But I don't like it. She's acting very strangely.'

'Oh?' His face darkened as he took off the rain-soaked macintosh and hung it on a peg in the vestibule where it dripped water on to the flagstones. 'Go on.'

'You don't think . . . you don't think she might have heard something?' As though suddenly fearing him, Diane stepped back a little then shook her head. 'No, of course not. It's just my imagination. Forget it.'

John stared at her for some time then, as though picking up on her thoughts, put on the mac once more and said, 'I have to go out again.'

'If it's to the windmill, you needn't bother,' she said. At his astonished look, she added, 'What you hid there, I now have safe.'

With the storm crashing overhead and rain slanting across the roads, Grant turned into Thornley's High Street. No lights shone in cottage windows or from the two street lamps. As he reached the watersplash a flash of lightning lit the scene. A startled duck flew out of his path as he drove on far too quickly and turned up the hill. 'Bloody power cut! That's all I need.'

Entering the drive slowly, he saw that the farmhouse too was in darkness. Having finally managed to contact the police, he glanced around in vain for a sign of them. The only car in sight was Terry's Austin.

With dread in his heart he rushed from the MG towards the front door and saw it was not quite closed. Under his gentle touch it yielded and he entered the darkened hall. For one moment the only sound he heard was the ticking of the grandfather clock then a voice made him start.

'Come in, Grant.' John appeared from the sitting room, holding a candle. His face in the amber glow was as expressionless as his voice. 'As you can see, we've had a power cut.'

'Where's Terry?' he wanted to know.

'In her room.' John smiled sardonically and said, 'What's all this then? Had a tiff, have you?'

Ignoring him, Grant bounded up to Terry's bedroom and slowly opened the door, dreading what he might find. Peering into darkness, he could see nothing. Only when John appeared behind him with the candle did its flickering light reveal Terry lying on top of the bed, still in her blue dress. Alarmed, Grant moved towards the bed, saw that she was sleeping, and felt a shudder of relief course through his body. He wanted to touch her, hold her, take her out of this place right now, but he held back. Any minute now the police would arrive. He should be here.

Turning, he faltered for a moment, knowing that as he left the room he would have to brush past this man who had murdered two innocent people. But John stood back to let him pass, then closed the door quietly.

*

Had she slept? Terry sat up and glanced at her watch. It was well after nine. The storm, although it had abated, was still circling around. She must have slept, but all she remembered was lying down on the bed and sobbing. She put out her hand and pressed the switch of her bedside lamp. The room remained deep in darkness.

Searching for the candle and holder which she always kept for the many power cuts that bedevilled Thornley, she lit it and moved out on to the landing. Raised voices drifted up to her from the sitting room. By the subdued light coming from it she knew the door was partly open. Creeping down the stairs, hand shielding the candle flame to prevent it from blowing out, she was about to enter the room when she heard Grant's voice.

'I didn't come here to warn you, I came because of Terry.'

Astonished that he was here, she stopped in her tracks and stood listening behind the door. Suddenly her mother cried out.

'Dear God! Do you seriously imagine we would harm a hair of her head? I'll fetch her down. Let her speak for herself.'

'No.' Grant was leaning against the door frame, his suit soaking wet, dark eyes watchful. 'Let her sleep. I don't want her to hear what you did, but for God's sake, tell me why you did it before I go out of my mind.'

'You already have!' John shouted seriously. 'Coming here with your idiotic accusations, expecting us to sit and calmly accept them. And all because of this strange woman. If you insist on believing her, then tell me this. Where the hell did John and Diane Fenton go?'

'Into a shallow grave,' said Grant. 'Where *you* put them.' He studied their shocked reaction to this and knew then that the nightmare was reality. They sank into chairs with stunned expressions on their faces.

Terry slowly crumpled on to the hall chair, unable to believe what she had just heard. Had Grant gone mad? How could he even think such a thing? She put the candle on the table beside her, wondering why her parents were not denying his dreadful accusation instead of letting him go on.

'The police have the Fentons' dental records and, I believe, the hospital notes detailing Diane's injuries after her accident.' Grant saw blue eyes fixed on him in surprise. 'Of course, you didn't know about that accident, did you?'

Too shocked to answer, she just stared at him in silence as he turned to John, saying, 'That you did it to gain a small farm beggars belief. From what I've heard of Peter Carlton he doesn't seem the type. For one thing he went to a lot of trouble with that family in Guernsey. Always agreeable, always ready with a helping hand and good sound advice. John Fenton hung on his every word and thought him such a friend. Somehow that seems more the mark of a confidence trickster than a cold-blooded killer, but then, I don't usually keep company with murderers. And you did kill John and Diane Fenton. Better if I address you by your true name, perhaps?' He saw rage in the man's eyes and his raised, threatening hand.

'Enough. I've heard enough. Now get out of here before I do something I might regret.' Grant stood his ground without flinching. 'I think you did that a long time ago.' The threatening hand was lowered.

'What the hell do you mean?'

Shooting to her feet, Diane rounded on him, crying, 'Stop it! For God's sake, stop it.' The cry choked on a sob. 'It's over, can't you see that? It's over.' For a moment she stood looking at him then said quietly, 'We always knew that one day it could happen. Well, now it has and you can't bluff your way out of it. Dental records.' A wry smile played on her lips. 'You thought of everything except that. And what was this accident I knew nothing about?'

'Shut up, you bloody fool!' raged Carlton. 'How do we know the police have any such records? We only have his word for it.'

Exhaustion getting the better of her, Diane made her way to the sofa and sat down. Head in hands, she murmured quietly, 'Why would Grant say it if he didn't know it? Why would he come here thinking we might have harmed Terry if the truth hadn't come out? No, it's over at last and it's as if I've been released. It's become harder and harder, living with that terrible memory, knowing that any day could bring discovery. Now the day has come and there's an end to it at last.'

She looked up, her tear-stained face turned to Grant in supplication. 'My one fear now is for Eliot and the girls. What's to become of them, the poor darlings? What's to become of my darling, golden son?' She turned away and covered her face with her hands once more, crying in anguish, 'Oh, God, I love him so much!'

It was hard not to pity her, and clear to Grant that she had been led by the nose into something so terrible that after twenty years of agonising over it she felt the need of expiation.

In the hallway Terry felt her stomach muscles tightening, thought she was about to faint and gripped the edge of the table in an effort to keep a hold on consciousness.

Grant asked Peter Carlton, 'Would you really kill two innocent people and steal their identities just to get your hands on a small farm?' He paused, looking puzzled. 'It doesn't make sense. Far too risky for one thing, and living a lie for the rest of your life would be impossible to pull off. Twenty years is a feat in itself.' He drew in a long breath then shook his head. 'No. The care and planning involved doesn't add up to the work of a common murderer.'

At this, Carlton's rage visibly diminished, almost as though Grant had paid him a compliment of sorts. He sat down once more and stared into the empty grate.

'You have good intuition, I'll give you that. I'm not a common murderer, I'm a carefully trained agent. As for owning a farm, I had no thought of it until the spring of 1939. Those two . . . out in the wood . . . well, they should be seen as casualties of war, not victims of murder. I was ordered to do what I did in order to establish a cover for my war work.'

Grant looked bemused. 'And what exactly was that?'

'Supplying German Intelligence with information.' Carlton smiled with wry amusement. 'What's the matter? Shocked at the thought of an Englishman spying for Nazi Germany? Never heard of divided loyalties?'

He got up, walked to the drinks table and poured himself a large whisky, then stood there staring down into the glass thoughtfully. 'You see, Mother was German, Father English. My early years were spent in a village outside Exeter where he had a small legal practice. After the Great War, my mother more or less gave up the ghost. Miserable and very homesick, she sold up when my father died and returned to Berlin, taking me with her. I was about fourteen and it was the worst time to be in Germany.'

He drank and grimaced at the memory. 'I grew to manhood as Hitler grew to power. When he became Chancellor, I knew the relief of seeing Germany move out of the doldrums into prosperity. And so, like all my friends, I joined the Nazi Party. It opened up new avenues to a bored young bank clerk. I got in with a wild crowd, went nightclubbing, soon fell into debt and borrowed a great deal of money from someone on the fringe of my group of friends. When he wanted me to settle my debt, I couldn't. Things looked ugly until he introduced me to a colleague of his who, as it turned out, was an official in the *Abwher*.'

He smiled at Grant. 'Clever, eh? Catch some poor sod whose got himself into a financial mess and offer him a loan in return for helping them. I was a very useful catch, being half-English with the right to carry a British passport. The job wasn't too onerous. They needed me to discover the locations of certain ordnance factories and depots in England. I came back to England briefly and returned to Berlin with the information.'

He sat down again, leaning restlessly forward, rubbing the tumbler between his hands, rolling it this way and that as he told Grant that after returning with the information, he still owed interest on the loan so did more work, then more, until it was paid off. In the end he had acquired a taste for espionage and was given proper training.

Drinking more quickly now, he allowed himself to grin. 'Besides, I was astute enough to wonder at the fate of a man who, in the likelihood of war between Britain and Germany, was not only half-English but knew too much about German Intelligence. My best hope of survival lay in throwing in my lot with them, so I did. I was sent back to England, collected a radio transmitter which had been smuggled across by boat, and spent three months here masquerading as a salesman while secretly locating armaments factories and airfields. Each evening I transmitted coded messages giving map references, co-ordinates, lay outs of fields, numbers of aircraft spotted, and so forth. In short, I warned the Germans of any build up of defences within the Home Counties.'

Grant glared at him in disgust. 'Didn't you have any sense of guilt? Spying on your own country?'

Carlton looked surprised at this. 'But I wasn't. Germany was my country by then. Oh, I had no hatred for England . . . nothing like that . . . just a belief in the Third Reich and its power that Britain could never match.' He smiled and shrugged. 'With divided loyalties you either sit on the sidelines or actively work for the winning side. When talk of war became rife I thought I had chosen the latter. Was that so terrible?'

Still hardly able to believe what she was hearing, Terry leaned against the wall, eyes staring ahead in the flickering light of the candle. It couldn't be true. Her father was teasing Grant, surely, playing some silly game to amuse himself? It had to be that, and Grant, bless his heart, was falling for it.

She did not hear the back door open nor did she see PC Kimber, his uniform and cape soaking wet, creep silently from the kitchen into the hall. Slowly becoming aware of a presence beside her, she turned her head in surprise then saw him put a finger to his lips as he heard voices from the sitting room.

Mouthing, 'Are you all right?' he saw her nod, even though her expression and the tense lines of her body told him she was anything but.

Ten minutes earlier he had been stopping a fight between local youths outside the Red Lion at Boxham. On returning home his wife had told him that Lowdham wanted him to check out a possible incident at the farm and to make certain that Miss Fenton was safe and well. He would have to go since a major car accident outside the town had tied up most of their force. Amazed at such an order, he had cycled as quickly as was possible in the storm, found the back door open and crept in. Now here she was, looking ill, her expression alarming, yet safe enough.

Wondering why he was here at all, he turned his attention to the conversation taking place in the sitting room.

'How did Guernsey come into all this?' Grant was asking.

'Strangely,' said John. 'I'd sailed those waters before, so I chartered a yacht and . . .'

'Put her on the rocks deliberately?'

John glanced at him in surprise. 'Ah, yes, Grace bloody Collinette. Of course. My, my, you two *did* have a long chat didn't you?' He drained his glass. 'But you're wrong. It was low tide, strong winds and a moment's inattention that put me on the rocks. Providentially as it turned out. Still, when the Fentons took me in I felt nothing more than relief at their kindness. Only in the following year, when war became inevitable, did I remember them and their lone cousin in Suffolk whose wife had died so tragically. The Fentons had never been in this part of the world or met Arthur, and they, like he, were without relatives here. Fortuitously for me.'

As Grant listened, Carlton continued with his story, saying that travelling back and forth across the Channel was becoming too dangerous. Ordered to set up operations in this country, he needed a strong cover under which to transmit information to Germany and await orders concerning his pre-invasion mission, should Britain declare war.

'That's when I thought of the plan. Thing was, could I pull it off? Would Arthur Fenton's death ensure that John Fenton inherited? The chances were good, but it was an idea which could go badly wrong. Still, it had to be tried.'

Having put his plan to his German superiors and gained their approval to go ahead, he then turned to the pretty young English Mosley supporter who, on visiting Berlin with friends, had fallen in love with Peter Carlton and stayed. She had no idea of his secret life and so he had trodden carefully as he drew her into his plans.

Diane's lips curled into a bitter smile. 'God, I was a pathetic creature in those days!' She addressed Grant, seemingly unable to bring herself to look at Carlton. 'How he must have laughed when I believed his lies! But then, he was my first true love and I couldn't live without him. I thought he cared for me and I would have done anything he asked.'

Ignoring this outburst, Carlton explained how he'd crossed to England, hired a car and left it in a quiet lane a mile or so from Thornley. With the help of an Ordnance Survey map, he made his way across the fields until arriving at a rundown windmill which, as luck would have it, bordered Fenton land. The mill house was locked and deserted but the door to the mill itself was unlocked. Inside it had become a dumping ground for old farm implements and such like, but from an upper window Carlton could see the large cornfield, the woods and part of the barn. It became his cover for three days, while he checked the area and the comings and goings on the farm.

'Only one very old dog. No others, thank God. Arthur Fenton I soon identified when he was talking to labourers in the field. Older than I'd expected.'

All this time Grant remained leaning on the door frame, his concentration fixed on this man whom Terry called Dad. 'And to get the Fentons here, you had to kill Arthur?'

In the hallway, Terry stifled a gasp of horror and glanced up at Kimber with appalled eyes. He gestured to her to be quiet. She ought to stop this, she thought. She ought to rush into the sitting room and shout that everything was being overhead but she couldn't move. She, like Grant, was gripped by the story, horrendous though it was.

Having a clear view of the house from the edge of the wood, Carlton watched each evening as Arthur settled the plough horses then checked around before retiring for the night. One evening when he was doing his last rounds, Carlton walked into the house, took the shotgun from a hook on the vestibule wall, found cartridges in the drawer of the hall table, loaded the gun then walked back into the wood and hid the weapon in undergrowth close to an area where trees had been felled. It gave him a reference point. He then returned to the windmill for the night.

He shook his head at the memory. 'Christ, it was cold! At first light, I slipped on my rucksack, made my way back to the edge of the wood and when Arthur showed up, stepped out and apologised for trespassing. I told him I was on a walking holiday but had become hopelessly lost and asked if he would be kind enough to help me find the public footpath to Boxham. He was so damned decent. It didn't make it any easier. And I'd never killed anyone before. We chatted casually as he led me through the wood. Then I bent down quickly, slid the gun from its hiding place and shot him at point blank range. After wiping off my finger prints, I placed the gun in his hand and positioned him to make it look as though he had tripped on a tree root. No one saw me come and no one saw me go. My only witness lay dead in the wood.'

Grant frowned. 'But how could you be certain the Fentons wouldn't attend Arthur's funeral?'

'I couldn't. If they had, then my plan would have been scuppered. However, there had to be an inquest into Arthur's death and an autopsy, all of which gave me time to return to Guernsey.'

'Where you made certain John Fenton wouldn't go to the funeral but would take up his inheritance? He and Diane left St Peter Port in July. What happened then?'

'I'd told him I would contact him when he reached Suffolk and, under pretext of writing down this address and telephone number from the solicitor's letter, managed to note the address and telephone number of the solicitor himself. I phoned this man later and asked him to arrange for Arthur Fenton's car to be left at Ipswich station with the keys in the glove compartment, so John could drive his family home.'

Diane shuddered and turned dead-looking eyes on to Grant. 'He asked me to pretend to be his wife for a little while. We were to step into the shoes of a married couple with two children who were taking on a farm in a place where no one had ever seen them. We were to raise the children as our own, until they could be returned to their true parents after Germany had invaded England.'

She twisted her hands in a washing motion and went on, 'I was uncertain, but he said that if I loved him I would do this for him so that when the Nazis took power here and he was raised to a high position, I would be honoured as his wife. I believed in him as much as I believed that Fascism was the only way out of the terrible Depression. I didn't want to do anything to harm or betray my country, but he made me understand that to refuse would make us traitors to Germany and the reckoning would come when they took power. As for our plan, he promised me faithfully that no one would be harmed as a consequence of our actions. After all, it would only be for a few months.'

Her stricken expression told Grant that every word she said she had believed at that time. 'And what exactly were those actions, Diane?'

'Virginia,' snapped Carlton. 'Her real name is Virginia Sharp.'

She blinked and shook her head. 'No, Virginia vanished a long time ago. Stupid, silly woman that she was.' She turned to Grant. 'I've been Mrs Diane Fenton for twenty years. I can't be anyone else now. So please go on calling me Diane.'

Carlton shook his head impatiently. 'The wedding ring was just a prop. We were acting our parts, that's all.'

Fighting down the urge to strike the man, Grant looked at Diane and thought how old and diminished she looked suddenly. In that moment he knew her likely fate. Her grip on reality would fade and she would end her days in a twilight world surrounded by female wardens who would show little understanding or kindness to someone who had helped to betray this country during the war. Was that any kinder than execution, if executing women for treason was still a possibility? How did one judge these things?

Turning to the woman who had loved him, hated him, and loved him again for over twenty years, Carlton suddenly realised that he loved her too, only until this moment he had never seen it. In that same moment he also saw what Grant had seen and turned to him with rage in his eyes, whispering, 'You bastard! You bloody bastard. Why did you have to pry? What good has it done?'

Wondering why the police were taking so long in arriving, he spoke to Diane once more. 'What happened on the night the Fentons arrived?'

'There was a storm, a dreadful storm, even worse than the one tonight.' Her voice was weak and trembling. 'I was told to go to Ipswich station and wait inside the car for the Fentons. It was late and very dark when they finally arrived, tired after their journey, struggling with babies and luggage. It was a pitiful sight and I suddenly wanted to warn them both. But I was afraid; afraid of what he would do, afraid of him yet loving him all at the same time . . . I was so mixed up. In the end I told them that I lived in Thornley and had been sent by Mrs Shotley to drive them home.'

Starting at a loud clap of thunder, she took a cigarette from the wooden box on the coffee table and paused with it in her trembling fingers. Searching the air for a light, she found it, unaware that Grant had stepped forward with his lighter. After inhaling deeply, she went on.

'They were so grateful. Grateful and exhausted, poor things. Mr Fenton sat in the front passenger seat, his wife and children in the back. Marisa was then just two and a half and Terry about seven months, I think. I'm not sure. The babies slept. The rain was almost torrential at times and the thunder and lightning terrified me. I could hardly see where I was driving and thought I would get lost, even though I'd been over the route six times.'

'Didn't you wonder, even at that moment, what the fate of this family would be?' asked Grant.

She stared at the hearth for a long time before answering. 'I had been told they would be taken to a place of safety. I wanted to believe it . . . *had* to believe it . . . so I concentrated on asking questions about the children, the youngest especially. Was she weaned? – and so forth. A very loud thunder clap woke Marisa and she started crying. At that moment I saw a light ahead. It was the signal so I stopped the car. The torchlight came towards us, dazzling me. Then he was tapping on the window. I lowered it. We were in the lane . . . at the gate to the wood.'

In the silence that followed, Carlton worked his bottom jaw before describing how, wearing his collar up and trilby low so as not to be recognised, he said his car had skidded into a small ditch and needed help. John got out, walked a few paces ahead and was shot in the head with a Luger. Returning to the car, Carlton heard the toddler screaming and told the mother that her husband had been slightly hurt and needed her. Recognising their old friend, a bewildered Diane asked what was going on and left the car with him.

'I had to be sure no blood would get on to the upholstery, you see, so I led her three paces forward then shot her too. She fell beside her husband. The damned toddler kept on screaming and screaming. I almost felt like killing her as well.' His voice broke off and he poured another large whisky, drinking it down as though to drive out the memory.

In the hallway Terry covered her face with her hands and recalled Mrs Shotley's words. 'Marisa was so frightened, poor little mite ... kept kicking and screaming, pushing away from your mother ... I thought later there was something very wrong ... wrong in her head.'

She felt Kimber's firm but gentle hand on her shoulder and looked up at him with tears streaming down her face. He touched her lips with one finger, warning her to remain silent.

Wishing to God the police would arrive, Grant stood looking at Carlton with ill-concealed disgust. 'Then you buried the poor devils in the woods.' He turned to Diane. 'And you were a party to all this, yet you claim innocence?'

'He made me help him,' she murmured. 'I was so appalled, so shocked, he had to prise my fingers from the steering wheel. I had expected another car to take them on, not ... not that. He slapped me and said I was now a party to murder and would die with him if found out.'

'She was bloody hysterical!' snapped Carlton. 'We dragged the bodies to the grave I'd dug earlier that day. When it was done, we tried removing the mud from our shoes then drove on to the house where Mrs Shotley was waiting for John and Diane Fenton.'

'Marisa wouldn't stop crying,' said Diane in a faltering voice. 'She had seen her parents taken from her and was now in the company of strangers. It went on and on. Her rages, her constant sobbing. We worried about her. She only had a few words then, thank goodness. By the time she could speak properly, she'd forgotten everything.'

Had she, though? Tears falling down her cheeks, Terry thought of Marisa's dream of something dark and terrifying behind the light. It was no dream but a subconscious memory, and it had damaged her.

Oh, God, if only she could go to bed, sleep soundly and wake to find all this had truly just been a dream. But the man she called Dad was now saying how well his plan had worked. How soon he'd learned to play the new farmer, in need of guidance from Arthur's old labourers, and how in the first months of the war, he used his 'wife and children' as cover to drive around East Anglia checking bomber stations and transmitting their co-ordinates and strength to Germany.

'The windmill was perfect to transmit from. It was higher than the house and far enough away so that should the receiver ever be located, I would not necessarily be suspect. After all, anyone could have got into the mill as I was pretty lax about keeping it locked. But the invasion failed, and we found ourselves trapped here in our roles.'

He lit a cigarette and shook his head. 'I couldn't believe it at first and told myself it was just a hiccup. When England's fighting strength had been diminished, the invasion would go ahead. So, to be on the safe side, I kept transmitting, giving the Germans anything I thought might be of interest. That's where Elsie came in. She proved to be a treasure house of information with all her airmen friends. Not one of those men could have dreamed he was giving anything away . . . he didn't know he had information to give . . . but from little things said, from a date suddenly cancelled, I knew from Elsie when there was something big on. I counted the bombers out and counted them back, transmitting the losses back to Germany.'

Flicking ash into the glass ashray, he went on, 'One day I stopped sending and buried the radio transmitter beside the windmill. Recently, after the Fentons were found, I dug it up, drove to Woodbridge and sailed down river where I dropped it over the side into the deepest channel.'

At this Terry twisted away from David Kimber's attempts at restraining her and entered the sitting room. He followed close behind.

'And what was our fate to be if the Germans had invaded?' She stood trembling, looking from the woman she called Mother to the man she still found it hard to believe was not her father. 'Well, what would have happened to us then?'

Moving quickly towards her, Grant pulled her close to him but Terry seemed unaware of it and screamed at Carlton: 'Would you have killed us too?'

Shocked at Terry's appearance, Diane rose to her feet, face stricken with despair. 'Oh, my dear. You heard ... you heard all this?' She swayed a little then clutched the back of an armchair for support. 'Whatever we did ... I swear to you now that we came to love you both and to think of you as our own children. We both wanted to make it up to you ... to give you what your true parents would have given you: love, a decent upbringing, a good education and a happy life. You are as much to us as Eliot is.'

Rigid in Grant's arms, Terry stared at her. 'But what if the Germans had come? What would you have done with us then?'

Carlton answered in a cool manner, 'You would have gone into an orphanage. But the invasion didn't happen. And in the end I was glad.'

Terry blinked. 'Sorry. What was that? You were glad?'

'Yes, Terry. I mark my sea change from the moment the Lancaster crashed. Seeing those boys laid out in my barn ... I knew then that I would send no more messages.' He turned to Kimber. 'And how long have you been standing out there?'

'A good ten minutes, sir.' Still finding the whole thing unbelievable, the PC glanced at Terry, so ashen-faced and shattered, and wondered how she would ever be able to live with all she had learned tonight.

Carlton stood glaring at him. 'And just why did you enter my premises without leave or a search warrant?'

'I was ordered to ascertain that Miss Fenton was safe and well.'

'Who made the police think she wouldn't be?' Carlton glared at Grant. At that moment headlights shone into the room accompanied by the sounds of car doors slamming. He smiled sardonically. 'They took their time. You must have been worried. You needn't have been. You were no more in danger than Terry was. Do you really think I would help to raise a memorial to your brother and his crew then try to harm you? I'm not a monster, I'm just a man who once obeyed orders.'

Grant looked at him. 'And where have I heard that one before?'

Carlton sighed and suddenly it seemed the reality of his plight had caught up with him at last. 'A few days ago I was hoping you would be our son-in-law.' He shrugged. 'Well . . . all I can hope for now is that you'll take care of Terry and that she will take care of Eliot.'

Kimber walked to the front door, opened it and stood back as Detective Sergeant Hopwood and another officer entered. Those in the sitting room heard muffled voices from the hall and Grant held a shaking Terry closer to him.

PC Kimber was finishing his verbal report to a surprised Hopwood. 'I'll make as many notes as I can. It's a very long story. The confession was willingly made. I don't think there'll be any resistance to arrest, sir.' He frowned and said, 'No wonder he didn't want a path through the wood! Can't believe it, really. They're such a nice family.'

Still trying to take it all in, Hopwood picked up the telephone, got through to his superior and explained everything. With instructions ringing in his ears, he replaced the receiver, saw Grant and wondered what on earth this man had done or said to bring about such an extraordinary result.

'Chief Inspector Lytton will be here as soon as possible,' he said to PC Kimber, then walked into the sitting room.

Carlton bade him good evening civilly then sank back in his chair and listened as formal arrests were made and cautions delivered. When it was done he turned to Grant and said, 'Odd thing, you know. I mean . . . what's a mile or so from the air? A fraction to port, a fraction to starboard, and that bomber could have come down on any field but mine.' He paused, his mouth working again. 'It's fanciful but I do sometimes wonder if the men in that plane were pointing a finger right at me.' He looked at Grant and smiled. 'Fate, wouldn't you call it?'

Grant returned his look coldly. 'No, justice.'

Diane stood, looking grey-faced, weak and exhausted. 'Please, I feel very unwell. I must go up to the bathroom.' For one moment Hopwood hesitated, then took pity on her. 'Very well.'

As she left the room, Carlton turned to Grant and smiled grimly. 'And the most bloody ironic thing of all is that three months after that bomber crashed, the RAF built a runway at Woodbridge especially for damaged aircraft to land on. Had it been there that August, your brother and his crew might well have made it. There would have been no memorial, you would never have come into our lives, and we would have continued them without anyone ever learning the truth. Now *that* surely has to be fate?'

'You're forgetting Grace Collinette.'

'Her word against ours? Who would believe her? No, the memorial and you were the two things that tipped our world on its axis.' Suddenly sounding the worse for drink, Carlton stood up, stumbled a little and murmured, 'Must see if Diane's all right. Think I'm about to throw up myself.'

Alarmed at the thought, Hopwood gave his permission, followed Carlton into the hall and watched him slowly climb the stairs. Then he ordered Kimber to guard the front entrance while the other constable guarded the rear.

Walking back to the sitting room, he recalled his Inspector's admonishment that he should have gone out on a limb without informing his superiors. 'You could have blown the whole case.' Hopwood smiled to himself. What case? Until Grace Collinette had made her remarkable statement there had been no case as such, just a long and tedious trawl back through missing persons' files. No one had been interested and although the file was still open, the case was all but abandoned. Now he had a murderer and a traitor on his hands. How quickly the world turns!

He looked from PC Kimber to Grant who had his arms around a distraught Terry. 'Right, who's going to fill me in before the Chief Inspector arrives?'

In the bedroom, meanwhile, Diane had reached under some blankets at the top of the wardrobe. She was holding the Luger she had retrieved from the windmill when the door opened and Carlton walked in.

The storm had circled and was now crashing overhead as Marisa peered through the windscreen, wondering why she had decided to head for home instead of telling Alastair to jump in the lake. Perhaps it was the row that had followed their bedroom spat, perhaps the knowledge that he would stay in the house, causing an atmosphere too thick for her to bear. Whatever it was, she had decided to pack a small case and drive to Suffolk, leaving him to stew.

Peace, she thought. Please God, just a few days of peace before picking up the reins once more and deciding how she would break the news to Julian. A short while ago she had not dreamed of the possibility for happiness which now awaited them both. It was all too much to take in.

Having driven into the worst storm she had known for years, she had been held up by a bad accident outside Lowdham. Police cars and two ambulances had blocked the road for thirty minutes until she was waved on through. Torrential rain slamming into the car made the headlights practically useless. Only when a flash of lightning lit the dark night did she realise she was past the gate to the wood and almost at the house.

Slowly she turned to enter the drive, then saw a small light waving about ahead. The light moved towards her, widening then dazzling. She blinked. Her hands clenched the wheel until her knuckles turned white. The light was blinding now and in it was the horror; the horror she had dreamed of all her life. She wanted to scream but, as in the dream, no sound escaped from her throat.

Hearing a tapping at the window, something else clicked in her memory. Terrified, she slowly turned her head and saw PC Kimber's face looking in at her. Overwhelmed with relief, she wound down the window. Rain splattered into the car as realisation dawned that Kimber was not given to paying social calls at this hour.

'What is it? What's happened?'

'Sorry, Mrs Hammond. I'll let you through but you must stay in the car.'

'Why? What's happened?'

'I can't tell you at the moment. Oh, it's all right, everyone is safe and well. But take my word for it, you must stay in the car. I'll direct you . . . follow me.' So saying he walked forward and flicked the torch to one side of the drive, indicating her parking spot and making room for the other cars when they arrived.

Worried and bemused, Marisa drove where he indicated and then switched off her engine and headlights and sat waiting and wondering.

In the bedroom, Carlton stood in the light of two candles, staring at the gun in Diane's hand.

'We always agreed what we would do when this day came,' she was saying. 'That's why I retrieved it from the windmill. Were you hiding it from me? Have you suddenly got cold feet?'

He stared at the Luger in stupefied silence, an overwhelming survival sense suddenly taking over from his earlier submission. He was neither drunk nor ill and said quite coherently, 'I hid the gun in case the police came back with a search warrant. As for what we agreed twenty years ago . . . the threat of interrogation is well behind us now. There's no need for dramatic suicides, woman. Give the thing to me.'

White-faced, she shook her head, saying, 'No. We must do it for the sake of the children. A sensational trial would destroy them, poor darlings.'

Glancing through the window Carlton saw Kimber's attention distracted by a car at the gate and said, 'This power cut is heaven-sent. If we don't take this chance, we might never have another. I'll go first and check that it's clear.'

Diane blinked in surprise. 'You've just made a long confession and now you want to escape? You've had far too much to drink and you're not thinking straight. There's nowhere for us to hide. Nowhere. Spare the children that undignified farce at least.'

But he wasn't listening. He opened the door, then beckoned for her to follow him. Slowly and quietly they crept down the stairs, paused in the candlelit hallway to see Hopwood's attention distracted by Grant, then moved quickly to the front door, opened it and rushed out into the deluge.

Having settled Marisa, Kimber turned just in time to see two figures caught in a lightning flash as they ran from the house towards the wood. Within a second they were lost in the darkness once more. A loud crack of thunder drowned the blast from his whistle. He tried again before the next stab of lightning, and rushed to the door of the house. It opened and Hopwood appeared, shouted an obscenity at him then headed after his escaped prisoners.

Climbing slowly from her car, Marisa stood transfixed with fear and bewilderment.

Inside the wood, trees swayed dangerously as Diane and Carlton ran towards the cornfield. When she deemed they were far enough from the house, Diane stopped and said breathlessly. 'This is it . . . this will do.'

Carlton stared back at her, gasping, 'Don't stop, you fool!'

Scornful laughter escaped her. 'You are ridiculous. Where exactly are you going? Oh, God, I wish I were as drunk as you. It's finished. There'll be no pitiful attempt at escape and no trial. Do you think I want to die? Do you think I want to leave my son?' Her voice choked on a sob. Then, pulling herself together with a supreme effort, she glared at him. 'Do you think I want to leave any of them? Those poor innocents, what will become of them! Now do you see how many lives you've destroyed?' She held up the Luger and levelled it at him.

Carlton raised his arm in alarm then, quite suddenly, lowered it and relaxed his shoulders. 'It isn't loaded. You took the gun from the windmill but not the bullets. They were in a separate case and well hidden. That gun is useless, believe me.'

'Always you ask me to believe you.' Diane smiled wryly, mimicking him. '*Believe me*, I know what I'm doing. It will be all right, *believe me*. Well, it isn't all right, is it? And I was a fool ever to believe you. I found the bullets and put eight in the chamber.' She glanced about and said, 'It seems fitting somehow to end it here, where you started it.'

She aimed the gun once more and released the safety catch. 'Stay perfectly still and it will soon be over.'

Carlton froze for a moment then tried to run. A shot rang out. He felt a searing pain below his left shoulder and stumbled away. Another shot rang out and he crashed to the ground with a shattered thigh.

Shocked at the recoil, Diane stared at his squirming body and silently screamed at the pain she was inflicting. At last he became still. For a moment she stood there stunned by her own actions then, raising the gun to her temple, she pulled the trigger for the last time.

Having lost the path, Grant was forcing his way through the bracken when he heard shots. Swinging in the direction of the sound, he felt his heart sink. From the moment Carlton and Diane had escaped the house, he had sensed their purpose and was desperate to stop them.

'Did you hear that?' cried Hopwood, scrambling through the undergrowth just behind. 'The bastard's shooting at us.'

'I don't think so,' said Grant. At that moment he felt a grab at his arm and turned to look down into Terry's shocked, terrified face. 'You should have stayed in the house! Don't follow,' he said firmly. 'I must go . . . I might be needed. Stay here, please, darling.'

Soaked and shivering, eyes staring like a wild thing, Terry wrapped her arms about her like a vice. For all the words she wanted to say, for all the questions and the accusations, she could say nothing. Her body was as rigid and immovable as Lot's wife.

'Over here, sir.'

Hating to leave her, Grant staggered on behind Hopwood to see Kimber's torch playing over a body. Bending to Diane, he grimaced at the sight and felt in vain for a pulse. Death would have been instantaneous. He had seen many sad things in his years but this made him want to cry.

Hopwood looked around and saw Kimber beckoning. 'There's the other one.'

Grant moved on to where Carlton lay, his chest and leg covered in blood. 'He's alive! Get an ambulance. Quickly!'

Kimber raced back to the house, passing Terry who now began to stagger forward to where Grant knelt beside the injured man. Her teeth were clenched and her whole body was shaking convulsively as she looked down.

Seeing her, Grant rose to his feet and tried to block her way. His arm went about her and he pulled her away, murmuring, 'No, don't look. Go back to the house.' Calling to the other constable, he asked him to take care of Terry while he tried to attend to the wounded man.

As the constable started helping her away, Terry suddenly caught sight of her mother lying in the bracken. From somewhere deep within her a sound forced its way to her throat and found release in a piercing scream. 'No! Oh, God, no . . . no . . .'

With ferocious strength she pushed the constable from her, ran to Diane's body and fell to her knees. Her cries of anguish filled the night as she saw what the bullet had done. As Grant tried to raise her up she turned on him, pummelling his chest and screaming, 'Dead . . . she's dead . . . they're dead . . . you killed them . . .' She collapsed in hysterics, resisting all attempts to lead her away 'You killed them . . . you killed my parents!'

Grant took her by the shoulders and shouted above her screams, '*They* killed your parents – and buried them in the wood.'

For one moment she stared at him then cried, 'I don't know those horrors from the wood. I don't know them . . .' With that she fell to convulsive sobbing as the constable led her back to the house, leaving a shattered Grant to administer what little first aid he could to Carlton.

'What are his chances?' asked Hopwood

'That depends on how quickly he reaches hospital.'

Hopwood cast his eye over the wounded man. 'Shoulder and thigh wound? He should make it all right.'

Still working to stem the blood pumping out of Carlton's body, Grant recalled a member of his patrol dying of a thigh wound in Malaya during his National Service days. He looked up at Hopwood and said, 'The entry wound looks small enough but if I moved him, you would see a large hole caused by its exit. When the bullet was fired it sucked in dirt from the air, shattered bone and tissue, severed the femoral artery and now I'm trying to prevent him from bleeding to death. The other bullet hit below the clavicle and is too close to the heart for comfort. Does Lowdham have good theatre facilities?'

Hopwood shook his head. 'None. It's just a cottage hospital. It has to be Ipswich.'

Grant sighed in despair. By the time Carlton reached there, sepsis would have set in. He felt his pulse and found it very weak. 'There's little else I can do here. Where's that bloody ambulance?'

As Grant went on trying to stem the flow of blood, Carlton opened his eyes and tried to push the helping hand away. His whisper was barely audible. 'We . . . planned this way out . . . I botched it.'

'Don't speak,' said Grant. 'Save your strength.'

'For the hangman?' The white lips moved into what might pass for a smile, then his eyes closed.

As he worked on, Grant wondered at the ethics of saving him to face trial, imprisonment and finally execution. Better surely to let him die now, as he wished to? But that went against his own oath and training.

Forty minutes later two ambulances arrived. Grant supervised Carlton's transfer on to a stretcher then walked beside him back through the woods as the second team followed with the blanket-covered body of Diane.

Following close behind, Hopwood said, 'I'm all at sea, Mr Kenway. What made you think Miss Fenton was in danger? I got a rather garbled message.'

Grant lowered his voice to a whisper and explained. When he had finished, he paused and added, 'I fully expected, and fervently hoped, that you would already have made your arrest. But when I got here there was no police presence. Christ, I thought you'd never come!'

As Hopwood listened his frown grew deeper. 'But I had no grounds on which to make an arrest. I only came in response to some message which finally filtered through to me from Lowdham.'

Grant stopped walking and turned to him, shock and confusion written all over his face. 'But the dental records? You have them, surely?'

Hopwood shrugged. 'Only just. Having them is one thing; awaiting results that would match them with the murder victims is quite another. It could be days yet.'

For a long time Grant stood staring at the Sergeant, trying to take this in. Then he let out a long, slow breath and said, 'Well, it's all rather academic now, isn't it?'

Chapter Eighteen

The storm had abated by the time they left the wood and crossed muddy ground towards the house. Grant saw lights shining from the two ambulances where the rear doors stood open. Police hovered beside the vehicles but there was no sign of Terry.

Heavy of heart, he became aware that his hands and shirt still had Carlton's blood on them and that by acting too quickly he could be said to have caused this terrible tragedy. Now he wondered how he could ever have thought Carlton would harm Terry. Yet he had thought it. Two hours ago it had been a reasonable suspicion for then the world had been black and white, and a man guilty of murder had seemed to him like a dangerous animal.

Now he knew that the world was not so black and white, that Terry was never in danger and that a man who had committed evil deeds need not necessarily think himself evil or be denied love. 'I don't know those horrors from the wood . . .' Grant put a hand over his eyes, realising that, despite the truth, Terry would always think of Carlton and Virginia as John and Diane Fenton, the parents who had raised her lovingly. Her cries filled his head still. 'They're dead . . . you killed them . . .'

Hardly knowing anything any more, he watched as Diane's body was placed in one ambulance, and felt a gnawing pain deep inside him. As the ambulance moved off silently he turned to Hopwood, saying, 'Miss Fenton's in no condition to be questioned or bothered in any way. She must leave this house at once. The Rashleighs at Thornley Hall will take her in, I'm sure. I want her doctor to look in on her.' He moved forward as Carlton was placed inside the other ambulance, checked that all that could be done at this point was being done, then stood back as the doors were closed.

'Fate, wouldn't you call it?'

'No, justice.'

The words returned to haunt him but were suddenly drowned out by clanging bells as the ambulance moved into the lane. Almost at once a police car entered the drive and from it emerged one uniformed officer and a tall man in a grey suit.

Chief Inspector Lytton homed in at once on the luckless Hopwood, who was already wondering how he was going to describe this evening's events to his superior. Certainly the identifications of dental records must now be given top priority.

Leaving them together, Grant entered the house and made his way to the sitting room. To his surprise he saw Marisa seated in an armchair, hands to her face, groaning over and over again, 'Why? I don't understand . . . tell me why?'

Too traumatised to help her sister, Terry sat shivering on the sofa, swathed in a blanket and staring into emptiness. She seemed quite unaware that Grant was standing close by her.

The Chief Inspector spoke to him quietly, asking him to remain here until he had given a statement. Grant asked him if the sisters could go to Thornley Hall for the night and when this was agreed, washed his hands in the utility room, went into the hall and dialled the Rashleighs' number.

At the sound of the telephone, Gerald Rashleigh roused himself from the fireside chair, walked slowly across the drawing room and picked up the receiver. He then listened in horrified silence to Grant's story. 'Oh, Lord . . . that's dreadful, utterly dreadful!'

Lydia was beside him at once, whispering, 'What's dreadful . . . who is it . . . what's happened?'

Twisting away from her as she tried to take the receiver from him, Gerald said, 'Yes, of course. I'll come for them at once.' He rang off then turned to his wife and shook his head in disbelief. 'The Fentons. Some kind of shooting accident. Diane's dead and John's in hospital. Don't know any more details. Call Tranmer. The girls are in shock. I'm bringing them here.'

Open-mouthed Lydia just stared at him. 'Did you just say that Diane was dead? What nonsense! She can't be. Are you sure?' As her husband headed towards the door, she followed him. 'What do you mean, a shooting accident? It isn't even the season . . .'

Before Lydia had finished the sentence she found herself alone and talking to thin air. Too stunned to think any more, she poured a brandy to get over the shock then remembered to call Dr Tranmer. After this she rang Alastair's number at Cadogan Place.

When the Land Rover arrived at the farmhouse Marisa was led out by PC Kimber and assisted into the vehicle. Grant tried to help Terry who stumbled slightly at first and hardly knew where she was being led. Then, as he spoke gently to her, the eyes that had been so empty suddenly blazed at him.

'Leave me!' she said vehemently. 'I hate you ... *hate* you. Don't come near me again.'

Stricken by her words and expression, he stood motionless as the Land Rover left the drive, taking all that he loved with it.

As Peter Carlton lay between life and death in a guarded hospital room, Terry and Marisa stayed within the sanctuary of the Hall. But when the news broke, just twenty-four hours later, filling the front pages of every newspaper in the land, an appalled Lydia wanted Alastair to take them away.

'Their presence here will turn the spotlight on us,' she said anxiously. 'It's bad enough you have to be dragged into it . . . but you would marry into that family.' Fiona's exclamations of horror had little effect on Lydia. 'The whole thing is too dreadful. Take them to London, Alastair, and don't forget to fetch their brother from Kingston first.'

After gaining police permision to collect some of Terry's and Eliot's clothing from the farmhouse, Fiona packed them neatly in a suitcase, then Alastair gathered up his charges and drove them to Cadogan Place. There, in spite of shock, he proved to be an unlikely source of comfort and quiet efficiency, handling all the details which 'the girls' would find it too upsetting to cope with.

Terry retreated behind a wall of shock and confusion, guarding herself from something she refused to believe had happened. Behind that wall she was unassailable, unable to think or feel anything, until she hardly knew herself any more.

Marisa spent silent hours staring into space, seeing only the light which loomed larger and larger, knowing now that the dark within it was her father killing her other father and other mother. She began to slip into a kind of madness, aware only that that her whole being cried out for Julian. He would make the horror go away. She wanted to flee to him, but Alastair kept her locked inside the house while he himself was everywhere, one minute talking for hours on the phone to his office in Coventry, or his racing team now preparing for Goodwood, and the next, being an elder brother to Eliot and attentive to Terry. Oh, so very attentive to Terry, Marisa thought bitterly. Even now . . . even now *she* was all that mattered to him.

The newspapers that had been hidden from Eliot and his sisters caused shock and consternation to the villagers of Thornley. How could it be, they asked each other, that two people who had lived in their midst all these years, two perfectly decent hard-working, church-going farmers, could turn out to be traitors and murderers?

In the pubs for miles around there was no other topic and those who refused to believe the story soon found themselves in heated arguments with those who said it had to be true because it was in the newspaper

Mrs Shotley alone said nothing, but made her way to the farm during Kimber's watch and insisted on checking that all was well inside the house. Once inside, the old lady looked around carefully, making sure everything was in order after the police had searched the place. With an aching heart she picked up the mail and placed each letter in a neat pile on the hall table before watering Diane's cherished houseplants.

She wept as she worked but doing these simple tasks was the only way she could handle the shock. If Terry were here, she thought, or Eliot or Marisa, then she could fuss over them as she had done in the old days.

The old days! It tore at her to think of them and there was one image she would give anything to erase from her mind; that of a man and a woman she had never seen before, standing in the hall with mud on their shoes, both soaked to the skin and struggling with a baby and a toddler who screamed and screamed and wouldn't be comforted.

Having been called on to operate in the middle of the night, Grant heard the knock on his door at seven which was accompanied by a cup of tea. It was the start of another day when he wondered if he could face the strain of concentrating on surgery at this, the worst time of his life.

On returning to London, late that fateful night, he had

telephoned Meg, revealing all that had happened.

Still trying to wake up, she had wondered at the catch in his voice and glanced at her watch. It was one-fifteen in the morning. When her mind had finally taken in the news, she closed her eyes in dismay and said, 'Stop blaming yourself. They murdered my cousin and her husband, and betrayed this country. The police should be grateful to you.'

'Then why do I feel so bad about it?'

That had been when . . . four days ago. And Carlton still hung on tenuously to life as the newspapers hung on to the story. Much to his relief, Grant realised that his name had not been mentioned and neither had Grace Collinette's. That was the only light in a world turned dark.

How could he live without Terry? How could he live with her suffering and the knowledge that now she hated him as once she had loved him. Summer was just a dream. Time to wake up to cold reality and somehow learn to live with it.

Quickly he showered, dressed, and all but managed a coffee in the Doctors' Mess before heading on to the wards. The minute he hit them there there wasn't a moment to spare between the gall bladders, perforated ulcers, ruptured appendixes, and examination of X-rays and medical notes.

Trying to trace Terry in between his duty hours was impossible. Obeying her instructions, the Rashleighs would only say she had gone to friends and they were not sure where. A protective curtain had been drawn around her to keep out unwelcome intruders. And that meant Grant as well as the press. Although he understood, it did nothing to alleviate the pain.

As Terry's protective wall crumbled and disbelief turned to grief, she recalled more of the events of that terrible evening and with them the words she had hurled at Grant. She hated him, she told herself, hated him with the same intensity with which she had once loved him. So why was his face always before her? Why could she not push him from her mind?

Now, as she sat at the breakfast table, struggling in vain to eat Mrs Mount's kedgeree, her mind was awakening to reality. 'They're not your parents,' Grant had said. 'They killed your parents and buried them in the wood.' Down went the fork with a clatter on the plate. She started shaking as emotion welled up and tears poured down her cheeks.

Alastair looked up from his plate and saw. At once he got up, walked to where she sat and placed an arm about her shoulders. She could not feel his touch or hear his words of comfort. Realising she was a world away, in some private hell of her own, he sat down again, aware of Marisa's cold stare fixed on him.

The telephone rang. With a sigh of impatience Alastair got up again. 'It could be one of a dozen things, the office, the factory, even the hospital, but I think we can hazard a guess at what it will be.' He picked up the receiver, face set in a grim expression as he listened and said, 'Very well. Yes, of course. Thanks for letting me know.' Returning to the table, he buttered some toast before glaring at his wife.

'Your very good *friends*, the Palmers, cancelling their party next week. Unforseen circumstances, apparently. They'll be in touch later. Just like all the others.' He smiled wryly. Did people really think they would go out to parties at such a time? Couldn't they understand? Couldn't they imagine anything beyond their own pathetic little world – who's in, who's out. The Hammonds were most definitely out. He thanked God for his colleagues in the motor racing world who were of a different breed.

Glancing at his wife, he wondered what was going on in that head of hers. In her more rational moments she seemed calm enough but the mood swings were becoming alarming. Being dropped by those she once called friends only served to fuel her simmering rage.

It was easy for her, thought Alastair. She could hide behind the protection he provided but he now had in-laws known to the world as murderous traitors and could hide nowhere. How damned unfair it was. Married to a woman he didn't love and who loved someone else, he was now inextricably part of her shame and new status – *persona non grata*. What now of the famous Hammond name? What of booming car sales? What of the workforce in the Coventry factory? Since this had happened he hadn't been near the place to test the reactions on the faces of those men and women and dreaded the day he would have to. Before him stretched a long dark tunnel. Married to Terry he could have borne it for her sake, but married to Marisa he could not.

Terry was in the drawing room when the doorbell rang. She tensed then moved towards the door and listened to muted voices from the hall below. Was it him? Had he found her at last? Did she want to be found? The voices were difficult to make out and the caller was not asked in. Then Mrs Mount was saying, 'No. No one of that name here. I'm sorry, I can't help you.'

Grant! It had to be. Rushing to the window Terry looked down at the old green MG parked outside the house. It was raining and the hood was up. He was walking slowly towards it, his demeanour a testimony to his disbelief. For one brief moment he stood there, turned and looked up. She pulled back swiftly. Then, with a mixture of emotions, watched him climb into the car and drive out of Cadogan Place. Suddenly she wanted to scream after him: 'Come back! Come back,' but he would never come back, not now.

With an ache in her heart she stood there thinking how desolate he'd seemed, how tired and drawn. All that they once had was gone forever. What other way could there be for them now?

In his room, where he spent most of his days weeping alone, Eliot wondered how both his parents could be victims of a shooting accident. If his father had been teaching his mother to use a gun, how could a stray bullet have killed her and wounded him? And why on earth did she suddenly want to learn about guns? Women didn't shoot. It was a man's sport, surely?

He remembered the day all too clearly when Alastair had arrived at Kingston with news of the accident and brought him here where his sisters behaved like ghosts, drifting through the house. All that Alastair had added was that it had happened in the wood. After that Eliot understood everything. The wood had claimed more victims. It was a place of evil and no one could stand against it.

Raedwald had warned him, warned him of something terrible to come. Well, what could be more terrible than this? Now that it had happened, the dreams had stopped and Raedwald was at rest once more.

Terry tried to comfort him, glad that Alastair had kept the full story from the boy. That was kind, but was it wise? He would have to know the truth sooner or later, and it must come from her. But how could she bring herself to tell him things she could hardly believe herself? Yet she must, for the new school year was about to start. He must be prepared for everything before returning to Kingsmead.

She spoke to him of returning to school, saying that he would find it a help and eventually the pain of loss would ease. She truly believed this, that given help and pastoral care from his Headmaster and tutors, he would rally. It would be hard facing the other boys, of course, but with diligent support from his tutors, any bullying would be curbed at once. Before he left for Kingsmead she must tell him the whole terrible story. When and how would have to wait until she could find the words.

With his school awaiting him and the Dame Edith awaiting her, it was time to face up to things, she told herself; time to return to the place she had thought never to see again. Much as she wished it otherwise, there was no getting away from her responsibilities. All their things were there, including Eliot's school uniform, cleaned and prepared by Diane just waiting to be put in his trunk. The two farm labourers who had been working Fenton land for as long as she could remember would need their wages and some indication of what their future would be. And what of Dauphine, the cats, the hens? Good God, who had been looking after the poor creatures? Had anyone? Time she forced herself back into the world, no matter how she longed to hide from it. Life must go on and the much dreaded return to Suffolk faced at last.

Alastair drove them to Thornley on a bright sunny September morning, thinking that the one good thing to come out of this tragedy was Terry's need to lean on him.

He glanced at her beside him, and remembered when they had first met. Had that dog not dashed across the road, had he been at the spot a few seconds earlier or later, then he would never have become involved with the Fentons at all. He had been driving this very Rover, which had once belonged to his mother, and Eliot had been in the back of Terry's car, presumably talking away happily. Today, the boy was as quiet as the grave, and Terry's brave attempts at conversation could not disguise her dread. He too had no desire to stay longer at the farm than was necessary. The whole thing gave him the creeps.

Marisa returned to the house in Cadogan Place late that evening and poured herself a large brandy. Earlier she had driven to Julian's flat, slipped her key into the lock and found it would not turn. She tried again, checked she had the right key, and slowly realised the lock had been changed. The light was on. He was there, thank goodness! She rang the doorbell. The light went out.

Marisa knocked on the door again and again but in vain. Frantic, she tore a leaf from her diary and scribbed on it in wild handwriting:

Julian! Do not desert me, or I shall kill myself.
Darling, I need you. Phone me. I'm alone this evening.

Now she could only wait. But waiting was not her forte. Snatching up the receiver, she dialled Julian's number. He answered in low, measured tones and chided her for making such a scene earlier.

'You changed the locks,' screamed Marisa. 'Good God . . . why?'

'You must know why. Marisa, I have no choice. We can't see each other again. My children . . . my career . . . I can't be connected with you now. Try to understand.' With that he rang off and left the receiver on the table top, knowing she would keep calling.

Finally tiring of the engaged tone, Marisa stopped dialling and sat numbly trying to come to terms with this betrayal. She had counted on Julian to take her away from this terrible void and the horrors which filled her mind when she was left alone. If he was not there for her . . . how could she go on?

Alastair pulled up at the flat in Lowdham where Terry wanted to check her mail before going on to Thornley. In the hallway she met her landlady who looked a shade embarrassed.

'Ah, Miss Fenton. I . . . I'm so sorry, but I've decided not to let the flat any longer. I need it for a relation. So, regretfully, I must ask you to leave.' At Terry's dumbfounded expression, she smiled weakly and went on, 'You do understand?'

Terry's eyes flashed dangerously. 'Yes, I believe I do. But I've paid a month's rent in advance.'

'Which I shall return in full at once. But I want to you leave as soon as possible.' Realising that her attempts at hiding the truth were farcical, she sighed. 'Please, Miss Fenton, do understand how very difficult this is for me. And I'm sorry about it, truly. You're a good tenant, I couldn't wish for better, but . . . as it is . . . I simply cannot have you coming in and out of this house. Not here on the Green where everyone can see.'

To Terry it was like being hit in the solar plexus. 'I must stay here tonight. I have my young brother with me and we can't possibly sleep at the farm. I'll collect his things and drive him to school tomorrow. After that, I'll find somewhere else.'

Where, though?

'Very well, Miss Fenton, but please wait until after dark before arriving and leave before light tomorrow.' With that the landlady walked back into her own drawing room and shut the door firmly.

The policeman at the gate held up his hand and Alastair stopped the car. When he explained who his passenger was he was allowed through. The constable waited until Terry and Alastair got out and approached them, saying, 'Sorry about that, but we've had so many sightseers. We've searched the house, but you'll find it's been left tidy. They only took the things they deemed necessary.'

Terry glared at him. 'Necessary! They have all they need, surely? A dead woman and a critically injured man should be enough without searching our personal belongings as well?'

'They're just doing their job,' murmured Alastair, taking her by the elbow and leading her towards the front door.

Terry thanked God they had stopped off at Mrs Shotley's house where she had wept on the old lady's shoulder and felt the warm comforting arms she had last felt as a child.

'Now you and Eliot are to stay here the night,' Mrs Shotley had insisted. 'And your landlady can get lost! I can manage very well. You can sleep on a camp bed in my room, Terry, while Eliot has the small back room. Stay as long as you like. Now have a bite to eat and leave him with me. Do what you have to do, then return here and I'll have dinner ready for you. You may eat with us too, Mr Hammond, but I don't see as how I can put you up.'

Alastair had thanked her but said he was calling in on his relations before driving straight back to London where a great many things awaited his attention. Marisa, primarily. Leaving her was a risk but Mrs Mount had promised to keep careful watch.

To Terry's anxious questions, Mrs Shotley replied that Fiona had looked after Dauphine and the cats, while the wife of one of the labourers was looking after the hens. 'Mrs Mundy's been a treasure. She wants you to look in on her before coming back here. They're dreadfully upset.'

Now, as Terry opened the front door, Alastair stepped back a pace and murmured, 'Well, you'll be wanting to be alone, I'm sure. I'll be at the Hall if you need me. Nothing to worry about with the bobby outside.'

After he had driven away Terry turned and looked across to the wood. It seemed impossible that sun-drenched trees, just turning to autumn shades, could hide a tale so terrible. 'Do you believe a place can be evil . . . of itself, I mean?' How long ago had she asked that of Grant?

She entered the house, wishing now that she hadn't let Alastair go. But then, he had hardly insisted on staying. For a moment she stood there, the silence broken only by the grandfather clock in the hall. For over a hundred years, through six reigning monarchs and two world wars, that clock had stood in the same place, ticking away the measure of a man's life and serving as the heartbeat of the house. Now she found comfort in the familiar sound and half-expected to hear her mother's voice from the sitting room.

But on entering it reality smacked her in the face. How cold and dead it all seemed now. How cold and dead everything seemed. Recalling snatches of that last terrible conversation, she gazed about her, remembering where each person had sat or stood before that final horror.

The room was too neat and tidy, she thought, but Mrs Shotley had always been thorough. Copies of *Wisden* lined the top shelf of the bookcase and caught at her heart. Her father had been a keen cricketer, playing for the local team and listenening avidly to broadcasts of Test matches. Her father? No . . . but he wasn't her father. Why was it so hard to remember that?

Swiftly she averted her eyes, only to see Diane's books on horses set neatly beside the hardback novels from her Book Club. Vaguely it occurred to Terry that she must cancel the subscription. Moving back into the hall, she saw the mail neatly piled on the table. Remembering her own letters taken from the flat, she added these to the others and took them into the kitchen to read. Homely cooking smells had been replaced by the stuffiness of windows too long closed. Terry sat down at the pine table, tried to push the anguish from her heart and voices from the past out of her mind as she opened the first letter.

It was a demand from the local dairy for prompt payment of milk bills. Never before had such a letter arrived in this house. The next came from the butcher who wanted his account settled at once. She was astonished. These were people she had known all her life, the butcher in particular playing in the same cricket team as her father. Their shock and disgust must be profound, she thought, trying to prevent other emotions from taking hold on her. Instead of rage she must come to terms with how it was for them, and how it would now be for her, Eliot and Marisa.

The third letter was from the family solicitor, the same man who had once served Arthur Fenton. He offered his help and advice, asking her to contact him at once. Thank God for that, she thought wondering about the legal mess that must be sorted out. She turned to the mail she had collected from her flat and saw on one envelope the letterhead of the Dame Edith Harting School for Girls.

Tearing it open, she expected condolences but Miss Yeats had not been in a sympathetic mood when dictating this to the school secretary. In dismissing Terry, she had gone on to say:

> I realise this will come as no surprise, and know you will understand why such a step has been necessary. Of course I discussed the situation with the Board of Governors and all were in complete agreement that it would not be in the interest of the school for you to remain. It goes without saying that pupils would be withdrawn if you returned.

After this her tone softened a little.

> I fully realise that no blame can be attached to you in any way and that your suffering must be terrible, but I have no choice in this matter. I am truly sorry to lose you and believe your girls will feel the same. That you should continue teaching them is, of course, now out of the question.
>
> I shall give you good references and wish you luck in finding another post . . .

Terry stared at the letter and asked herself why she was so surprised. The ruined social life of her sister and brother-in-law and the behaviour of her own landlady should have alerted her to such an eventuality. She and her siblings were guilty by association. They had been raised by traitors and murderers.

Her heart sank when she came to another formal-looking letter, this time from Eliot's Headmaster, enclosing the cheque sent in advance for the new term. He too was sorry but knew she would understand. Again it was the parents he feared. Eliot, he said, had shown great promise and he was sad to lose such a bright and likeable pupil. He hoped the boy would soon settle in a new school and wished him well.

Furious, Terry put a call through to the school office to be told by the secretary that the Head was not available at the moment. They were still sorting things out for the coming term.

This cold reply sent her into a blind rage. 'Then find him at once. Now. It's desperately urgent.' After she had held on for five minutes, a man's voice came on the line. 'Miss Fenton, you have received my letter, I hope? I did try calling but you were not at home.'

'Did you expect I would be?' said Terry thinly. 'Mr Cunningham, your letter has come as a great shock to me. What kind of school turns its back on a pupil who is suffering as my brother is suffering? He's depending on you to give him back some semblance of normality after all that's happened. He still doesn't know the entire truth, I've tried to keep it from him, and I was . . .'

'Miss Fenton, I understand very well, but I'm afraid it is entirely out of the question to have him back here. The Governors are adamant on this issue and I've already had anxious enquiries from parents who have threatened to remove their sons should I not act as I have done. In any case, it would not be in Eliot's own interest. That surely would be best served by finding him a school where he will not be connected with . . . with such terrible events? You do see that?'

'I see you are expelling an innocent boy for something beyond his control. What sort of world do we live in when children are made to pay for adults' crimes? You have no right . . .'

'Ah, but I do. This is not a state school. I have the right and you have the cheque. I'm sorry, Miss Fenton, there really is nothing more to be said. I hope you find Eliot a good school soon. Goodbye.'

She heard the click at the other end of the line and slammed down the phone. 'God . . . oh God . . . you horrible, creepy, little coward!'

Eliot, her poor brother. Why had she not foreseen this disaster? How could one have faith in human nature when humans were so fearful of their peers? Everyone said they understood and were sorry – before twisting the knife. It made her wonder how many people in this world acted according to their conscience. Grant had. And where had that ended? In tragedy and hateful cutting words; words that could never be taken back or forgotten. Yes, that was what people received when they stood by truth and their consciences.

Meanwhile she must help her brother, place him uppermost in her thoughts and find him shelter in a hostile world. Where? Why was that word haunting her so much today?

Someone knocked on the rear door and slowly it opened to reveal Bob Mundy and Ross Turner, the two farm workers who had served Arthur Fenton and then his successor.

Terry smiled apprehensively, wondering what they were thinking. Both of them then offered her their deepest sympathies, asked how her father was doing, and said how shocked they had been and that neither of them believed the wicked lies told in the press.

'That's kind of you, but the wicked lies appear to be true.' It was the first time she had said it aloud. Until this moment even thinking it had been an impossibility. 'They're true.' Terry swallowed hard and found it difficult to go on.

Bob shuffled awkwardly and said, 'And yet for all 'e done, I couldn't 'ave worked for a better man. Always good to us and no matter what . . . we shall miss 'im and Mrs Fenton. Well . . . that is . . .'

'I know . . . I know.' Terry bit back tears. 'Thank you. Thank you, Bob. And thank Mrs Mundy for looking after the hens. I do appreciate that. I wonder if she wouldn't mind continuing looking after them until I sort myself out?' How prosaic that sounded under the circumstances.

'Of course, Miss Fenton. But what's to 'appen now? To the farm, I mean? We got the 'arvest in before that storm. Fields're all ploughed and ready for the winter wheat.'

Terry frowned. 'I don't . . . I'm not sure. You haven't had your wages. I'm so sorry. I'll get on to the bank at once about that. I don't know much about these things, but I have to see the solicitor and he'll sort me out. Meanwhile I'm sure the bank will release money against the estate.'

'And the winter wheat?' asked Ross. 'Should be in soon.' His lined face was anxious. 'Corn merchants delivered before the . . . before the . . . well, anyway, it's all paid for. The fields are ploughed and waitin'. Only we dunno what to do about it.'

Looking into their kindly bewildered eyes, Terry suddenly felt a terrible burden of responsibility fall upon her. Both these men lived in tied cottages. Seeing them turned out was the last thing she wanted. But if the farm was sold, new owners might do just that and replace them with younger men. On the other hand it could take months to sell the farm. Meanwhile Bob and Ross must be paid their weekly wages and keep a roof over their heads. How was this to be done? It seemed to her then that, come what may, the farm must keep going.

She said firmly, 'If the wheat's here then go ahead and plant. Farms don't wait.' She watched as they walked towards the door and felt tears welling up as they kept doing these days. 'I know what a dreadful shock this has been for you, but thank you. Thank you for carrying on and . . . well . . . just being here. What has happened has been devastating for us. Knowing I can turn to you for guidance is comforting.'

Bob Mundy turned to her and frowned. 'Look, Miss Fenton. You shouldn't stay 'ere alone. Mrs Mundy can put you in our back room tonight.'

She smiled. 'That's very kind, but Mrs Shotley's putting us up. Eliot's with her now. Look, he doesn't know the whole truth. He will soon, of course, but I must make sure he hears it from me rather than anyone from the village.'

'We understand, Miss Fenton.' They walked out, shutting the door behind them, leaving her alone to ponder on the responsibility thrust on her young shoulders and wondering how she would cope.

Chapter Nineteen

Trusting that Marisa was safely asleep in her own bed, Alastair returned to Cadogan Place well after midnight.

Turning the key in the lock, he glanced up, saw the drawing-room light still on and felt his heart sink. Confrontation was the last thing he wanted right now.

He found Marisa seated on the sofa, brandy glass clutched tightly between her hands. Hunched and tense, she was wearing the figure-hugging dress he had always loathed but assumed that Julian liked; her make-up was hideously overdone and weeping had caused mascara to streak down her cheeks, giving her a clown-like appearance.

It was all too obvious that she had slipped Mrs Mount's guard and gone to the man he had hoped would offer both of them salvation. One look at Marisa told him that was not to be. 'So, he ditched you?' Alastair barked. 'Jumped ship, just like all the others.'

When Marisa made no reply he walked to the drinks table, poured himself a large brandy and said vehemently, 'And you thought he loved you. Marisa, he found you conveniently married and intended to keep it that way.'

A strangled cry escaped from her throat. 'He does! He does love me . . . I know it.'

'Not enough to be caught in the fall out, it seems. He's got his reputation to think of and so he's sorry, he can no longer have you in his life.'

But I must. Alastair drank, then rubbed his brow in despair. *I must because I can't be seen to desert my wife in her hour of need. Yet I'm the last man she wants. How bloody ironic! Together now until death us do part.* He turned to Marisa with an expression akin to hatred. 'For God's sake, go to bed. You look bloody awful.'

With that, he walked out of the room and up the stairs, leaving her staring after him in a trance-like state.

At seven in the morning, Mrs Mount entered the drawing room and drew back the heavy velvet curtains. Turning from the windows, she started a little to see Mrs Hammond slumped on the sofa. A glass lay on the floor, its contents having seeped into the carpet. Fearing the worst, the housekeeper peered at Marisa more closely then heaved a sigh of relief when it was obvious she was just the worse for drink. Fetching a blanket, Mrs Mount covered the sleeping woman and asked herself how she would react if her parents had turned out to be what Mrs Hammond's were? Perhaps she too would have drunk herself into oblivion.

Driving to Lowdham, Terry tried to concentrate on all the important things she had to discuss with the solicitor but her mind was filled with Grant. She missed him ... God, how she missed him. Missed his love, his strength and his sound common sense. Most of all, she missed the warmth of his arms about her. But she had said vile things to him and told him to stay out of her life and he, being he, would blame himself for what had happened and not pursue one who apparently hated him.

How wrong he was, she thought, how terribly wrong. But words once said could not be unsaid. He would go on hearing them all his life and so would she. It was probably just as well. Any association with her now would ruin his chances, for how could a man in his profession risk marriage to a woman raised by traitors and murderers? His career would suffer dreadfully, for being close to the Fentons was akin to being close to lepers in Biblical times.

Telling herself that she must bear the unbearable and resign herself to a bleak future, Terry thought of Eliot. She had to be strong for his sake now, be there to pick up the pieces when he learned the full truth. By then she hoped to be far away from this place, in London perhaps, where they would find anonymity among people who wouldn't notice them and care even less.

Entering Cornmarket Street, she parked outside Malling & Son, Solicitors, then walked inside the Victorian building and was shown into a large, rather depressing office.

Mr Malling sat behind his old desk, opened a file before him, and stared at Terry through horn-rimmed spectacles. He expressed his sorrow then came to the matter of the will. 'It is, of course, null and void because it wasn't made by John Fenton but by Peter Carlton, who did not inherit the farm.'

Mr Malling removed his glasses and turned them in his fingers as he spoke. 'Your true parents died intestate. In such a case the beneficiaries are you and your sister.

'And my brother, Eliot?'

'Mr Malling shook his head. 'Miss Fenton, you have no blood brother. Eliot is the natural son of Peter Carlton and Virginia Sharp. He is not family and doesn't inherit anything.'

Terry blinked. Until that moment, she had not considered Eliot to be anything other than her brother. To hear the truth pointed out in such a cold manner came as a considerable shock.

'I imagine you will want to sell the farm and divide the money between you?' Mr Malling was asking.

'What? Er . . . well . . . yes.'

'And is that the wish of Mrs Hammond also?'

'Terry thought of her sister's vacant stare and said, 'Mrs Hammond has said she will never return to this part of the world again. I shall leave also when our affairs are sorted out.'

'I understand that your sister is the elder and wonder why she isn't dealing with all this?'

'My sister is unwell at the moment. She cannot cope and . . .' Terry stopped speaking suddenly, the echo of her words circling her mind. 'She cannot cope'. Marisa, the strong one, admired for her beauty, wit, intelligence and sense of indepenence, unable to cope?

Mr Malling was saying how sorry he was to hear that. 'Of course, she must inform me of her wishes in writing.' He paused. 'You do realise that this whole business might make it difficult to sell the farm, and even if we found a buyer I doubt we would receive the correct asking price. There are those who will take advantage of you, Miss Fenton. Do not allow it. All in all, I fear you may have to wait some time.'

'Meanwhile what do I do about the farm?' She asked. 'It isn't like a house that can just be shuttered up until the next occupant comes along. Farms have to be worked and labourers paid.'

Mr Malling nodded, said he would arrange things with the bank and if Mrs Hammond was in agreement would contact the land agents with a view to auctioning the farm. Her other options were to let the fields to local farmers and sell the house separately, or else bring in a tenant farmer who would live in the house and work the land.

Terry thought about this and frowned. 'That would mean our link with the farm would not be broken. No, I want to make a fresh start a long way from this area. I need money to put a roof over our heads. Mine and Eliot's, I mean. We can't live at the farm, you must surely understand why not?'

'I see.' Mr Malling looked a little puzzled. 'But you do have your salary from teaching which will tide you over . . .'

'Not any more.'

He looked at her questioningly then sighed. 'I see. I'm very sorry.'

As he escorted her to the door, Terry paused. 'I wish to place something from our inheritance into a trust fund for Eliot. It will be needed for his education.

'Ah, he boards at a public school, I understand?'

Terry shook her head. 'Again, not any more.'

'That's iniquitous.'

'It's fear,' said Terry. 'Good morning, Mr Malling.'

Having spent much of the afternoon on the telephone to a sharp-toned woman at the offices of the local education authority, Terry's nerves had reached breaking point. Abandoning the search for a school for Eliot, she left the house and made her way along the path towards Dauphine's paddock.

Before she had time to open the gate, the chestnut mare had trotted over to her, glad to see a familiar face and nuzzling into her hand for affection. Placing an arm about the long glistening neck, Terry stroked it gently, murmuring, 'Did you miss me? I'm sorry. I'm sorry I went away and left you.' How could she have been so cruel? Yet Dauphine had forgiven her. Why weren't people more like horses? thought Terry bitterly.

Soon she would be forced to desert this mare whose soft brown eyes were so trusting, whose nature was so gentle, whose heart was strong and loyal; desert her because she could no longer afford her and, eventually, would have nowhere to keep her.

She glanced around, aching for a world that had vanished

overnight; a world of innocence which had seemed so secure; a world where all things were possible; a world of happiness which, until now, she had not truly appreciated. That world had been blown away and all was now desolation.

Suddenly she saw a tractor in the ploughed up field and felt her spirits lift briefly. They crashed to earth when she realised it was only Bob Mundy. For one silly moment she had thought it was her father, as though all that she wished had been granted by some modern-day Lilac Fairy with a magic wand.

Was it really only a year since she had stood on the edge of this field watching the harvest being gathered in, before that mad rush to Woodbridge station and the sailing trip which had ended in a car crash? Just one year? Unbelievable! Where would she be this time next year, and who would be harvesting the wheat? Where was Mother to be buried . . . no . . . Virginia . . . oh, God, her brain needed unscrambling. Meanwhile there was so much to do, so much to sort out. Never in her life had she felt so alone. She turned and walked back towards the house.

Bright sunlight streamed across the pathway ahead of her. Thomas the house cat was sitting in the middle of it, washing his face. He paused, looked up and, mewing a welcome, walked slowly towards Terry, rubbing against her legs and purring with pleasure. She stroked him and whispered, 'You too? Missing us all? What am I to do about you then? Oh, I know you're a good mouser and the land will provide, but who's to provide the comforts of home and hearth in the winter months? Mrs Mundy perhaps? Yes, I think she would give you a good home.'

With lazy bees humming around her, she approached the house, intending to ring the hospital yet again for news. Every time she had done this, the cool tones of the Ward Sister informed her that the infamous and well-guarded patient was dangerously ill but that no visitors could be allowed.

The policeman at the gate raised a hand to her; she paused, then heard a familiar voice.

'Cooee! Only me.' With Max pulling on his lead, Fiona's bulk came into sight. Breathless from being hauled along behind the powerful dog, she peered at Terry and frowned.

'Lord, you shouldn't be here alone. It isn't right, so I've come to help. Put me to work. There must be heaps of things I can do.'

Terry smiled, suddenly realising that she had never doubted

Fiona's firm friendship no matter what the rest of the world said. 'Just being here is help enough.' There was so much to sort out . . . but sorting out would be slow and painful and she felt she would rather do that alone. Getting used to this empty house filled with heart-breaking memories, and one more dark than any, was the first hurdle she must overcome. 'Let's just talk.'

Following Terry into the kitchen, Fiona felt an involuntary shudder course through her. It had been hard enough entering this place to collect Terry's clothes, but then her father had been with her and a policeman had stood in the doorway. Today it was different, worse somehow. Still, she thought, at least the shooting hadn't happened here. That particular horror remained in the wood, along with others. The wood! Dear God, had all this really started because of the need for a path through the wood? How utterly unbelievable it seemed now.

'What are your plans?' she asked Terry as they entered the kitchen. 'What do you intend to do?'

'Sell up.'

'But . . . leave Thornley?'

'I can't stay.' Terry bit her bottom lip, forcing back tears, and went on, 'Which means I'm going to have to sell Dauphine. But I can't bear her to go to someone who might not love her as we all have. You said you were looking for a dependable horse for your new riding school. If I gave her to you, would you take her?'

Fiona nodded. 'She knows me and that will make things a little easier on her. But of course I shall buy her.'

Terry breathed a sigh of relief, then shook her head. 'No. I'm only too grateful that she'll be in your care.' The tears welled up once more, as they kept doing these days. 'I couldn't bear some stranger taking her away in a horse box to God knows where.'

Having had the foresight to bring a bottle of milk with her, Fiona made a pot of tea and, as they sat talking in the way they always had, Terry could almost tell herself that everything was normal and this just another ordinary day. They spoke of practicalities, avoiding any mention of events which were too painful for words. Fiona longed to ask whether Grant had been in touch since that night, but something in Terry's eyes told her that this too was a taboo subject.

Once only did Terry break down, and was comforted by her old friend. Capable and not given to sentimentality, Fiona's practical manner was the very thing she needed just now. She stayed for an hour, finally driven away by the sight of the Vicar arriving on his bike.

Taking Terry's hand in his, the Reverend Clements murmured words of comfort which brought none. She listened politely as he then raised the delicate issue of re-interment for her true parents. He would make all the arrangements on her behalf, he said.

Terry listened dispassionately. He could be talking about anyone; any two strangers. She thanked him and insisted on complete privacy. 'No one in the village is to know. I don't want curious onlookers who have no reason to be there.'

The Vicar left, thinking how strangely unmoved she seemed by the tragic little funeral he was arranging. It shocked him as the whole terrible business had done. Perhaps he needed to spend more time with this particular parishioner and bring her to understand that God tries people in different ways? On the other hand, maybe he should wait a while.

When he had gone the telephone rang. Pausing with her hand on the receiver, Terry wondered if it was Grant. If so what would she say to him or he to her? For some time she let it ring on then picked it up, telling herself she was a fool for doing so.

It was Meg, who had tried to reach her time and again to say how dreadfully sorry she was that bringing her mother to Thornley had ended in a drama no one could have anticipated.

Wishing now that she had never met the Collinettes, Terry nevertheless felt obliged to explain about the forthcoming interment. 'I rather think your mother would wish to be there. I shall be the only other mourner, Marisa's too unwell to attend.'

Meg agreed that her mother would want to be there then went on to say: 'Terry, your friend Grant Kenway is looking everywhere for you. He's tried the farm but either the police answer or the phone just rings and rings. He's tried me, he's tried the Rashleighs, he's even been politely turned away from Cadogan Place. It seems you don't want to be found. But, Terry, I happen to know how dreadful he feels about all that happened and that he blames himself. I don't know why, because it was Mum who insisted on calling the police in the first place. Grant knew from the pathologist's report that your true parents were dead and that dental records would merely confirm that.'

Meg paused then said, 'Are you there still?'

'Yes, I'm here,' answered Terry in a quiet voice.

'I was the one who told him the police had the records. He knew then what was going to happen. I think he was afraid for you. Don't blame him, Terry. He's too busy blaming himself.'

Replacing the receiver, she tried to turn her mind to 'sorting out', but could only think of Grant. Meg was right, of course. Blaming him for what had happened was an instinctive reaction which she now bitterly regretted. Having found himself at the farm ahead of the police, Grant had been honest enough to confront the man she called her father who had opened his heart and mind to him. That must say something for the esteem in which he held Grant. They might even have become in-laws, had she never read that fateful letter in the first place.

'I think he was afraid for you.' Those words kept going round and round in her head as she wandered through the rooms, unable to settle to anything. Finally, she gave up, walked out of the house, locked the door and lifted her face to the golden September evening. The air was full of woodsmoke and with it came memories of helping Diane to bottle tomatoes and apples in large Kilner jars for the winter months to come.

Don't think of it. This time will pass, this terrible time must pass.

When her car refused to start, Terry set off on foot for the village, feeling a sense of guilt that she had left poor Eliot alone for so long. Devastated that he could not return to school next week, her brother had listened to her explanation that it was considered the best thing for him in the long run, and then asked why.

'Why is it better? When Packham's mother died he returned so why can't I?'

That was the moment she should have told him the truth, but even though she tried the words would not form. The look on his face would remain with her for the rest of her days. He knew there was more and that she had ducked the issue. After that he had followed her into the garden, saying again and again that she should explain the difference between him and Packham, but she couldn't, she simply couldn't.

Reaching Mrs Shotley's cottage at last, she saw Eliot at the far end of the long rear garden, guarding the remains of a bonfire which had been lit earlier. There was an all-pervading smell of casserole cooking in the oven.

Terry spoke of the Vicar's visit, adding, 'Why is it that I feel nothing for my true parents? Nothing at all. It's wicked . . . wicked.'

Mrs Shotley shook her head. 'You never knew them.'

'Even so, I should feel something. But I don't. What happened to them might have happened to strangers so far as I'm concerned.' Her face shadowed in puzzlement as though she was no longer sure of anything. 'But their deaths weren't at the hands of strangers, so how can it be right, or natural, for me to grieve more for their assailants than for them?'

'It isn't.' Mrs Shotley took Terry's hand and patted it lightly. 'But this is hardly a natural situation, so stop torturing yourself or you'll go out of your mind. If you must know I'm having much the same thoughts myself, so you're not alone.'

Deeply troubled nevertheless, Terry opened the sideboard drawer and drew from it a starched white linen tablecloth. It dawned on her then that it was the first time she had openly admitted that the parents who'd raised her had killed. She turned to Mrs Shotley again, saying, 'I asked Mr Clements about my mother . . . my other mother . . . and my other father . . . if he doesn't live. He looked taken aback, and said he would make enquiries since it was a situation he was not familiar with.' Her hand clenched the tablecloth leaving creases. 'One thing's certain. They won't be buried at Thornley.' Her voice cracked, then sobs wracked her body as though the pain would never leave it.

It was some time before she pulled away from Mrs Shotley's comforting arms, lifted her head and said, 'Oh, yes. He also reminded me that this Sunday was Harvest Festival and hoped Eliot and I would attend the service, as we always had done. I wondered if he was barking mad! When I said I wouldn't be there to have people staring at me, he said I must give them a chance to be charitable. Charitable!'

She threw the tablecloth over the dining table and smoothed it out, face hard with anger, voice raised. 'I walked through the village just now and people pretended they hadn't seen me. They crossed the street or looked the other way, as if I were a total stranger. Charitable! He lives in cloud cuckooland does our Reverend Clements. So no, I won't be going to church this Sunday or any other Sunday come to that.'

Mrs Shotley poured her a glass of sherry and said calmly, 'Here, drink this it'll calm your nerves. I know it's too sweet for you, but it's all I keep in the house. I've had it since Christmas.' She handed the glass to Terry and went on, 'You're wrong, you know. I don't think it's a matter of people being unkind, more not knowing what to say. Well, think about it. What can they say to you? How can they comfort you? They don't mean to seem uncaring, they're just afraid they might upset you.'

'Upset me!' Terry looked astonished. Her true parents had been murdered by her adoptive ones who were also traitors to their country. One has died by her own hand and had injured the other, forced to this act by the man Terry loved who had now vanished from her life for ever. Her sister was half-mad, and who could say how her brother would react when he knew the truth?

Yet the good people of Thornley did not wish to upset her!

Like a bear with a sore head Alastair was heading through a misty Sunday dawn towards Goodwood, his recent row with Denholm Ward, the team's driver, still on his mind.

It had started a week earlier when Alastair accused Ward of holding back all the time and not pushing the car to its full potential. It ended last night with Ward resigning in disgust and Alastair deciding to drive the car himself.

To hell with what his father said, to hell with his mad wife, to hell with the whole bloody world, he thought. For once he would do something he wanted to do and no one was going to stop him. And what he wanted to do was win.

Marisa sat alone, her thoughts twisting in on themselves; alone with memories of Julian's betrayal and Alastair's harsh words; alone with the light, the bright expanding light that hid the darkness within it. If only she could cut that light out of her mind she might know peace.

Peace! She stroked her cheek thoughtfully, smiled, then wrote a note to Alastair. Placing it on the drawing-room mantlepiece, she slipped on a loose cream woollen coat with large pockets, and when she was sure Mrs Mount was busy in the kitchen, crept along the hallway and left the house.

Having given up her day off to look after Mrs Hammond, the housekeeper heard the front door slam shut and rushed outside just in time to see her charge getting into a taxi. Too late to stop her, Mrs Mount could only watch as the taxi pulled away.

Appalled, she returned to the kitchen, knowing she had failed Mr Alastair yet again, failed in her promise to keep the sick woman from leaving the house. She continued her tasks, unable to shake off the feeling of foreboding sweeping over her. Forty minutes later she walked into the drawing room to remove the flowers and rearrange them. Her eyes fell on the envelope standing against the mantelpiece clock. Finding it unsealed, she hesitated briefly then drew out the note and read it.

After calls to Lynwood Farm where no one replied, and calls to Thornley Hall where a punctiliously polite Lydia pleaded ignorance of Terry's whereabouts, Grant drove to Cadogan Place once more even though he knew he would receive the same reply as before.

But he felt a lightening of the intense strain he had been under for today was the first of his much-needed two weeks' leave; two precious weeks longed for during the summer when he and Terry could have spent them together without constantly having to say goodbye. Now at least they gave him time to search for her.

Turning into Cadogan Place, he wondered if she was staring through the window watching as he arrived. Would she still be there watching as he left? The last time he had called, he could feel her eyes on him. Perhaps this was where she wanted to remain. Once she had loved Alastair and now it was he who was comforting and caring for her.

He rang the doorbell and Mrs Mount appeared, her face pale and anxious as she recognised him. 'Mr Kenway, isn't it?'

'Yes. I must speak to Miss Fenton. Please, please tell her that I'm here.'

'Miss Fenton has left.' Mrs Mount's troubled eyes looked into his and she knew that for all she had been forced to turn this man away he was someone she could trust. 'Mr Hammond drove her and her brother to Suffolk. But ... please ... would you step inside for a moment? You see, I'm desperately worried about Mrs Hammond.'

As he followed her into the hall and upstairs to the drawing room, she said, 'I'm told you're in the medical profession and that's the only reason I'm confiding in you.' She handed him the note, saying, 'I don't know what to do.'

As Grant tried to make sense of the hastily scrawled writing, the housekeeper explained that Alastair was at Goodwood for the motor racing while Marisa had taken off in a taxi when she should be here.

'She's unwell, you see. Very unwell . . . emotionally and mentally. I tried to hear what she said to the taxi driver and thought it sounded like . . . Liverpool. I can only think she meant Liverpool Street station, which would mean she was going to Suffolk. And yet she was adamant at she would never go home again.'

Grant re-read the note and could see why Mrs Mount was worried.

It can't go on. I intend to release us both.
Marisa

He tried to sound casual as he asked about the state of her marriage to Alastair. 'Only she could be referring to divorce . . .'

Mrs Mount shook her head. 'It's not for me to speak about their marriage. In any case, I don't think that's what she means. She doesn't mention suicide but it's implied just the same. I don't know what to do. She's not . . . all there, you see.'

Remembering what Clayton had said about the toddler screaming, Grant could well understand why Marisa was 'not all there', as Mrs Mount put it. She now knew she had witnessed the murder of her parents. People were driven out of their minds by less than that. He smiled at the housekeeper reassuringly.

'Whatever Mrs Hammond said about never returning to her home, she's obviously heading that way. I'll ring the farm.' With hopes raised, he tensed as he heard the endless ringing tone. After five minutes he replaced the receiver. 'Miss Fenton doesn't seem to be at the house.' He tried Terry's Lowdham number with the same result. 'Not there either.' His heart sank at the thought. Where the hell was she then?

It was Mrs Mount who recalled that Marisa had telephoned the hospital early that morning and had then gone into her bedroom without a word. 'She seemed very odd at breakfast, but then she is odd these days so I didn't take much notice. After that she left the house.'

'The hospital?' Had Clayton's condition worsened suddenly? Had he died?

'But she wouldn't go there,' said Mrs Mount. 'They won't allow any visitors. Every time she and her sister rang, they were told that. So why would she go all that way for nothing?'

'Maybe she feels a desire to be near her . . . near him.' Unlikely, though, Grant told himself. Nevertheless . . .

He moved quickly towards the door. 'I'm heading for Suffolk right now and will call in at the hospital. Don't worry, I'll find her.' More comforting words, he thought wryly.

As she accompanied Grant to the door, Mrs Mount was still perturbed. 'She shouldn't be going. That man's a monster.'

Grant said nothing to this but started down the steps, trying to sound more confident than he felt. 'Maybe she's simply going to find her sister and do what she can to help her?'

And pigs might fly, thought Mrs Mount as she watched him drive away. If Mrs Hammond was in a mood to help anyone then she really *had* flipped her lid.

Once out of London, Grant was able to put his foot down. The country roads were clear and the air keen with pale sunlight slowly dissolving the morning mist. How very different it was from that last fateful journey through the storm. His fears were the same, though. What would he find when he arrived?

The policeman seated on duty outside Carlton's hospital room was bored. He had read the Sunday paper from cover to cover and now thought of the hundred and one other things he would rather be doing than sitting in this dreary corridor waiting for some kind nurse to bring him the occasional coffee.

The doctor and ward sister arrived, looked in on the infamous patient and wondered how much longer this sad routine would be necessary. Carlton lay in a bare white room drifting in and out of consciousness. The medical staff had done all they could, but there was only one way for him now. The doctor made his examination, checked the chart then stepped away with a sigh. 'He's not fighting back. But then, what has he to live for?'

As he and the sister left the room they heard the click of high heels heading down the corridor towards them. Into sight came an attractive woman wearing an expensive-looking cream woollen coat, her dark hair falling loosely to her shoulders. Carrying a large bunch of flowers, Marisa smiled at the doctor and let tears fill her eyes as she asked to be allowed to see 'my father'.

'I'm afraid that won't be possible,' the doctor replied. 'Police orders.' His expression softened. 'He's very near the end. You must prepare yourself.'

'Yes,' sniffed Marisa, hand to her eyes. 'I phoned this morning. That's why I've come from London to see him for the last time. You couldn't refuse me that, surely?'

To the young doctor it seemed cruel to deny this beautiful and distressed woman the chance to say goodbye. Even a man such as Peter Carlton, it seemed, was loved. He glanced at the guard and said, 'Well, what harm can it do now?'

The PC looked wary for the moment, remembering his orders, but she did look so distraught that his heart softened. 'Very well, but keep it short.' He winked at all three of them saying, 'Don't tell anyone or they'll have my guts for garters.'

Marisa entered the room and closed the door behind her. No one saw the change in her expression as she walked over to where Carlton lay, dumped the flowers on a table and sat on the chair beside him.

His eyes opened slowly and he stared up at the ceiling for a moment. then, turning his head slightly, he focussed on Marisa. Surprised and perturbed, he tried to speak but was too weak to utter a sound. She spoke instead.

'They say you're dying and that's why they let me in.' Her voice was cold and matter-of-fact. 'I'm glad you're conscious and can see me. Can you hear me too? Yes . . . I can see by that flicker of your eyes that you can. How dreadful to be imprisoned in a body that won't function. Now I don't have much time, so I'll be brief.'

She opened her handbag and produced a large bottle of sleeping tablets. Laying it on the bed, she reached back into her coat pocket and pulled out a half bottle of Scotch. Taking the glass from his locker, she filled it to the brim with whisky and shook several tablets into the palm of her hand. The look of agitation in his eyes gave her a sense of triumph as she put the pills in her mouth and washed them down with the drink.

'You're an evil man,' she said. 'You took everything from me – my true parents, my friends, my dignity, and finally the man I love.' More whisky was swallowed along with another handful of tablets. She watched his eyes dart from side to side, heard his strangled cry and saw his attempts to reach out for the bell. Failing to reach it, the hand fell heavily to his side once more.

Marisa went on swallowing the pills and drinking the whisky, watching the horror on his face and the eyes urging her to stop.

'Strange how I never liked you. But then, somewhere inside I always knew. I knew what you were. You sensed that and so you couldn't love me as you loved Terry. You and Mother both . . . ready to let me die while she must live.'

She paused, beginning to feel strange. The bottle was empty now, and the pills mostly gone. She reached into her other pocket and opened a second half bottle. Gagging on the remaining pills, she forced the drink down her throat. It dribbled on to her chin; she wiped her mouth with the back of her hand then saw his eyes staring in horror, lips moving. She could barely hear what he was saying nor did she care. Again he tried to reach the bell but fell back weakly.

'The torchlight . . .' Marisa managed to murmur. 'You . . . the monster behind the light.' Her mind went to another light: sunlight above clouds streaming past the small windows of the Comet. She should never have left that world where she had been happy.

Dropping the empty bottle to the floor, Marisa let the pill container fall on to the bed and rested her head on his blanket-covered legs, a smile on her ashen face. Her breathing was laboured, her heart pounding. She felt so sleepy that forming words became a problem.

'Oh, Dad . . . watching me die . . . can't be . . . so terrible for you?' After a long pause her voice could barely be heard. 'I want you . . . to watch . . . just the same.'

Her eyes rolled then closed and she lay still on the bed, no longer able to see the horror in his eyes.

Chapter Twenty

It had been hard sorting out Diane's clothes, but Terry had steeled herself to the task and now they stood in tidy piles, ready to be sent to a charity.

As she had worked, Terry kept wondering who could have been trying to get through to her while she was struggling with her key in the lock. By the time she'd reached the telephone, the caller had rung off. Thinking it could have been Grant she had been tempted to call his number, but fought the temptation. What would she say? What could she say? And if he hadn't been the caller, the outcome would be abject embarrassment all round. She had told him to go, and he had gone. It was over, and best for him that it was.

Suddenly she had to get out of the house; close the door on it as she must try to close the door on the past. As she stepped out into warm sunshine, the church bells stopped pealing. The Harvest Festival service had begun.

'Come, ye thankful people, come'. She closed her eyes, heard the hymn in her mind and saw the procession of children setting down on the altar steps plaited loaves, fruit, vegetables and sheaves of corn, as she had done in her schooldays. 'Raise the song of Harvest-home ...' The church would be crowded. It always was on this particular Sunday. 'All is safely gather'd in ...' Oh, God, if only everything could be as it used to be.

The anguished thought was pushed firmly aside as she went down to the hen house and, scattering feed, wondered what to do about them now. Give them to Mrs Mundy perhaps? Leave them in her care for the new occupants of the farm? Kill them? No, that was out of the question, she knew all twenty-three by name and they had been Diane's pride and joy. Good laying hens would surely find a home. It was yet another problem to be solved before she left Thornley.

After feeding the farm cats, and giving Dauphine her bucket of water, she walked back towards the house. A young girl was heading along the drive towards the front door. Blue jacket over blue pleated skirt, with dark hair neatly combed back from her face instead of the usual plaits, Margaret Temple was hardly recognisable to Terry at first.

Terry quickened her pace, unable to believe her eyes. 'Margaret? What on earth are you doing here?'

The girl walked towards her, mouth pursed and tense, eyes big and tearful.

'They say you've left the school, Miss Fenton? That you won't be teaching us any more.'

Astonished, Terry glanced at the PC on the gate, who smiled back and waved casually. 'Margaret, have you come all the way from Lowdham? Do your parents know you're here?'

The girl shook her head. 'I'm supposed to be at church, but I caught the bus instead when there was no reply from your flat.'

Sighing, Terry shook her head. 'How do you know where my flat is?'

'I saw you one day. The house is visible from the hotel.'

'Ah, yes, of course. Your parents manage the Swan. Well, you'd better come inside.'

As they entered the sitting room Margaret became more and more emotional, asking Terry why she was leaving and begging her not to go. 'We thought you liked us? I thought you liked me?' Terry sat beside her on the sofa. 'I do like you and I'm going to miss you all dreadfully, but I must leave. Try to understand. It's simply no longer possible for me to stay. You know what's happened, surely?'

Margaret nodded, took the clean handkerchief that Terry was offering, wiped her tears and nose then sniffed. 'It was in the newspapers, but my parents wouldn't let me read them. My mother told me, though, and I'm very sorry about the gun accident and that your mother died. It's sad for you, but I still don't see why you're leaving us?'

Despair overwhelmed Terry once more. Margaret, like Eliot, had been fed a lie and when school started next week, she would be shaken to the core. 'No, Margaret, there's more to it than that, which is why it's better for the school that I go away. I don't want to leave, believe me, but there it is.'

Margaret stared up at her in puzzlement. 'But . . . what's going to happen to me? I can't read without you, and then I'll be sent away.'

Remembering Miss Yeats's threat, so recently lifted, Terry touched her brow wearily. The fall out from this terrible affair had a long reach, it seemed. 'Now look, you know perfectly well that your reading has improved tremendously and that's because of your own hard work. I can only guide. You yourself make it happen. And, yes, we both accept there is a problem but it's not insoluble. You say you can't read without me? That's nonsense, Margaret, and you'll soon come to realise it. Miss Beddoes understands and I'm sure will carry on helping you. I'll contact her and ask. I'm sure she'll be happy to do this.'

But Margaret was becoming hysterical now. 'She's not you . . . it's all no good without you!'

For ten minutes Terry tried to calm her pupil and when she had succeeded said, 'Now, let's think about this. We've done the worst already. Yes, you still have difficulty with silent letters, but you'll conquer that too, in good time. You know how; we've gone all through it. So then, let's see how you get on this morning.' All her suitable material being at the flat, she searched the bookcase for the volume of poetry which had been there as long as she could recall. Finally settling on a passage by Housman she handed the book to Margaret, saying, 'This is from a poem called 'A Shropshire Lad'. Look at it first, then read it aloud to me.' She moved across to the sitting-room window and stared out, waiting in silence until Margaret finally and ponderously spoke each word.

'"Into my heart an air that kills
From yon far country blows;
What are those blue remembered hills,
What spires, what farms are those?"'

As she listened to the young voice, Terry felt anguish overwhelm her and could not fight back the tears.

'"That is the land of lost content,
I see it shining plain,
The happy . . ."'

There was a pause, as Terry had known there would be at this point. Still staring out of the window, she tried to fight back her emotion and said,

'"The happy highways where I went
And cannot come again."'

Her voice ended on a sob. She pulled herself together and turned to see Margaret staring up at her with anxiety. 'So now, look at the word 'highways', remember what I told you, and how we deal with this. Then read that passage again.'

This time Margaret read more confidently and after chatting together for twenty minutes, during which Terry convinced the girl that she could carry on from the firm base they had built together, Margaret seemed happier, suddenly realising that if she didn't catch the next bus to Lowdham, she would be stranded in Thornley until half-past three.

With only six minutes to spare, Terry rushed her down the hill, waited until the girl was safely on the single-decker then waved goodbye. As the bus pulled away she saw Margaret drying her eyes and prayed Miss Yeats would give her the chance she deserved.

The Goodwood circuit on the Sussex Downs was well attended on such a lovely day. But Alastair hardly saw the fields around him or the distant hills. His nerves at breaking point, he strode about the paddocks, barking at the rest of his team, and only settled down after the qualifying laps were over.

Now, as he waited for the race, he felt he had come home and began to relax at last. It was good to meet old comrades again, good to feel that here he counted and that this time he would be at the wheel instead of lily-livered Ward.

How tedious the wretched man had become, complaining incessantly of this and that and always the cornering. Each problem had been worked on and put right yet still the complaints came thick and fast as well as the holding back, so that the new model always finished well behind to everyone's bitter disappointment. When Alastair had driven the car himself on the test circuit, he'd found it faultless and decided Ward was blaming the machine rather than his own performance. Thank God he had gone!

Having done extremely well in the qualifying laps for the Modified Sports Car class, Alastair knew he had been right all along. Not bad for someone who had been out of the game for almost a year. With the adrenalin flowing now, he wondered if he could push it further in the race to come? He told himself he could; he told himself he would. Winning was everything now. It was all that was left to him. Nothing else mattered. Better this way than the slow death of being chained to a mad-woman and a life of dark whispers and insults. Life or death . . . it was in God's hands now.

Clad in overalls, he climbed into the car, put on his helmet and started the engine. As he had a last word with his mechanic, he noticed a man running towards them. Sean spoke to the man, then turned and looked at Alastair with a worried expression. Whatever was going on, he had no time to ponder it as he drove off to the starting grid.

The race started without incident and Alastair headed down to Madgwick Corner, took the left hander into St Mary's, rounded Lavant with five cars ahead of him then into the straight where he felt a surge of power shoot him forward to overtake two cars before rounding Woodcote Corner. By the second lap he was third in the field, by the third he was in second place and the adrenalin was pumping. Speed was all now, winning everything, and life a poor second. Like a man possessed he flew around the circuit, thrilling the crowds, until he had closed up behind the leading car.

'Heaven take me or give me victory,' he murmured.

Watching from the paddocks, Sean's knuckles whitened. 'Easy! Take it easy . . .'

'What the hell's got into him?' asked the mechanic.

After swinging left into St Mary's, Alastair was making a move to overtake when the lead car suddenly swung across his path. In an effort to avoid it his wheels locked. The car spun uncontrollably off the track and rolled over and over. Trying to protect his head, he closed his eyes and thought, This is it.

Suddenly the car stopped; the rolling sky was still again and, without knowing how, he found himself stumbling through a strangely still and silent world. Was this death? Looking up he realised how blue the sky was, how green the meadows and trees around him. On the distant Downs lay a misty autumn haze. It was all so incredibly beautiful. He looked to his left and saw a heap of straw stacks now scattered around the wreck of a burning car.

The stillness was broken by officials rushing around with fire extinguishers, but still the world was silent. For one horrible moment he thought his body might still be inside that car, then he felt a sharp pain in his left leg and another in his shoulder. Touching his face, he saw blood on his driving gloves.

How did he get out of the car? He had no memory of it. Officials were running towards him, Sean foremost among them. Alastair just stared. A moment ago he had challenged The Grim Reaper and long bony fingers had reached out to him only to be withdrawn in disdain. *Et tu, Brute?*

Suddenly he wanted to laugh. He was alive and it was bloody marvellous! Alive! At the moment the car rolled he had known that he wanted to live, and he had. Offering up a prayer of thanks, he thought of all the years that stretched before him and vowed that never again would he test that fine margin between life and death. He was alive and wanted to kiss the wonderful ground.

Suddenly the world burst in on him as his ears cleared. The roar of engines told him the race was still going on without him. It didn't matter. But for his leg and the pain in his shoulder, he was miraculously in one piece.

With his arm about Sean's shoulders he hobbled off slowly towards an ambulance, protesting that he was all right. Inwardly he told himself he had driven his last race.

'We'll get you attended to,' a relieved Sean was saying, 'then we'll contact the hospital.'

'I don't need a hospital.'

Sean stopped walking and looked at his brother. 'Marisa. It's Marisa. You're to contact Ipswich Hospital urgently. We'll phone from Goodwood House.'

Alastair stared at him. If Sean had said such a thing to him yesterday he might have remained unmoved. Now he felt panic welling up, his mind seeing again her tragic clown-like face and hearing the cruel words he had said to her. Marisa!

Inside the ambulance Sean was silent while Alastair felt a churning in his stomach. 'Didn't they say anything else? She should be at home, not in a hospital. Was it a car accident? Is she alive or dead? Christ, they should have said something. Get me to Ipswich, Sean. Get me there right now.'

'Look, phone first, then get that leg of yours . . .'

'To the devil with my leg.' Alastair leaned back and closed his eyes. God help him if anything had happened to Marisa. She was ill and he had left her. He had said terrible things and caused her more pain when she was already badly wounded. Hell, he wouldn't treat an animal the way he had treated her. 'For God's sake, Sean, get me to Ipswich at once.' And pray, he thought. Pray.

A golden afternoon sunlight bathed the Suffolk countryside. It fell on fruit trees in cottage gardens and apples ripening in orchards and brought with it that fruity woodsmoke smell that would deepen before evening.

It was no time to die, thought Grant as he drove along the narrow country lanes towards Thornley. The world about him seemed so calm and peaceful, so picturesque and beautiful, that it was hard for him to believe the scene that had greeted him when he'd entered Carlton's room. Finding it had been difficult enough and the policeman on duty outside had refused him entry. Only when he'd asked if there had been any other visitors was it obvious from the PC's expression that a certain visitor was still there.

A picture of Marisa lying half on and half off the bed would remain with him forever. So too would the expression on Carlton's face. Dead as he was, his eyes told the whole story. The sting in her tail, he thought. Marisa, scorpion-like, had turned it on herself to inflict the maximum hurt on the man who had robbed her of her parents, then dared to love her in their place.

Having told the hospital staff where Alastair could be located, Grant still found it hard to accept that any man would leave his wife at such a time as this. God help him! If Marisa had been right about Terry's initial attraction to Alastair, then Terry had been very lucky to lose him. Right now Grant would like to punch the bastard on the jaw.

He was approaching Thornley and passing the village green. By the old war memorial a group of youths were fooling around. On looking closer, however, he realised they were punching and kicking a smaller boy who was trying to shield himself from the blows raining down on him.

Stopping the car, Grant leaped from it and threw himself into the fray with a shout that caused the youths to jump back. 'What the hell do you think you're doing?'

There was a moment's pause before the boys ran off, jeering and shouting obscenities. Grant turned his attention to their victim whose face was covered with blood. Taking a clean handkerchief from his pocket, he used it to stem the bleeding, then frowned in recognition.

'Eliot? What the devil . . .? Come on, I'll take you home.'

'No.' The panicky voice was barely recognisable through his badly swollen lip. 'Mithis Thotley.'

Between Mrs Shotley's consternation and Grant's ministrations, a shocked and tearful Eliot was cleaned up and now lay on his bed, handkerchief held firmly to his nose which was still bleeding. His face was badly bruised as was his hip which had borne the brunt of the kicks, but it was not these wounds that hurt so much as what the youths had shouted as they attacked him.

'Murderers! Spies!' With each word another blow, another kick.

He lay quiet as Grant tended his painful, swollen face, thankful he had arrived on the scene. But why had the village boys turned on him so violently? What had he done? What was all that about spies and murderers?

Looking up at Grant, Eliot began to feel calmer. Nothing bad could happen while this man was here. He hoped he would stay. But as he felt those gentle fingers cleaning him up, the words the hooligans had shouted set his mind turning. Just why had his school refused to have him back, and why had Terry ducked that very question? He tried to speak but found it too painful and sensed that even if he could ask questions they would still go unanswered.

He thought next of those summer days when he had sailed with Grant and Terry; fun-filled days of laughter and looks between his sister and this man that had told him they were very much in love. So why had Grant not visited them before this? He lived in London and they had been in London, why hadn't he been to see them and offer his condolences? Only then did it dawn on Eliot that no one had called on them at the London house, no one at all.

Grant walked with Mrs Shotley into the sitting room and said angrily, 'I'd no idea! Dear God, I'd no idea. No bones broken. Keep him in bed, though, and let him rest.' He wondered whether he should tell her about Marisa, then decided against it. 'I have to find Terry. Where is she?'

'At the house.'

'Alone? She's there alone?' Grant found the thought horrendous. What on earth must she be going through? 'Has she been treated to a sample of Thornley hospitality as well?'

At the door, Mrs Shotley took his arm, almost in tears as she whispered, 'People here aren't all like that, you know. But every village has its problem family and the Mallocks happen to be ours. Rough lot; live a mile or so out in a rundown slum they like to call their smallholding. Inbred and thick as two short planks, the lot of them. Poor Eliot. When you get up to the farm, contact the police and tell them what's happened. Time those sods were called to account.'

She glanced back towards the boy's bedroom, her face filled with sorrow. 'I wonder what they said to him? Terry did try to tell him the truth but in the end it proved too hard for her. Just how do you tell a boy a thing like that? The danger was that someone else would, which was why I told him to stay in while I was at church this morning. He did, but slipped out when I was in the garden after lunch.'

Watching as Grant drove off, she recalled how the Vicar had departed from his usual Harvest Sermon to speak of the 'tragic and dreadful events which have devastated the village'. He had then asked the congregation to think how much more shocking and devastating they had been for Terry, Marisa and Eliot, who had grown up among them and whose lives had been so cruelly shattered. 'A kind word, an offer of help, an understanding smile, might lessen the isolation they must feel.' With that he'd asked the congregation to join in a prayer for them.

She had found difficulty in holding back the tears as after the service ended people gathered around her, asking if she would convey their sympathies and concern for Terry and her brother and sister. She only wished Terry had been there to hear for herself.

Terry was just leaving Dauphine's paddock when she heard the distant sound of a car in the lane. She looked along the track, listening for the engine to fade away as it journeyed on past the house, but the car had stopped. Would David Kimber allow it in? Not unless he knew the caller. Turning sightseers and reporters away had been a full-time job, but with press interest waning the attention was lessening too and Lowdham could no longer spare manpower to guard the farm.

The car engine could be heard once more and from the sound it made, she knew it had turned into the drive. Her heart lurched. She wanted to run towards the house, but her legs wouldn't move. For some moments she stood watching, waiting, and then he came into sight, jacket slung over his shoulder, ambling along the rutted track towards her.

She drew a quick breath and stood like stone, hardly daring to believe it. After the terrible things she had said to him and the way she had behaved, he had returned when any other man would have given up on her.

Grant drew close then stopped. She saw how dark and troubled his eyes were, and wanted to reach out to him. Why couldn't she move?

'Even though you didn't want to be found, did you imagine I would stop looking?' he said thickly.

She couldn't speak, only reach out for him. He clasped his arms about her and held her close. Head resting on his chest, she could hear his heart beating and never wanted him to let her go. He was here, and everything was going to be all right. Suddenly, with a shuddering release, all the fear and the built-up tension fell away. Avalanche-like, her emotions swept her along as she wept in his arms.

Afterwards she listened in silence as he told her his toned down version of what had happened at the hospital.

'She's going to be fine, Terry. The hospital staff got to her in time and were marvellous. I was at Cadogan Place looking for you when Mrs Mount showed me a note Marisa had left. I chased off to Ipswich and we got to her in time. I think it was more a cry for help than anything. After all, if you really want to take your own life, you don't choose to do it in a hospital, surely?'

'How was she when you left?'

'I'm not sure. Pretty cross, I should think. So would you be after having your stomach pumped out.' He smiled and stroked her face gently, saying, 'They're keeping her in to give her a good night's rest. Her husband should know by now and is probably on his way to her from Goodwood.'

'And Dad?' She looked up and saw the answer in his eyes. Quickly she turned her head away, but he took it gently in his hands and made her face him.

'He's at peace,' said Grant as he saw the tears. 'Neither of them ever intended to live through what had to come. They had always planned it this way. He told me that himself.'

He held her close, his mind returning to the moment when, having found Marisa slumped on the bed, he had rung the bell quickly, yelled for the policeman to get help then, slapping Marisa's face several times to bring her round, hauled her to her feet and tried to make her walk. The Ward Sister arrived, quickly followed by a young doctor who removed Marisa to the treatment room. Only later did Grant learn that she had been so close to death that had he arrived a few minutes afterwards it would have been too late.

One look at Carlton had told him everything. Even now it shocked him to the core that Marisa could exact such a terrible revenge. Watching his adopted daughter dying slowly, and being unable to stop her, must have been unendurable torture. So much so that his heart finally gave out.

As he held Terry, stroking her head and murmuring comforting words, Grant swore to himself that the truth of what had happened this morning would never reach her ears so long as he had breath in his body.

They walked on, hardly realising where they were walking as they made their way along the edge of the cornfield towards the memorial. She told him all that had happened; how Eliot had no school to go to and how she had been dismissed. On top of all this there were a hundred and one things to do on the farm and she didn't know how she could cope.

Grant told her he would take most of it off her shoulders and that he didn't want her up here all alone with such terrible memories. 'When all is settled, we'll go back to London together, the three of us. Let me look after you. Marry me?'

Looking out over the ploughed field, Terry leaned back in his arms and felt the relief of having him here. How tired she was suddenly. Tired to the point of exhaustion. Now she could rest at last. Then she knew it couldn't be. 'I can't marry you. I can't.'

She stepped from his arms and turned to look up at him. 'Why do you think Marisa tried to take her own life? It's because we are tainted and no one will have anything to do with us now. You can't have a wife who was raised by murderers and traitors. That's the phrase being bandied about. I'm guilty by association and so will you be if you're seen with me. Your career will come to a very abrupt end. Oh, darling, I love you but you must forget me.'

'What utter rubbish!' he said firmly.

Her eyes searched his face. 'You're not thinking straight. What we want, what we long for, can never be. You have no idea what people are like.' She smiled wryly. 'You once laughingly said we had no plague victims. Well, you were wrong. You'll perish too if you don't run from me.'

Grant smiled and lifted her face to his. 'Oh, I'll risk it. But I won't risk losing you again. So there's nothing more to be said on that subject.' He kissed her again. Struggling with herself to be strong, she finally wrapped her arms about him and gave herself up to this moment.

They walked on with Terry setting her desire to have Grant beside her for the rest of her days against the price he would pay for loving her. There was only one way out. They must leave England and make their lives in a country where he could continue his career. She bit back the remark as they came to the memorial. How could he leave the land of his birth, the land his brother had died to defend? No. That she could never ask of him.

They stood quietly looking at that stone with the seven names carved on it and remembered Peter Carlton's words about the crashed Lancaster and how he had stopped his spying then. It seemed so long ago yet it was just eleven days.

'We shall never return to Thornley again,' she said. 'So who will look after this site?'

'The villagers,' said Grant. 'It's theirs now and so is the ground we're standing on. The relatives will come here from time to time; the schoolchildren will tend the plants, and no doubt Brigadier Rashleigh will make sure everything is done with all due respect. They won't forget.'

After a long silence he said, 'Two days ago I had a letter from Australia informing me that since my mother will never return to England, the house in Richmond has been given to me. The tenant is leaving and so I can either sell it or live in it.' He held her hands tightly and said, 'Say you will live in it with me? Say you will because I'm damned if I'm returning to London without you.'

As Terry listened to him her strong resolve to martyr herself was weakening rapidly. She knew she couldn't go through her life without this man, just as he knew he couldn't go on without her.

Seeing her troubled eyes, he held her again and kissed the top of her head. 'Darling, we have all the time in the world, so let's take things step by step. And the first of these steps is a quiet wedding in London.'

Her shoulders relaxed. There was so much she wanted to say, but it could wait. As shadows lengthened before them, they walked slowly back along the edge of the field. No more was said about the future. For now there was only the present. A moment in time when all the lies and dark memories were set aside so that peace could finally settle on their unquiet hearts.

STOCK CIRCULATION

G1+F BOx 6/04			
TWI 6/04			